PENG

The Comple
Volume One

Roald Dahl is best known for his mischievous, wildly inventive stories for children. But throughout his life he was also a prolific and acclaimed writer of stories for adults. These sinister, surprising tales continue to entertain, amuse and shock generations of readers even today.

The Complete Short Stories

Volume One

ROALD DAHL

PENGUIN BOOKS

PENGUIN BOOKS

Published by the Penguin Group
Penguin Books Ltd, 80 Strand, London WC2R ORL, England
Penguin Group (USA) Inc., 375 Hudson Street, New York, New York 10014, USA
Penguin Group (Canada), 90 Eglinton Avenue East, Suite 700, Toronto, Ontario, Canada M4P 2Y3
(a division of Pearson Penguin Canada Inc.)
Penguin Ireland, 25 St Stephen's Green, Dublin 2, Ireland (a division of Penguin Books Ltd)
Penguin Group (Australia), 707 Collins Street, Melbourne, Victoria 3008, Australia
(a division of Pearson Australia Group Pty Ltd)
Penguin Books India Pvt Ltd, 11 Community Centre, Panchsheel Park, New Delhi – 110 017, India
Penguin Group (NZ), 67 Apollo Drive, Rosedale, Auckland 0632, New Zealand
(a division of Pearson New Zealand Ltd)
Penguin Books (South Africa) (Pty) Ltd, Block D, Rosebank Office Park,
181 Jan Smuts Avenue, Parktown North, Gauteng 2193, South Africa

Penguin Books Ltd, Registered Offices: 80 Strand, London WC2R ORL, England

www.penguin.com

These stories have been previously published in a variety of publications.
Details of each story's original publication are provided at the start of
each chapter and constitute an extension of this copyright page
This collection first published in Penguin Books 2013
001

Set in 12.5/14.75pt Garamond MT Std
Typeset by Jouve (UK), Milton Keynes
Printed in Great Britain by Clays Ltd, St Ives plc

ISBN: 978-1-405-93705-4

www.greenpenguin.co.uk

MIX
Paper from
responsible sources
FSC www.fsc.org FSC™ C018179

Penguin Books is committed to a sustainable
future for our business, our readers and our planet.
This book is made from Forest Stewardship
Council™ certified paper.

Contents

Introduction
by Charlie Higson

'I ought to warn you, if you haven't read any of my stories, that you may be a little disturbed by some of the things that happen in them . . .'

I remember the first time I saw Roald Dahl. It was 1979, and there on my television was a bald man in his sixties, sitting in an armchair by a roaring fire, with a tray across his lap, introducing a new series based on some of the short stories he had written. I'd seen *Willy Wonka and the Chocolate Factory*. I'd read the book that it was based on. I'd also read some of his adult stories. But I hadn't really made the connection that the same person was behind them all. 'Roald Dahl' was not yet the reliable brand name that it is today, so familiar that we can look at it without thinking what an *odd* name it is (unless, I suppose, you're Norwegian). Nowadays everybody knows who Roald Dahl is – one of the most popular children's writers in the world – but I am from the generation who first became aware of him sitting there in his cardigan introducing the TV series *Tales of the Unexpected*.

For a while there were two Roald Dahls in people's consciousness. One – the *Tales of the Unexpected* Dahl – who wrote slightly sinister, blackly humorous adult stories with a sting in the tail. The other – the Willy Wonka Dahl – who wrote slightly sinister, blackly humorous children's stories illustrated by Quentin Blake. And back in 1979 the TV Dahl, the *Tales of the Unexpected* Dahl, took over for a while. After all, he had yet to write many of his most popular kids' books, like *The Twits*, *The BFG*, *Matilda* and *The Witches*. But there is a third Roald Dahl, and that is the one you will find in these pages – quite simply the master of the short-story form – because there is so much more to these tales than 'the unexpected', a label that has perhaps been too often applied to his adult work and which gives too narrow a view of its appeal. If every story consisted of nothing more than a twist we would read them once, perhaps skipping through to the big reveal, and then forget all about them. But you never forget a Dahl short story. This volume starts with ones based on his experiences as a fighter pilot in the Second World War and ends with ones of country life. In between there is horror, comedy, science fiction, satire and sex. Yes, many of them do end with a final drop of acid, but the pleasure goes far beyond the punchline.

Dahl's introduction to the very first *Tales of the Unexpected* is, like his stories, instantly captivating, short, sharp, dry and to the point, and it gives an excellent insight into his approach to writing:

> When I'm writing a short story I'm haunted by the thought that I've got to hold the reader's attention for literally every second, otherwise I'm dead.

That is a sentence that should be carved into the forehead of anybody starting out as a writer. In fact it should be carved into the foreheads of many established literary novelists and critics who believe it is the job of the reader, not the writer, to make the effort in a story. Each of the stories in this collection draws you in and plays with you, even though, on the surface, nothing much seems to be happening. They are written in a deceptively straightforward style. They may be about warfare and madness, of cows suckling snakes, of husbands contemplating killing their wives, and wives calmly murdering their husbands, of bullying, revenge and mutilation – indeed, many of them verge on horror – but the writing never strays into overblown histrionics and Dahl avoids any Gothic flourishes. There are no thunderstorms and old dark houses. The stories mostly play out in sunlight. But it is a pitiless bright light that exposes everything it touches. Dahl's style is always understated and matter-of-fact, which is what gives it its cold, hard kick. It is the epitome of the British stiff upper lip: a calm, polite exterior that thinly masks the seething turmoil and suppressed violence underneath. This idea is perfectly depicted in this description of an airman from the story 'Madame Rosette'.

> Stuffy noticed that the Stag was being polite. There was always trouble for somebody when he was like that. Back in the squadron, when he was leading a flight, when they sighted the enemy and when there was going to be a battle, the Stag never gave an order without saying 'Please' and he never received a message without saying 'Thank you.' He was saying 'Thank you' now to Abdul.

No matter how normal things might appear on the surface, we somehow know that it's not going to end well.

Dahl will shine his light on to the secrets and lies and pathetic aspirations of his perfectly drawn and desperate characters. They are brutal, these stories, and yet you finish reading each one with a smile, or maybe even a hollow laugh, certainly a shiver of gratification, because the conclusion always seems so *right*. Justice has been served. It is not a civilized Christian justice at work, though. It is something older and darker, the same justice that runs through Dahl's children's books. It is the child-torturing justice of Willy Wonka, or the aunt-crushing justice of *James and the Giant Peach*.

The stories in this book are arranged chronologically, in the order they were first published, and what is extraordinary is just how polished the early ones are, despite the fact that Dahl had shown no real literary skills at school and no real interest in writing. You might expect to find a writer feeling his way, grasping for his themes and even experimenting with his style, but no, right from the off the writing is amazingly assured. Again, in his introduction to *Tales of the Unexpected* from 1979, Dahl gives an insight into the care he took over his stories:

> The one you're going to see now is the first of a series based on stories that have taken me thirty-five years to write. I find them difficult to do well so I work slowly, about two a year.

In 'Lucky Break' Dahl tells how it all came about when he was approached by the writer C. S. Forester – famous for his Hornblower adventure novels – in Washington during the war. Dahl was working as a British cultural attaché, having been wounded in Africa, and Forester needed material for stories to publish in American magazines. Too old to fight, he was, instead, a propagandist and was writing pieces sympathetic to the British to make sure we received as much American support as possible. He asked Dahl to jot down some notes for him about his experiences of being shot down over Libya. Dahl duly obliged, but when he got Dahl's notes Forester wrote back to him, 'You were meant to give me notes. I'm bowled over. Your piece is marvellous. It is the work of a gifted writer. I didn't touch a word of it.'

The piece was duly published under Dahl's name and he never looked back. Overnight he had become a writer. (That story, later rewritten, appears in this volume as 'A Piece of Cake'.) When asking for notes, Forester gave Dahl a piece of advice that really stuck with him:

> Let me have plenty of detail. That's what counts in our business, tiny little details, like you had a broken shoelace on your left shoe, or a fly settled on the rim of your glass at lunch . . .

That attention to detail is evident in all these stories, and it's what makes them so powerful. It is the little things that convince the reader that Dahl had to be there to know all this. The early flying stories are full of such details – local Greek peasants hiding a makeshift runway with branches, the particular smell of Cairo, the intense brief dog-fight in 'Death of an Old Old Man' that took 'perhaps as long as it would take you to light a cigarette'.

And the small scale – the fly on the rim of the glass – keeps cropping up, like the description of the boy in 'The Wish' picking at a scab on his knee. Working in miniature like this, Dahl manages to cram whole lives into his stories. In lesser hands each one might have been a full-length novel, but Dahl has boiled them down to their essence.

When faced with a fat volume like this you might wonder where to start. Well, I would turn to either 'Man from the South' or 'Lamb to the Slaughter'. They are quintessential Dahl short stories and probably the best known. One makes you ask how much you would be prepared to gamble to get what you wanted, and the other hangs on the thought we've all had when taking a joint of meat from the freezer: 'You could do a lot of damage with this.' Having read these two, you'll want to go right back to page one and read the rest of the stories from the beginning. And you won't want to stop until you get to the end, where you will find 'Claud's Dog', four tales of the countryside. This is not the cosy, sentimental countryside of James Herriot, however. It is an alarming place full of horrible things hidden in the hayricks, maggot farms and a ghastly ratcatcher who has stepped straight out of a horror film. Writing of these stories in 1989, Dahl said that 're-reading them again now fills me with acute nostalgia and with vivid memories of those sweet days many years ago'. Which only goes to show that Dahl's idea of sweet nostalgia is perhaps different from the rest of ours, and is probably why his stories are still so compelling today.

Katina

First published in *Ladies' Home Journal*
(March 1944)

Some brief notes about the last days of
RAF fighters in the first Greek campaign.

Peter saw her first.

She was sitting on a stone, quite still, with her hands resting on her lap. She was staring vacantly ahead, seeing nothing, and all around, up and down the little street, people were running backwards and forwards with buckets of water, emptying them through the windows of the burning houses.

Across the street on the cobblestones, there was a dead boy. Someone had moved his body close in to the side so that it would not be in the way.

A little farther down an old man was working on a pile of stones and rubble. One by one he was carrying the stones away and dumping them to the side. Sometimes he would bend down and peer into the ruins, repeating a name over and over again.

All around there was shouting and running and fires and buckets of water and dust. And the girl sat quietly on the stone, staring ahead, not moving. There was blood running down the left side of her face. It ran down from her forehead and dripped from her chin on to the dirty print dress she was wearing.

Peter saw her and said, 'Look at that little girl.'

We went up to her and Fin put his hand on her shoulder, bending down to examine the cut. 'Looks like a piece of shrapnel,' he said. 'She ought to see the Doc.'

Peter and I made a chair with our hands and Fin lifted her up on to it. We started back through the streets and out towards the aerodrome, the two of us walking a little awkwardly, bending down, facing our burden. I could feel Peter's fingers clasped tightly in mine and I could feel the buttocks of the little girl resting lightly on my wrists. I was on the left side and the blood was dripping down from her face on to the arm of my flying suit, running down the waterproof cloth on to the back of my hand. The girl never moved or said anything.

Fin said, 'She's bleeding rather fast. We'd better walk a bit quicker.'

I couldn't see much of her face because of the blood, but I could tell that she was lovely. She had high cheekbones and large round eyes, pale blue like an autumn sky, and her hair was short and fair. I guessed she was about nine years old.

This was in Greece in early April 1941, at Paramythia. Our fighter squadron was stationed on a muddy field near the village. We were in a deep valley and all around us were the mountains. The freezing winter had passed, and now, almost before anyone knew it, spring had come. It had come quietly and swiftly, melting the ice on the lakes and brushing the snow off the mountain tops; and all over the airfield we could see the pale-green shoots of grass pushing up through the mud, making a carpet for our landings. In our valley there were warm winds and wild flowers.

The Germans, who had pushed in through Yugoslavia a few days before, were now operating in force, and that afternoon they had come over very high with about thirty-five Dorniers and bombed the village. Peter and Fin and I were off duty for a while, and the three of us had gone down to see if there was anything we could do in the way of rescue work. We had spent a few hours digging around in the ruins and helping to put out fires, and we were on our way back when we saw the girl.

Now, as we approached the landing field, we could see the Hurricanes circling around coming in to land, and there was the Doc standing out in front of the dispersal tent, just as he should have been, waiting to see if anyone had been hurt. We walked towards him, carrying the child, and Fin, who was a few yards in front, said, 'Doc, you lazy old devil, here's a job for you.'

The Doc was young and kind and morose except when he got drunk. When he got drunk he sang very well.

'Take her into the sick bay,' he said. Peter and I carried her in and put her down on a chair. Then we left her and wandered over to the dispersal tent to see how the boys had got along.

It was beginning to get dark. There was a sunset behind the ridge over in the west, and there was a full moon, a bombers' moon, climbing up into the sky. The moon shone upon the shoulders of the tents and made them white; small white pyramids, standing up straight, clustering in little orderly groups around the edges of the aerodrome. They had a scared-sheep look about them the way they clustered themselves together, and they had a human look about them the way they stood up close to one another, and it seemed almost as though they knew that there was going to be trouble, as though someone had warned them that they might be forgotten and left behind. Even as I looked, I thought I saw them move. I thought I saw them huddle just a fraction nearer together.

And then, silently, without a sound, the mountains crept a little closer into our valley.

For the next two days there was much flying. There was the getting up at dawn, there was the flying, the fighting and the sleeping; and there was the retreat of the Army. That was about all there was or all there was time for. But on the third day the clouds dropped down over the mountains and slid into the valley. And it rained, so we sat around in the mess-tent drinking beer and resinato, while the rain made a noise like a sewing machine on the roof. Then lunch. For the first time in days the whole squadron was present. Fifteen pilots at a long table with benches on either side and Monkey, the CO, sitting at the head.

We were still in the middle of our fried corned beef when the flap of the tent opened and in came the Doc with an enormous dripping raincoat over his head. And with him, under the coat, was the little girl. She had a bandage round her head.

The Doc said, 'Hello. I've brought a guest.' We looked around and suddenly, automatically, we all stood up.

The Doc was taking off his raincoat and the little girl was standing there with her hands hanging loose by her sides looking at the men, and the men were all looking at her. With her fair hair and pale skin she looked less like a Greek than anyone I've ever seen. She was frightened by the fifteen scruffy-looking foreigners who had suddenly stood up when she came in, and for a moment she half turned as if she were going to run away out into the rain.

Monkey said, 'Hallo. Hallo there. Come and sit down.'

'Talk Greek,' the Doc said. 'She doesn't understand.'

Fin and Peter and I looked at one another and Fin said, 'Good God, it's our little girl. Nice work, Doc.'

She recognized Fin and walked round to where he was standing. He took her by the hand and sat her down on the bench, and everyone else sat down too. We gave her some fried corned beef and she ate it slowly, looking down at her plate while she ate. Monkey said, 'Get Pericles.'

Pericles was the Greek interpreter attached to the squadron. He was a wonderful man we'd picked up at Yanina, where he had been the local schoolteacher. He had been out of work ever since the war started. 'The children do not come to school,' he said. 'They are up in the mountains and fight. I cannot teach sums to the stones.'

Pericles came in. He was old, with a beard, a long pointed nose and sad grey eyes. You couldn't see his mouth, but his beard had a way of smiling when he talked.

'Ask her her name,' said Monkey.

He said something to her in Greek. She looked up and said, 'Katina.' That was all she said.

'Look, Pericles,' Peter said, 'ask her what she was doing sitting by that heap of ruins in the village.'

Fin said, 'For God's sake, leave her alone.'

'Ask her, Pericles,' said Peter.

'What should I ask?' said Pericles, frowning.

Peter said, 'What she was doing sitting on that heap of stuff in the village when we found her.'

Pericles sat down on the bench beside her and he talked to her again. He spoke gently and you could see that his beard was smiling a little as he spoke, helping her. She listened and it seemed a long time before she answered. When she spoke, it was only a few words, and the old man translated: 'She says that her family were under the stones.'

Outside the rain was coming down harder than ever. It beat upon the roof of the mess-tent so that the canvas shivered as the water bounced upon it. I got up and walked over and lifted the flap of the tent. The mountains were invisible behind the rain, but I knew they were around us on every side. I had a feeling that they were laughing at us, laughing at the smallness of our numbers and at the hopeless courage of the pilots. I felt that it was the mountains, not us, who were the clever ones. Had not the hills that very morning turned and looked northwards towards Tepelene, where they had seen a thousand German aircraft gathered under the shadow of Olympus? Was it not true that the snow on the top of Dodona had melted away in a day, sending little rivers of water running down across our landing field? Had not Kataphidi buried his head in a cloud so that our pilots might be tempted to fly through the whiteness and crash against his rugged shoulders?

And as I stood there looking at the rain through the tent flap, I knew for certain that the mountains had turned against us. I could feel it in my stomach.

I went back into the tent and there was Fin, sitting beside Katina, trying to teach her English words. I don't know whether he made much progress, but I do know that once he made her laugh and that was a wonderful thing for him to have done. I remember the sudden sound of her high laughter and how we all looked up and saw her face; how we saw how different it was to what it had been before. No one but Fin could have done it. He was so gay himself that it was difficult to be serious in his presence. He was gay and tall and black-haired, and he was sitting there on the bench, leaning forward, whispering and smiling, teaching Katina to speak English and teaching her how to laugh.

The next day the skies cleared and once again we saw the mountains. We did a patrol over the troops which were already retreating slowly towards Thermopylae, and we met some Messerschmitts and Ju-87s dive-bombing the soldiers. I think we got a few of them, but they got Sandy. I saw him going down. I sat quite still for thirty seconds and watched his plane spiralling gently downwards. I sat and waited for the parachute. I remember switching over my radio and saying quietly, 'Sandy, you must jump now. You must jump; you're getting near the ground.' But there was no parachute.

When we landed and taxied in, there was Katina, standing outside the dispersal tent with the Doc; a tiny shrimp of a girl in a dirty print dress, standing there watching the machines as they came in to land. To Fin, as he walked in, she said, '*Tha girisis xana*.'

Fin said, 'What does it mean, Pericles?'

'It just means "You are back again,"' and he smiled.

The child had counted the aircraft on her fingers as they took off, and now she noticed that there was one missing. We were standing around taking off our parachutes and she was trying to ask us about it, when suddenly someone said, 'Look out. Here they come.' They came through a gap in the hills, a mass of thin, black silhouettes, coming down upon the aerodrome.

There was a scramble for the slit trenches and I remember seeing Fin catch Katina round the waist and carry her off with us, and I remember seeing her fight like a tiger the whole way to the trenches.

As soon as we got into the trench and Fin had let her go, she jumped out and ran over on to the airfield. Down came the Messerschmitts with their guns blazing, swooping so low that you could see the noses of the pilots sticking out under their goggles. Their bullets threw up spurts of dust all around and I saw one of our Hurricanes burst into flames. I saw Katina standing right in the middle of the field, standing firmly with her legs astride and her back to us, looking up at the Germans as they dived past. I have never seen anything smaller and more angry and more fierce in my life. She seemed to be shouting at them, but the noise was great and one could hear nothing at all except the engines and the guns of the aeroplanes.

Then it was over. It was over as quickly as it had begun, and no one said very much except Fin, who said, 'I wouldn't have done that, ever; not even if I was crazy.'

That evening Monkey got out the squadron records and added Katina's name to the list of members, and the equipment officer was ordered to provide a tent for her. So, on 11 April 1941, she became a member of the squadron.

In two days she knew the first name or nickname of every pilot and Fin had already taught her to say 'Any luck?' and 'Nice work.'

But that was a time of much activity, and when I try to think of it hour by hour, the whole period becomes hazy in my mind. Mostly, I remember, it was escorting the Blenheims to Valona, and if it wasn't that, it was a ground-strafe of Italian trucks on the Albanian border or an SOS from the Northumberland Regiment saying they were having the hell bombed out of them by half the aircraft in Europe.

None of that can I remember. I can remember nothing of that time clearly, save for two things. The one was Katina and how she was with us all the time; how she was everywhere and how wherever she went the people were pleased to see her. The other thing that I remember was when the Bull came into the mess-tent one evening after a lone patrol. The Bull was an enormous man with massive, slightly hunched shoulders and his chest was like the top of an oak table. Before the war he had done many things, most of them things which one could not do unless one conceded beforehand that there was no difference between life and death. He was quiet and casual and when he came into a room or into a tent, he always looked as though he had made a mistake and hadn't really meant to come in at all. It was getting dark and we were sitting round in the tent playing shove-halfpenny when the Bull came in. We knew that he had just landed.

He glanced around a little apologetically, then he said, 'Hello,' and wandered over to the bar and began to get out a bottle of beer.

Someone said, 'See anything, Bull?'

The Bull said, 'Yes,' and went on fiddling with the bottle of beer.

I suppose we were all very interested in our game of shove-halfpenny because no one said anything else for about five minutes. Then Peter said, 'What did you see, Bull?'

The Bull was leaning against the bar, alternately sipping his beer and trying to make a hooting noise by blowing down the neck of the empty bottle.

Peter said, 'What did you see?'

The Bull put down the bottle and looked up. 'Five S-79s,' he said.

I remember hearing him say it, but I remember also that our game was exciting and that Fin had one more shove to win. We all watched him miss it and Peter said, 'Fin, I think you're going to lose.' And Fin said, 'Go to hell.'

We finished the game, then I looked up and saw the

Bull still leaning against the bar making noises with his beer bottle.

He said, 'This sounds like the old *Mauretania* coming into New York harbour,' and he started blowing into the bottle again.

'What happened with the S-79s?' I said.

He stopped his blowing and put down the bottle.

'I shot them down.'

Everyone heard it. At that moment eleven pilots in that tent stopped what they were doing and eleven heads flicked around and looked at the Bull. He took another drink of his beer and said quietly, 'At one time I counted eighteen parachutes in the air together.'

A few days later he went on patrol and did not come back.

Shortly afterwards Monkey got a message from Athens. It said that the squadron was to move down to Elevsis and from there do a defence of Athens itself and also cover the troops retreating through the Thermopylae Pass.

Katina was to go with the trucks and we told the Doc he was to see that she arrived safely. It would take them a day to make the journey. We flew over the mountains towards the south, fourteen of us, and at two thirty we landed at Elevsis. It was a lovely aerodrome with runways and hangars; and best of all, Athens was only twenty-five minutes away by car.

That evening, as it was getting dark, I stood outside my tent. I stood with my hands in my pockets watching the sun go down and thinking of the work which we were to do. The more that I thought of it, the more impossible I knew it to be. I looked up, and once again I saw the mountains. They were closer to us here, crowding in upon us on all sides, standing shoulder to shoulder, tall and naked, with their heads in the clouds, surrounding us everywhere save in the south, where lay Piraeus and the open sea. I knew that each night, when it was very dark, when we were all tired and sleeping in our tents, those mountains would move forward, creeping a little closer, making no noise, until at last on the appointed day they would tumble forward with one great rush and push us into the sea.

Fin emerged from his tent.

'Have you seen the mountains?' I said.

'They're full of gods. They aren't any good,' he answered.

'I wish they'd stand still,' I said.

Fin looked up at the great crags of Parnes and Pentelikon.

'They're full of gods,' he said. 'Sometimes, in the middle of the night, when there is a moon, you can see the gods sitting on the summits. There was one on Kataphidi when we were at Paramythia. He was huge, like a house but without any shape and quite black.'

'You saw him?'

'Of course I saw him.'

'When?' I said. 'When did you see him, Fin?'

Fin said, 'Let's go into Athens. Let's go and look at the women in Athens.'

The next day the trucks carrying the ground staff and the equipment rumbled on to the aerodrome, and there was Katina sitting in the front seat of the leading vehicle with the Doc beside her. She waved to us as she jumped down, and she came running towards us, laughing and calling our names in a curious Greek way. She still had on the same dirty print dress and she still had a bandage round her forehead; but the sun was shining in her hair.

We showed her the tent which we had prepared for her and we showed her the small cotton nightdress which Fin had obtained in some mysterious way the night before in Athens. It was white with a lot of little blue birds embroidered on the front and we all thought that it was very beautiful. Katina wanted to put it on at once and it took a long time to persuade her that it was meant only for sleeping in. Six times Fin had to perform a complicated act which consisted of pretending to put on the nightdress, then jumping on to the bed and falling fast asleep. In the end she nodded vigorously and understood.

For the next two days nothing happened, except that the remnants of another squadron came down from the north and joined us. They brought six Hurricanes, so that altogether we had about twenty machines.

Then we waited.

On the third day German reconnaissance aircraft appeared, circling high over Piraeus, and we chased after them but never got up in time to catch them. This was understandable, because our radar was of a very special type. It is obsolete now, and I doubt whether it will ever be used again. All over the country, in all the villages, up on the mountains and out on the islands, there were

Greeks, all of whom were connected to our small operations room by field telephone.

We had no operations officer, so we took it in turns to be on duty for the day. My turn came on the fourth day, and I remember clearly what happened.

At six thirty in the morning the phone buzzed.

'This is A-7,' said a very Greek voice. 'This is A-7. There are noises overhead.'

I looked at the map. There was a little ring with 'A-7' written inside it just beside Yanina. I put a cross on the celluloid which covered the map and wrote 'Noises' beside it, as well as the time: '0631 hours.'

Three minutes later the phone went again.

'This is A-4. This is A-4. There are many noises above me,' said an old quavering voice, 'but I cannot see because there are thick clouds.'

I looked at the map. A-4 was Mount Karava. I made another cross on the celluloid and wrote 'Many noises – 0634,' and then I drew a line between Yanina and Karava. It pointed towards Athens, so I signalled the 'readiness' crew to scramble, and they took off and circled the city. Later they saw a Ju-88 on reconnaissance high above them, but they never caught it. It was in such a way that one worked the radar.

That evening when I came off duty I could not help thinking of the old Greek, sitting all alone in a hut up at A-4; sitting on the slope of Karava looking up into the whiteness and listening all day and all night for noises in the sky. I imagined the eagerness with which he seized the telephone when he heard something, and the joy he must have felt when the voice at the other end repeated his message and thanked him. I thought of his clothes and wondered if they were warm enough and I thought, for some reason, of his boots, which almost certainly had no soles left upon them and were stuffed with tree bark and paper.

That was April seventeenth. It was the evening when Monkey said, 'They say the Germans are at Lamia, which means that we're within range of their fighters. Tomorrow the fun should start.'

It did. At dawn the bombers came over, with the fighters circling around overhead, watching the bombers, waiting to pounce, but doing nothing unless someone interfered with the bombers.

I think we got eight Hurricanes into the air just before they arrived. It was not my turn to go up, so with Katina standing by my side I watched the battle from the ground. The child never said a word. Now and again she moved her head as she followed the little specks of silver dancing high above in the sky. I saw a plane coming down in a trail of black smoke and I looked at Katina. The hatred which was on the face of the child was the fierce burning hatred of an old woman who has hatred in her heart; it was an old woman's hatred and it was strange to see it.

In that battle we lost a sergeant called Donald.

At noon Monkey got another message from Athens. It said that morale was bad in the capital and that every available Hurricane was to fly in formation low over the city in order to show the inhabitants how strong we were and how many aircraft we had. Eighteen of us took off. We flew in tight formation up and down the main streets just above the roofs of the houses. I could see the people looking up, shielding their eyes from the sun, looking at us as we flew over, and in one street I saw an old woman who never looked up at all. None of them waved, and I knew then that they were resigned to their fate. None of them waved, and I knew, although I could not see their faces, that they were not even glad as we flew past.

Then we headed out towards Thermopylae, but on the way we circled the Acropolis twice. It was the first time I had seen it so close.

I saw a little hill – a mound almost, it seemed – and on the top of it I saw the white columns. There were a great number of them, grouped together in perfect order, not crowding one another, white in the sunshine, and I wondered, as I looked at them, how anyone could have put so much on top of so small a hill in such an elegant way.

Then we flew up the great Thermopylae Pass and I saw long lines of vehicles moving slowly southwards towards the sea. I saw occasional puffs of white smoke where a shell landed in the valley and I saw a direct hit on the road which made a gap in the line of trucks. But we saw no enemy aircraft.

When we landed Monkey said, 'Refuel quickly and get in the air again; I think they're waiting to catch us on the ground.'

But it was no use. They came down out of the sky five minutes after we had landed. I remember I was in the pilots' room in Number Two Hangar, talking to Fin and to a big tall man with rumpled hair called Paddy. We heard the bullets on the corrugated-iron roof of the hangar, then we heard explosions and the three of us dived under the little wooden table in the middle of the room. But the table upset. Paddy set it up again and crawled underneath. 'There's something about being under a table,' he said. 'I don't feel safe unless I'm under a table.'

Fin said, 'I never feel safe.' He was sitting on the floor watching the bullets making holes in the corrugated-iron wall of the room. There was a great clatter as the bullets hit the tin.

Then we became brave and got up and peeped outside the door. There were many Messerschmitt 109s circling the aerodrome, and one by one they straightened out and dived past the hangars, spraying the ground with their guns. But they did something else. They slid back their cockpit hoods and as they came past they threw out small bombs which exploded when they hit the ground and fiercely flung quantities of large lead balls in every direction. Those were the explosions which we had heard, and it was a great noise that the lead balls made as they hit the hangar.

Then I saw the men, the ground crews, standing up in their slit trenches firing at the Messerschmitts with rifles, reloading and firing as fast as they could, cursing and shouting as they shot, aiming ludicrously, hopelessly, aiming at an aeroplane with just a rifle. At Elevsis there were no other defences.

Suddenly the Messerschmitts all turned and headed for home, all except one, which glided down and made a smooth belly landing on the aerodrome.

Then there was chaos. The Greeks around us raised a shout and jumped on to the fire tender and headed out towards the crashed German aeroplane. At the same time more Greeks streamed out from every corner of the field, shouting and yelling and crying for the blood of the pilot. It was a mob intent upon vengeance and one could not blame them; but there were other considerations. We wanted the pilot for questioning, and we wanted him alive.

Monkey, who was standing on the tarmac, shouted to us, and Fin and Paddy and I raced with him towards the station wagon which was standing fifty yards away. Monkey was inside like a flash, started the engine and drove off just as the three of us jumped on the running board. The fire tender with the Greeks on it was not fast and it still had two hundred yards to go, and the other people had a long way to run. Monkey drove quickly and we beat them by about fifty yards.

We jumped up and ran over to the Messerschmitt, and there, sitting in the cockpit, was a fair-haired boy with pink cheeks and blue eyes. I have never seen anyone whose face showed so much fear.

He said to Monkey in English, 'I am hit in the leg.'

We pulled him out of the cockpit and got him into the car, while the Greeks stood around watching. The bullet had shattered the bone in his shin.

We drove him back and as we handed him over to the Doc, I saw Katina standing close, looking at the face of the German. This kid of nine was standing there looking at the German and she could not speak; she could not even move. She clutched the skirt of her dress in her hands and stared at the man's face. 'There is a mistake somewhere,' she seemed to be saying. 'There must be a mistake. This one has pink cheeks and fair hair and blue eyes. This cannot possibly be one of them. This is an ordinary boy.' She watched him as they put him on a stretcher and carried him off, then she turned and ran across the grass to her tent.

In the evening at supper I ate my fried sardines, but I could not eat the bread or the cheese. For three days I had been conscious of my stomach, of a hollow feeling such as one gets just before an operation or while waiting to have a tooth out in the dentist's house. I had had it all day for three days, from the moment I woke up to the time I fell asleep. Peter was sitting opposite me and I asked him about it.

'I've had it for a week,' he said. 'It's good for the bowels. It loosens them.'

'German aircraft are like liver pills,' said Fin from the bottom of the table. 'They are very good for you, aren't they, Doc?'

The Doc said, 'Maybe you've had an overdose.'

'I have,' said Fin, 'I've had an overdose of German liver pills. I didn't read the instructions on the bottle. Take two before retiring.'

Peter said, 'I would love to retire.'

After supper three of us walked down to the hangars with Monkey, who said, 'I'm worried about this ground-strafing. They never attack the hangars because they know that we never put anything inside them. Tonight I think we'll collect four of the aircraft and put them into Number Two Hangar.'

That was a good idea. Normally the Hurricanes were dispersed all over the edge of the aerodrome, but they were being picked off one by one, because it was impossible to be in the air the whole time. The four of us took a machine each and taxied it into Number Two Hangar, and then we pulled the great sliding doors together and locked them.

The next morning, before the sun had risen from behind the mountains, a flock of Ju-87s came over and blew Number Two Hangar right off the face of the earth. Their bombing was good and they did not even hit the hangars on either side of it.

That afternoon they got Peter. He went off towards a village called Khalkis, which was being bombed by Ju-88s, and no one ever saw him again. Gay, laughing Peter, whose mother lived on a farm in Kent and who used to write to him in long, pale-blue envelopes which he carried about in his pockets.

I had always shared a tent with Peter, ever since I came to the squadron, and that evening after I had gone to bed he came back to that tent. You need not believe me; I do not expect you to, but I am telling you what happened.

I always went to bed first, because there is not room in one of those tents for two people to be turning around at the same time. Peter usually came in two or three minutes afterwards. That evening I went to bed and I lay thinking that tonight he would not be coming. I wondered whether his body lay tangled in the wreckage of his aircraft on the side of some bleak mountain or whether it was at the bottom of the sea, and I hoped only that he had had a decent funeral.

Suddenly I heard a movement. The flap of the tent opened and it shut again. But there were no footsteps. Then I heard him sit down on his bed. It was a noise that I had heard every night for weeks past and always it had been the same. It was just a thump and a creaking of the wooden legs of the camp bed. One after the other the flying boots were pulled off and dropped upon the ground, and as always one of them took three times as long to get off as the other. After that there was the gentle rustle of a blanket being pulled back and then the creakings of the rickety bed as it took the weight of a man's body.

They were sounds I had heard every night, the same sounds in the same order, and now I sat up in bed and said, 'Peter.' It was dark in the tent. My voice sounded very loud.

'Hallo, Peter. That was tough luck you had today.' But there was no answer.

I did not feel uneasy or frightened, but I remember at the time touching the tip of my nose with my finger to make sure that I was there; then because I was very tired, I went to sleep.

In the morning I looked at the bed and saw it had been slept in. But I did not show it to anyone, not even to Fin. I put the blankets back in place myself and patted the pillow.

It was on that day, 20 April 1941, that we fought the Battle of Athens. It was perhaps the last of the great dog-fighting air battles that will ever be fought, because nowadays the planes fly always in great formations of wings and squadrons, and attack is carried out methodically and scientifically upon the orders of the leader. Nowadays one does not dog-fight at all over the sky except upon very rare occasions. But the Battle of Athens was a long and beautiful dog-fight in which fifteen Hurricanes fought for half an hour with between one hundred and fifty and two hundred German bombers and fighters.

The bombers started coming over early in the afternoon. It was a lovely spring day and for the first time the sun had in it a trace of real summer warmth. The sky was blue, save for a few wispy clouds here and there and the mountains stood out black and clear against the blue of the sky.

Pentelikon no longer hid his head in the clouds. He stood over us, grim and forbidding, watching every move and knowing that each thing we did was of little purpose. Men were foolish and were made only so that they should die, while mountains and rivers went on for ever and did not notice the passing of time. Had not Pentelikon himself many years ago looked down upon Thermopylae and seen a handful of Spartans defending the pass against the invaders; seen them fight until there was not one man left alive among them? Had he not seen the Persians cut to pieces by Leonidas at Marathon, and had he not looked down upon Salamis and upon the sea when Themistocles and the Athenians drove the enemy from their shores, causing them to lose more than two hundred sail? All these things and many more he had seen, and now he looked down upon us, we were as nothing in his eyes. Almost there was a look of scorn upon the face of the mountain, and I thought for a moment that I could hear the laughter of the gods. They knew so well that we were not enough and that in the end we must lose.

The bombers came over just after lunch, and at once we saw that there were a great number of them. We looked up and saw that the sky was full of little silver specks and the sunlight danced and sparkled upon a hundred different pairs of wings.

There were fifteen Hurricanes in all and they fought like a storm in the sky. It is not easy to remember much about such a battle, but I remember looking up and seeing in the sky a mass of small black dots. I remember thinking to myself that those could not be aeroplanes; they simply could not be aeroplanes, because there were not so many aeroplanes in the world.

Then they were on us, and I remember that I applied a little flap so that I should be able to turn in tighter circles; then I remember only one or two small incidents which photographed themselves upon my mind. There were the spurts of flame from the guns of a Messerschmitt as he attacked from the frontal quarter of my starboard side. There was the German whose parachute was on fire as it opened. There was the German who flew up beside me and made rude signs at me with his fingers. There was the Hurricane which collided with a Messerschmitt. There was the aeroplane which collided with a man who was descending in a parachute, and which went into a crazy frightful spin towards the earth with the man and the parachute dangling from its port wing. There were the two bombers which collided while swerving to avoid a fighter, and I remember distinctly seeing a man being thrown clear out of the smoke and debris of the collision, hanging in mid-air with his arms outstretched and his legs apart. I tell you there was nothing that did not happen in that battle. There was the moment when I saw a single Hurricane doing tight turns around the summit of Mt Parnes with nine Messerschmitts on its tail and then I remember that suddenly the skies seemed to clear. There were no longer any aircraft in sight. The battle was over. I turned around and headed back towards Elevsis, and as I went I looked down and saw Athens and Piraeus and the rim of the sea as it curved around the gulf and travelled southward towards the Mediterranean. I saw the port of Piraeus where the bombs had fallen and I saw the smoke and fire rising above the docks. I saw the narrow coastal plain, and on it I saw tiny bonfires, thin columns of black smoke curling upward and drifting away to the east. They were the fires of aircraft which had been shot down, and I hoped only that none of them were Hurricanes.

Just then I ran straight into a Junkers 88; a straggler, the last bomber returning from the raid. He was in trouble and there was black smoke streaming from one of his engines. Although I shot at him, I don't think that it made any difference. He was coming down anyway. We were over the sea and I could tell that he wouldn't make the land. He didn't. He came down smoothly on his belly in the blue Gulf of Piraeus, two miles from the shore. I followed him and circled, waiting to make sure that the crew got out safely into their dinghy.

Slowly the machine began to sink, dipping its nose under the water and lifting its tail into the air. But there was no sign of the crew. Suddenly, without any warning, the rear gun started to fire. They opened up with their rear gun and the bullets made small jagged holes in my starboard wing. I swerved away and I remember shouting at them. I slid back the hood of the cockpit and shouted, 'You lousy brave bastards. I hope you drown.' The bomber sank soon backwards.

When I got back they were all standing around outside the hangars counting the score, and Katina was sitting on a box with tears rolling down her cheeks. But she was not crying, and Fin was kneeling down beside her, talking to her in English, quietly and gently, forgetting that she could not understand.

We lost one third of our Hurricanes in that battle, but the Germans lost more.

The Doc was dressing someone who had been burned and he looked up and said, 'You should have heard the Greeks on the aerodrome cheering as the bombers fell out of the sky.'

As we stood around talking, a truck drove up and a Greek got out and said that he had some pieces of body inside. 'This is the watch,' he said, 'that was on the arm.' It was a silver wristwatch with a luminous dial, and on the back there were some initials. We did not look inside the truck.

Now we had, I think, nine Hurricanes left.

That evening a very senior RAF officer came out from Athens and said, 'Tomorrow at dawn you will all fly to Megara. It is about ten miles down the coast. There is a small field there on which you can land. The Army is working on it throughout the night. They have two big rollers there and they are rolling it smooth. The moment you land you must hide your aircraft in the olive grove which is on the south side of the field. The ground staff are going farther south to Argos and you can join them later, but you may be able to operate from Megara for a day or two.'

Fin said, 'Where's Katina? Doc, you must find Katina and see that she gets to Argos safely.'

The Doc said, 'I will,' and we knew that we could trust him.

At dawn the next morning, when it was still dark, we took off and flew to the little field at Megara, ten miles away. We landed and hid our Hurricanes in the olive grove and broke off branches of the trees and put them over the aircraft. Then we sat down on the slope of a small hill and waited for orders.

As the sun rose up over the mountains we looked across the field and saw a mass of Greek villagers coming down from the village of Megara, coming down towards our field. There were many hundreds of them, women and children mostly, and they all came down towards our field, hurrying as they came.

Fin said, 'What the hell,' and we sat up on our little hill and watched, wondering what they were going to do.

They dispersed all around the edge of the field and gathered armfuls of heather and bracken. They carried it out on to the field, and forming themselves into long lines, they began to scatter the heather and the bracken over the grass. They were camouflaging our landing field. The rollers, when they had rolled out the ground and made it flat for landing, had left marks which were easily visible from above, and so the Greeks came out of their village, every man, woman and child, and began to put matters right. To this day I do not know who told them to do it. They stretched in a long line across the field, walking forward slowly and scattering the heather, and Fin and I went out and walked among them.

They were old women and old men mostly, very small and very sad-looking, with dark, deeply wrinkled faces, and they worked slowly scattering the heather. As we walked by, they would stop their work and smile, saying something in Greek which we could not understand. One of the children gave Fin a small pink flower and he did not know what to do with it, but walked around carrying it in his hand.

Then we went back to the slope of the hill and waited. Soon the field telephone buzzed. It was the very senior officer speaking. He said that someone must fly back to Elevsis at once and collect important messages and money. He said also that all of us must leave our little field at Megara and go to Argos that evening. The others said that they would wait until I came back with the money so that we could all fly to Argos together.

At the same time, someone had told the two Army men

who were still rolling our field to destroy their rollers so that the Germans would not get them. I remember, as I was getting into my Hurricane, seeing the two huge rollers charging towards each other across the field, and I remember seeing the Army men jump aside just before they collided. There was a great crash and I saw all the Greeks who were scattering heather stop in their work and look up. For a moment they stood rock still, looking at the rollers. Then one of them started to run. It was an old woman and she started to run back to the village as fast as she could, shouting something as she went, and instantly every man, woman and child in the field seemed to take fright and ran after her. I wanted to get out and run beside them and explain to them; to say I was sorry but that there was nothing else we could do. I wanted to tell them that we would not forget them and that one day we would come back. But it was no use. Bewildered and frightened, they ran back to their homes, and they did not stop running until they were out of sight, not even the old men.

I took off and flew to Elevsis. I landed on a dead aerodrome. There was not a soul to be seen. I parked my Hurricane, and as I walked over to the hangars the bombers came over once again. I hid in a ditch until they had finished their work, then got up and walked over to the small operations room. The telephone was still on the table, so for some reason I picked up the receiver and said, 'Hallo.'

A rather German voice at the other end answered.

I said, 'Can you hear me?' and the voice said: 'Yes, yes, I can hear you.'

'All right,' I said, 'Listen carefully.'

'Yes, continue please.'

'This is the RAF speaking. And one day we will come back, do you understand? One day we will come back.'

Then I tore the telephone from its socket and threw it through the glass of the closed window. When I went outside there was a small man in civilian clothes standing near the door. He had a revolver in one hand and a small bag in the other.

'Do you want anything?' he said in quite good English.

I said, 'Yes, I want important messages and papers which I am to carry back to Argos.'

'Here you are,' he said, as he handed me the bag. 'And good luck.'

I flew back to Megara. There were two Greek destroyers standing offshore, burning and sinking. I circled our field and the others taxied out, took off and we all flew off towards Argos.

The landing ground at Argos was just a kind of small field. It was surrounded by thick olive groves into which we taxied our aircraft for hiding. I don't know how long the field was, but it was not easy to land upon it. You had to come in low hanging on the prop, and the moment you touched down you had to start putting on the brake, jerking it on and jerking it off again the moment she started to nose over. But only one man overshot and crashed.

The ground staff had arrived already and as we got out of our aircraft Katina came running up with a basket of black olives, offering them to us and pointing to our stomachs, indicating that we must eat.

Fin bent down and ruffled her hair with his hand. He said, 'Katina, one day we must go into town and buy you a new dress.' She smiled at him but did not understand and we all started to eat black olives.

Then I looked around and saw that the wood was full of aircraft. Around every corner there was an aeroplane hidden in the trees, and when we asked about it we learned that the Greeks had brought the whole of their air force down to Argos and parked them in that little wood. They were peculiar ancient models, not one of them less than five years old, and I don't know how many dozen there were there.

That night we slept under the trees. We wrapped Katina up in a large flying suit and gave her a flying helmet for a pillow, and after she had gone to sleep we sat around eating black olives and drinking resinato out of an enormous cask. But we were very tired, and soon we fell asleep.

All the next day we saw the truckloads of troops moving down the road towards the sea, and as often as we could we took off and flew above them.

The Germans kept coming over and bombing the road near by, but they had not yet spotted our airfield.

Later in the day we were told that every available Hurricane was to take off at six p.m. to protect an important shipping move, and the nine machines, which were all that were now left, were refuelled and got ready. At three minutes to six we began to taxi out of the olive grove on to the field.

The first two machines took off, but just as they left the ground something black swept down out of the sky and shot them both down in flames. I looked around and saw at least fifty Messerschmitt 110s circling our field, and even as I looked some of them turned and came down upon the remaining seven Hurricanes which were waiting to take off.

There was no time to do anything. Each one of our aircraft was hit in that first swoop, although funnily enough only one of the pilots was hurt. It was impossible now to take off, so we jumped out of our aircraft, hauled the wounded pilot out of his cockpit and ran with him back to the slit trenches, to the wonderful big, deep zigzagging slit trenches which had been dug by the Greeks.

The Messerschmitts took their time. There was no opposition either from the ground or from the air, except that Fin was firing his revolver.

It is not a pleasant thing to be ground-strafed, especially if they have cannon in their wings; and unless one has a deep slit trench in which to lie, there is no future in it. For some reason, perhaps because they thought it was a good joke, the German pilots went for the slit trenches before they bothered about the aircraft. The first ten minutes was spent rushing madly around the corners of the trenches so as not to be caught in a trench which ran parallel with the line of flight of the attacking aircraft. It was a hectic, dreadful ten minutes, with everyone shouting, 'Here comes another,' and scrambling and rushing to get around the corner into the other section of the trench.

Then the Germans went for the Hurricanes and at the same time for the mass of old Greek aircraft parked all around the olive grove, and one by one, methodically and systematically, they set them on fire. The noise was terrific, and everywhere – in the trees, on the rocks and on the grass – the bullets splattered.

I remember peeping cautiously over the top of our trench and seeing a small white flower growing just a few inches away from my nose. It was pure white and it had three petals. I remember looking past it and seeing three of the Germans diving on my own Hurricane which was parked on the other side of the field and I remember shouting at them, although I do not know what I said.

Then suddenly I saw Katina. She was running out from the far corner of the aerodrome, running right out into the middle of this mass of blazing guns and burning aircraft, running as fast as she could. Once she stumbled, but she scrambled to her feet again and went on running. Then she stopped and stood looking up, raising her fists at the planes as they flew past.

Now as she stood there, I remember seeing one of the Messerschmitts turning and coming in low straight towards her and I remember thinking that she was so small that she could not be hit. I remember seeing the spurts of flame from his guns as he came, and I remember seeing the child, for a split second, standing quite still, facing the machine. I remember that the wind was blowing in her hair.

Then she was down.

The next moment I shall never forget. On every side, as if by magic, men appeared out of the ground. They swarmed out of their trenches and like a crazy mob poured on to the aerodrome, running towards the tiny little bundle which lay motionless in the middle of the field. They ran fast, crouching as they went, and I remember jumping up out of my slit trench and joining with them. I remember thinking of nothing at all and watching the boots of the man in front of me, noticing that he was a little bow-legged and that his blue trousers were much too long.

I remember seeing Fin arrive first, followed closely by a sergeant called Wishful, and I remember seeing the two of them pick up Katina and start running with her back towards the trenches. I saw her leg, which was just a lot of blood and bones, and I saw her chest where the blood was spurting out on to her white print dress; I saw, for a moment, her face, which was white as the snow on top of Olympus.

I ran beside Fin, and as he ran, he kept saying, 'The lousy bastards, the lousy, bloody bastards'; and then as we got to our trench I remember looking round and finding that there was no longer any noise or shooting. The Germans had gone.

Fin said, 'Where's the Doc?' and suddenly there he was, standing beside us, looking at Katina – looking at her face.

The Doc gently touched her wrist and without looking up he said, 'She is not alive.'

They put her down under a little tree, and when I turned away I saw on all sides the fires of countless burning aircraft. I saw my own Hurricane burning near by and I stood staring hopelessly into the flames as they danced around the engine and licked against the metal of the wings.

I stood staring into the flames, and as I stared, the fire became a deeper red and I saw beyond it not a tangled mass of smoking wreckage, but the flames of a hotter and intenser fire which now burned and smouldered in the hearts of the people of Greece.

Still I stared, and as I stared I saw in the centre of the fire, whence the red flames sprang, a bright, white heat, shining bright and without any colour.

As I stared, the brightness diffused and became soft and yellow like sunlight, and through it, beyond it, I saw a young child standing in the middle of a field with the sunlight shining in her hair. For a moment she stood looking up into the sky, which was clear and blue and without any clouds; then she turned and looked towards me, and as she turned I saw that the front of her white print dress was stained deep red, the colour of blood.

Then there was no longer any fire or any flames and I saw before me only the glowing twisted wreckage of a burned-out plane. I must have been standing there for quite a long time.

Only This

First published in *Ladies' Home Journal*
(September 1944)

That night the frost was very heavy. It covered the hedges and whitened the grass in the fields so that it seemed almost as though it had been snowing. But the night was clear and beautiful and bright with stars, and the moon was nearly full.

The cottage stood alone in a corner of the big field. There was a path from the front door which led across the field to a stile and on over the next field to a gate which opened on to the lane about three miles from the village. There were no other houses in sight and the country around was open and flat and many of the fields were under the plough because of the war.

The light of the moon shone upon the cottage. It shone through the open window into the bedroom where the woman was asleep. She slept lying on her back, with her face upturned to the ceiling, with her long hair spread out around her on the pillow, and although she was asleep, her face was not the face of someone who is resting. Once she had been beautiful, but now there were thin furrows running across her forehead and there was a tightness about the way in which her skin was stretched over the cheekbones. But her mouth was still gentle, and as she slept, she did not close her lips.

The bedroom was small, with a low ceiling, and for furniture there was a dressing-table and an armchair. The clothes of the woman lay over the back of the armchair where she had put them when she undressed. Her black shoes were on the floor beside the chair. On the dressing-table there was a hairbrush, a letter and a large photograph of a young boy in uniform who wore a pair of wings on the left side of his tunic. It was a smiling photograph, the kind that one likes to send to one's mother, and it had a thin, black frame made of wood. The moon shone through the open window and the woman slept her restless sleep. There was no noise anywhere save for the soft, regular noise of her breathing and the rustle of the bedclothes as she stirred in her sleep.

Then, from far away, there came a deep, gentle rumble which grew and grew and became louder and louder until soon the whole sky seemed to be filled with a great noise which throbbed and throbbed and kept on throbbing and did not stop.

Right at the beginning, even before it came close, the woman had heard the noise. In her sleep she had been waiting for it, listening for the noise and dreading the moment when it would come. When she heard it, she opened her eyes and for a while she lay quite still, listening. Then she sat up, pushed the bedclothes aside and got out of bed. She went over to the window and placing her hands on the window sill, she leaned out, looking up into the sky; and her long hair fell down over her shoulders, over the thin cotton nightdress which she wore. For many minutes she stood there in the cold, leaning out of the window, hearing the noise, looking up and searching the sky; but she saw only the bright moon and the stars.

'God keep you,' she said aloud. 'Oh dear God keep you safe.'

Then she turned and went quickly over to the bed, pulled the blankets away and wrapped them round her shoulders like a shawl. She slipped her bare feet into the black shoes and walked over to the armchair and pushed it forward so that it was right up in front of the window. Then she sat down.

The noise and the throbbing overhead was very great. For a long time it continued as the huge procession of bombers moved towards the south. All the while the woman sat huddled in her blankets, looking out of the window into the sky.

Then it was over. Once more the night became silent. The frost lay heavy on the field and on the hedges and it seemed as though the whole countryside was holding its breath. An army was marching in the sky. All along the route people had heard the noise and knew what it was; they knew that soon, even before they had gone to sleep, there would be a battle. Men drinking beer in the pubs had stopped their talking in order to listen. Families in their houses had turned off the radio and gone out into their gardens, where they stood looking up into the sky. Soldiers arguing in their tents had stopped their shouting, and men and women walking home at night from the factories had stood still on the road, listening to the noise.

It is always the same. As the bombers move south across the country at night, the people who hear them become strangely silent. For those women whose men are with the planes, the moment is not an easy one to bear.

Now they had gone, and the woman lay back in the armchair and closed her eyes, but she did not sleep. Her face was white and the skin seemed to have been drawn tightly over her cheeks and gathered up in wrinkles around her eyes. Her lips were parted and it was as though she were listening to someone talking. Almost she could hear the sound of his voice as he used to call to her from outside the window when he came back from working in the fields. She could hear him saying he was hungry and asking what there was for supper, and then when he came in he would put his arm around her shoulder and talk to her about what he had been doing all day. She would bring in the supper and he would sit down and start to eat and always he would say, Why don't you have some, and she never knew what to answer except that she wasn't hungry. She would sit and watch him and pour out his tea, and after a while she would take his plate and go out into the kitchen to get him some more.

It was not easy having only one child. The emptiness when he was not there and the knowing all the time that something might happen; the deep conscious knowing that there was nothing else to live for except this; that if something did happen, then you too would be dead. There would be no use in sweeping the floor or washing the dishes or cleaning the house; there would be no use in gathering wood for the fire or in feeding the hens; there would be no use in living.

Now, as she sat there by the open window she did not

feel the cold; she felt only a great loneliness and a great fear. The fear took hold of her and grew upon her so that she could not bear it, and she got up from the chair and leaned out of the window again, looking up into the sky. And as she looked the night was no longer beautiful; it was cold and clear and immensely dangerous. She did not see the fields or the hedges or the carpet of frost upon the countryside; she saw only the depths of the sky and the danger that was there.

Slowly she turned and sank down again into her chair. Now the fear was great. She could think of nothing at all except that she must see him and be with him, that she must see him now because tomorrow would be too late. She let her head rest against the back of the chair and when she closed her eyes she saw the aircraft; she saw it clearly in the moonlight, moving forward through the night like a great, black bird. She was close to it and she could see the way in which the nose of the machine reached out far ahead of everything, as though the bird was craning its neck in the eagerness of its passage. She could see the markings on the wings and on the body and she knew that he was inside. Twice she called to him, but there was no answer; then the fear and the longing welled up within her so that she could stand it no longer and it carried her forward through the night and on and on until she was with him, beside him, so close that she could have touched him had she put out her hand.

He was sitting at the controls with gloves on his hands, dressed in a great bulky flying suit which made his body look huge and shapeless and twice its normal size. He was looking straight ahead at the instruments on the panel, concentrating upon what he was doing and thinking of nothing except flying the machine.

Now she called to him again and he heard her. He looked around and when he saw her, he smiled and stretched out a hand and touched her shoulder, and then all the fear and the loneliness and the longing went out of her and she was happy.

For a long time she stood beside him watching him as he flew the machine. Every now and then he would look around and smile at her, and once he said something, but she could not hear what it was because of the noise of the engines. Suddenly he pointed ahead through the glass windshield of the aeroplane and she saw that the sky was full of searchlights. There were many hundreds of them; long white fingers of light travelling lazily across the sky, swaying this way and that, working in unison so that sometimes several of them would come together and meet in the same spot and after a while they would separate and meet again somewhere else, all the time searching the night for the bombers which were moving in on the target.

Behind the searchlights she saw the flak. It was coming up from the town in a thick many-coloured curtain, and the flash of the shells as they burst in the sky lit up the inside of the bomber.

He was looking straight ahead now, concentrating upon the flying, weaving through the searchlights and going directly into this curtain of flak, and she watched and waited and did not dare to move or to speak lest she distract him from his task.

She knew that they had been hit when she saw the flames from the nearest engine on the left side. She watched them through the glass of the side panel, licking against the surface of the wing as the wind blew them backwards, and she watched them take hold of the wing and come dancing over the black surface until they were right up under the cockpit itself. At first she was not frightened. She could see him sitting there, very cool, glancing continually to one side, watching the flames and flying the machine, and once he looked quickly around and smiled at her and she knew then that there was no danger. All around she saw the searchlights and the flak and the explosions of the flak and the colours of the tracer, and the sky was not a sky but just a small confined space which was so full of lights and explosions that it did not seem possible that one could fly through it.

But the flames were brighter now on the left wing. They had spread over the whole surface. They were alive and active, feeding on the fabric, leaning backwards in the wind which fanned them and encouraged them and gave them no chance of going out.

Then came the explosion. There was a blinding white flash and a hollow *crumph* as though someone had burst a blown-up paper bag; then there was nothing but flames and thick whitish-grey smoke. The flames were coming up through the floor and through the sides of the cockpit; the smoke was so thick that it was difficult to see and almost impossible to breathe. She became terrified and panicky because he was still sitting there at the controls, flying the machine, fighting to keep it on an even keel, turning the wheel first to one side, then to the other, and suddenly there was a blast of cold air and she had a vague impression of urgent crouching figures scrambling past her and throwing themselves away from the burning aircraft.

Now the whole thing was a mass of flames and through the smoke she could see him still sitting there, fighting with the wheel while the crew got out, and as he did so he held one arm up over his face because the heat was so great. She rushed forward and took him by the shoulders and shook him and shouted, 'Come on, quickly, you must get out, quickly, quickly.'

Then she saw that his head had fallen forward upon his chest and that he was limp and unconscious. Frantically she tried to pull him out of the seat and towards the door, but he was too limp and heavy. The smoke was filling her lungs and her throat so that she began to retch and gasp for breath. She was hysterical now, fighting against death and against everything, and she managed to get her hands under his arms and drag him a little way towards the door. But it was impossible to get him farther. His legs were tangled around the wheel and there was a buckle somewhere which she could not undo. She knew then that it was impossible, that there was no hope because of the smoke and the fire and because there was no time; and suddenly all the strength drained out of her body. She fell down on top of him and began to cry as she had never cried before.

Then came the spin and the fierce rushing dive downwards and she was thrown forward into the fire so that the last she knew was the bright yellow of the flames and the smell of the burning.

Her eyes were closed and her head was resting against the back of the chair. Her hands were clutching the edges of the blankets as though she were trying to pull them tighter around her body and her long hair fell down over her shoulders.

Outside the moon was low in the sky. The frost lay heavier than ever on the fields and on the hedges and there was no noise anywhere. Then from far away in the south came a deep gentle rumble which grew and grew and became louder and louder until soon the whole sky was filled with the noise and the singing of those who were coming back.

But the woman who sat by the window never moved. She had been dead for some time.

Beware of the Dog

First published in *Harper's* (October 1944)

Down below there was only a vast white undulating sea of cloud. Above there was the sun, and the sun was white like the clouds, because it is never yellow when one looks at it from high in the air.

He was still flying the Spitfire. His right hand was on the stick and he was working the rudder bar with his left leg alone. It was quite easy. The machine was flying well. He knew what he was doing.

Everything is fine, he thought. I'm doing all right. I'm doing nicely. I know my way home. I'll be there in half an hour. When I land I shall taxi in and switch off my engine and I shall say, Help me to get out, will you. I shall make my voice sound ordinary and natural and none of them will take any notice. Then I shall say, Someone help me to get out. I can't do it alone because I've lost one of my legs. They'll all laugh and think that I'm joking and I shall say, All right, come and have a look, you unbelieving bastards. Then Yorky will climb up on to the wing and look inside. He'll probably be sick because of all the blood and the mess. I shall laugh and say, For God's sake, help me get out.

He glanced down again at his right leg. There was not much of it left. The cannon-shell had taken him on the thigh, just above the knee, and now there was nothing but a great mess and a lot of blood. But there was no pain. When he looked down, he felt as though he were seeing something that did not belong to him. It had nothing to do with him. It was just a mess which happened to be there in the cockpit; something strange and unusual and rather interesting. It was like finding a dead cat on the sofa.

He really felt fine, and because he still felt fine, he felt excited and unafraid.

I won't even bother to call up on the radio for the blood-wagon, he thought. It isn't necessary. And when I land I'll sit there quite normally and say, Some of you fellows come and help me out, will you, because I've lost one of my legs. That will be funny. I'll laugh a little while I'm saying it; I'll say it calmly and slowly, and they'll think I'm joking. When Yorky comes up on to the wing and gets sick, I'll say, Yorky, you old son of a bitch, have you fixed my car yet? Then when I get out I'll make my report. Later I'll go up to London. I'll take that half bottle of whisky with me and I'll give it to Bluey. We'll sit in her room and drink it. I'll get the water out of the bathroom tap. I won't say much until it's time to go to bed, then I'll say, Bluey I've got a surprise for you. I lost a leg today. But I don't mind so long as you don't. It doesn't even hurt. We'll go everywhere in cars. I always hated walking except when I walked down the street of the coppersmiths in Baghdad, but I could go in a rickshaw. I could go home and chop wood, but the head always flies off the axe. Hot water, that's what it needs; put it in the bath and make the handle swell. I chopped lots of wood last time I went home and I put the axe in the bath . . .

Then he saw the sun shining on the engine cowling of his machine. He saw the sun shining on the rivets in the metal, and he remembered the aeroplane and he remembered where he was. He realized that he was no longer feeling good; that he was sick and giddy. His head kept falling forward on to his chest because his neck seemed no longer to have any strength. But he knew that he was flying the Spitfire. He could feel the handle of the stick between the fingers of his right hand.

I'm going to pass out, he thought. Any moment now I'm going to pass out.

He looked at his altimeter. Twenty-one thousand. To test himself he tried to read the hundreds as well as the thousands. Twenty-one thousand and what? As he looked the dial became blurred and he could not even see the needle. He knew then that he must bale out; that there was not a second to lose, otherwise he would become unconscious. Quickly, frantically, he tried to slide back the hood with his left hand, but he had not the strength. For a second he took his right hand off the stick and with both hands he managed to push the hood back. The rush of cold air on his face seemed to help. He had a moment of great clearness. His actions became orderly and precise. That is what happens with a good pilot. He took some quick deep breaths from his oxygen mask, and as he did so, he looked out over the side of the cockpit. Down below there was only a vast white sea of cloud and he realized that he did not know where he was.

It'll be the Channel, he thought. I'm sure to fall in the drink.

He throttled back, pulled off his helmet, undid his straps and pushed the stick hard over to the left. The Spitfire dipped its port wing and turned smoothly over on to its back. The pilot fell out.

As he fell, he opened his eyes, because he knew that he must not pass out before he had pulled the cord. On one side he saw the sun; on the other he saw the whiteness of the clouds, and as he fell, as he somersaulted in the air, the white clouds chased the sun and the sun chased the clouds. They chased each other in a small circle; they ran faster and faster and there was the sun and the clouds and the clouds and the sun, and the clouds came nearer until suddenly there was no longer any sun but only a great whiteness. The whole world was white and there was nothing in it. It was so white that sometimes it looked black, and after a time it was either white or black, but mostly it was white. He watched it as it turned from white to black, then back to white again, and the white stayed for a long time, but the black lasted only for a few seconds. He got into the habit of going to sleep during the white periods, of waking up just in time to see the world when it was black. The black was very quick. Sometimes it was only a flash, a flash of black lightning. The white was slow and in the slowness of it, he always dozed off.

One day, when it was white, he put out a hand and he touched something. He took it between his fingers and crumpled it. For a time he lay there, idly letting the tips of his fingers play with the thing which they had touched. Then slowly he opened his eyes, looked down at his hand and saw that he was holding something which was white.

It was the edge of a sheet. He knew it was a sheet because he could see the texture of the material and the stitchings on the hem. He screwed up his eyes and opened them again quickly. This time he saw the room. He saw the bed in which he was lying: he saw the grey walls and the door and the green curtains over the window. There were some roses on the table by his bed.

Then he saw the basin on the table near the roses. It was a white enamel basin and beside it there was a small medicine glass.

This is a hospital, he thought. I am in a hospital. But he could remember nothing. He lay back on his pillow, looking at the ceiling and wondering what had happened. He was gazing at the smooth greyness of the ceiling which was so clean and grey, and then suddenly he saw a fly walking upon it. The sight of this fly, the suddenness of seeing this small black speck on a sea of grey, brushed the surface of his brain, and quickly, in that second, he remembered everything. He remembered the Spitfire and he remembered the altimeter showing twenty-one thousand feet. He remembered the pushing back of the hood with both hands and he remembered the baling out. He remembered his leg.

It seemed all right now. He looked down at the end of the bed, but he could not tell. He put one hand underneath the bedclothes and felt for his knees. He found one of them, but when he felt for the other, his hand touched something which was soft and covered in bandages.

Just then the door opened and a nurse came in.

'Hello,' she said. 'So you've waked up at last.'

She was not good-looking, but she was large and clean. She was between thirty and forty and she had fair hair. More than that he did not notice.

'Where am I?'

'You're a lucky fellow. You landed in a wood near the beach. You're in Brighton. They brought you in two days ago, and now you're all fixed up. You look fine.'

'I've lost a leg,' he said.

'That's nothing. We'll get you another one. Now you must go to sleep. The doctor will be coming to see you in about an hour.' She picked up the basin and the medicine glass and went out.

But he did not sleep. He wanted to keep his eyes open because he was frightened that if he shut them again everything would go away. He lay looking at the ceiling. The fly was still there. It was very energetic. It would run forward very fast for a few inches, then it would stop. Then it would run forward again, stop, run forward, and every now and then it would take off and buzz around viciously in small circles. It always landed back in the same place on the ceiling and started running and stopping all over again. He watched it for so long that after a while it was no longer a fly, but only a black speck upon a sea of grey, and he was still watching it when the nurse opened the door, and stood aside while the doctor came in. He was an Army doctor, a major, and he had some last-war ribbons on his chest. He was bald and small, but he had a cheerful face and kind eyes.

'Well, well,' he said. 'So you've decided to wake up at last. How are you feeling?'

'I feel all right.'

'That's the stuff. You'll be up and about in no time.'

The doctor took his wrist to feel his pulse.

'By the way,' he said, 'some of the lads from your squadron were ringing up and asking about you. They wanted to come along and see you, but I said that they'd better wait a day or two. Told them you were all right and that they could come and see you a little later on. Just lie quiet and take it easy for a bit. Got something to read?' He glanced at the table with the roses. 'No. Well, Nurse will look after you. She'll get you anything you want. With that he waved his hand and went out, followed by the large clean nurse.

When they had gone, he lay back and looked at the ceiling again. The fly was still there and as he lay watching it he heard the noise of an aeroplane in the distance. He lay listening to the sound of its engines. It was a long way away. I wonder what it is, he thought. Let me see if I can place it. Suddenly he jerked his head sharply to one side. Anyone who has been bombed can tell the noise of a Junkers 88. They can tell most other German bombers for that matter, but especially a Junkers 88. The engines seem to sing a duet. There is a deep vibrating bass voice and with it there is a high-pitched tenor. It is the singing of the tenor which makes the sound of a Ju-88 something which one cannot mistake.

He lay listening to the noise and he felt quite certain about what it was. But where were the sirens and where the guns? That German pilot certainly had a nerve coming near Brighton alone in daylight.

The aircraft was always far away and soon the noise

faded away into the distance. Later on there was another. This one, too, was far away, but there was the same deep undulating bass and the high swinging tenor and there was no mistaking it. He had heard that noise every day during the Battle.

He was puzzled. There was a bell on the table by the bed. He reached out his hand and rang it. He heard the noise of footsteps down the corridor. The nurse came in.

'Nurse, what were those aeroplanes?'

'I'm sure I don't know. I didn't hear them. Probably fighters or bombers. I expect they were returning from France. Why, what's the matter?'

'They were Ju-88s. I'm sure they were Ju-88s. I know the sound of the engines. There were two of them. What were they doing over here?'

The nurse came up to the side of his bed and began to straighten out the sheets and tuck them in under the mattress.

'Gracious me, what things you imagine. You mustn't worry about a thing like that. Would you like me to get you something to read?'

'No, thank you.'

She patted his pillow and brushed back the hair from his forehead with her hand.

'They never come over in daylight any longer. You know that. They were probably Lancasters or Flying Fortresses.'

'Nurse.'

'Yes.'

'Could I have a cigarette?'

'Why certainly you can.'

She went out and came back almost at once with a packet of Players and some matches. She handed one to him and when he had put it in his mouth, she struck a match and lit it.

'If you want me again,' she said, 'just ring the bell,' and she went out.

Once towards evening he heard the noise of another aircraft. It was far away, but even so he knew that it was a single-engined machine. It was going fast; he could tell that. He could not place it. It wasn't a Spit, and it wasn't a Hurricane. It did not sound like an American engine either. They make more noise. He did not know what it was, and it worried him greatly. Perhaps I am very ill, he thought. Perhaps I am imagining things. Perhaps I am a little delirious. I simply do not know what to think.

That evening the nurse came in with a basin of hot water and began to wash him.

'Well,' she said, 'I hope you don't think that we're being bombed.'

She had taken off his pyjama top and was soaping his right arm with a flannel. He did not answer.

She rinsed the flannel in the water, rubbed more soap on it, and began to wash his chest.

'You're looking fine this evening,' she said. 'They operated on you as soon as you came in. They did a marvellous job. You'll be all right. I've got a brother in the RAF,' she added. 'Flying bombers.'

He said, 'I went to school in Brighton.'

She looked up quickly. 'Well, that's fine,' she said. 'I expect you'll know some people in the town.'

'Yes,' he said, 'I know quite a few.'

She had finished washing his chest and arms. Now she turned back the bedclothes so that his left leg was uncovered. She did it in such a way that his bandaged stump remained under the sheets. She undid the cord of his pyjama trousers and took them off. There was no trouble because they had cut off the right trouser-leg so that it could not interfere with the bandages. She began to wash his left leg and the rest of his body. This was the first time he had had a bed-bath and he was embarrassed. She laid a towel under his leg and began washing his foot with the flannel. She said, 'This wretched soap won't lather at all. It's the water. It's as hard as nails.'

He said, 'None of the soap is very good now and, of course, with hard water it's hopeless.' As he said it he remembered something. He remembered the baths which he used to take at school in Brighton, in the long stone-floored bathroom which had four baths in a row. He remembered how the water was so soft that you had to take a shower afterwards to get all the soap off your body, and he remembered how the foam used to float on the surface of the water, so that you could not see your legs underneath. He remembered that sometimes they were given calcium tablets because the school doctor used to say that soft water was bad for the teeth.

'In Brighton,' he said, 'the water isn't . . .'

He did not finish the sentence. Something had occurred to him; something so fantastic and absurd that for a moment he felt like telling the nurse about it and having a good laugh.

She looked up. 'The water isn't what?' she said.

'Nothing,' he answered. 'I was dreaming.'

She rinsed the flannel in the basin, wiped the soap off his leg and dried him with a towel.

'It's nice to be washed,' he said. 'I feel better.' He was feeling his face with his hand. 'I need a shave.'

'We'll do that tomorrow,' she said. 'Perhaps you can do it yourself then.'

That night he could not sleep. He lay awake thinking of the Junkers 88s and of the hardness of the water. He could think of nothing else. They were Ju-88s, he said to himself. I know they were. And yet it is not possible, because they would not be flying around so low over here in broad daylight. I know that it is true and yet I know that it is impossible. Perhaps I am ill. Perhaps I am behaving like a fool and do not know what I am doing or saying. Perhaps I am delirious. For a long time he lay awake thinking these things, and once he sat up in bed and said aloud, 'I will prove that I am not crazy. I will make a little speech about something complicated and intellectual. I will talk about what to do with Germany after the war.' But before he had time to begin, he was asleep.

He woke just as the first light of day was showing through the slit in the curtains over the window. The room was still dark, but he could tell that it was already beginning to get light outside. He lay looking at the grey light which was showing through the slit in the curtain and as he lay there he remembered the day before. He remembered the Junkers 88s and the hardness of the water; he remembered the large pleasant nurse and the kind doctor, and now a small grain of doubt took root in his mind and it began to grow.

He looked around the room. The nurse had taken the roses out the night before. There was nothing except the table with a packet of cigarettes, a box of matches and an ashtray. The room was bare. It was no longer warm or friendly. It was not even comfortable. It was cold and empty and very quiet.

Slowly the grain of doubt grew, and with it came fear, a light, dancing fear that warned but did not frighten; the kind of fear that one gets not because one is afraid, but because one feels that there is something wrong. Quickly the doubt and the fear grew so that he became restless and angry, and when he touched his forehead with his hand, he found that it was damp with sweat. He knew then that he must do something; that he must find some way of proving to himself that he was either right or wrong, and he looked up and saw again the window and the green curtains. From where he lay, that window was right in front of him, but it was fully ten yards away. Somehow he must reach it and look out. The idea became an obsession with him and soon he could think of nothing except the window. But what about his leg? He put his hand underneath the bedclothes and felt the thick bandaged stump which was all that was left on the right-hand side. It seemed all right. It didn't hurt. But it would not be easy.

He sat up. Then he pushed the bedclothes aside and put his left leg on the floor. Slowly, carefully, he swung his body over until he had both hands on the floor as well;

then he was out of bed, kneeling on the carpet. He looked at the stump. It was very short and thick, covered with bandages. It was beginning to hurt and he could feel it throbbing. He wanted to collapse, lie down on the carpet and do nothing, but he knew that he must go on.

With two arms and one leg, he crawled over towards the window. He would reach forward as far as he could with his arms, then he would give a little jump and slide his left leg along after them. Each time he did it, it jarred his wound so that he gave a soft grunt of pain, but he continued to crawl across the floor on two hands and one knee. When he got to the window he reached up, and one at a time he placed both hands on the sill. Slowly he raised himself up until he was standing on his left leg. Then quickly he pushed aside the curtains and looked out.

He saw a small house with a grey tiled roof standing alone beside a narrow lane, and immediately behind it there was a ploughed field. In front of the house there was an untidy garden, and there was a green hedge separating the garden from the lane. He was looking at the hedge when he saw the sign. It was just a piece of board nailed to the top of a short pole, and because the hedge had not been trimmed for a long time, the branches had grown out around the sign so that it seemed almost as though it had been placed in the middle of the hedge. There was something written on the board with white paint. He pressed his head against the glass of the window, trying to read what it said. The first letter was a G, he could see that. The second was an A, and the third was an R. One after another he managed to see what the letters were. There were three words, and slowly he spelled the letters out aloud to himself as he managed to read them. G-A-R-D-E A-U C-H-I-E-N, *Garde au chien.* That is what it said.

He stood there balancing on one leg and holding tightly to the edges of the window sill with his hands, staring at the sign and at the whitewashed lettering of the words. For a moment he could think of nothing at all. He stood there looking at the sign, repeating the words over and over to himself. Slowly he began to realize the full meaning of the thing. He looked up at the cottage and at the ploughed field. He looked at the small orchard on the left of the cottage and he looked at the green countryside beyond. 'So this is France,' he said. 'I am in France.'

Now the throbbing in his right thigh was very great. It felt as though someone was pounding the end of his stump with a hammer and suddenly the pain became so intense that it affected his head. For a moment he thought he was going to fall. Quickly he knelt down again, crawled back to the bed and hoisted himself in. He pulled the bedclothes over himself and lay back on the pillow, exhausted. He could still think of nothing at all except the small sign by the hedge and the ploughed field and the orchard. It was the words on the sign that he could not forget.

It was some time before the nurse came in. She came carrying a basin of hot water and she said, 'Good morning, how are you today?'

He said, 'Good morning, Nurse.'

The pain was still great under the bandages, but he did

not wish to tell this woman anything. He looked at her as she busied herself with getting the washing things ready. He looked at her more carefully now. Her hair was very fair. She was tall and big-boned and her face seemed pleasant. But there was something a little uneasy about her eyes. They were never still. They never looked at anything for more than a moment and they moved too quickly from one place to another in the room. There was something about her movements also. They were too sharp and nervous to go well with the casual manner in which she spoke.

She set down the basin, took off his pyjama top and began to wash him.

'Did you sleep well?'

'Yes.'

'Good,' she said. She was washing his arms and his chest.

'I believe there's someone coming down to see you from the Air Ministry after breakfast,' she went on. 'They want a report or something. I expect you know all about it. How you got shot down and all that. I won't let him stay long, so don't worry.'

He did not answer. She finished washing him and gave him a toothbrush and some toothpowder. He brushed his teeth, rinsed his mouth and spat the water out into the basin.

Later she brought him his breakfast on a tray, but he did not want to eat. He was still feeling weak and sick and he wished only to lie still and think about what had happened. And there was a sentence running through his head. It was a sentence which Johnny, the intelligence officer of his squadron, always repeated to the pilots every day before they went out. He could see Johnny now, leaning against the wall of the dispersal hut with his pipe in his hand, saying, 'And if they get you, don't forget, just your name, rank and number. Nothing else. For God's sake, say nothing else.'

'There you are,' she said as she put the tray on his lap. 'I've got you an egg. Can you manage all right?'

'Yes.'

She stood beside the bed. 'Are you feeling all right?'

'Yes.'

'Good. If you want another egg I might be able to get you one.'

'This is all right.'

'Well, just ring the bell if you want any more.' And she went out.

He had just finished eating, when the nurse came in again.

She said, 'Wing Commander Roberts is here. I've told him that he can only stay for a few minutes.'

She beckoned with her hand and the wing commander came in.

'Sorry to bother you like this,' he said.

He was an ordinary RAF officer, dressed in a uniform which was a little shabby. He wore wings and a DFC. He was fairly tall and thin with plenty of black hair. His teeth, which were irregular and widely spaced, stuck out a little even when he closed his mouth. As he spoke he took a printed form and a pencil from his pocket and he pulled up a chair and sat down.

'How are you feeling?'

There was no answer.

'Tough luck about your leg. I know how you feel. I hear you put up a fine show before they got you.'

The man in the bed was lying quite still, watching the man in the chair.

The man in the chair said, 'Well, let's get this stuff over. I'm afraid you'll have to answer a few questions so that I can fill in this combat report. Let me see now, first of all, what was your squadron?'

The man in the bed did not move. He looked straight at the wing commander and he said, 'My name is Peter Williamson, my rank is squadron leader and my number is nine seven two four five seven.'

An African Story

First published in *Over to You* (1945)

For England, the war began in September 1939. The people on the island knew about it at once and began to prepare themselves. In farther places the people heard about it a few minutes afterwards, and they too began to prepare themselves.

And in East Africa, in Kenya Colony, there was a young man who was a white hunter, who loved the plains and the valleys and the cool nights on the slopes of Kilimanjaro. He too heard about the war and began to prepare himself. He made his way over the country to Nairobi, and he reported to the RAF and asked that they make him a pilot. They took him in and he began his training at Nairobi Airport, flying in little Tiger Moths and doing well with his flying.

After five weeks he nearly got court-martialled because he took his plane up and instead of practising spins and stall-turns as he had been ordered to do, he flew off in the direction of Nakuru to look at the wild animals on the plain. On the way, he thought he saw a Sable antelope, and because these are rare animals, he became excited and flew down low to get a better view. He was looking down at the antelope out of the left side of the cockpit, and because of this he did not see the giraffe on the other side. The leading edge of the starboard wing struck the neck of the giraffe just below the head and cut clean through it. He was flying as low as that. There was damage to the wing, but he managed to get back to Nairobi, and as I said, he was nearly court-martialled, because you cannot explain away a thing like that by saying you hit a large bird, not when there are pieces of giraffe skin and giraffe hair sticking to the wing and the stays.

After six weeks he was allowed to make his first solo cross-country flight, and he flew off from Nairobi to a place called Eldoret, which is a little town eight thousand feet up in the Highlands. But again he was unlucky. This time he had engine failure on the way, due to water in the fuel tanks. He kept his head and made a beautiful forced landing without damaging the aircraft, not far from a little shack which stood alone on the highland plain with no other habitation in sight. That is lonely country up there.

He walked over to the shack, and there he found an old man, living alone, with nothing but a small patch of sweet potatoes, some brown chickens and a black cow.

The old man was kind to him. He gave him food and milk and a place to sleep, and the pilot stayed with him for two days and two nights, until a rescue plane from Nairobi spotted his aircraft on the ground, landed beside it, found out what was wrong, went away and came back with clean petrol which enabled him to take off and return.

But during his stay, the old man, who was lonely and had seen no one for many months, was glad of his company and of the opportunity to talk. He talked much and the pilot listened. He talked of the lonely life, of the lions that came in the night, of the rogue elephant that lived over the hill in the west, of the hotness of the days and of the silence that came with the cold at midnight.

On the second night he talked about himself. He told a long, strange story, and as he told it, it seemed to the pilot that the old man was lifting a great weight off his shoulders in the telling. When he had finished, he said that he had never told that to anyone before, and that he would never tell it to anyone again, but the story was so strange that the pilot wrote it down on paper as soon as he got back to Nairobi. He wrote it not in the old man's words, but in his own words, painting it as a picture with the old man as a character in the picture, because that was the best way to do it. He had never written a story before, and so naturally there were mistakes. He did not know any of the tricks with words which writers use, which they have to use just as painters have to use tricks with paint, but when he had finished writing, when he put down his pencil and went over to the airmen's canteen for a pint of beer, he left behind him a rare and powerful tale.

We found it in his suitcase two weeks later when we were going through his belongings after he had been killed in training, and because he seemed to have no relatives, and because he was my friend, I took the manuscript and looked after it for him.

This is what he wrote.

The old man came out of the door into the bright sunshine, and for a moment he stood leaning on his stick, looking around him, blinking at the strong light. He stood with his head on one side, looking up, listening for the noise which he thought he had heard.

He was small and thick and well over seventy years old, although he looked nearer eighty-five, because rheumatism had tied his body into knots. His face was covered with grey hair, and when he moved his mouth, he moved it only on one side of his face. On his head, whether indoors or out, he wore a dirty white topee.

He stood quite still in the bright sunshine, screwing up his eyes, listening for the noise.

Yes, there it was again. The head of the old man flicked around and he looked towards the small wooden hut standing a hundred yards away on the pasture. This time there was no doubt about it: the yelp of a dog, the high-pitched, sharp-piercing yelp of pain which a dog gives when he is in great danger. Twice more it came and this time the noise was more like a scream than a yelp. The note was higher and more sharp, as though it were wrenched quickly from some small place inside the body.

The old man turned and limped fast across the grass towards the wooden shed where Judson lived, pushed open the door and went in.

The small white dog was lying on the floor and Judson was standing over it, his legs apart, his black hair falling all over his long, red face; standing there tall and skinny, muttering to himself and sweating through his greasy white shirt. His mouth hung open in an odd way, a lifeless way, as though his jaw was too heavy for him, and he was dribbling gently down the middle of his chin. He stood there looking at the small white dog which was lying on the floor, and with one hand he was slowly twisting his left ear; in the other he held a heavy bamboo.

The old man ignored Judson and went down on his knees beside his dog, gently running his thin hands over its body. The dog lay still, looking up at him with watery eyes. Judson did not move. He was watching the dog and the man.

Slowly the old man got up, rising with difficulty, holding the top of his stick with both hands and pulling himself to his feet. He looked around the room. There was a dirty rumpled mattress lying on the floor in the far corner; there was a wooden table made of packing cases and on it a Primus stove and a chipped blue-enamelled saucepan. There were chicken feathers and mud on the floor.

The old man saw what he wanted. It was a heavy iron bar standing against the wall near the mattress, and he hobbled over towards it, thumping the hollow wooden floorboards with his stick as he went. The eyes of the dog followed his movements as he limped across the room. The old man changed his stick to his left hand, took the iron bar in his right, hobbled back to the dog and, without pausing, he lifted the bar and brought it down hard upon the animal's head. He threw the bar to the ground and looked up at Judson, who was standing there with his legs apart, dribbling down his chin and twitching around the corners of his eyes. He went right up to him and began to speak. He spoke very quietly and slowly, with a terrible anger, and as he spoke he moved only one side of his mouth.

'You killed him,' he said. 'You broke his back.'

Then, as the tide of anger rose and gave him strength, he found more words. He looked up and spat them into the face of the tall Judson, who twitched around the corners of his eyes and backed away towards the wall.

'You lousy, mean, dog-beating bastard. That was my dog. What the hell right have you got beating my dog, tell me that. Answer me, you slobbering madman. Answer me.'

Judson was slowly rubbing the palm of his left hand up and down on the front of his shirt, and now the whole of his face began to twitch. Without looking up, he said, 'He wouldn't stop licking that old place on his paw. I couldn't stand the noise it made. You know I can't stand noises like that, licking, licking, licking. I told him to stop. He looked up and wagged his tail; but then he went on licking. I couldn't stand it any longer, so I beat him.'

The old man did not say anything. For a moment it looked as though he were going to hit this creature. He half raised his arm, dropped it again, spat on the floor, turned around and hobbled out of the door into the sunshine. He went across the grass to where a black cow was standing in the shade of a small acacia tree, chewing its cud, and the cow watched him as he came limping across the grass from the shed. But it went on chewing, munching its cud, moving its jaws regularly, mechanically, like a metronome in slow time. The old man came limping up and stood beside it, stroking its neck. Then he leaned against its shoulder and scratched its back with the butt-end of his stick. He stood there for a long time, leaning against the cow, scratching it with his stick; and now and again he would speak to it, speaking quiet little words, whispering them almost, like a person telling a secret to another.

It was shady under the acacia tree, and the country around him looked lush and pleasant after the long rains, for the grass grows green up in the Highlands of Kenya; and at this time of year, after the rains, it is as green and rich as any grass in the world. Away in the north stood Mount Kenya itself, with snow upon its head, with a thin white plume trailing from its summit where the icy winds made a storm and blew the white powder from the top of the mountain. Down below, upon the slopes of that same mountain there were lion and elephant, and sometimes during the night one could hear the roar of the lions as they looked at the moon.

The days passed and Judson went about his work on the farm in a silent, mechanical kind of way, taking in the corn, digging the sweet potatoes and milking the black cow, while the old man stayed indoors away from the fierce African sun. Only in the late afternoon when the air began to get cool and sharp did he hobble outside, and always he went over to his black cow and spent an hour with it under the acacia tree. One day when he came out he found Judson standing beside the cow, regarding it strangely, standing in a peculiar attitude with one foot in front of the other and gently twisting his ear with his right hand.

'What is it now?' said the old man as he came limping up.

'Cow won't stop chewing,' said Judson.

'Chewing her cud,' said the old man. 'Leave her alone.'

Judson said, 'It's the noise, can't you hear it? Crunchy noise like she was chewing pebbles, only she isn't; she's chewing grass and spit. Look at her, she goes on and on crunching, crunching, crunching, and it's just grass and spit. Noise goes right into my head.'

'Get out,' said the old man. 'Get out of my sight.'

At dawn the old man sat, as he always did, looking out of his window, watching Judson coming across from his hut to milk the cow. He saw him coming sleepily across the field, talking to himself as he walked, dragging his feet, making a dark-green trail in the wet grass, carrying in his hand the old four-gallon kerosene tin which he used as a milk pail. The sun was coming up over the escarpment and making long shadows behind the man, the cow and the little acacia tree. The old man saw Judson put down the tin and he saw him fetch the box from beside the acacia tree and settle himself upon it, ready for the milking. He saw him suddenly kneeling down, feeling the udder of the cow with his hands and at the same time the old man noticed from where he sat that the animal had no milk. He saw Judson get up and come walking fast towards the shack. He came and stood under the window where the old man was sitting and looked up.

'Cow's got no milk,' he said.

The old man leaned through the open window, placing both his hands on the sill.

'You lousy bastard, you've stole it.'

'I didn't take it,' said Judson. 'I bin asleep.'

'You stole it.' The old man was leaning farther out of the window, speaking quietly with one side of his mouth. 'I'll beat the hell out of you for this,' he said.

Judson said, 'Someone stole it in the night, a native, one of the Kikuyu. Or maybe she's sick.'

It seemed to the old man that he was telling the truth. 'We'll see,' he said, 'if she milks this evening; and now for Christ's sake, get out of my sight.'

By evening the cow had a full udder and the old man watched Judson draw two quarts of good thick milk from under her.

The next morning she was empty. In the evening she was full. On the third morning she was empty once more.

On the third night the old man went on watch. As soon as it began to get dark, he stationed himself at the open window with an old twelve-bore shot-gun lying on his lap, waiting for the thief who came and milked his cow in the night. At first it was pitch dark and he could not see the cow even, but soon a three-quarter moon came over the hills and it became light, almost as though it was daytime. But it was bitter cold because the Highlands are seven thousand feet up, and the old man shivered at his post and pulled his brown blanket closer around his shoulders. He could see the cow well now, just as well as in daylight, and the little acacia tree threw a deep shadow across the grass, for the moon was behind it.

All through the night the old man sat there watching the cow, and save when he got up once and hobbled back into the room to fetch another blanket, his eyes never left her. The cow stood placidly under the small tree, chewing her cud and gazing at the moon.

An hour before dawn her udder was full. The old man could see it; he had been watching it the whole time, and although he had not seen the movement of its swelling any more than one can see the movement of the hour hand of a watch, yet all the time he had been conscious of the filling as the milk came down. It was an hour before dawn. The moon was low, but the light had not gone. He could see the cow and the little tree and the greenness of the grass around the cow. Suddenly he jerked his head. He heard something. Surely that was a noise he heard. Yes, there it was again, a rustling in the grass right underneath the window where he was sitting. Quickly he pulled himself up and looked over the sill on to the ground.

Then he saw it. A large black snake, a mamba, eight feet long and as thick as a man's arm, was gliding through the wet grass, heading straight for the cow and going fast. Its small pear-shaped head was raised slightly off the ground and the movement of its body against the wetness made a clear hissing sound like gas escaping from a jet. He raised his gun to shoot. Almost at once he lowered it again, why he did not know, and he sat there not moving, watching the mamba as it approached the cow, listening to the noise it made as it went, watching it come up close to the cow and waiting for it to strike.

But it did not strike. It lifted its head and for a moment let it sway gently back and forth; then it raised the front part of its black body into the air under the udder of the cow, gently took one of the thick teats into its mouth and began to drink.

The cow did not move. There was no noise anywhere, and the body of the mamba curved gracefully up from the ground and hung under the udder of the cow. Black snake and black cow were clearly visible out there in the moonlight.

For half an hour the old man watched the mamba taking the milk of the cow. He saw the gentle pulsing of its black body as it drew the liquid out of the udder and he saw it, after a time, change from one teat to another until at last there was no longer any milk left. Then the mamba gently lowered itself to the ground and slid back through the grass in the direction whence it came. Once more it made a clear hissing noise as it went, and once more it passed underneath the window where the old man sat, leaving a thin dark trail in the wet grass where it had gone. Then it disappeared behind the shack.

Slowly the moon went down behind the ridge of Mount Kenya. Almost at the same time the sun rose up out of the escarpment in the east and Judson came out of his hut with the four-gallon kerosene tin in his hand, walking sleepily towards the cow, dragging his feet in the heavy dew as he went. The old man watched him coming and waited. Judson bent down and felt the udder with his hand and, as he did so, the old man shouted at him. Judson jumped at the sound of the old man's voice.

'It's gone again,' said the old man.

Judson said, 'Yes, cow's empty.'

'I think,' said the old man slowly, 'I think that it was a Kikuyu boy. I was dozing a bit and only woke up as he was making off. I couldn't shoot because the cow was in the way. He made off behind the cow. I'll wait for him tonight. I'll get him tonight,' he added.

Judson did not answer. He picked up his four-gallon tin and walked back to his hut.

That night the old man sat up again by the window watching the cow. For him there was this time a certain pleasure in the anticipation of what he was going to see. He knew that he would see the mamba again, but he wanted to make quite certain. And so, when the great black snake slid across the grass towards the cow an hour before sunrise, the old man leaned over the window sill and followed the movements of the mamba as it approached the cow. He saw it wait for a moment under the belly of the animal, letting its head sway slowly backwards and forwards half a dozen times before finally raising its body from the ground to take the teat of the cow into its mouth. He saw it drink the milk for half an hour, until there was none left, and he saw it lower its body and slide smoothly back behind the shack whence it came. And while he watched these things, the old man began laughing quietly with one side of his mouth.

Then the sun rose up from behind the hills, and Judson came out of his hut with the four-gallon tin in his hand, but this time he went straight to the window of the shack where the old man was sitting wrapped up in his blankets.

'What happened?' said Judson.

The old man looked down at him from his window. 'Nothing,' he said. 'Nothing happened. I dozed off again and the bastard came and took it while I was asleep. Listen, Judson,' he added, 'we got to catch this boy, otherwise you'll be going short of milk, not that that would do you any harm. But we got to catch him. I can't shoot because he's too clever; the cow's always in the way. You'll have to get him.'

'Me get him? How?'

The old man spoke very slowly. 'I think,' he said, 'I think you must hide beside the cow, right beside the cow. That is the only way you can catch him.'

Judson was rumpling his hair with his left hand.

'Today,' continued the old man, 'you will dig a shallow trench right beside the cow. If you lie in it and if I cover you over with hay and grass, the thief won't notice you until he's right alongside.'

'He may have a knife,' Judson said.

'No, he won't have a knife. You take your stick. That's all you'll need.'

Judson said, 'Yes, I'll take my stick. When he comes, I'll jump up and beat him with my stick.' Then suddenly he seemed to remember something. 'What about her chewing?' he said. 'Couldn't stand her chewing all night, crunching and crunching, crunching spit and grass like it was pebbles. Couldn't stand that all night,' and he began twisting again at his left ear with his hand.

'You'll do as you're bloody well told,' said the old man.

That day Judson dug his trench beside the cow which was to be tethered to the small acacia tree so that she could not wander about the field. Then, as evening came and as he was preparing to lie down in the trench for the night, the old man came to the door of his shack and said, 'No point in doing anything until early morning. They won't come till the cow's full. Come in here and wait; it's warmer than your filthy little hut.'

Judson had never been invited into the old man's shack before. He followed him in, happy that he would not have to lie all night in the trench. There was a candle burning in the room. It was stuck into the neck of a beer bottle and the bottle was on the table.

'Make some tea,' said the old man, pointing to the Primus stove standing on the floor. Judson lit the stove and made tea. The two of them sat down on a couple of wooden boxes and began to drink. The old man drank his hot and made loud sucking noises as he drank. Judson kept blowing on his, sipping it cautiously and watching the old man over the top of his cup. The old man went on sucking away at his tea until suddenly Judson said, 'Stop.' He said it quietly, plaintively almost, and as he said it he began to twitch around the corners of his eyes and around his mouth.

'What?' said the old man.

Judson said, 'That noise, that sucking noise you're making.'

The old man put down his cup and regarded the other quietly for a few moments, then he said, 'How many dogs you killed in your time, Judson?'

There was no answer.

'I said how many? How many dogs?'

Judson began picking the tea leaves out of his cup and sticking them on to the back of his left hand. The old man was leaning forward on his box.

'How many dogs, Judson?'

Judson began to hurry with his tea leaves. He jabbed his fingers into his empty cup, picked out a tea leaf, pressed it quickly on to the back of his hand and quickly went back for another. When there were not many left and he did not find one immediately, he bent over and peered closely into the cup, trying to find the ones that remained. The back of the hand which held the cup was covered with wet black tea leaves.

'Judson!' The old man shouted, and one side of his mouth opened and shut like a pair of tongs. The candle flame flickered and became still again.

Then quietly and very slowly, coaxingly, as someone to a child. 'In all your life, how many dogs has it been?'

Judson said, 'Why should I tell you?' He did not look up. He was picking the tea leaves off the back of his hand one by one and returning them to the cup.

'I want to know, Judson.' The old man was speaking very gently. 'I'm getting keen about this too. Let's talk about it and make some plans for more fun.'

Judson looked up. A ball of saliva rolled down his chin, hung for a moment in the air, snapped and fell to the floor.

'I only kill 'em because of a noise.'

'How often've you done it? I'd love to know how often.'

'Lots of times long ago.'

'How? Tell me how you used to do it. What way did you like best?'

No answer.

'Tell me, Judson. I'd love to know.'

'I don't see why I should. It's a secret.'

'I won't tell. I swear I won't tell.'

'Well, if you'll promise.' Judson shifted his seat closer

and spoke in a whisper. 'Once I waited till one was sleeping, then I got a big stone and dropped it on his head.'

The old man got up and poured himself a cup of tea. 'You didn't kill mine like that.'

'I didn't have time. The noise was so bad, the licking, and I just had to do it quick.'

'You didn't even kill him.'

'I stopped the noise.'

The old man went over to the door and looked out. It was dark. The moon had not yet risen, but the night was clear and cold with many stars. In the east there was a little paleness in the sky, and as he watched, the paleness grew and it changed from a paleness into a brightness, spreading over the sky so that the light was reflected and held by the small drops of dew upon the grass along the Highlands; and slowly, the moon rose up over the hills. The old man turned and said, 'Better get ready. Never know; they might come early tonight.'

Judson got up and the two of them went outside. Judson lay down in the shallow trench beside the cow and the old man covered him over with grass, so that only his head peeped out above the ground. 'I shall be watching, too,' he said, 'from the window. If I give a shout, jump up and catch him.'

He hobbled back to the shack, went upstairs, wrapped himself in blankets and took up his position by the window. It was early still. The moon was nearly full and it was climbing. It shone upon the snow on the summit of Mount Kenya.

After an hour the old man shouted out of the window, 'Are you still awake, Judson?'

'Yes,' he answered, 'I'm awake.'

'Don't go to sleep,' said the old man. 'Whatever you do, don't go to sleep.'

'Cow's crunching all the time,' said Judson.

'Good, and I'll shoot you if you get up now,' said the old man.

'You'll shoot me?'

'I said, "I'll shoot you if you get up now." '

A gentle sobbing noise came up from where Judson lay, a strange gasping sound as though a child was trying not to cry, and in the middle of it, Judson's voice, 'I've got to move; please let me move. This crunching.'

'If you get up,' said the old man, 'I'll shoot you in the belly.'

For another hour or so the sobbing continued, then quite suddenly it stopped.

Just before four o'clock it began to get very cold and the old man huddled deeper into his blankets and shouted, 'Are you cold out there, Judson? Are you cold?'

'Yes,' came the answer. 'So cold. But I don't mind because cow's not crunching any more. She's asleep.'

The old man said, 'What are you going to do with the thief when you catch him?'

'I don't know.'

'Will you kill him?'

A pause.

'I don't know. I'll just go for him.'

'I'll watch,' said the old man. 'It ought to be fun.' He was leaning out of the window with his arms resting on the sill.

Then he heard the hiss under the window sill, and looked over and saw the black mamba, sliding through the grass towards the cow, going fast and holding its head just a little above the ground as it went.

When the mamba was five yards away, the old man shouted. He cupped his hands to his mouth and shouted, 'Here he comes, Judson; here he comes. Go and get him.'

Judson lifted his head quickly and looked up. As he did so he saw the mamba and the mamba saw him. There was a second, or perhaps two, when the snake stopped, drew back and raised the front part of its body in the air. Then the stroke. Just a flash of black and a slight thump as it took him in the chest. Judson screamed, a long, high-pitched scream which did not rise or fall, but held its note until gradually it faded into nothingness and there was silence. Now he was standing up, ripping open his shirt, feeling for the place in his chest, whimpering quietly, moaning and breathing hard with his mouth wide open. And all the while the old man sat quietly at the open window, leaning forward and never taking his eyes away from the one below.

Everything comes very quick when one is bitten by a black mamba, and almost at once the poison began to work. It threw him to the ground, where he lay humping his back and rolling around on the grass. He no longer made any noise. It was all very quiet, as though a man of great strength was wrestling with a giant whom one could not see, and it was as though the giant was twisting him and not letting him get up, stretching his arms through the fork of his legs and pushing his knees up under his chin.

Then he began pulling up the grass with his hands and soon after that he lay on his back kicking gently with his legs. But he didn't last very long. He gave a quick wriggle, humped his back again, turning over as he did it, then he lay on the ground quite still, lying on his stomach with his right knee drawn up underneath his chest and his hands stretched out above his head.

Still the old man sat by the window, and even after it was all over, he stayed where he was and did not stir. There was a movement in the shadow under the acacia tree and the mamba came forward slowly towards the cow. It came forward a little, stopped, raised its head, waited, lowered its head, and slid forward again right under the belly of the animal. It raised itself into the air and took one of the brown teats in its mouth and began to drink. The old man sat watching the mamba taking the milk of the cow, and once again he saw the gentle pulsing of its body as it drew the liquid out of the udder.

While the snake was still drinking, the old man got up and moved away from the window.

'You can have his share,' he said quietly. 'We don't mind you having his share,' and as he spoke he glanced back and saw again the black body of the mamba curving upwards from the ground, joining with the belly of the cow.

'Yes,' he said again, 'we don't mind your having his share.'

Yesterday Was Beautiful

First published in *Over to You* (1945)

He bent down and rubbed his ankle where it had been sprained with the walking so that he couldn't see the ankle bone. Then he straightened up and looked around him. He felt in his pocket for a packet of cigarettes, took one out and lit it. He wiped the sweat from his forehead with the back of his hand and he stood in the middle of the street looking around him.

'Dammit, there must be someone here,' he said aloud, and he felt better when he heard the sound of his voice.

He walked on, limping, walking on the toe of his injured foot, and when he turned the next corner he saw the sea and the way the road curved around between the ruined houses and went on down the hill to the edge of the water. The sea was calm and black. He could clearly make out the line of hills on the mainland in the distance and he estimated that it was about eight miles away. He bent down again to rub his ankle. 'God dammit,' he said. 'There must be some of them still alive.' But there was no noise anywhere, and there was a stillness about the buildings and about the whole village which made it seem as though the place had been dead for a thousand years.

Suddenly he heard a little noise as though someone had moved his feet on the gravel and when he looked around he saw the old man. He was sitting in the shade on a stone beside a water trough, and it seemed strange that he hadn't seen him before.

'Health to you,' said the pilot. '*Ghia sou.*'

He had learned Greek from the people up around Larissa and Yanina.

The old man looked up slowly, turning his head but not moving his shoulders. He had a greyish-white beard. He had a cloth cap on his head and he wore a shirt which had no collar. It was a grey shirt with thin black stripes. He looked at the pilot and he was like a blind man who looks towards something but does not see.

'Old man, I am glad to see you. Are there no other people in the village?'

There was no answer.

The pilot sat down on the edge of the water trough to rest his ankle.

'I am *Inglese*,' he said. 'I am an aviator who has been shot down and jumped out by the parachute. I am *Inglese*.'

The old man moved his head slowly up and down. '*Inglesus*,' he said quietly. 'You are *Inglesus*.'

'Yes, I am looking for someone who has a boat. I wish to go back to the mainland.'

There was a pause, and when he spoke, the old man seemed to be talking in his sleep. 'They come over all the time,' he said. 'The *Germanoi* they come over all the time.' The voice had no expression. He looked up into the sky, then he turned and looked behind him in the sky. 'They will come again today, *Inglese*. They will come again soon.' There was no anxiety in his voice. There was no expression whatsoever. 'I do not understand why they come to us,' he added.

The pilot said, 'Perhaps not today. It is late now. I think they have finished for today.'

'I do not understand why they come to us, *Inglese*. There is no one here.'

The pilot said, 'I am looking for a man who has a boat who can take me across to the mainland. Is there a boat owner now in the village?'

'A boat?'

'Yes.' There was a pause while the question was considered.

'There is such a man.'

'Could I find him? Where does he live?'

'There is a man in the village who owns a boat.'

'Please tell me what is his name?'

The old man looked up again at the sky. 'Joannis is the one here who has a boat.'

'Joannis who?'

'Joannis Spirakis,' and he smiled. The name seemed to have a significance for the old man and he smiled.

'Where does he live?' the pilot said. 'I am sorry to be giving you this trouble.'

'Where he lives?'

'Yes.'

The old man considered this too. Then he turned and looked down the street towards the sea. 'Joannis was living in the house nearest to the water. But his house isn't any more. The *Germanoi* hit it this morning. It was early and it was still dark. You can see the house isn't any more. It isn't any more.'

'Where is he now?'

'He is living in the house of Antonina Angelou. That house there with the red colour on the window.' He pointed down the street.

'Thank you very much. I will go and call on the boat owner.'

'Ever since he was a boy,' the old man went on, 'Joannis has had a boat. His boat is white with a blue line around the top,' and he smiled again. 'But at the moment I do not think he will be in the house. His wife will be there. Anna will be there, with Antonina Angelou. They will be home.'

'Thank you again. I will go and speak to his wife.'

The pilot got up and started to go down the street, but almost at once the man called after him, '*Inglese*.'

The pilot turned.

'When you speak to the wife of Joannis – when you speak to Anna . . . you should remember something.' He paused, searching for words. His voice wasn't expressionless any longer and he was looking up at the pilot.

'Her daughter was in the house when the *Germanoi* came. It is just something that you should remember.'

The pilot stood on the road waiting.

'Maria. Her name was Maria.'

'I will remember,' answered the pilot. 'I am sorry.'

He turned away and walked down the hill to the house with the red windows. He knocked and waited. He knocked again louder and waited. There was the noise of footsteps and the door opened.

It was dark in the house and all he could see was that the woman had black hair and that her eyes were black like her hair. She looked at the pilot who was standing out in the sunshine.

'Health to you,' he said. 'I am *Inglese*.'

She did not move.

'I am looking for Joannis Spirakis. They say that he owns a boat.'

Still she did not move.

'Is he in the house?'

'No.'

'Perhaps his wife is here. She could know where he is.'

At first there was no answer. Then the woman stepped back and held open the door. 'Come in, *Inglesus*,' she said.

He followed her down the passage and into a back room. The room was dark because there was no glass in the windows – only patches of cardboard. But he could see the old woman who was sitting on the bench with her arms resting on the table. She was tiny. She was small like a child and her face was like a little screwed-up ball of brown paper.

'Who is it?' she said in a high voice.

The first woman said, 'This is an *Inglesus*. He is looking for your husband because he requires a boat.'

'Health to you, *Inglesus*,' the old woman said.

The pilot stood by the door, just inside the room. The first woman stood by the window and her arms hung down by her sides.

The old woman said, 'Where are the *Germanoi*?' Her voice seemed bigger than her body.

'Now they are around Lamia.'

'Lamia.' She nodded. 'Soon they will be here. Perhaps tomorrow they will be here. But I do not care. Do you hear me, *Inglesus*, I do not care.' She was leaning forward a little in her chair and the pitch of her voice was becoming higher. 'When they come it will be nothing new. They have already been here. Every day they have been here. Every day they come over and they bom bom bom and you shut your eyes and you open them again and you get up and you go outside and the houses are just dust – and the people.' Her voice rose and fell.

She paused, breathing quickly, then she spoke more quietly. 'How many have you killed, *Inglesus*?'

The pilot put out a hand and leaned against the door to rest his ankle.

'I have killed some,' he said quietly.

'How many?'

'As many as I could, old woman. We cannot count the number of men.'

'Kill them all,' she said softly. 'Go and kill every man and every woman and every baby. Do you hear me, *Inglesus*? You must kill them all.' The little brown ball of paper became smaller and more screwed up. 'The first one I see I shall kill.' She paused. 'And then, *Inglesus*, and then later, his family will hear that he is dead.'

The pilot did not say anything. She looked up at him and her voice was different. 'What is it you want, *Inglesus*?'

He said, 'About the *Germanoi*, I am sorry. But there is not much we can do.'

'No,' she answered, 'there is nothing. And you?'

'I am looking for Joannis. I wish to use his boat.'

'Joannis,' she said quietly, 'he is not here. He is out.'

Suddenly she pushed back the bench, got to her feet and went out of the room. 'Come,' she said. He followed her down the passage towards the front door. She looked even smaller when she was standing than when she was sitting down and she walked quickly down the passage towards the door and opened it. She stepped out into the sunshine and for the first time he saw how very old she was.

She had no lips. Her mouth was just wrinkled skin like the rest of her face and she screwed up her eyes at the sun and looked up the road.

'There he is,' she said. 'That's him.' She pointed at the old man who was sitting beside the drinking trough.

The pilot looked at the man. Then he turned to speak to the old woman, but she had disappeared into the house.

A Piece of Cake

Revised and retitled version of 'Shot Down over Libya', published in *Over to You* (1945)

I do not remember much of it; not beforehand anyway; not until it happened.

There was the landing at Fouka, where the Blenheim boys were helpful and gave us tea while we were being refuelled. I remember the quietness of the Blenheim boys, how they came into the mess-tent to get some tea and sat down to drink it without saying anything; how they got up and went out when they had finished drinking and still they did not say anything. And I knew that each one was holding himself together because the going was not very good right then. They were having to go out too often, and there were no replacements coming along.

We thanked them for the tea and went out to see if they had finished refuelling our Gladiators. I remember that there was a wind blowing which made the windsock stand out straight, like a signpost, and the sand was blowing up around our legs and making a rustling noise as it swished against the tents, and the tents flapped in the wind so that they were like canvas men clapping their hands.

'Bomber boys unhappy,' Peter said.

'Not unhappy,' I answered.

'Well, they're browned off.'

'No. They've had it, that's all. But they'll keep going. You can see they're trying to keep going.'

Our two old Gladiators were standing beside each other in the sand and the airmen in their khaki shirts and shorts seemed still to be busy with the refuelling. I was wearing a thin white cotton flying suit and Peter had on a blue one. It wasn't necessary to fly with anything warmer.

Peter said, 'How far away is it?'

'Twenty-one miles beyond Charing Cross,' I answered, 'on the right side of the road.' Charing Cross was where the desert road branched north to Mersah Matruh. The Italian Army was outside Mersah, and they were doing pretty well. It was about the only time, so far as I know, that the Italians have done pretty well. Their morale goes up and down like a sensitive altimeter, and right then it was at forty thousand because the Axis was on top of the world. We hung around waiting for the refuelling to finish.

Peter said, 'It's a piece of cake.'

'Yes. It ought to be easy.'

We separated and I climbed into my cockpit. I have always remembered the face of the airman who helped me to strap in. He was oldish, about forty, and bald except for a neat patch of golden hair at the back of his head. His face was all wrinkles, his eyes were like my grandmother's eyes, and he looked as though he had spent his life helping to strap in pilots who never came back. He stood on the wing pulling my straps and said, 'Be careful. There isn't any sense not being careful.'

'Piece of cake,' I said.

'Like hell.'

'Really. It isn't anything at all. It's a piece of cake.'

I don't remember much about the next bit; I only remember about later on. I suppose we took off from Fouka and flew west towards Mersah, and I suppose we flew at about eight hundred feet. I suppose we saw the sea to starboard, and I suppose – no, I am certain – that it was blue and that it was beautiful, especially where it rolled up on to the sand and made a long thick white line east and west as far as you could see. I suppose we flew over Charing Cross and flew on for twenty-one miles to where they had said it would be, but I do not know. I know only that there was trouble, lots and lots of trouble, and I know that we had turned round and were coming back when the trouble got worse. The biggest trouble of all was that I was too low to bale out, and it is from that point on that my memory comes back to me. I remember the dipping of the nose of the aircraft and I remember looking down the nose of the machine at the ground and seeing a little clump of camel-thorn growing there all by itself. I remember seeing some rocks lying in the sand beside the camel-thorn, and the camel-thorn and the sand and the rocks leaped out of the ground and came to me. I remember that very clearly.

Then there was a small gap of not-remembering. It might have been one second or it might have been thirty; I do not know. I have an idea that it was very short, a second perhaps, and next I heard a *crumph* on the right as the starboard wing tank caught fire, then another *crumph* on the left as the port tank did the same. To me that was not significant, and for a while I sat still, feeling comfortable, but a little drowsy. I couldn't see with my eyes, but that was not significant either. There was nothing to worry about. Nothing at all. Not until I felt the hotness around my legs. At first it was only a warmness and that was all right too, but all at once it was a hotness, a very stinging scorching hotness up and down the sides of each leg.

I knew that the hotness was unpleasant, but that was all I knew. I disliked it, so I curled my legs up under the seat and waited. I think there was something wrong with the telegraph system between the body and the brain. It did not seem to be working very well. Somehow it was a bit slow in telling the brain all about it and in asking for instructions. But I believe a message eventually got through, saying, 'Down here there is a great hotness. What shall we do? (Signed) Left Leg and Right Leg.' For a long time there was no reply. The brain was figuring the matter out.

Then slowly, word by word, the answer was tapped over the wires. 'The – plane – is – burning. Get – out – repeat – get – out – get – out.' The order was relayed to the whole system, to all the muscles in the legs, arms and body, and the muscles went to work. They tried their best; they pushed a little and pulled a little, and they strained greatly, but it wasn't any good. Up went another telegram, 'Can't get out. Something holding us in.' The answer to this one took even longer in arriving, so I just sat there waiting for it to come, and all the time the hotness increased. Something was holding me down and it was up to the brain to find out what it was. Was it giants' hands pressing on my shoulders, or heavy stones or houses or steam rollers or filing cabinets or gravity or was it ropes?

Wait a minute. Ropes – ropes. The message was beginning to come through. It came very slowly. 'Your – straps. Undo – your – straps.' My arms received the message and went to work. They tugged at the straps, but they wouldn't undo. They tugged again and again, a little feebly, but as hard as they could, and it wasn't any use. Back went the message, 'How do we undo the straps?'

This time I think that I sat there for three or four minutes waiting for the answer. It wasn't any use hurrying or getting impatient. That was the one thing of which I was sure. But what a long time it was all taking. I said aloud, 'Bugger it. I'm going to be burned. I'm . . .' but I was interrupted. The answer was coming – no, it wasn't – yes, it was, it was slowly coming through. 'Pull – out – the – quick – release – pin – you – bloody – fool – and – hurry.'

Out came the pin and the straps were loosed. Now, let's get out. Let's get out, let's get out. But I couldn't do it. I simply couldn't lift myself out of the cockpit. Arms and legs tried their best but it wasn't any use. A last desperate message was flashed upwards and this time it was marked 'Urgent'.

'Something else is holding us down,' it said. 'Something else, something else, something heavy.'

Still the arms and legs did not fight. They seemed to know instinctively that there was no point in using up their strength. They stayed quiet and waited for the answer, and oh what a time it took. Twenty, thirty, forty hot seconds. None of them really white-hot yet, no sizzling of flesh or smell of burning meat, but that would come any moment now, because those old Gladiators aren't made of stressed steel like a Hurricane or a Spit.

They have taut canvas wings, covered with magnificently inflammable dope, and underneath there are hundreds of small thin sticks, the kind you put under the logs for kindling, only these are drier and thinner. If a clever man said, 'I am going to build a big thing that will burn better and quicker than anything else in the world,' and if he applied himself diligently to his task, he would probably finish up by building something very like a Gladiator. I sat still waiting.

Then suddenly the reply, beautiful in its briefness, but at the same time explaining everything. 'Your – parachute – turn – the – buckle.'

I turned the buckle, released the parachute harness and with some effort hoisted myself up and tumbled over the side of the cockpit. Something seemed to be burning, so I rolled about a bit in the sand, then crawled away from the fire on all fours and lay down.

I heard some of my machine-gun ammunition going off in the heat and I heard some of the bullets thumping into the sand near by. I did not worry about them; I merely heard them.

Things were beginning to hurt. My face hurt most. There was something wrong with my face. Something had happened to it. Slowly I put up a hand to feel it. It was sticky. My nose didn't seem to be there. I tried to feel my teeth, but I cannot remember whether I came to any conclusion about them. I think I dozed off.

All of a sudden there was Peter. I heard his voice and I heard him dancing around and yelling like a madman and shaking my hand and saying, 'Jesus, I thought you were still inside. I came down half a mile away and ran like hell. Are you all right?'

I said, 'Peter, what has happened to my nose?'

I heard him striking a match in the dark. The night comes quickly in the desert. There was a pause.

'It actually doesn't seem to be there very much,' he said. 'Does it hurt?'

'Don't be a bloody fool, of course it hurts.'

He said he was going back to his machine to get some morphia out of his emergency pack, but he came back again soon, saying he couldn't find his aircraft in the dark.

'Peter,' I said, 'I can't see anything.'

'It's night,' he answered. 'I can't see either.'

It was cold now. It was bitter cold, and Peter lay down close alongside so that we could both keep a little warmer. Every now and then he would say, 'I've never seen a man without a nose before.' I kept spewing a lot of blood and every time I did it, Peter lit a match. Once he gave me a cigarette, but it got wet and I didn't want it anyway.

I do not know how long we stayed there and I remember only very little more. I remember that I kept telling Peter that there was a tin of sore-throat tablets in my pocket, and that he should take one, otherwise he would catch my sore throat. I remember asking him where we were and him saying, 'We're between the two armies,' and then I remember English voices from an English patrol asking if we were Italians. Peter said something to them; I cannot remember what he said.

Later I remember hot thick soup and one spoonful making me sick. And all the time the pleasant feeling that

Peter was around, being wonderful, doing wonderful things and never going away. That is all that I can remember.

The men stood beside the aeroplane painting away and talking about the heat.

'Painting pictures on the aircraft,' I said.

'Yes,' said Peter. 'It's a great idea. It's subtle.'

'Why?' I said. 'Just you tell me.'

'They're funny pictures,' he said. 'The German pilots will all laugh when they see them; they'll shake so with their laughing that they won't be able to shoot straight.'

'Oh baloney, baloney, baloney.'

'No, it's a great idea. It's fine. Come and have a look.'

We ran towards the line of aircraft. 'Hop, skip, jump,' said Peter. 'Hop, skip, jump, keep in time.'

'Hop, skip, jump,' I said. 'Hop, skip, jump,' and we danced along.

The painter on the first aeroplane had a straw hat on his head and a sad face. He was copying the drawing out of a magazine, and when Peter saw it he said, 'Boy oh boy look at that picture,' and he began to laugh. His laugh began with a rumble and grew quickly into a belly-roar and he slapped his thighs with his hands both at the same time and went on laughing with his body doubled up and his mouth wide open and his eyes shut. His silk top hat fell off his head on to the sand.

'That's not funny,' I said.

'Not funny!' he cried. 'What d'you mean, "not funny"? Look at me. Look at me laughing. Laughing like this I couldn't hit anything. I couldn't hit a hay wagon or a house or a louse.' And he capered about on the sand, gurgling and shaking with laughter. Then he seized me by the arm and we danced over to the next aeroplane. 'Hop, skip, jump,' he said. 'Hop, skip, jump.'

There was a small man with a crumpled face writing a long story on the fuselage with a red crayon. His straw hat was perched right on the back of his head and his face was shiny with sweat.

'Good morning,' he said. 'Good morning, good morning,' and he swept his hat off his head in a very elegant way.

Peter said, 'Shut up,' and bent down and began to read what the little man had been writing. All the time Peter was spluttering and rumbling with laughter, and as he read he began to laugh afresh. He rocked from one side to the other and danced around on the sand slapping his thighs with his hands and bending his body. 'Oh my, what a story, what a story, what a story. Look at me. Look at me laughing,' and he hopped about on his toes, shaking his head and chortling like a madman. Then suddenly I saw the joke and I began to laugh with him. I laughed so much that my stomach hurt and I fell down and rolled around on the sand and roared and roared because it was so funny that there was nothing else I could do.

'Peter, you're marvellous,' I shouted. 'But can all those German pilots read English?'

'Oh hell,' he said. 'Oh hell. Stop,' he shouted. 'Stop your work,' and the painters all stopped their painting and turned round slowly and looked at Peter. They did a little caper on their toes and began to chant in unison. 'Rubbishy things – on all the wings, on all the wings, on all the wings,' they chanted.

'Shut up,' said Peter. 'We're in a jam. We must keep calm. Where's my top hat?'

'What?' I said.

'You can speak German,' he said. 'You must translate for us. He will translate for you,' he shouted to the painters. 'He will translate.'

Then I saw his black top hat lying in the sand. I looked away, then I looked around and saw it again. It was a silk opera hat and it was lying there on its side in the sand.

'You're mad,' I shouted. 'You're madder than hell. You don't know what you're doing. You'll get us all killed. You're absolutely plumb crazy, do you know that? You're crazier than hell. My God, you're crazy.'

'Goodness, what a noise you're making. You mustn't shout like that; it's not good for you.' This was a woman's voice. 'You've made yourself all hot,' she said, and I felt someone wiping my forehead with a handkerchief. 'You mustn't work yourself up like that.'

Then she was gone and I saw only the sky, which was pale blue. There were no clouds and all around were the German fighters. They were above, below and on every side and there was no way I could go; there was nothing I could do. They took it in turns to come in to attack and they flew their aircraft carelessly, banking and looping and dancing in the air. But I was not frightened, because of the funny pictures on my wings. I was confident and I thought, I am going to fight a hundred of them alone and

I'll shoot them all down. I'll shoot them while they are laughing; that's what I'll do.

Then they flew closer. The whole sky was full of them. There were so many that I did not know which ones to watch and which ones to attack. There were so many that they made a black curtain over the sky and only here and there could I see a little of the blue showing through. But there was enough to patch a Dutchman's trousers, which was all that mattered. So long as there was enough to do that, then everything was all right.

Still they flew closer. They came nearer and nearer, right up in front of my face so that I saw only the black crosses which stood out brightly against the colour of the Messerschmitts and against the blue of the sky; and as I turned my head quickly from one side to the other I saw more aircraft and more crosses and then I saw nothing but the arms of the crosses and the blue of the sky. The arms had hands and they joined together and made a circle and danced around my Gladiator, while the engines of the Messerschmitts sang joyfully in a deep voice. They were playing Oranges and Lemons and every now and then two would detach themselves and come out into the middle of the floor and make an attack and I knew then that it was Oranges and Lemons. They banked and swerved and danced upon their toes and they leaned against the air first to one side, then to the other. 'Oranges and lemons said the bells of St Clements,' sang the engines.

But I was still confident. I could dance better than they and I had a better partner. She was the most beautiful girl in the world. I looked down and saw the curve of her neck and the gentle slope of her pale shoulders and I saw her slender arms, eager and outstretched.

Suddenly I saw some bullet-holes in my starboard wing and I got angry and scared both at the same time; but mostly I got angry. Then I got confident and I said, 'The German who did that had no sense of humour. There's always one man in a party who has no sense of humour. But there's nothing to worry about; there's nothing at all to worry about.'

Then I saw more bullet-holes and I got scared. I slid back the hood of the cockpit and stood up and shouted, 'You fools, look at the funny pictures. Look at the one on my tail; look at the story on my fuselage. Please look at the story on my fuselage.'

But they kept on coming. They tripped into the middle of the floor in twos, shooting at me as they came. And the engines of the Messerschmitts sang loudly. 'When will you pay me, said the bells of Old Bailey?' sang the engines, and as they sang the black crosses danced and swayed to the rhythm of the music. There were more holes in my wings, in the engine cowling and in the cockpit.

Then suddenly there were some in my body.

But there was no pain, even when I went into a spin, when the wings of my plane went flip flip, flip flip, faster and faster, when the blue sky and the black sea chased each other round and round until there was no longer any sky or sea but just the flashing of the sun as I turned. But the black crosses were following me down, still dancing and still holding hands and I could still hear the singing of their engines. 'Here comes a candle to light you to bed, here comes a chopper to chop off your head,' sang the engines.

Still the wings went flip flip, flip flip, and there was neither sky nor sea around me, but only the sun.

Then there was only the sea. I could see it below me and I could see the white horses, and I said to myself, Those are white horses riding a rough sea. I knew then that my brain was going well because of the white horses and because of the sea. I knew that there was not much time because the sea and the white horses were nearer, the white horses were bigger and the sea was like a sea and like water, not like a smooth plate. Then there was only one white horse, rushing forward madly with his bit in his teeth, foaming at the mouth, scattering the spray with his hooves and arching his neck as he ran. He galloped on madly over the sea, riderless and uncontrollable, and I could tell that we were going to crash.

After that it was warmer, and there were no black crosses and there was no sky. But it was only warm because it was not hot and it was not cold. I was sitting in a great red chair made of velvet and it was evening. There was a wind blowing from behind.

'Where am I?' I said.

'You are missing. You are missing, believed killed.'

'Then I must tell my mother.'

'You can't. You can't use that phone.'

'Why not?'

'It goes only to God.'

'What did you say I was?'

'Missing, believed killed.'

'That's not true. It's a lie. It's a lousy lie because here I am and I'm not missing. You're just trying to frighten me and you won't succeed. You won't succeed, I tell you, because I know it's a lie and I'm going back to my squadron. You can't stop me because I'll just go. I'm going, you see, I'm going.'

I got up from the red chair and began to run.

'Let me see those X-rays again, Nurse.'

'They're here, Doctor.' This was the woman's voice again, and now it came closer. 'You have been making a noise tonight, haven't you? Let me straighten your pillow for you, you're pushing it on to the floor.' The voice was close and it was very soft and nice.

'Am I missing?'

'No, of course not. You're fine.'

'They said I was missing.'

'Don't be silly; you're fine.'

Oh everyone's silly, silly, silly, but it was a lovely day, and I did not want to run but I couldn't stop. I kept on running across the grass and I couldn't stop because my legs were carrying me and I had no control over them. It was as if they did not belong to me, although when I looked down I saw that they were mine, that the shoes on the feet were mine and that the legs were joined to my body. But they would not do what I wanted; they just went on running across the field and I had to go with them. I ran and ran and ran, and although in some places the field was rough and bumpy, I never stumbled. I ran past trees and hedges and in one field there were some sheep which stopped their eating and scampered off as I ran past them.

Once I saw my mother in a pale-grey dress bending down picking mushrooms, and as I ran past she looked up and said, 'My basket's nearly full; shall we go home soon?' but my legs wouldn't stop and I had to go on.

Then I saw the cliff ahead and I saw how dark it was beyond the cliff. There was this great cliff and beyond it there was nothing but darkness, although the sun was shining in the field where I was running. The light of the sun stopped dead at the edge of the cliff and there was only darkness beyond. That must be where the night begins, I thought, and once more I tried to stop but it was not any good. My legs began to go faster towards the cliff and they began to take longer strides, and I reached down with my hand and tried to stop them by clutching the cloth of my trousers, but it did not work; then I tried to fall down. But my legs were nimble, and each time I threw myself I landed on my toes and went on running.

Now the cliff and the darkness were much nearer and I could see that unless I stopped quickly I should go over the edge. Once more I tried to throw myself to the ground and once more I landed on my toes and went on running.

I was going fast as I came to the edge and I went straight on over it into the darkness and began to fall.

At first it was not quite dark. I could see little trees growing out of the face of the cliff, and I grabbed at them with my hands as I went down. Several times I managed to catch hold of a branch, but it always broke off at once because I was so heavy and because I was falling so fast, and once I caught a thick branch with both hands and the tree leaned forward and I heard the snapping of the roots one by one until it came away from the cliff and I went on falling. Then it became darker because the sun and the day were in the fields far away at the top of the cliff, and as I fell I kept my eyes open and watched the darkness turn from grey-black to black, from black to jet black and from jet black to pure liquid blackness which I could touch with my hands but which I could not see. But I went on falling, and it was so black that there was nothing anywhere and it was not any use doing anything or caring or thinking because of the blackness and because of the falling. It was not any use.

'You're better this morning. You're much better.' It was the woman's voice again.

'Hallo.'

'Hallo; we thought you were never going to get conscious.'

'Where am I?'

'In Alexandria; in hospital.'

'How long have I been here?'

'Four days.'

'What time is it?'

'Seven o'clock in the morning.'

'Why can't I see?'

I heard her walking a little closer.

'Oh, we've just put a bandage around your eyes for a bit.'

'How long for?'

'Just for a while. Don't worry. You're fine. You were very lucky, you know.'

I was feeling my face with my fingers but I couldn't feel it; I could only feel something else.

'What's wrong with my face?'

I heard her coming up to the side of my bed and I felt her hand touching my shoulder.

'You mustn't talk any more. You're not allowed to talk. It's bad for you. Just lie still and don't worry. You're fine.'

I heard the sound of her footsteps as she walked across the floor and I heard her open the door and shut it again.

'Nurse,' I said. 'Nurse.'

But she was gone.

They Shall Not Grow Old

First published in *Ladies' Home Journal*
(March 1945)

The two of us sat outside the hangar on wooden boxes.

It was noon. The sun was high and the heat of the sun was like a close fire. It was hotter than hell out there by the hangar. We could feel the hot air touching the inside of our lungs when we breathed and we found it better if we almost closed our lips and breathed in quickly; it was cooler that way. The sun was upon our shoulders and upon our backs, and all the time the sweat seeped out from our skin, trickled down our necks, over our chests and down our stomachs. It collected just where our belts were tight around the tops of our trousers and it filtered under the tightness of our belts where the wet was very uncomfortable and made prickly heat on the skin.

Our two Hurricanes were standing a few yards away, each with that patient, smug look which fighter planes have when the engine is not turning, and beyond them the thin black strip of the runway sloped down towards the beaches and towards the sea. The black surface of the runway and the white grassy sand on the sides of the runway shimmered and shimmered in the sun. The heat-haze hung like a vapour over the aerodrome.

The Stag looked at his watch.

'He ought to be back,' he said.

The two of us were on readiness, sitting there for orders to take off. The Stag moved his feet on the hot ground.

'He ought to be back,' he said.

It was two and a half hours since Fin had gone and he certainly should have come back by now. I looked up into the sky and listened. There was the noise of airmen talking beside the petrol wagon and there was the faint pounding of the sea upon the beaches; but there was no sign of an aeroplane. We sat a little while longer without speaking.

'It looks as though he's had it,' I said.

'Yep,' said the Stag. 'It looks like it.'

The Stag got up and put his hands into the pockets of his khaki shorts. I got up too. We stood looking northwards into the clear sky, and we shifted our feet on the ground because of the softness of the tar and because of the heat.

'What was the name of that girl?' said the Stag, without turning his head.

'Nikki,' I answered.

The Stag sat down again on his wooden box, still with his hands in his pockets, and he looked down at the ground between his feet. The Stag was the oldest pilot in the squadron; he was twenty-seven. He had a mass of coarse ginger hair which he never brushed. His face was pale, even after all this time in the sun, and covered with freckles. His mouth was wide and tight closed. He was not tall but his shoulders under his khaki shirt were broad and thick like those of a wrestler. He was a quiet person.

'He'll probably be all right,' he said, looking up. 'And anyway, I'd like to meet the Vichy Frenchman who can get Fin.'

We were in Palestine fighting the Vichy French in Syria. We were at Haifa, and three hours before the Stag, Fin and I had gone on readiness. Fin had flown off in response to an urgent call from the Navy, who had phoned up and said that there were two French destroyers moving out of Beyrouth harbour. Please go at once and see where they are going, said the Navy. Just fly up the coast and have a look and come back quickly and tell us where they are going.

So Fin had flown off in his Hurricane. The time had gone by and he had not returned. We knew that there was no longer much hope. If he hadn't been shot down, he would have run out of petrol some time ago.

I looked down and I saw his blue RAF cap, which was lying on the ground where he had thrown it as he ran to his aircraft, and I saw the oil stains on top of the cap and the shabby bent peak. It was difficult now to believe that he had gone. He had been in Egypt, in Libya and in Greece. On the aerodrome and in the mess we had had him with us all of the time. He was gay and tall and full of laughter, this Fin, with black hair and a long straight nose which he used to stroke up and down with the tip of his finger. He had a way of listening to you while you were telling a story, leaning back in his chair with his face to the ceiling but with his eyes looking down on the ground, and it was only last night at supper that he had suddenly said,

'You know, I wouldn't mind marrying Nikki. I think she's a good girl.'

The Stag was sitting opposite him at the time, eating baked beans.

'You mean just occasionally,' he said.

Nikki was in a cabaret in Haifa.

'No,' said Fin. 'Cabaret girls make fine wives. They are never unfaithful. There is no novelty for them in being unfaithful; that would be like going back to the old job.'

The Stag had looked up from his beans. 'Don't be such a bloody fool,' he said. 'You wouldn't really marry Nikki.'

'Nikki,' said Fin with great seriousness, 'comes of a fine family. She is a good girl. She never uses a pillow when she sleeps. Do you know why she never uses a pillow when she sleeps?'

'No.'

The others at the table were listening now. Everyone was listening to Fin talking about Nikki.

'Well, when she was very young she was engaged to be married to an officer in the French Navy. She loved him greatly. Then one day when they were sunbathing together on the beach he happened to mention to her that he never used a pillow when he slept. It was just one of those little things which people say to each other for the sake of conversation. But Nikki never forgot it. From that time onwards she began to practise sleeping without a pillow. One day the French officer was run over by a truck and killed; but although to her it was very uncomfortable, she still went on sleeping without a pillow to preserve the memory of her lover.'

Fin took a mouthful of beans and chewed them slowly. 'It is a sad story,' he said. 'It shows that she is a good girl. I think I would like to marry her.'

That was what Fin had said last night at supper. Now he was gone and I wondered what little thing Nikki would do in his memory.

The sun was hot on my back and I turned instinctively in order to take the heat upon the other side of my body. As I turned, I saw Carmel and the town of Haifa. I saw the steep pale-green slope of the mountain as it dropped down towards the sea, and below it I saw the town and the bright colours of the houses shining in the sun. The houses with their whitewashed walls covered the sides of Carmel and the red roofs of the houses were like a rash on the face of the mountain.

Walking slowly towards us from the grey corrugated-iron hangar came the three men who were the next crew on readiness. They had their yellow Mae Wests slung over their shoulders and they came walking slowly towards us, holding their helmets in their hands as they came.

When they were close, the Stag said, 'Fin's had it,' and they said, 'Yes, we know.' They sat down on the wooden boxes which we had been using, and immediately the sun was upon their shoulders and upon their backs and they began to sweat. The Stag and I walked away.

The next day was a Sunday and in the morning we flew up the Lebanon valley to ground-strafe an aerodrome called Rayak. We flew past Hermon, who had a hat of snow upon his head, and we came down out of the sun on to Rayak and on to the French bombers on the aerodrome and began our strafing. I remember that as we flew past, skimming low over the ground, the doors of the French bombers opened. I remember seeing a whole lot of women in white dresses running out across the aerodrome; I remember particularly their white dresses.

You see, it was a Sunday and the French pilots had asked their ladies out from Beyrouth to look over the bombers. The Vichy pilots had said, Come out on Sunday morning and we will show you our aeroplanes. It was a very Vichy French thing for them to do.

So when we started shooting, they all tumbled out and began to run across the aerodrome in their white Sunday dresses.

I remember hearing Monkey's voice over the radio, saying, 'Give them a chance, give them a chance,' and the whole squadron wheeled around and circled the aerodrome once while the women ran over the grass in every direction. One of them stumbled and fell twice and one of them was limping and being helped by a man, but we gave them time. I remember watching the small bright flashes of a machine gun on the ground and thinking that they should at least have stopped their shooting while we were waiting for their white-dressed women to get out of the way.

That was the day after Fin had gone. The next day the Stag and I sat once more at readiness on the wooden boxes outside the hangar. Paddy, a big fair-haired boy, had taken Fin's place and was sitting with us.

It was noon. The sun was high and the heat of the sun was like a close fire. The sweat ran down our necks, down inside our shirts, over our chests and stomachs, and we sat there waiting for the time when we would be relieved. The Stag was sewing the strap on to his helmet with a needle and cotton and telling of how he had seen Nikki the night before in Haifa and of how he had told her about Fin.

Suddenly we heard the noise of an aeroplane. The Stag stopped his talking and we all looked up. The noise was coming from the north, and it grew louder and louder as the aeroplane flew closer, and then the Stag said suddenly, 'It's a Hurricane.'

The next moment it was circling the aerodrome, lowering its wheels to land.

'Who is it?' said the fair-haired Paddy. 'No one's gone out this morning.'

Then, as it glided past us on to the runway, we saw the number on the tail of the machine, H.4427, and we knew that it was Fin.

We were standing up now, watching the machine as it taxied towards us, and when it came up close and swung round for parking we saw Fin in the cockpit. He waved his hand at us, grinned and got out. We ran up and shouted at him, 'Where've you been?' 'Where in the hell have you been?' 'Did you force-land and get away again?' 'Did you find a woman in Beyrouth?' 'Fin, where in the hell have you been?'

Others were coming up and crowding around him now, fitters and riggers and the men who drove the fire tender, and they all waited to hear what Fin would say. He stood there pulling off his helmet, pushing back his black hair with his hand, and he was so astonished at our behaviour that at first he merely looked at us and did not speak. Then he laughed and he said, 'What in the hell's the matter? What's the matter with all of you?'

'Where have you been?' we shouted. 'Where have you been for two days?'

Upon the face of Fin there was a great and enormous astonishment. He looked quickly at his watch.

'Five past twelve,' he said. 'I left at eleven, one hour and five minutes ago. Don't be a lot of damn fools. I must go and report quickly. The Navy will want to know that those destroyers are still in the harbour at Beyrouth.'

He started to walk away; I caught his arm.

'Fin,' I said quietly, 'you've been away since the day before yesterday. What's the matter with you?'

He looked at me and laughed.

'I've seen you organize much better jokes than this one,' he said. 'It isn't so funny. It isn't a bit funny.' And he walked away.

We stood there, the Stag, Paddy and I, the fitters, the riggers and the men who drove the fire-engine, watching Fin as he walked away. We looked at each other, not knowing what to say or to think, understanding nothing, knowing nothing except that Fin had been serious when he spoke and that what he said he had believed to be true. We knew this because we knew Fin, and we knew it because when one has been together as we had been together, then there is never any doubting of anything that anyone says when he is talking about his flying: there can only be a doubting of one's self. These men were doubting themselves, standing there in the sun doubting themselves, and the Stag was standing by the wing of Fin's machine peeling off with his fingers little flakes of paint which had dried up and cracked in the sun.

Someone said, 'Well, I'll be buggered,' and the men turned and started to walk quietly back to their jobs. The next three pilots on readiness came walking slowly towards us from the grey corrugated-iron hangar, walking slowly under the heat of the sun and swinging their helmets in their hands as they came. The Stag, Paddy and I walked over to the pilots' mess to have a drink and lunch.

The mess was a small white wooden building with a veranda. Inside there were two rooms, one a sitting-room with armchairs and magazines and a hole in the wall through which you could buy drinks, and the other a dining-room with one long wooden table. In the sitting-room we found Fin talking to Monkey, our CO. The other pilots were sitting around listening and everybody was drinking beer. We knew that it was really a serious business in spite of the beer and the armchairs; that Monkey was doing what he had to do and doing it in the only way possible. Monkey was a rare man, tall with a handsome face, an Italian bullet wound in his leg and a casual friendly efficiency. He never laughed out loud, he just choked and grunted deep in his throat.

Fin was saying, 'You must go easy, Monkey; you must help me to stop thinking that I've gone mad.'

Fin was being serious and sensible, but he was worried as hell.

'I have told you all I know,' he said. 'That I took off at eleven o'clock, that I climbed up high, that I flew to Beyrouth, saw the two French destroyers and came back, landing at five past twelve. I swear to you that that is all I know.'

He looked around at us, at the Stag and me, at Paddy and Johnny and the half-dozen other pilots in the room, and we smiled at him and nodded to show him that we were with him, not against him, and that we believed what he said.

Monkey said, 'What in the hell am I going to say to Headquarters at Jerusalem? I reported you missing. Now I've got to report your return. They'll insist on knowing where you've been.'

The whole thing was getting to be too much for Fin. He was sitting upright, tapping with the fingers of his left hand on the leather arm of his chair, tapping with quick sharp taps, leaning forward, thinking, thinking, fighting to think, tapping on the arm of the chair and then he began tapping the floor with his foot as well. The Stag could stand it no longer.

'Monkey,' he said, 'Monkey, let's just leave it all for a bit. Let's leave it and perhaps Fin will remember something later on.'

Paddy, who was sitting on the arm of the Stag's chair, said, 'Yes, and meanwhile we could tell HQ that Fin had force-landed in a field in Syria, taken two days to repair his aircraft, then flown home.'

Everybody was helping Fin. The pilots were all helping him. In the mind of each of us was the certain knowledge that here was something that concerned us greatly. Fin knew it, although that was all he knew, and the others knew it because one could see it upon their faces. There was a tension, a fine high-drawn tension in the room, because here for the first time was something which was neither bullets nor fire nor the coughing of an engine nor burst tyres nor blood in the cockpit nor yesterday nor today, nor even tomorrow. Monkey felt it too, and he said, 'Yes, let's have another drink and leave it for a bit. I'll tell HQ that you force-landed in Syria and managed to get off again later.'

We had some more beer and went in to lunch. Monkey ordered bottles of Palestine white wine with the meal to celebrate Fin's return.

After that no one mentioned the thing at all; we did not even talk about it when Fin wasn't there. But each one of us continued to think about it secretly, knowing for certain that it was something important and that it was not finished. The tension spread quickly through the squadron and it was with all the pilots.

Meanwhile the days went by and the sun shone upon the aerodrome and upon the aircraft and Fin took his place among us flying in the normal way.

Then one day, I think it was about a week later, we did another ground-strafe of Rayak aerodrome. There were six of us, with Monkey leading and Fin flying on his starboard side. We came in low over Rayak and there was plenty of light flak, and as we went in on the first run, Paddy's machine was hit. As we wheeled for the second run we saw his Hurricane wing gently over and dive straight to the ground at the edge of the aerodrome. There was a great billow of white smoke as it hit, then the flames, and as the flames spread the smoke turned from white to black and Paddy was with it. Immediately there was a crackle over the radio and I heard Fin's voice, very excited, shouting into his microphone, shouting, 'I've remembered it. Hello, Monkey, I've remembered it all,' and Monkey's calm slow reply, 'OK, Fin, OK; don't forget it.'

We did our second run and then Monkey led us quickly away, weaving in and out of the valleys, with the bare grey-brown hills far above us on either side, and all the way home, all through the half-hour's flight, Fin never stopped shouting over the RT. First he would call to Monkey and say, 'Hello, Monkey, I've remembered it, all of it; every bit of it.' Then he would say, 'Hello, Stag, I've remembered it, all of it; I can't forget it now.' He called me and he called Johnny and he called Wishful; he called us all separately over and over again, and he was so excited that sometimes he shouted too loudly into his mike and we could not hear what he was saying.

When we landed, we dispersed our aircraft and because Fin for some reason had to park his at the far side of the aerodrome, the rest of us were in the operations room before him.

The ops room was beside the hangar. It was a bare place with a large table in the middle of the floor on which there was a map of the area. There was another smaller table with a couple of telephones, a few wooden chairs and benches and at one end the floor was stacked with

Mae Wests, parachutes and helmets. We were standing there taking off our flying clothing and throwing it on to the floor at the end of the room when Fin arrived. He came quickly into the doorway and stopped. His black hair was standing up straight and untidy because of the way in which he had pulled off his helmet; his face was shiny with sweat and his khaki shirt was dark and wet. His mouth was open and he was breathing quickly. He looked as though he had been running. He looked like a child who had rushed downstairs into a room full of grown-ups to say that the cat has had kittens in the nursery and who does not know how to begin.

We had all heard him coming because that was what we had been waiting for. Everyone stopped what they were doing and stood still, looking at Fin.

Monkey said, 'Hello, Fin,' and Fin said, 'Monkey, you've got to believe this because it's what happened.'

Monkey was standing over by the table with the telephones; the Stag was near him, square short ginger-haired Stag, standing up straight, holding a Mae West in his hand, looking at Fin. The others were at the far end of the room. When Fin spoke, they began to move up quietly until they were closer to him, until they reached the edge of the big map table which they touched with their hands. There they stood, looking at Fin, waiting for him to begin.

He started at once, talking quickly, then calming down and talking more slowly as he got into his story. He told everything, standing there by the door of the ops room, with his yellow Mae West still on him and with his helmet and oxygen mask in his hand. The others stayed where they were and listened, and as I listened to him, I forgot that it was Fin speaking and that we were in the ops room at Haifa; I forgot everything and went with him on his journey, and did not come back until he had finished.

'I was flying at about twenty thousand,' he said. 'I flew over Tyre and Sidon and over the Damour River and then I flew inland over the Lebanon hills, because I intended to approach Beyrouth from the east. Suddenly I flew into cloud, thick white cloud which was so thick and dense that I could see nothing except the inside of my cockpit. I couldn't understand it, because a moment before everything had been clear and blue and there had been no cloud anywhere.

'I started to lose height to get out of the cloud and I went down and down and still I was in it. I knew that I must not go too low because of the hills, but at six thousand the cloud was still around me. It was so thick that I could see nothing, not even the nose of my machine nor the wings, and the cloud condensed on the windshield and little rivers of water ran down the glass and got blown away by the slipstream. I have never seen cloud like that before. It was thick and white right up to the edges of the cockpit. I felt like a man on a magic carpet, sitting there alone in this little glass-topped cockpit, with no wings, no tail, no engine and no aeroplane.

'I knew that I must get out of this cloud, so I turned and flew west over the sea away from the mountains; then I came down low by my altimeter. I came down to five hundred feet, four hundred, three hundred, two hundred, one hundred, and the cloud was still around me. For a moment I paused. I knew that it was unsafe to go lower. Then, quite suddenly, like a gust of wind, came the feeling that there was nothing below me; no sea nor earth nor anything else, and slowly, deliberately, I opened the throttle, pushed the stick hard forward and dived.

'I did not watch the altimeter; I looked straight ahead through the windshield at the whiteness of the cloud and I went on diving. I sat there pressing the stick forward, keeping her in the dive, watching the vast clinging whiteness of the cloud and I never once wondered where I was going. I just went.

'I do not know how long I sat there; it may have been minutes and it may have been hours; I know only that as I sat there and kept her diving, I was certain that what was below me was neither mountains nor rivers nor earth nor sea and I was not afraid.

'Then I was blinded. It was like being half asleep in bed when someone turns on the light.

'I came out of the cloud so suddenly and so quickly that I was blinded. There was no space of time between being in it and being out of it. One moment I was in it and the whiteness was thick around me and in that same moment I was out of it and the light was so bright that I was blinded. I screwed up my eyes and held them tight closed for several seconds.

'When I opened them everything was blue, more blue than anything that I had ever seen. It was not a dark blue, nor was it a bright blue; it was a blue blue, a pure shining colour which I had never seen before and which I cannot describe. I looked around. I looked up above me and behind me. I sat up and peered below me through the glass of the cockpit and everywhere it was blue. It was bright and clear, like pleasant sunlight, but there was no sun.

'Then I saw them.

'Far ahead and above I saw a long thin line of aircraft flying across the sky. They were moving forward in a single black line, all at the same speed, all in the same direction, all close up, following one behind the other, and the line stretched across the sky as far as the eye could see. It was the way they moved ahead, the urgent way in which they pressed forward forward forward like ships sailing before a great wind, it was from this that I knew everything. I do not know why or how I knew it, but I knew as I looked at them that these were the pilots and air crews who had been killed in battle, who now, in their own aircraft were making their last flight, their last journey.

'As I flew higher and closer I could recognize the machines themselves. I saw in that long procession nearly every type there was. I saw Lancasters and Dorniers, Halifaxes and Hurricanes, Messerschmitts, Spitfires, Stirlings, Savoia 79s, Junkers 88s, Gladiators, Hampdens, Macchi 200s, Blenheims, Focke Wulfs, Beaufighters, Swordfish and Heinkels. All these and many more I saw, and the moving line reached across the blue sky both to the one side and to the other until it faded from sight.

'I was close to them now and I began to sense that I was being sucked towards them regardless of what I wished to do. There was a wind which took hold of my machine, blew it over and tossed it about like a leaf and I was pulled and sucked as by a giant vortex towards the other aeroplanes. There was nothing I could do for I was in the vortex and in the arms of the wind. This all happened very quickly, but I remember it clearly. I felt the pull on my aircraft becoming stronger; I was whisked forward faster and faster, and then suddenly I was flying in the procession itself, moving forward with the others, at the same speed and on the same course. Ahead of me, close enough for me to see the colour of the paint on its wings, was a Swordfish, an old Fleet Air Arm Swordfish. I could see the heads and helmets of the observer and the pilot as they sat in their cockpits, the one behind the other. Ahead of the Swordfish there was a Dornier, a Flying Pencil, and beyond the Dornier there were others which I could not recognize from where I was.

'We flew on and on. I could not have turned and flown away even if I had wanted to. I do not know why, although it may have been something to do with the vortex and with the wind, but I knew that it was so. Moreover, I was not really flying my aircraft; it flew itself. There was no manoeuvring to reckon with, no speed, no height, no throttle, no stick, no nothing. Once I glanced down at my instruments and saw that they were all dead, just as they are when the machine is sitting on the ground.

'So we flew on. I had no idea how fast we went. There was no sensation of speed and for all I know, it was a million miles an hour. Now I come to think of it, I never once during that time felt either hot or cold or hungry or thirsty; I felt none of those things. I felt no fear, because I knew nothing of which to be afraid. I felt no worry, because I could remember nothing or think of nothing about which to be worried. I felt no desire to do anything that I was not doing or to have anything that I did not have, because there was nothing that I wished to do and there was nothing that I wished to have. I felt only pleasure at being where I was, at seeing the wonderful light and the beautiful colour around me. Once I caught sight of my face in the cockpit mirror and I saw that I was smiling, smiling with my eyes and with my mouth, and when I looked away I knew that I was still smiling, simply because that was the way I felt. Once, the observer in the Swordfish ahead of me turned and waved his hand. I slid back the roof of my cockpit and waved back. I remember that even when I opened the cockpit, there was no rush of air and no rush of cold or heat, nor was there any pressure of the slipstream on my hand. Then I noticed that they were all waving at each other, like children on a roller-coaster, and I turned and waved at the man in the Macchi behind me.

'But there was something happening along the line. Far up in front I could see that the aeroplanes had changed course, were wheeling around to the left and losing height. The whole procession, as it reached a certain point, was banking around and gliding downwards in a wide, sweeping circle. Instinctively I glanced down over the cockpit, and there I saw spread out below me a vast green plain. It was green and smooth and beautiful; it reached to the far edges of the horizon where the blue of the sky came down and merged with the green of the plain.

'And there was the light. Over to the left, far away in the

distance, was a bright white light, shining bright and without any colour. It was as though the sun, but something far bigger than the sun, something without shape or form whose light was bright but not blinding, was lying on the far edge of the green plain. The light spread outwards from a centre of brilliance and it spread far up into the sky and far out over the plain. When I saw it, I could not at first look away from it. I had a desire to go towards it, into it, and almost at once the desire and the longing became so intense that several times I tried to pull my aircraft out of the line and fly straight towards it; but it was not possible and I had to fly with the rest.

'As they banked around and lost height I went with them, and we began to glide down towards the green plain below. Now that I was closer, I could see the great mass of aircraft upon the plain itself. They were everywhere, scattered over the ground like currants upon a green carpet. There were hundreds and hundreds of them, and each minute, each second almost, their number grew as those in front of me landed and taxied to a standstill.

'Quickly we lost height. Soon I saw that the ones just in front of me were lowering their wheels and preparing to land. The Dornier next but one to me levelled off and touched down. Then the old Swordfish. The pilot turned a little to the left out of the way of the Dornier and landed beside him. I turned to the left of the Swordfish and levelled off. I looked out of the cockpit at the ground, judging the height, and I saw the green of the ground blurred as it rushed past me and below me.

'I waited for my aircraft to sink and to touch down. It

seemed to take a long time. "Come on," I said. "Come on, come on." I was only about six feet up, but she would not sink. "Get down," I shouted, "please *get down*." I began to panic. I became frightened. Suddenly I noticed that I was gaining speed. I cut all the switches but it made no difference. The aircraft was gathering speed, going faster and faster, and I looked around and saw behind me the long procession of aircraft dropping down out of the sky and sweeping in to land. I saw the mass of machines upon the ground, scattered far across the plain, and away on one side I saw the light, that shining white light which shone so brightly over the great plain and to which I longed to go. I know that had I been able to land, I would have started to run towards that light the moment I got out of my aircraft.

'And now I was flying away from it. My fear grew. As I flew faster and farther away, the fear took hold of me until soon I was fighting crazy mad, pulling at the stick, wrestling with the aeroplane, trying to turn it around, back towards the light. When I saw that it was impossible, I tried to kill myself. I really wanted to kill myself then. I tried to dive the aircraft into the ground, but it flew on straight. I tried to jump out of the cockpit, but there was a hand upon my shoulder which held me down. I tried to bang my head against the sides of the cockpit, but it made no difference and I sat there fighting with my machine and with everything until suddenly I noticed that I was in cloud. I was in the same thick white cloud as before; and I seemed to be climbing. I looked behind me, but the cloud had closed in all round. There was nothing now but this vast impenetrable whiteness. I began to feel sick and giddy. I did not care any longer what happened one way or the other, I just sat there limply, letting the machine fly on by itself.

'It seemed a long time and I am sure that I sat there for many hours. I must have gone to sleep. As I slept, I dreamed. I dreamed not of the things that I had just seen, but of the things of my ordinary life, of the squadron, of Nikki and of the aerodrome here at Haifa. I dreamed that I was sitting at readiness outside the hangar with two others, that a request came from the Navy for someone to do a quick recco over Beyrouth; and because I was first up, I jumped into my Hurricane and went off. I dreamed that I passed over Tyre and Sidon and over the Damour River, climbing up to twenty thousand as I went. Then I turned inland over the Lebanon hills, swung around and approached Beyrouth from the east. I was above the town, peering over the side of the cockpit, looking for the harbour and trying to find the two French destroyers. Soon I saw them, saw them clearly, tied up close alongside each other by the wharf, and I banked around and dived for home as fast as I could.

'The Navy's wrong, I thought to myself as I flew back. The destroyers are still in the harbour. I looked at my watch. An hour and a half. "I've been quick," I said. "They'll be pleased." I tried to call up on the radio to give the information, but I couldn't get through.

'Then I came back here. When I landed, you all crowded around me and asked me where I had been for two days, but I could remember nothing. I did not remember anything except the flight to Beyrouth until just now, when I saw Paddy being shot down. As his machine hit the ground, I found myself saying, "You lucky bastard. You lucky, lucky bastard," and as I said it, I knew why I was saying it and remembered everything. That was when I shouted to you over the radio. That was when I remembered.'

Fin had finished. No one had moved or said anything all the time that he had been talking. Now it was only Monkey who spoke. He shuffled his feet on the floor, turned and looked out of the window and said quietly, almost in a whisper, 'Well, I'll be damned,' and the rest of us went slowly back to the business of taking off our flying clothing and stacking it in the corner of the room on the floor; all except the Stag, square short Stag, who stood there watching Fin as Fin walked slowly across the room to put away his clothing.

After Fin's story, the squadron returned to normal. The tension which had been with us for over a week disappeared. The aerodrome was a happier place in which to be. But no one ever mentioned Fin's journey. We never once spoke about it together, not even when we got drunk in the evening at the Excelsior in Haifa.

The Syrian campaign was coming to an end. Everyone could see that it must finish soon, although the Vichy people were still fighting fiercely south of Beyrouth. We were still flying. We were flying a great deal over the fleet, which was bombarding the coast, for we had the job of protecting them from the Junkers 88s which came over from Rhodes. It was on the last one of these flights over the fleet that Fin was killed.

We were flying high above the ships when the Ju-88s came over in force and there was a battle. We had only six Hurricanes in the air; there were many of the Junkers and it was a good fight. I do not remember much about what went on at the time. One never does. But I remember that it was a hectic, chasing fight, with the Junkers diving for the ships, with the ships barking at them, throwing up everything into the air so that the sky was full of white flowers which blossomed quickly and grew and blew away with the wind. I remember the German who blew up in mid-air, quickly, with just a white flash, so that where the bomber had been, there was nothing left except tiny little pieces falling slowly downwards. I remember the one that had its rear turret shot away, which flew along with the gunner hanging out of the tail by his straps, struggling to get back into the machine. I remember one, a brave one who stayed up above to fight us while the others went down to dive-bomb. I remember that we shot him up and I remember seeing him turn slowly over on to his back, pale-green belly upwards like a dead fish, before finally he spun down.

And I remember Fin.

I was close to him when his aircraft caught fire. I could see the flames coming out of the nose of his machine and dancing over the engine cowling. There was black smoke coming from the exhaust of his Hurricane.

I flew up close and I called to him over the RT. 'Hello, Fin,' I called, 'you'd better jump.'

His voice came back, calm and slow. 'It's not so easy.'

'Jump,' I shouted. 'Jump quickly.'

I could see him sitting there under the glass roof of the cockpit. He looked towards me and shook his head.

'It's not so easy,' he answered. 'I'm a bit shot up. My arms are shot up and I can't undo the straps.'

'Get out,' I shouted. 'For God's sake, get out,' but he did not answer. For a moment his aircraft flew on, straight and level, then gently, like a dying eagle, it dipped a wing and dived towards the sea. I watched it as it went; I watched the thin trail of black smoke which it made across the sky, and as I watched, Fin's voice came again over the radio, clear and slow. 'I'm a lucky bastard,' he was saying. 'A lucky, lucky bastard.'

Madame Rosette

First published in *Harper's* (August 1945)

'Oh Jesus, this is wonderful,' said the Stag.

He was lying back in the bath with a scotch and soda in one hand and a cigarette in the other. The water was right up to the brim and he was keeping it warm by turning the tap with his toes.

He raised his head and took a little sip of his whisky, then he lay back and closed his eyes.

'For God's sake, get out,' said a voice from the next room. 'Come on, Stag, you've had over an hour.' Stuffy was sitting on the edge of the bed with no clothes on, drinking slowly and waiting his turn.

The Stag said, 'All right. I'm letting the water out now,' and he stretched out a leg and flipped up the plug with his toes.

Stuffy stood up and wandered into the bathroom, holding his drink in his hand. The Stag lay in the bath for a few moments more, then, balancing his glass carefully on the soap rack, he stood up and reached for a towel. His body was short and square, with strong thick legs and exaggerated calf muscles. He had coarse curly ginger hair and a thin, rather pointed face covered with freckles. There was a layer of pale-ginger hair on his chest.

'Jesus,' he said, looking down into the bath tub, 'I've brought half the desert with me.'

Stuffy said, 'Wash it out and let me get in. I haven't had a bath for five months.'

This was back in the early days when we were fighting the Italians in Libya. One flew very hard in those days because there were not many pilots. They certainly could not send any out from England because there they were fighting the Battle of Britain. So one remained for long periods out in the desert, living the strange unnatural life of the desert, living in the same dirty little tent, washing and shaving every day in a mugful of one's own spat-out tooth water, all the time picking flies out of one's tea and out of one's food, having sandstorms which were as much in the tents as outside them so that placid men became bloody-minded and lost their tempers with their friends and with themselves; having dysentery and gippy tummy and mastoid and desert sores, having some bombs from the Italian S-79s, having no water and no women; having no flowers growing out of the ground; having very little except sand sand sand. One flew old Gloster Gladiators against the Italian CR42s, and when one was not flying, it was difficult to know what to do.

Occasionally one would catch scorpions, put them in empty petrol cans and match them against each other in fierce mortal combat. Always there would be a champion scorpion in the squadron, a sort of Joe Louis who was invincible and won all his fights. He would have a name; he would become famous and his training diet would be a great secret known only to the owner. Training diet was considered very important with scorpions. Some were trained on corned beef, some on a thing called

Machonachies, which is an unpleasant canned meat stew, some on live beetles, and there were others who were persuaded to take a little beer just before the fight, on the premise that it made the scorpion happy and gave him confidence. These last ones always lost. But there were great battles and great champions, and in the afternoons when the flying was over, one could often see a group of pilots and airmen standing around in a circle on the sand, bending over with their hands on their knees, watching the fight, exhorting the scorpions and shouting at them as people shout at boxers or wrestlers in a ring. Then there would be a victory, and the man who owned the winner would become excited. He would dance around in the sand, yelling, waving his arms in the air and extolling in a loud voice the virtues of the victorious animal. The greatest scorpion of all was owned by a sergeant called Wishful who fed him only on marmalade. The animal had an unmentionable name, but he won forty-two consecutive fights and then died quietly in training just when Wishful was considering the problem of retiring him to stud.

So you can see that because there were no great pleasures while living in the desert, the small pleasures became great pleasures and the pleasures of children became the pleasures of grown men. That was true for everyone; for the pilots, the fitters, the riggers, the corporals who cooked the food and the men who kept the stores. It was true for the Stag and for Stuffy, so true that when the two of them wangled a forty-eight-hour pass and a lift by air into Cairo, and when they got to the hotel, they were feeling about having a bath rather as you would feel on the first night of your honeymoon.

The Stag had dried himself and was lying on the bed with a towel round his waist, with his hands up behind his head, and Stuffy was in the bath, lying with his head against the back of the bath, groaning and sighing with ecstasy.

The Stag said, 'Stuffy.'

'Yes.'

'What are we going to do now?'

'Women,' said Stuffy. 'We must find some women to take out to supper.'

The Stag said, 'Later. That can wait till later.' It was early afternoon.

'I don't think it can wait,' said Stuffy.

'Yes,' said the Stag, 'it can wait.'

The Stag was very old and wise; he never rushed any fences. He was twenty-seven, much older than anyone else in the squadron, including the CO, and his judgement was much respected by the others.

'Let's do a little shopping first,' he said.

'Then what?' said the voice from the bathroom.

'Then we can consider the other situation.'

There was a pause.

'Stag?'

'Yes.'

'Do you know any women here?'

'I used to. I used to know a Turkish girl with very white skin called Wenka, and a Yugoslav girl who was six inches taller than I, called Kiki, and another who I think was Syrian. I can't remember her name.'

'Ring them up,' said Stuffy.

'I've done it. I did it while you were getting the whisky. They've all gone. It isn't any good.'

'It's never any good,' Stuffy said.

The Stag said, 'We'll go shopping first. There is plenty of time.'

In an hour Stuffy got out of the bath. They both dressed themselves in clean khaki shorts and shirts and wandered downstairs, through the lobby of the hotel and out into the bright hot street. The Stag put on his sunglasses.

Stuffy said, 'I know. I want a pair of sunglasses.'

'All right. We'll go and buy some.'

They stopped a gharri, got in and told the driver to go to Cicurel. Stuffy bought his sunglasses and the Stag bought some poker dice, then they wandered out again on to the hot crowded street.

'Did you see that girl?' said Stuffy.

'The one that sold us the sunglasses?'

'Yes. That dark one.'

'Probably Turkish,' said Stag.

Stuffy said, 'I don't care what she was. She was terrific. Didn't you think she was terrific?'

They were walking along the Sharia Kasr-el-Nil with their hands in their pockets, and Stuffy was wearing the sunglasses which he had just bought. It was a hot dusty afternoon, and the sidewalk was crowded with Egyptians and Arabs and small boys with bare feet. The flies followed the small boys and buzzed around their eyes, trying to get at the inflammation which was in them, which was there because their mothers had done something terrible to those eyes when the boys were young, so that they would not be eligible for military conscription when they grew older. The small boys pattered along beside the Stag and Stuffy shouting, 'Baksheesh, baksheesh,' in shrill insistent voices, and the flies followed the small boys. There was the smell of Cairo, which is not like the smell of any other city. It comes not from any one thing or from any one place; it comes from everything everywhere; from the gutters and the sidewalks, from the houses and the shops and the things in the shops and the food cooking in the shops, from the horses and the dung of the horses in the streets and from the drains; it comes from the people and the way the sun bears down upon the people and from the way the sun bears down upon the gutters and the drains and the horses and the food and the refuse in the streets. It is a rare, pungent smell, like something which is sweet and rotting and hot and salty and bitter all at the same time, and it is never absent, even in the cool of the early morning.

The two pilots walked slowly among the crowd.

'Didn't you think she was terrific?' said Stuffy. He wanted to know what the Stag thought.

'She was all right.'

'Certainly she was all right. You know what, Stag?'

'What?'

'I would like to take that girl out tonight.'

They crossed over a street and walked on a little farther.

The Stag said, 'Well, why don't you? Why don't you ring up Rosette?'

'Who in the hell's Rosette?'

'Madame Rosette,' said the Stag. 'She is a great woman.'

They were passing a place called Tim's Bar. It was run by an Englishman called Tim Gilfillan who had been a quartermaster sergeant in the last war and who had somehow managed to get left behind in Cairo when the Army went home.

'Tim's,' said the Stag. 'Let's go in.'

There was no one inside except for Tim, who was arranging his bottles on shelves behind the bar.

'Well, well, well,' he said, turning around. 'Where you boys been all this time?'

'Hello, Tim.'

He did not remember them, but he knew by their looks that they were in from the desert.

'How's my old friend Graziani?' he said, turning round and leaning his elbows on the counter.

'He's bloody close,' said the Stag. 'He's outside Mersah.'

'What you flying now?'

'Gladiators.'

'Hell, they had those here eight years ago.'

'Same ones still here,' said the Stag. 'They're clapped out.'

They got their whisky and carried the glasses over to a table in the corner.

Stuffy said, 'Who's this Rosette?'

The Stag took a long drink and put down the glass.

'She's a great woman,' he said.

'Who is she?'

'She's a filthy old whore.'

'All right,' said Stuffy, 'all right, but what about her?'

'Well,' said Stag, 'I'll tell you. Madame Rosette runs the biggest brothel in the world. It is said that she can get you any girl that you want in the whole of Cairo.'

'Bullshit.'

'No, it's true. You just ring her up and tell her where you saw the woman, where she was working, what shop and at which counter, together with an accurate description, and she will do the rest.'

'Don't be such a bloody fool,' said Stuffy.

'It's true. It's absolutely true. Thirty-three Squadron told me about her.'

'They were pulling your leg.'

'All right. You go and look her up in the phone book.'

'She wouldn't be in the phone book under that name.'

'I'm telling you she is,' said Stag. 'Go and look her up under Rosette. You'll see I'm right.'

Stuffy did not believe him, but he went over to Tim and asked him for a telephone directory and brought it back to the table. He opened it and turned the pages until he came to R-o-s. He ran his finger down the column. Roseppi . . . Rosery . . . Rosette. There it was, Rosette, Madame, and the address and number, clearly printed in the book. The Stag was watching him.

'Got it?' he said.

'Yes, here it is. Madame Rosette.'

'Well, why don't you go and ring her up?'

'What shall I say?'

The Stag looked down into his glass and poked the ice with his finger.

'Tell her you are a colonel,' he said. 'Colonel Higgins; she mistrusts pilot officers. And tell her that you have seen a beautiful dark girl selling sunglasses at Cicurel's and that you would like, as you put it, to take her out to dinner.'

'There isn't a telephone here.'

'Oh yes there is. There's one over there.'

Stuffy looked around and saw the telephone on the wall at the end of the bar.

'I haven't got a piastre piece.'

'Well, I have,' said Stag. He fished in his pocket and put a piastre on the table.

'Tim will hear everything I say.'

'What the hell does that matter? He probably rings her up himself. You're windy,' he added.

'You're a shit,' said Stuffy.

Stuffy was just a child. He was nineteen; seven whole years younger than the Stag. He was fairly tall and he was thin, with a lot of black hair and a handsome wide-mouthed face which was coffee brown from the sun of the desert. He was unquestionably the finest pilot in the squadron, and already in these early days his score was fourteen Italians confirmed destroyed. On the ground he moved slowly and lazily like a tired person and he thought slowly and lazily like a sleepy child, but when he was up in the air his mind was quick and his movements were quick, so quick that they were like reflex actions. It seemed, when he was on the ground, almost as though he was resting, as though he was dozing a little in order to make sure that when he got into the cockpit he would wake up fresh and quick, ready for that two hours of high concentration. But Stuffy was away from the aerodrome now and he had something on his mind which had waked him up almost like flying. It might not last, but for the moment anyway, he was concentrating.

He looked again in the book for the number, got up and walked slowly over to the telephone. He put in the piastre, dialled the number and heard it ringing at the other end. The Stag was sitting at the table looking at him and Tim was still behind the bar arranging his bottles. Tim was only about five yards away and he was obviously going to listen to everything that was said. Stuffy felt rather foolish. He leaned against the bar and waited, hoping that no one would answer.

Then click, the receiver was lifted at the other end and he heard a woman's voice saying, 'Allo.'

He said, 'Hello, is Madame Rosette there?' He was watching Tim. Tim went on arranging his bottles, pretending to take no notice, but Stuffy knew that he was listening.

'This ees Madame Rosette. Oo ees it?' Her voice was petulant and gritty. She sounded as if she did not want to be bothered with anyone just then.

Stuffy tried to sound casual. 'This is Colonel Higgins.'

'Colonel oo?'

'Colonel Higgins.' He spelled it.

'Yes, Colonel. What do you want?' She sounded impatient. Obviously this was a woman who stood no nonsense. He still tried to sound casual.

'Well, Madame Rosette, I was wondering if you could help me over a little matter.'

Stuffy was watching Tim. He was listening all right. You can always tell if someone is listening when he is pretending not to. He is careful not to make any noise about what he is doing and he pretends that he is concentrating very hard upon his job. Tim was like that now, moving the bottles quickly from one shelf to another, watching the bottles, making no noise, never looking around into the room. Over in the far corner the Stag was leaning forward with his elbows on the table, smoking a cigarette. He was watching Stuffy, enjoying the whole business and knowing that Stuffy was embarrassed because of Tim. Stuffy had to go on.

'I was wondering if you could help me,' he said. 'I was in Cicurel's today buying a pair of sunglasses and I saw a girl there whom I would very much like to take out to dinner.'

'What's 'er name?' The hard, rasping voice was more businesslike than ever.

'I don't know,' he said sheepishly.

'What's she look like?'

'Well, she's got dark hair, and tall and, well, she's very beautiful.'

'What sort of a dress was she wearing?'

'Er, let me see. I think it was a kind of white dress with red flowers printed all over it.' Then, as a brilliant afterthought, he added, 'She had a red belt.' He remembered that she had been wearing a shiny red belt.

There was a pause. Stuffy watched Tim, who wasn't making any noise with the bottles; he was picking them up carefully and putting them down carefully.

Then the loud gritty voice again, 'It may cost you a lot.'

'That's all right.' Suddenly he didn't like the conversation any more. He wanted to finish it and get away.

'Might cost you six pounds, might cost you eight or ten. I don't know till I've seen her. That all right?'

'Yes yes, that's all right.'

'Where you living, Colonel?'

'Metropolitan Hotel,' he said without thinking.

'All right, I give you a ring later.' And she put down the receiver, bang.

Stuffy hung up, went slowly back to the table and sat down.

'Well,' said Stag, 'that was all right, wasn't it?'

'Yes, I suppose so.'

'What did she say?'

'She said that she would call me back at the hotel.'

'You mean she'll call Colonel Higgins at the hotel.'

Stuffy said, 'Oh Christ.'

Stag said, 'It's all right. We'll tell the desk that the Colonel is in our room and put his calls through to us. What else did she say?'

'She said it may cost me a lot, six or ten pounds.'

'Rosette will take ninety per cent of it,' said Stag. 'She's a filthy old whore.'

'How will she work it?' Stuffy said.

He was really a gentle person and now he was feeling worried about having started something which might become complicated.

'Well,' said Stag, 'she'll dispatch one of her pimps to locate the girl and find out who she is. If she's already on the books, then it's easy. If she isn't, the pimp will proposition her there and then over the counter at Cicurel's. If the girl tells him to go to hell, he'll up the price, and if she still tells him to go to hell, he'll up the price still more, and in the end she'll be tempted by the cash and probably agree. Then Rosette quotes you a price three times as high and takes the balance herself. You have to pay her, not the girl. Of course after that the girl goes on Rosette's books, and once she's in her clutches, she's finished. Next time Rosette will dictate the price and the girl will not be in a position to argue.'

'Why?'

'Because if she refuses, Rosette will say, "All right, my girl, I shall see that your employers, that's Cicurel's, are told about what you did last time, how you've been working for me and using their shop as a market place. Then they'll fire you." That's what Rosette will say, and the wretched girl will be frightened and do what she's told.'

Stuffy said, 'Sounds like a nice person.'

'Who?'

'Madame Rosette.'

'Charming,' said Stag. 'She's a charming person.'

It was hot. Stuffy wiped his face with his handkerchief.

'More whisky,' said Stag. 'Hi, Tim, two more of those.'

Tim brought the glasses over and put them on the table without saying anything. He picked up the empty glasses and went away at once. To Stuffy it seemed as though he was different from what he had been when they first came in. He wasn't cheery any more, he was quiet and offhand. There wasn't any more 'Hi, you fellows, where you been all this time' about him now, and when he got back behind the counter, he turned his back and went on arranging the bottles.

The Stag said, 'How much money you got?'

'Nine pounds, I think.'

'May not be enough. You gave her a free hand, you know. You ought to have set a limit. She'll sting you now.'

'I know,' Stuffy said.

They went on drinking for a little while without talking. Then Stag said, 'What you worrying about, Stuffy?'

'Nothing,' he answered. 'Nothing at all. Let's go back to the hotel. She may ring up.'

They paid for their drinks and said good-bye to Tim, who nodded but didn't say anything. They went back to the Metropolitan and as they went past the desk, the Stag said to the clerk, 'If a call comes in for Colonel Higgins, put it through to our room. He'll be there.' The Egyptian said, 'Yes, sir,' and made a note of it.

In the bedroom, the Stag lay down on his bed and lit a cigarette. 'And what am I going to do tonight?' he said.

Stuffy had been quiet all the way back to the hotel. He hadn't said a word. Now he sat down on the edge of the other bed with his hands still in his pockets and said, 'Look, Stag, I'm not very keen on this Rosette deal any more. It may cost too much. Can't we put it off?'

The Stag sat up. 'Hell no,' he said. 'You're committed. You can't fool about with Rosette like that. She's probably working on it at this moment. You can't back out now.'

'I may not be able to afford it,' Stuffy said.

'Well, wait and see.'

Stuffy got up, went over to the parachute bag and took out the bottle of whisky. He poured out two, filled the glasses with water from the tap in the bathroom, came back and gave one to the Stag.

'Stag,' he said. 'Ring up Rosette and tell her that Colonel Higgins has had to leave town urgently, to rejoin his regiment in the desert. Ring her up and tell her that. Say the colonel asked you to deliver the message because he didn't have time.'

'Ring her up yourself.'

'She'd recognize my voice. Come on, Stag, you ring her.'

'No,' he said, 'I won't.'

'Listen,' said Stuffy suddenly. It was the child Stuffy speaking. 'I don't want to go out with that woman and I don't want to have any dealings with Madame Rosette tonight. We can think of something else.'

The Stag looked up quickly. Then he said, 'All right. I'll ring her.'

He reached for the phone book, looked up her number and spoke it into the telephone. Stuffy heard him get her on the line and he heard him giving her the message from the colonel. There was a pause, then the Stag said, 'I'm sorry, Madame Rosette, but it's nothing to do with me. I'm merely delivering a message.' Another pause; then the Stag said the same thing over again and that went on for quite a long time, until he must have got tired of it, because in the end he put down the receiver and lay back on his bed. He was roaring with laughter.

'The lousy old bitch,' he said, and he laughed some more.

Stuffy said, 'Was she angry?'

'Angry,' said Stag. 'Was she angry? You should have heard her. Wanted to know the colonel's regiment and God knows what else and said he'd have to pay. She said you boys think you can fool around with me but you can't.'

'Hooray,' said Stuffy. 'The filthy old whore.'

'Now what are we going to do?' said the Stag. 'It's six o'clock already.'

'Let's go out and do a little drinking in some of those Gyppi places.'

'Fine. We'll do a Gyppi pub crawl.'

They had one more drink, then they went out. They went to a place called the Excelsior, then they went to a place called the Sphinx, then to a small place called by an Egyptian name, and by ten o'clock they were sitting happily in a place which hadn't got a name at all, drinking beer and watching a kind of stage show. At the Sphinx they had picked up a pilot from 33 Squadron, who said that his name was William. He was about the same age as Stuffy, but his face was younger, for he had not been flying so long. It was especially around his mouth that he was younger. He had a round schoolboy face and a small turned-up nose and his skin was brown from the desert.

The three of them sat happily in the place without a name drinking beer, because beer was the only thing that they served there. It was a long wooden room with an unpolished wooden sawdust floor and wooden tables and chairs. At the far end there was a raised wooden stage where there was a show going on. The room was full of

Egyptians, sitting drinking black coffee with the red tarbooshes on their heads. There were two fat girls on the stage dressed in shiny silver pants and silver brassières. One was waggling her bottom in time to the music. The other was waggling her bosom in time to the music. The bosom waggler was the more skilful. She could waggle one bosom without waggling the other and sometimes she would waggle her bottom as well. The Egyptians were spellbound and kept giving her a big hand. The more they clapped the more she waggled and the more she waggled the faster the music played, and the faster the music played, the faster she waggled, faster and faster and faster, never losing the tempo, never losing the fixed brassy smile that was upon her face, and the Egyptians clapped more and more and louder and louder as the speed increased. Everyone was very happy.

When it was over William said, 'Why do they always have those dreary fat women? Why don't they have beautiful women?'

The Stag said, 'The Gyppies like them fat. They like them like that.'

'Impossible,' said Stuffy.

'It's true,' Stag said. 'It's an old business. It comes from the days when there used to be lots of famines here, and all the poor people were thin and all the rich people and the aristocracy were well fed and fat. If you got someone fat you couldn't go wrong; she was bound to be high class.'

'Bullshit,' said Stuffy.

William said, 'Well, we'll soon find out. I'm going to ask

those Gyppies.' He jerked his thumb towards two middle-aged Egyptians who were sitting at the next table, only four feet away.

'No,' said Stag. 'No, William. We don't want them over here.'

'Yes,' said Stuffy.

'Yes,' said William. 'We've got to find out why the Gyppies like fat women.'

He was not drunk. None of them was drunk, but they were happy with a fair amount of beer and whisky, and William was the happiest. His brown schoolboy face was radiant with happiness, his turned-up nose seemed to have turned up a little more and he was probably relaxing for the first time in many weeks. He got up, took three paces over to the table of the Egyptians and stood in front of them, smiling.

'Gentlemen,' he said, 'my friends and I would be honoured if you would join us at our table.'

The Egyptians had dark greasy skin and podgy faces. They were wearing the red hats and one of them had a gold tooth. At first, when William addressed them, they looked a little alarmed. Then they caught on, looked at each other, grinned and nodded.

'Pleess,' said one.

'Pleess,' said the other, and they got up, shook hands with William and followed him over to where the Stag and Stuffy were sitting.

William said, 'Meet my friends. This is the Stag. This is Stuffy. I am William.'

The Stag and Stuffy stood up, they all shook hands, the

Egyptians said 'Pleess' once more and then everyone sat down.

The Stag knew that their religion forbade them to drink. 'Have a coffee,' he said.

The one with the gold tooth grinned broadly, raised his hands, palms upward and hunched his shoulders a little. 'For me,' he said, 'I am accustomed. But for my frient,' and he spread out his hands towards the other, 'for my frient – I cannot speak.'

The Stag looked at the friend. 'Coffee?' he asked.

'Pleess,' he answered. 'I am accustomed.'

'Good,' said Stag. 'Two coffees.'

He called a waiter. 'Two coffees,' he said. 'And, wait a minute. Stuffy, William, more beer?'

'For me,' Stuffy said, 'I am accustomed. But for my friend,' and he turned towards William, 'for my friend – I cannot speak.'

William said, 'Please. I am accustomed.' None of them smiled.

The Stag said, 'Good. Waiter, two coffees and three beers.' The waiter fetched the order and the Stag paid. The Stag lifted his glass towards the Egyptians and said, 'Bung ho.'

'Bung ho,' said Stuffy.

'Bung ho,' said William.

The Egyptians seemed to understand and they lifted their coffee cups. 'Pleess,' said the one. 'Thank you,' said the other. They drank.

The Stag put down his glass and said, 'It is an honour to be in your country.'

'You like?'

'Yes,' said the Stag. 'Very fine.'

The music had started again and the two fat women in silver tights were doing an encore. The encore was a knockout. It was surely the most remarkable exhibition of muscle control that has ever been witnessed; for although the bottom-waggler was still just waggling her bottom, the bosom-waggler was standing like an oak tree in the centre of the stage with her arms above her head. Her left bosom she was rotating in a clockwise direction and her right bosom in an anti-clockwise direction. At the same time she was waggling her bottom and it was all in time to the music. Gradually the music increased its speed, and as it got faster, the rotating and the waggling got faster and some of the Egyptians were so spellbound by the contra-rotating bosoms of the woman that they were unconsciously following the movements of the bosoms with their hands, holding their hands up in front of them and describing circles in the air. Everyone stamped their feet and screamed with delight and the two women on the stage continued to smile their fixed brassy smiles.

Then it was over. The applause gradually died down.

'Remarkable,' said the Stag.

'You like?'

'Please, it was remarkable.'

'Those girls,' said the one with the gold tooth, 'very special.'

William couldn't wait any longer. He leaned across the table and said, 'Might I ask you a question?'

'Pleess,' said Golden Tooth. 'Pleess.'

'Well,' said William, 'how do you like your women? Like this – slim?' and he demonstrated with his hands. 'Or like this – fat?'

The gold tooth shone brightly behind a big grin. 'For me, I like like this, fat,' and a pair of podgy hands drew a big circle in the air.

'And your friend?' said William.

'For my frient,' he answered, 'I cannot speak.'

'Pleess,' said the friend. 'Like this.' He grinned and drew a fat girl in the air with his hands.

Stuffy said, 'Why do you like them fat?'

Golden Tooth thought for a moment, then he said, 'You like them slim, eh?'

'Please,' said Stuffy. 'I like them slim.'

'Why you like them slim? You tell me.'

Stuffy rubbed the back of his neck with the palm of his hand. 'William,' he said, 'why do we like them slim?'

'For me,' said William, 'I am accustomed.'

'So am I,' Stuffy said. 'But why?'

William considered. 'I don't know,' he said. 'I don't know why we like them slim.'

'Ha,' said Golden Tooth. 'You don't know.' He leaned over the table towards William and said triumphantly, 'And me, I do not know either.'

But that wasn't good enough for William. 'The Stag,' he said, 'says that all rich people in Egypt used to be fat and all poor people were thin.'

'No,' said Golden Tooth, 'No no no. Look those girls up there. Very fat; very poor. Look Queen of Egypt, Queen Farida. Very thin; very rich. Quite wrong.'

'Yes, but what about years ago?' said William.

'What is this, years ago?'

William said, 'Oh all right. Let's leave it.'

The Egyptians drank their coffee and made noises like the last bit of water running out of the bath tub. When they had finished, they got up to go.

'Going?' said the Stag.

'Pleess,' said Golden Tooth.

William said, 'Thank you.' Stuffy said, 'Pleess.' The other Egyptian said, 'Pleess,' and the Stag said, 'Thank you.' They all shook hands and the Egyptians departed.

'Ropey types,' said William.

'Very,' said Stuffy. 'Very ropey types.'

The three of them sat on drinking happily until midnight, when the waiter came up and told them that the place was closing and that there were no more drinks. They were still not really drunk because they had been taking it slowly, but they were feeling healthy.

'He says we've got to go.'

'All right. Where shall we go? Where shall we go, Stag?'

'I don't know. Where do you want to go?'

'Let's go to another place like this,' said William. 'This is a fine place.'

There was a pause. Stuffy was stroking the back of his neck with his hand. 'Stag,' he said slowly, 'I know where I want to go. I want to go to Madame Rosette's and I want to rescue all the girls there.'

'Who's Madame Rosette?' William said.

'She's a great woman,' said the Stag.

'She's a filthy old whore,' said Stuffy.

'She's a lousy old bitch,' said the Stag.

'All right,' said William. 'Let's go. But who is she?'

They told him who she was. They told him about their telephone calls and about Colonel Higgins, and William said, 'Come on, let's go. Let's go and rescue all the girls.'

They got up and left. When they went outside, they remembered that they were in a rather remote part of the town.

'We'll have to walk a bit,' said Stag. 'No gharries here.'

It was a dark starry night with no moon. The street was narrow and blacked-out. It smelled strongly with the smell of Cairo. It was quiet as they walked along, and now and again they passed a man or sometimes two men standing back in the shadow of a house, leaning against the wall of the house, smoking.

'I say,' said William, 'ropey, what?'

'Very,' said Stuffy. 'Very bad types.'

They walked on, the three of them walking abreast; square short ginger-haired Stag, tall dark Stuffy and tall young William who went barehead because he had lost his cap. They headed roughly towards the centre of town where they knew that they would find a gharri to take them on to Rosette.

Stuffy said, 'Oh, won't the girls be pleased when we rescue them?'

'Jesus,' said the Stag, 'it ought to be a party.'

'Does she actually keep them locked up?' William said.

'Well, no,' said Stag. 'Not exactly. But if we rescue them now, they won't have to work any more tonight anyway. You see, the girls she has at her place are nothing but ordinary shop girls who still work during the day in the shops. They have all of them made some mistake or other which Rosette either engineered or found out about, and now she has put the screws on them; she makes them come along in the evening. But they hate her and they do not depend on her for a living. They would kick her in the teeth if they got the chance.'

Stuffy said, 'We'll give them the chance.'

They crossed over a street. William said, 'How many girls will there be there, Stag?'

'I don't know. I suppose there might be thirty.'

'Good God,' said William. 'This *will* be a party. Does she really treat them very badly?'

The Stag said, 'Thirty-three Squadron told me that she pays them nothing, about twenty akkers a night. She charges the customers a hundred or two hundred akkers each. Every girl earns for Rosette between five hundred and a thousand akkers every night.'

'Good God,' said William. 'A thousand piastres a night and thirty girls. She must be a millionaire.'

'She is. Someone calculated that not even counting her outside business, she makes the equivalent of about fifteen hundred pounds a week. That's, let me see, that's between five and six thousand pounds a month. Sixty thousand pounds a year.'

Stuffy came out of his dream. 'Jesus,' he said, 'Jesus Christ. The filthy old whore.'

'The lousy old bitch,' said William.

They were coming into a more civilized section of the town, but still there were no gharries.

The Stag said, 'Did you hear about Mary's House?'

'What's Mary's House?' said William.

'It's a place in Alexandria. Mary is the Rosette of Alex.'

'Lousy old bitch,' said William.

'No,' Stag said. 'They say she's a good woman. But anyway, Mary's House was hit by a bomb last week. The Navy was in port at the time and the place was full of sailors, nautic types.'

'Killed?'

'Lots of them killed. And d'you know what happened? They posted them as killed in action.'

'The admiral is a gentleman,' said Stuffy.

'Magnificent,' said William.

Then they saw a gharri and hailed it.

Stuffy said, 'We don't know the address.'

'He'll know it,' said Stag. 'Madame Rosette,' he said to the driver.

The driver grinned and nodded. Then William said, 'I'm going to drive. Give me the reins, driver, and sit up here beside me and tell me where to go.'

The driver protested vigorously, but when William gave him ten piastres, he gave him the reins. William sat high up on the driver's seat with the driver beside him. The Stag and Stuffy got in the back of the carriage.

'Take off,' said Stuffy. William took off. The horses began to gallop.

'No good,' shrieked the driver. 'No good. Stop.'

'Which way Rosette?' shouted William.

'Stop,' shrieked the driver.

William was happy. 'Rosette,' he shouted. 'Which way?'

The driver made a decision. He decided that the only way to stop this madman was to get him to his destination. 'This way,' he shrieked. 'Left.' William pulled hard on the left rein and the horses swerved round the corner. The gharri took it on one wheel.

'Too much bank,' shouted Stuffy from the back seat.

'Which way now?' shouted William.

'Left,' shrieked the driver. They took the next street to the left, then they took one to the right, two more to the left, then one to the right again and suddenly the driver yelled, 'Here pleess, here Rosette. Stop.'

William pulled hard on the reins and gradually the horses raised their heads with the pulling and slowed down to a trot.

'Where?' said William.

'Here,' said the driver. 'Pleess.' He pointed to a house twenty yards ahead. William brought the horses to a stop right in front of it.

'Nice work, William,' said Stuffy.

'Jesus,' said the Stag. 'That was quick.'

'Marvellous,' said William. 'Wasn't it?' He was very happy.

The driver was sweating through his shirt and he was too frightened to be angry.

William said, 'How much?'

'Pleess, twenty piastres.'

William gave him forty and said, 'Thank you very much. Fine horses.' The little man took the money, jumped up on to the gharri and drove off. He was in a hurry to get away.

They were in another of those narrow, dark streets, but the houses, what they could see of them, looked huge and prosperous. The one which the driver had said was Rosette's was wide and thick and three storeys high, built of grey concrete, and it had a large thick front door which stood wide open. As they went in, the Stag said, 'Now leave this to me. I've got a plan.'

Inside there was a cold grey dusty stone hall, lit by a bare electric light bulb in the ceiling, and there was a man standing in the hall. He was a mountain of a man, a huge Egyptian with a flat face and two cauliflower ears. In his wrestling days he had probably been billed as Abdul the Killer or The Poisonous Pasha, but now he wore a dirty white cotton suit.

The Stag said, 'Good evening. Is Madame Rosette here?'

Abdul looked hard at the three pilots, hesitated, then said, 'Madame Rosette top floor.'

'Thank you,' said Stag. 'Thank you very much.' Stuffy noticed that the Stag was being polite. There was always trouble for somebody when he was like that. Back in the squadron, when he was leading a flight, when they sighted the enemy and when there was going to be a battle, the Stag never gave an order without saying 'Please' and he never received a message without saying 'Thank you'. He was saying 'Thank you' now to Abdul.

They went up the bare stone steps, which had iron railings. They went past the first landing and the second landing, and the place was as bare as a cave. At the top of the third flight of steps, there was no landing; it was walled off, and the stairs ran up to a door. The Stag pressed the bell. They waited a while, then a little panel in the door slid back and a pair of small black eyes peeked through. A woman's voice said, 'What you boys want?' Both the Stag and Stuffy recognized the voice from the telephone. The Stag said, 'We would like to see Madame Rosette.' He pronounced the Madame in the French way because he was being polite.

'You officers? Only officers here,' said the voice. She had a voice like a broken board.

'Yes,' said Stag. 'We are officers.'

'You don't look like officers. What kind of officers?'

'RAF.'

There was a pause. The Stag knew that she was considering. She had probably had trouble with pilots before, and he hoped only that she would not see William and the light that was dancing in his eyes; for William was still feeling the way he had felt when he drove the gharri. Suddenly the panel closed and the door opened.

'All right, come in,' she said. She was too greedy, this woman, even to pick her customers carefully.

They went in and there she was. Short, fat, greasy, with wisps of untidy black hair straggling over her forehead; a large, mud-coloured face, a large wide nose and a small fish mouth, with just the trace of a black moustache above the mouth. She had on a loose black satin dress.

'Come into the office, boys,' she said, and started to waddle down the passage to the left. It was a long wide passage, about fifty yards long and four or five yards wide. It ran through the middle of the house, parallel with the street, and as you came in from the stairs, you had to turn left along it. All the way down there were doors, about eight or ten of them on each side. If you turned right as you came in from the stairs, you ran into the end of the passage, but there was one door there too, and as the three of them walked in, they heard a babble of female voices from behind that door. The Stag noted that it was the girls' dressing-room.

'This way, boys,' said Rosette. She turned left and slopped down the passage, away from the door with the voices. The three followed her, Stag first, then Stuffy, then William, down the passage, which had a red carpet on the floor and huge pink lampshades hanging from the ceiling. They got about halfway down the passage when there was a yell from the dressing-room behind them. Rosette stopped and looked around.

'You go on, boys,' she said, 'into the office, last door on the left. I won't be a minute.' She turned and went back towards the dressing-room door. They didn't go on. They stood and watched her, and just as she got to the door, it opened and a girl rushed out. From where they stood, they could see that her fair hair was all over her face and that she had on an untidy-looking green evening dress. She saw Rosette in front of her and she stopped. They heard Rosette say something, something angry and quick-spoken, and they heard the girl shout something back at her. They saw Rosette raise her right arm and they saw her hit the girl smack on the side of the face with the palm of her hand. They saw her draw back her hand and hit her again in the same place. She hit her hard. The girl put her hands up to her face and began to cry. Rosette opened the door of the dressing-room and pushed her back inside.

'Jesus,' said the Stag. 'She's tough.' William said, 'So am I.' Stuffy didn't say anything.

Rosette came back to them and said, 'Come along, boys. Just a bit of trouble, that's all.' She led them to the end of the passage and in through the last door on the left. This was the office. It was a medium-sized room with two red plush sofas, two or three red plush armchairs and a thick red carpet on the floor. In one corner was a small desk, and Rosette sat herself behind it, facing the room.

'Sit down, boys,' she said.

The Stag took an armchair, Stuffy and William sat on a sofa.

'Well,' she said, and her voice became sharp and urgent. 'Let's do business.'

The Stag leaned forward in his chair. His short ginger hair looked somehow wrong against the bright red plush. 'Madame Rosette,' he said, 'it is a great pleasure to meet you. We have heard so much about you.' Stuffy looked at the Stag. He was being polite again. Rosette looked at him too, and her little black eyes were suspicious. 'Believe me,' the Stag went on, 'we've really been looking forward to this for quite a time now.'

His voice was so pleasant and he was so polite that Rosette took it.

'That's nice of you boys,' she said. 'You'll always have a good time here. I see to that. Now – business.'

William couldn't wait any longer. He said slowly, 'The Stag says that you're a great woman.'

'Thanks, boys.'

Stuffy said, 'The Stag says that you're a filthy old whore.'

William said quickly, 'The Stag says that you're a lousy old bitch.'

'And I know what I'm talking about,' said the Stag.

Rosette jumped to her feet. 'What's this?' she shrieked, and her face was no longer the colour of mud; it was the colour of red clay. The men did not move. They did not smile or laugh; they sat quite still, leaning forward a little in their seats, watching her.

Rosette had had trouble before, plenty of it, and she knew how to deal with it. But this was different. They didn't seem drunk, it wasn't about money and it wasn't about one of her girls. It was about herself and she didn't like it.

'Get out,' she yelled. 'Get out unless you want trouble.' But they did not move.

For a moment she paused, then she stepped quickly from behind her desk and made for the door. But the Stag was there first and when she went for him, Stuffy and William each caught one of her arms from behind.

'We'll lock her in,' said the Stag. 'Let's get out.'

Then she really started yelling and the words which she used cannot be written down on paper, for they were terrible words. They poured out of her small fish mouth in one long unbroken high-pitched stream, and little bits of spit and saliva came out with them. Stuffy and William pulled her back by the arms towards one of the big chairs and she fought and yelled like a large fat pig being dragged to the slaughter. They got her in front of the chair and gave her a quick push so that she fell backwards into it. Stuffy nipped across to her desk, bent down quickly and jerked the telephone cord from its connection. The Stag had the door open and all three of them were out of the room before Rosette had time to get up. The Stag had taken the key from the inside of the door, and now he locked it. The three of them stood outside in the passage.

'Jesus,' said the Stag. 'What a woman!'

'Mad as hell,' William said. 'Listen to her.'

They stood outside in the passage and they listened. They heard her yelling, then she began banging on the door, but she went on yelling and her voice was not the voice of a woman, it was the voice of an enraged but articulate bull.

The Stag said, 'Now quick. The girls. Follow me. And from now on you've got to act serious. You've got to act serious as hell.'

He ran down the passage towards the dressing-room, followed by Stuffy and William. Outside the door he stopped, the other two stopped and they could still hear Rosette yelling from her office. The Stag said, 'Now don't say anything. Just act serious as hell,' and he opened the door and went in.

There were about a dozen girls in the room. They all looked up. They stopped talking and looked up at the Stag, who was standing in the doorway. The Stag clicked his heels and said, 'This is the Military Police. *Les Gendarmes Militaires.*'

He said it in a stern voice and with a straight face and he was standing there in the doorway at attention with his cap on his head. Stuffy and William stood behind him.

'This is the Military Police,' he said again, and he produced his identification card and held it up between two fingers.

The girls didn't move or say anything. They stayed still in the middle of what they were doing and they were like a tableau because they stayed still. One had been pulling on a stocking and she stayed like that, sitting on a chair with her leg out straight and the stocking up to her knee with her hands on the stocking. One had been doing her hair in front of a mirror and when she looked round she kept her hands up to her hair. One was standing up and had been applying lipstick and she raised her eyes to the Stag but still held the lipstick to her mouth. Several were just sitting around on plain wooden chairs, doing nothing, and they raised their heads and turned them to the door, but they went on sitting. Most of them were in some sort of shiny evening dress, one or two were half clothed, but most of them were in shiny green or shiny blue or shiny red or shiny gold, and when they turned to look at the Stag, they were so still that they were like a tableau.

The Stag paused. Then he said, 'I am to state on behalf of the authorities that they are sorry to disturb you. My apologies, Mesd'moiselles. But it is necessary that you come with us for purposes of registration, et cetera. Afterwards you will be allowed to go. It is a mere formality. But now you must come, please. I have conversed with Madame.'

The Stag stopped speaking, but still the girls did not move.

'Please,' said the Stag, 'get your coats. We are the military.' He stepped aside and held open the door. Suddenly the tableau dissolved, the girls got up, puzzled and murmuring, and two or three of them moved towards the door. The others followed. The ones that were half clothed quickly slipped into dresses, patted their hair with their hands and came too. None of them had coats.

'Count them,' said the Stag to Stuffy as they filed out of the door. Stuffy counted them aloud and there were fourteen.

'Fourteen, sir,' said Stuffy, who was trying to talk like a sergeant-major.

The Stag said, 'Correct,' and he turned to the girls who were crowded in the passage. 'Now, Mesd'moiselles, I have the list of your names from Madame, so please do not try to run away. And do not worry. This is merely a formality of the military.'

William was out in the passage opening the door which led to the stairs, and he went out first. The girls followed and the Stag and Stuffy brought up the rear. The girls were quiet and puzzled and worried and a little frightened and they didn't talk, none of them talked except for a tall one with black hair who said, '*Mon Dieu*, a formality of the military. *Mon Dieu, mon Dieu*, what next?' But that was all and they went on down. In the hall they met the Egyptian who had a flat face and two cauliflower ears. For a moment it looked as though there would be trouble. But the Stag waved his identification card in his face and said, 'The

Military Police,' and the man was so surprised that he did nothing and let them pass.

And so they came out into the street and the Stag said, 'It is necessary to walk a little way, but only a very little way,' and they turned right and walked along the sidewalk with the Stag leading, Stuffy at the rear and William walking out on the road, guarding the flank. There was some moon now. One could see quite well and William tried to keep in step with Stag and Stuffy tried to keep in step with William, and they swung their arms and held their heads up high and looked very military, and the whole thing was a sight to behold. Fourteen girls in shiny evening dresses, fourteen girls in the moonlight in shiny green, shiny blue, shiny red, shiny black and shiny gold, marching along the street with the Stag in front, William alongside and Stuffy at the rear. It was a sight to behold.

The girls had started chattering. The Stag could hear them, although he didn't look around. He marched on at the head of the column and when they came to the crossroads he turned right. The others followed and they had walked fifty yards down the block when they came to an Egyptian café. The Stag saw it and he saw the lights burning behind the blackout curtains. He turned around and shouted, 'Halt!' The girls stopped, but they went on chattering and anyone could see now that there was mutiny in the ranks. You can't make fourteen girls in high heels and shiny evening dresses march all over town with you at night, not for long anyway, not for long, even if it is a formality of the military. The Stag knew it and now he was speaking.

'Mesd'moiselles,' he said, 'listen to me.' But there was mutiny in the ranks and they went on talking and the tall one with dark hair was saying, '*Mon Dieu*, what is this? What in hell's name sort of a thing is this, oh *mon Dieu*?'

'Quiet,' said the Stag. 'Quiet!', and the second time he shouted it as a command. The talking stopped.

'Mesd'moiselles,' he said, and now he became polite. He talked to them in his best way and when the Stag was polite there wasn't anyone who didn't take it. It was an extraordinary thing because he could make a kind of smile with his voice without smiling with his lips. His voice smiled while his face remained serious. It was a most forcible thing because it gave people the impression that he was being serious about being nice.

'Mesd'moiselles,' he said, and his voice was smiling. 'With the military there always has to be formality. It is something unavoidable. It is something that I regret exceedingly. But there can be chivalry also. And you must know that with the RAF there is great chivalry. So now it will be a pleasure if you will all come in here and take with us a glass of beer. It is the chivalry of the military.' He stepped forward, opened the door of the café and said, 'Oh for God's sake, let's have a drink. Who wants a drink?'

Suddenly the girls saw it all. They saw the whole thing as it was, all of them at once. It took them by surprise. For a second they considered. Then they looked at one another, then they looked at the Stag, then they looked around at Stuffy and at William, and when they looked at those two they caught their eyes and the laughter that was in them. All at once the girls began to laugh and William laughed and Stuffy laughed and they moved forward and poured into the café.

The tall one with dark hair took the Stag by the arm and said, '*Mon Dieu*, Military Police, *mon Dieu*, oh *mon Dieu*,' and she threw her head back and laughed and the Stag laughed with her. William said, 'It is the chivalry of the military,' and they moved into the café.

The place was rather like the one that they had been in before, wooden and sawdusty, and there were a few coffee-drinking Egyptians sitting around with the red tarbooshes on their heads. William and Stuffy pushed three round tables together and fetched chairs. The girls sat down. The Egyptians at the other tables put down their coffee cups, turned around in their chairs and gaped. They gaped like so many fat muddy fish, and some of them shifted their chairs round facing the party so that they could get a better view, and they went on gaping.

A waiter came up and the Stag said, 'Seventeen beers. Bring us seventeen beers.' The waiter said, 'Pleess,' and went away.

As they sat waiting for the drinks the girls looked at the three pilots and the pilots looked at the girls. William said, 'It is the chivalry of the military,' and the tall dark girl said, '*Mon Dieu*, you are crazy people, oh *mon Dieu*.'

The waiter brought the beer. William raised his glass and said, 'To the chivalry of the military.' The dark girl said, 'Oh *mon Dieu*.' Stuffy didn't say anything. He was busy looking around at the girls, sizing them up, trying to decide now which one he liked best so that he could go to work at once. The Stag was smiling and the girls were sitting there in their shiny evening dresses, shiny red, shiny gold, shiny blue, shiny green, shiny black and shiny silver, and once again it was almost a tableau, certainly it was a picture, and the girls were sitting there sipping their beer, seeming quite happy, not seeming suspicious any more because to them the whole thing now appeared exactly as it was and they understood.

'Jesus,' said the Stag. He put down his glass and looked around him. 'Oh Jesus, there's enough here for the whole squadron. How I wish the whole squadron was here!' He took another drink, stopped in the middle of it and put down his glass quickly. 'I know what,' he said. 'Waiter, oh waiter.'

'Pleess.'

'Get me a big piece of paper and a pencil.'

'Pleess.' The waiter went away and came back with a sheet of paper. He took a pencil from behind his ear and handed it to the Stag. The Stag banged the table for silence.

'Mesd'moiselles,' he said, 'for the last time there is a formality. It is the last of all the formalities.'

'Of the military,' said William.

'Oh *mon Dieu*,' said the dark girl.

'It is nothing,' the Stag said. 'You are required to write your name and your telephone number on this piece of paper. It is for my friends in the squadron. It is so that they can be as happy as I am now, but without the same trouble beforehand.' The Stag's voice was smiling again. One could see that the girls liked his voice. 'You would be very kind if you would do that,' he went on, 'for they too would like to meet you. It would be a pleasure.'

'Wonderful,' said William.

'Crazy,' said the dark girl, but she wrote her name and number on the paper and passed it on. The Stag ordered another round of beer. The girls certainly looked funny sitting there in their dresses, but they were writing their names down on the paper. They looked happy and William particularly looked happy, but Stuffy looked serious because the problem of choosing was a weighty one and it was heavy on his mind. They were good-looking girls, young and good-looking, all different, completely different from each other, because they were Greek and Syrian and French and Italian and light Egyptian and Yugoslav and many other things, but they were good-looking, all of them were good-looking and handsome.

The piece of paper had come back to the Stag now and they had written on it; fourteen strangely written names and fourteen telephone numbers. The Stag looked at it slowly. 'This will go on the squadron notice-board,' he said, 'and I will be regarded as a great benefactor.'

William said, 'It should go to Headquarters. It should be mimeographed and circulated to all squadrons. It would be good for morale.'

'Oh *mon Dieu*,' said the dark girl. 'You are crazy.'

Slowly Stuffy got to his feet, picked up his chair, carried it round to the other side of the table and pushed it between two of the girls. All he said was, 'Excuse me. Do you mind if I sit here?' At last he had made up his mind, and now he turned towards the one on his right and quietly went to work. She was very pretty; very dark and very pretty and she had plenty of shape. Stuffy began to talk to her, completely oblivious to the rest of the company, turning towards her and leaning his head on his hand. Watching him, it was not so difficult to understand why he was the greatest pilot in the squadron. He was a young concentrator, this Stuffy; an intense athletic concentrator who moved towards what he wanted in a dead-straight line. He took hold of winding roads and carefully he made them straight, then he moved over them with great speed and nothing stopped him. He was like that, and now he was talking to the pretty girl but no one could hear what he was saying.

Meanwhile the Stag was thinking. He was thinking about the next move, and when everyone was getting towards the end of their third beer, he banged the table again for silence.

'Mesd'moiselles,' he said, 'it will be a pleasure for us to escort you home. I will take five of you' – he had worked it all out – 'Stuffy will take five, and Jamface will take four. We will take three gharries and I will take five of you in mine and I will drop you home one at a time.'

William said, 'It is the chivalry of the military.'

'Stuffy,' said the Stag. 'Stuffy, is that all right? You take five. It's up to you whom you drop off last.'

Stuffy looked around. 'Yes,' he said. 'Oh yes. That suits me.'

'William, you take four. Drop them home one by one; you understand.'

'Perfectly,' said William. 'Oh perfectly.'

They all got up and moved towards the door. The tall one with dark hair took the Stag's arm and said, 'You take me?'

'Yes,' he answered. 'I take you.'

'You drop me off last?'

'Yes. I drop you off last.'

'Oh *mon Dieu*,' she said. 'That will be fine.'

Outside they got three gharries and they split up into parties. Stuffy was moving quickly. He got his girls into the carriage quickly, climbed in after them and the Stag saw the gharri drive off down the street. Then he saw William's gharri move off, but it seemed to start away with a sudden jerk, with the horses breaking into a gallop at once. The Stag looked again and he saw William perched high up on the driver's seat with the reins in his hands.

The Stag said, 'Let's go,' and his five girls got into their gharri. It was a squash, but everyone got in. The Stag sat back in his seat and then he felt an arm pushing up and under and linking with his. It was the tall one with dark hair. He turned and looked at her.

'Hello,' he said. 'Hello, you.'

'Ah,' she whispered. 'You are such goddam crazy people.' And the Stag felt a warmness inside him and he began to hum a little tune as the gharri rattled on through the dark streets.

Death of an Old Old Man

First published in *Ladies' Home Journal*
(September 1945)

Oh God, how I am frightened.

Now that I am alone I don't have to hide it; I don't have to hide anything any longer. I can let my face go because no one can see me; because there's twenty-one thousand feet between me and them and because now that it's happening again I couldn't pretend any more even if I wanted to. Now I don't have to press my teeth together and tighten the muscles of my jaw as I did during lunch when the corporal brought in the message; when he handed it to Tinker and Tinker looked up at me and said, 'Charlie, it's your turn. You're next up.' As if I didn't know that. As if I didn't know that I was next up. As if I didn't know it last night when I went to bed, and at midnight when I was still awake and all the way through the night, at one in the morning and at two and three and four and five and six and at seven o'clock when I got up. As if I didn't know it while I was dressing and while I was having breakfast and while I was reading the magazines in the mess, playing shove-halfpenny in the mess, reading the notices in the mess, playing billiards in the mess. I knew it then and I knew it when we went in to lunch, while we were eating that mutton for lunch. And when the corporal came into the room with the message – it wasn't anything at all. It wasn't anything more than when it begins to rain because there is a black cloud in the sky. When he handed the paper to Tinker I knew what Tinker was going to say before he had opened his mouth. I knew exactly what he was going to say.

So that wasn't anything either.

But when he folded the message up and put it in his pocket and said, 'Finish your pudding. You've got plenty of time,' that was when it got worse, because I knew for certain then that it was going to happen again, that within half an hour I would be strapping myself in and testing the engine and signalling to the airmen to pull away the chocks. The others were all sitting around eating their pudding; mine was still on my plate in front of me, and I couldn't take another mouthful. But it was fine when I tightened my jaw muscles and said, 'Thank God for that. I'm tired of sitting around here picking my nose.' It was certainly fine when I said that. It must have sounded like any of the others just before they started off. And when I got up to leave the table and said, 'See you at teatime,' that must have sounded all right too.

But now I don't have to do any of that. Thank Christ I don't have to do that now. I can just loosen up and let myself go. I can do or say anything I want so long as I fly this aeroplane properly. It didn't use to be like this. Four years ago it was wonderful. I loved doing it because it was exciting, because the waiting on the aerodrome was nothing more than the waiting before a football game or before going in to bat; and three years ago it was all right too. But then always the three months of resting and the going back again and the resting and the going back; always going back and always getting away with it, everyone saying what a fine pilot, no one knowing what a near thing it was that time near Brussels and how lucky it was that time over Dieppe and how bad it was that other time over Dieppe and how lucky and bad and scared I've been every minute of every trip every week this year. No one knows that. They all say, 'Charlie's a great pilot,' 'Charlie's a born flyer,' 'Charlie's terrific.'

I think he was once, but not any longer.

Each time now it gets worse. At first it begins to grow upon you slowly, coming upon you slowly, creeping up on you from behind, making no noise, so that you do not turn round and see it coming. If you saw it coming, perhaps you could stop it, but there is no warning. It creeps closer and closer, like a cat creeps closer stalking a sparrow, and then when it is right behind you, it doesn't spring like the cat would spring; it just leans forward and whispers in your ear. It touches you gently on the shoulder and whispers to you that you are young, that you have a million things to do and a million things to say, that if you are not careful you will buy it, that you are almost certain to buy it sooner or later, and that when you do you will not be anything any longer; you will just be a charred corpse. It whispers to you about how your corpse will look when it is charred, how black it will be and how it will be twisted and brittle, with the face black and the fingers black and the shoes off the feet because the shoes always come off the feet when you die like that. At first it whispers to you only at night, when you are lying awake in bed at night. Then it whispers to you at odd moments during the day, when you are doing your teeth or drinking a beer or when you are walking down the passage; and in the end it becomes so that you hear it all day and all night all the time.

There's Ijmuiden. Just the same as ever, with the little knob sticking out just beside it. There are the Frisians, Texel, Vlieland, Terschelling, Ameland, Juist and Norderney. I know them all. They look like bacteria under a microscope. There's the Zuider Zee, there's Holland, there's the North Sea, there's Belgium, and there's the world; there's the whole bloody world right there, with all the people who aren't going to get killed and all the houses and the towns and the sea with all the fish. The fish aren't going to get killed either. I'm the only one that's going to get killed. I don't want to die. Oh God, I don't want to die. I don't want to die today anyway. And it isn't the pain. Really it isn't the pain. I don't mind having my leg mashed or my arm burned off; I swear to you that I don't mind that. But I don't want to die. Four years ago I didn't mind. I remember distinctly not minding about it four years ago. I didn't mind about it three years ago either. It was all fine and exciting; it always is when it looks as though you may be going to lose, as it did then. It is always fine to fight when you are going to lose everything anyway, and that was how it was four years ago. But now we're going to win. It is so different when you are going to win. If I die now I lose fifty years of life, and I don't want to lose that. I'll lose anything except that because that would be all the things I want to do and all the things I want to see; all the things like going on sleeping with Joey. Like going home sometimes. Like walking through a wood. Like pouring out a drink from a bottle. Like looking forward to weekends and like being alive every hour every day every year for fifty years. If I die now I will miss all that, and I will miss everything else. I will miss the things that I don't know about. I think those are really the things I am frightened of missing. I think the reason I do not want to die is because of the things I hope will happen. Yes, that's right. I'm sure that's right. Point a revolver at a tramp, at a wet shivering tramp on the side of the road, and say, 'I'm going to shoot you,' and he will cry, 'Don't shoot. Please don't shoot.' The tramp clings to life because of the things he hopes will happen. I am clinging to it for the same reason; but I have clung for so long now that I cannot hold on much longer. Soon I will have to let go. It is like hanging over the edge of a cliff, that's what it is like; and I've been hanging on too long now, holding on to the top of the cliff with my fingers, not being able to pull myself back up, with my fingers getting more and more tired, beginning to hurt and to ache, so that I know that sooner or later I will have to let go. I dare not cry out for help; that is one thing that I dare not do; so I go on hanging over the side of this cliff, and as I hang I keep kicking a little with my feet against the side of the cliff, trying desperately to find a foothold, but it is steep and smooth like the side of a ship, and there isn't any foothold. I am kicking now, that's what I am doing. I am kicking against the smooth side of the cliff, and there isn't any foothold. Soon I shall have to let go. The longer I hang on the more certain I am of that, and so each hour, each day, each night, each week, I become more and more frightened. Four years ago I wasn't hanging over the edge like this. I was running about in the field above, and although I knew that there was a cliff somewhere and that I might fall over it, I did not mind. Three years ago it was the same, but now it is different.

I know that I am not a coward. I am certain of that. I will always keep going. Here I am today, at two o'clock in the afternoon, sitting here flying a course of one hundred and thirty-five at three hundred and sixty miles an hour and flying well; and although I am so frightened that I can hardly think, yet I am going on to do this thing. There was never any question of not going or of turning back. I would rather die than turn back. Turning back never enters into it. It would be easier if it did. I would prefer to have to fight that than to have to fight this fear.

There's Wassalt. Little camouflaged group of buildings and great big camouflaged aerodrome, probably full of 109s and 190s. Holland looks wonderful. It must be a lovely place in the summer. I expect they are haymaking down there now. I expect the German soldiers are watching the Dutch girls haymaking. Bastards. Watching them haymaking, then making them come home with them afterwards. I would like to be haymaking now. I would like to be haymaking and drinking cider.

The pilot was sitting upright in the cockpit. His face was nearly hidden by his goggles and by his oxygen mask. His right hand was resting lightly upon the stick, and his left hand was forward on the throttle. All the time he was looking around him into the sky. From force of habit his head never ceased to move from one side to the other, slowly, mechanically, like clockwork, so that each moment almost, he searched every part of the blue sky, above, below and all around. But it was into the light of the sun itself that he looked twice as long as he looked anywhere else; for that is the place where the enemy hides and waits before he jumps upon you. There are only two places in which you can hide yourself when you are up in the sky. One is in cloud and the other is in the light of the sun.

He flew on; and although his mind was working upon many things and although his brain was the brain of a frightened man, yet his instinct was the instinct of a pilot who is in the sky of the enemy. With a quick glance, without stopping the movement of his head, he looked down and checked his instruments. The glance took no more than a second, and like a camera can record a dozen things at once with the opening of a shutter, so he at a glance recorded with his eyes his oil pressure, his petrol, his oxygen, his rev counter, boost and his air-speed, and in the same instant almost he was looking up again into the sky. He looked at the sun, and as he looked, as he screwed up his eyes and searched into the dazzling brightness of the sun, he thought that he saw something. Yes, there it was; a small black speck moving slowly across the bright surface of the sun, and to him the speck was not a speck but a life-size German pilot sitting in a Focke Wulf which had cannon in its wings.

He knew that he had been seen. He was certain that the one above was watching him, taking his time, sure of being hidden in the brightness of the sun, watching the Spitfire and waiting to pounce. The man in the Spitfire did not take his eye away from the small speck of black. His head was quite still now. He was watching the enemy, and as he watched, his left hand came away from the throttle and began to move delicately around the cockpit. It moved quickly and surely, touching this thing and that, switching on his reflector sight, turning his trigger button from 'safe' over to 'fire' and pressing gently with his thumb upon a lever which increased, ever so slightly, the pitch of the airscrew.

There was no thought in his head now save for the thought of battle. He was no longer frightened or thinking of being frightened. All that was a dream, and as a sleeper who opens his eyes in the morning and forgets his dream, so this man had seen the enemy and had forgotten that he was frightened. It was always the same. It had happened a hundred times before, and now it was happening again. Suddenly, in an instant, he had become cool and precise, and as he prepared himself, as he made ready his cockpit, he watched the German, waiting to see what he would do.

This man was a great pilot. He was great because when the time came, whenever the moment arrived, his coolness was great and his courage was great, and more than anything else his instinct was great, greater by far than his coolness or his courage or his experience. Now he eased open the throttle and pulled the stick gently backwards, trying to gain height, trying to gain a little of the five-thousand-feet advantage which the German had over him. But there was not much time. The Focke Wulf came out of the sun with its nose down and it came fast. The pilot saw it coming and he kept going straight on, pretending that he had not seen it, and all the time he was looking over his shoulder, watching the German, waiting for the moment to turn. If he turned too soon, the German would turn with him, and he would be duck soup. If he turned too late, the German would get him anyway, provided that he could shoot straight, and he would be duck soup then too. So he watched and waited, turning his head and looking over his shoulder, judging his distance; and as the German came within range, as he was about to press his thumb upon the trigger button, the pilot swerved. He yanked the stick hard back and over to the left, he kicked hard with his left foot upon the rudder bar, and like a leaf which is caught up and carried away by a gust of wind, the Spitfire flipped over on to its side and changed direction. The pilot blacked out.

As his sight came back, as the blood drained away from his head and from his eyes, he looked up and saw the German fighter way ahead, turning with him, banking hard, trying to turn tighter and tighter in order to get back on the tail of the Spitfire. The fight was on. Here we go, he said to himself. Here we go again, and he smiled once, quickly, because he was confident and because he had done this so many times before and because each time he had won.

The man was a beautiful pilot. But the German was good too, and when the Spitfire applied a little flap in order to turn in tighter circles, the Focke Wulf appeared to do the same, and they turned together. When the Spitfire throttled back suddenly and got on his tail, the Focke Wulf half rolled and dived out and under and was away, pulling up again in a loop and rolling off the top, so that he came in again from behind. The Spitfire half rolled and dived away, but the Focke Wulf anticipated him, and half rolled and dived with him, behind him on his tail, and here he took a quick shot at the Spitfire, but he missed. For at least fifteen minutes the two small aircraft rolled and dived around each other in the sky. Sometimes they would separate, wheeling around and around in tight turns, watching one another, circling and watching like two boxers circling each other in the ring, waiting for an opening or for the dropping of a guard; then there would be a stall-turn and one would attack the other, and the diving and the rolling and the zooming would start all over again.

All the time the pilot of the Spitfire sat upright in his cockpit, and he flew his aircraft not with his hands but with the tips of his fingers, and the Spitfire was not a Spitfire but a part of his own body; the muscles of his arms and legs were in the wings and in the tail of the machine so that when he banked and turned and dived and climbed he was not moving his hands and his legs, but only the wings and the tail and the body of the aeroplane; for the body of the Spitfire was the body of the pilot, and there was no difference between the one and the other.

So it went on, and all the while, as they fought and as they flew, they lost height, coming down nearer and nearer to the fields of Holland, so that soon they were fighting only three thousand feet above the ground, and one could see the hedges and the small trees and shadows which the small trees made upon the grass.

Once the German tried a long shot, from a thousand yards, and the pilot of the Spitfire saw the tracer streaming past in front of the nose of his machine. Once, when they flew close past each other, he saw, for a moment, the head and shoulders of the German under the glass roof of his cockpit, the head turned towards him, with the brown helmet, the goggles, the nose and the white scarf. Once when he blacked out from a quick pull-out, the black-out lasted longer than usual. It lasted maybe five seconds, and when his sight came back, he looked quickly around for the Focke Wulf and saw it half a mile away, flying straight at him on the beam, a thin inch-long black line which grew quickly, so that almost at once it was no longer an inch, but an inch and a half, then two inches, then six and then a foot. There was hardly any time. There was a second or perhaps two at the most, but it was enough because he did not have to think or to wonder what to do; he had only to allow his instinct to control his arms and his legs and the wings and the body of the aeroplane. There was only one thing to do, and the Spitfire did it. It banked steeply and turned at right angles towards the Focke Wulf, facing it and flying straight towards it for a head-on attack.

The two machines flew fast towards each other. The pilot of the Spitfire sat upright in his cockpit, and now, more than ever, the aircraft was a part of his body. His eye was upon the reflector sight, the small yellow electric-light dot which was projected up in front of the windshield, and it was upon the thinness of the Focke Wulf beyond. Quickly, precisely, he moved his aircraft a little this way and that, and the yellow dot, which moved with the aircraft, danced and jerked this way and that, and then suddenly it was upon the thin line of the Focke Wulf and there it stayed. His right thumb in the leather glove felt for the firing-button; he squeezed it gently, as a rifleman squeezes a trigger, his guns fired, and at the same time, he saw the small spurts of flame from the cannon in the nose of the Focke Wulf. The whole thing, from beginning to end, took perhaps as long as it would take you to light a cigarette. The German pilot came straight on at him and he had a sudden, vivid, colourless view of the round nose and the thin outstretched wings of the Focke Wulf. Then there was a crack as their wing-tips met, and there was a splintering as the port wing of the Spitfire came away from the body of the machine.

The Spitfire was dead. It fell like a dead bird falls, fluttering a little as it died; continuing in the direction of its flight as it fell. The hands of the pilot, almost in a single movement, undid his straps, tore off his helmet and slid back the hood of the cockpit; then they grasped the edges of the cockpit and he was out and away, falling, reaching for the ripcord, grasping it with his right hand, pulling on it so that his parachute billowed out and opened and the straps jerked him hard between the fork of his legs.

All of a sudden the silence was great. The wind was blowing on his face and in his hair and he reached up a hand and brushed the hair away from his eyes. He was about a thousand feet up, and he looked down and saw flat green country with fields and hedges and no trees. He could see some cows in the field below him. Then he looked up, and as he looked, he said, 'Good God,' and his right hand moved quickly to his right hip, feeling for his revolver, which he had not brought with him. For there, not more than five hundred yards away, parachuting down at the same time and at the same height, was another man, and he knew when he saw him that it could be only the German pilot. Obviously his plane had been damaged at the same time as the Spitfire in the collision. He must have got out quickly too; and now here they were, both of them parachuting down so close to each other that they might even land in the same field.

He looked again at the German, hanging there in his straps with his legs apart, his hands above his head grasping the cords of the parachute. He seemed to be a small man, thickly built and by no means young. The German was looking at him too. He kept looking, and when his body swung around the other way, he turned his head, looking over his shoulder.

So they went on down. Both men were watching each other, thinking about what would happen soon, and the German was the king because he was landing in his own territory. The pilot of the Spitfire was coming down in enemy country; he would be taken prisoner, or he would be killed, or he would kill the German, and if he did that, he would escape. I will escape anyway, he thought. I'm sure I can run faster than the German. He does not look as though he could run very fast. I will race him across the fields and get away.

The ground was close now. There were not many seconds to go. He saw that the German would almost certainly land in the same field as he, the field with the cows. He looked down to see what the field was like and whether the hedges were thick and whether there was a gate in the hedge, and as he looked, he saw below him in the field a small pond, and there was a small stream running through the pond. It was a cow-drinking pond, muddy round the edges and muddy in the water. The pond was right below him. He was no more than the height of a horse above it and he was dropping fast; he was dropping right into the middle of the pond. Quickly he grasped the cords above his head and tried to spill the parachute to one side so that he would change direction, but he was too late; it wasn't any good. All at once something brushed the surface of his brain and the top of his stomach, and the fear which he had forgotten in the fighting was upon him again. He saw the pond and the black surface of the water of the pond, and the pond was not a pond, and the water was not water; it was a small black hole in the surface of the earth which went on down and down for miles and miles, with steep smooth sides like the sides of a ship, and it was so deep that when you fell into it, you went on falling and falling and you fell for ever. He saw the mouth of the hole and the deepness of it, and he was only a small brown pebble which someone had picked up and thrown into the air so that it would fall into the hole. He was a pebble which someone had picked up in the grass of the field. That was all he was and now he was falling and the hole was below him.

Splash. He hit the water. He went through the water and his feet hit the bottom of the pond. They sank into the mud on the bottom and his head went under the water, but it came up again and he was standing with the water up to his shoulders. The parachute was on top of him; his head was tangled in a mass of cords and white silk and he pulled at them with his hands, first this way and then that, but it only got worse, and the fear got worse because the white silk was covering his head so that he could see nothing but a mass of white cloth and a tangle of cords. Then he tried to move towards the bank, but his feet were stuck in the mud; he had sunk up to his knees in the mud. So he fought the parachute and the tangled cords of the parachute, pulling at them with his hands and trying to get them clear of his head; and as he did so he heard the sound of footsteps running on the grass. He heard the noise of the footsteps coming closer and the German must have jumped, because there was a splash and he was knocked over by the weight of a man's body.

He was under the water, and instinctively he began to struggle. But his feet were still stuck in the mud, the man was on top of him and there were hands around his neck holding him under and squeezing his neck with strong fingers. He opened his eyes and saw brown water. He noticed the bubbles in the water, small bright bubbles rising slowly upwards in the brown water. There was no noise or shouting or anything else, but only the bright bubbles moving upwards in the water, and suddenly, as he watched them, his mind became clear and calm like a sunny day. I won't struggle, he thought. There is no point in struggling, for when there is a black cloud in the sky, it is bound to rain.

He relaxed his body and all the muscles in his body because he had no farther wish to struggle. How nice it is not to struggle, he thought. There is no point in struggling. I was a fool to have struggled so much and for so long; I was a fool to have prayed for the sun when there was a black cloud in the sky. I should have prayed for rain; I should have shouted for rain. I should have shouted, Let it rain, let it rain in solid sheets and I will not care. Then it would have been easy. It would have been so easy then. I have struggled for five years and now I don't have to do it any more. This is so much better; this is ever so much better, because there is a wood somewhere that I wish to walk through, and you cannot walk struggling through a wood. There is a girl somewhere that I wish to sleep with, and you cannot sleep struggling with a girl. You cannot do anything struggling; especially you cannot live struggling, and so now I am going to do all the things that I want to do, and there will be no more struggling.

See how calm and lovely it is like this. See how sunny it is and what a beautiful field this is, with the cows and the little pond and the green hedges with primroses growing in the hedges. Nothing will worry me any more now, nothing nothing nothing; not even that man splashing in the water of the pond over there. He seems very puffed and out of breath. He seems to be dragging something out of the pond, something heavy. Now he's got it to the side and he's pulling it up on to the grass. How funny; it's a body. It's a body of a man. As a matter of fact, I think it's me. Yes, it is me. I know it is because of that smudge of yellow paint on the front of my flying suit. Now he's kneeling down, searching in my pockets, taking out my money and my identification card. He's found my pipe and the letter I got this morning from my mother. He's taking off my watch. Now he's getting up. He's going away. He's going to leave my body behind, lying on the grass beside the pond. He's walking quickly away across the field towards the gate. How wet and excited he looks. He ought to relax a bit. He ought to relax like me. He can't be enjoying himself that way. I think I will tell him.

'Why don't you relax a bit?'

Goodness, how he jumped when I spoke to him. And his face; just look at his face. I've never seen a man look as frightened as that. He's starting to run. He keeps looking back over his shoulder, but he keeps on running. But just look at his face; just look how unhappy and frightened he is. I do not want to go with him. I think I'll leave him. I think I'll stay here for a bit. I think I'll go along the hedges and find some primroses, and if I am lucky I may find some white violets. Then I will go to sleep. I will go to sleep in the sun.

Someone Like You

First published in *Town & Country*
(November 1945)

'Beer?'

'Yes, beer.'

I gave the order and the waiter brought the bottles and two glasses. We poured out our own, tipping the glasses and holding the tops of the bottles close to the glass.

'Cheers,' I said.

He nodded. We lifted our glasses and drank.

It was five years since I had seen him, and during that time he had been fighting the war. He had been fighting it right from the beginning up to now and I saw at once how he had changed. From being a young, bouncing boy, he had become someone old and wise and gentle. He had become gentle like a wounded child. He had become old like a tired man of seventy years. He had become so different and he had changed so much that at first it was embarrassing for both of us and it was not easy to know what to say.

He had been flying in France in the early days and he was in Britain during the Battle. He was in the Western Desert when we had nothing and he was in Greece and Crete. He was in Syria and he was at Habbaniya during the rebellion. He was at Alamein. He had been flying in Sicily and in Italy and then he had gone back and flown again from England. Now he was an old man.

He was small, not more than five feet six, and he had a pale, wide-open face which did not hide anything, and a sharp pointed chin. His eyes were bright and dark. They were never still unless they were looking into your own. His hair was black and untidy. There was a wisp of it always hanging down over his forehead; he kept pushing it back with his hand.

For a while we were awkward and did not speak. He was sitting opposite me at the table, leaning forward a little, drawing lines on the dew of the cold beer glass with his finger. He was looking at the glass, pretending to concentrate upon what he was doing, and to me it seemed as though he had something to say, but that he did not know how to say it. I sat there and picked nuts out of the plate and munched them noisily, pretending that I did not care about anything, not even about making a noise while eating.

Then without stopping his drawing on the glass and without looking up, he said quietly and very slowly, 'Oh God, I wish I was a waiter or a whore or something.'

He picked up his glass and drank the beer slowly and all at once, in two swallows. I knew now that there was something on his mind and I knew that he was gathering courage so that he could speak.

'Let's have another,' I said.

'Yes, let's have a whisky.'

'All right, whisky.'

I ordered two double Scotches and some soda, and we poured the soda into the Scotch and drank. He picked up his glass and drank, put it down, picked it up again and drank some more. As he put down the glass the second time, he leaned forward and quite suddenly he began to talk.

'You know,' he said, 'you know I keep thinking during a raid, when we are running over the target, just as we are going to release our bombs, I keep thinking to myself, Shall I just jink a little; shall I swerve a fraction to one side, then my bombs will fall on someone else. I keep thinking, Whom shall I make them fall on; whom shall I kill tonight? Which ten, twenty or a hundred people shall I kill tonight? It is all up to me. And now I think about this every time I go out.'

He had taken a small nut and was splitting it into pieces with his thumb-nail as he spoke, looking down at what he was doing because he was embarrassed by his own talk.

He was speaking very slowly. 'It would just be a gentle pressure with the ball of my foot upon the rudder bar; a pressure so slight that I would hardly know that I was doing it, and it would throw the bombs on to a different house and on to other people. It is all up to me, the whole thing is up to me, and each time that I go out I have to decide which ones shall be killed. I can do it with the gentle pressure of the ball of my foot upon the rudder bar. I can do it so that I don't even notice that it is being done. I just lean a little to one side because I am shifting my sitting position. That is all I am doing, and then I kill a different lot of people.'

Now there was no dew left upon the face of the glass, but he was still running the fingers of his right hand up and down the smooth surface.

'Yes,' he said, 'it is a complicated thought. It is very far-reaching; and when I am bombing I cannot get it out of my mind. You see it is such a gentle pressure with the ball of the foot; just a touch on the rudder bar and the bomb-aimer wouldn't even notice. Each time I go out, I say to myself, Shall it be these or shall it be those? Which ones are the worst? Perhaps if I make a little skid to the left I will get a houseful of lousy women-shooting German soldiers, or perhaps if I make that little skid I will miss getting the soldiers and get an old man in a shelter. How can I know? How can anyone know these things?'

He paused and pushed his empty glass away from him into the middle of the table.

'And so I never jink,' he added, 'at least hardly ever.'

'I jinked once,' I said, 'ground-strafing. I thought I'd kill the ones on the other side of the road instead.'

'Everybody jinks,' he said. 'Shall we have another drink?'

'Yes, let's have another.'

I called the waiter and gave the order, and while we were waiting, we sat looking around the room at the other people. The place was starting to fill up because it was about six o'clock and we sat there looking at the people who were coming in. They were standing around looking for tables, sitting down, laughing and ordering drinks.

'Look at that woman,' I said. 'The one just sitting down over there.'

'What about her?'

'Wonderful figure,' I said. 'Wonderful bosom. Look at her bosom.'

The waiter brought the drinks.

'Did I ever tell you about Stinker?' he said.

'Stinker who?'

'Stinker Sullivan in Malta.'

'No.'

'About Stinker's dog?'

'No.'

'Stinker had a dog, a great big Alsatian, and he loved that dog as though it was his father and his mother and everything else he had, and the dog loved Stinker. It used to follow him around everywhere he went, and when he went on ops it used to sit on the tarmac outside the hangars waiting for him to come back. It was called Smith. Stinker really loved that dog. He loved it like his mother and he used to talk to it all day long.'

'Lousy whisky,' I said.

'Yes, let's have another.'

We got some more whisky.

'Well, anyway,' he went on, 'one day the squadron got orders to fly to Egypt. We had to go at once; not in two hours or later in the day, but at once. And Stinker couldn't find his dog. Couldn't find Smith anywhere. Started running all over the aerodrome yelling for Smith and going mad yelling at everyone asking where he was and yelling, "Smith Smith," all over the aerodrome. Smith wasn't anywhere.'

'Where was he?' I said.

'He wasn't there and we had to go. Stinker had to go without Smith and he was mad as a hatter. His crew said he kept calling up over the radio asking if they'd found him. All the way to Heliopolis he kept calling up Malta saying, Have you got Smith, and Malta kept saying, No, they hadn't.'

'This whisky is really terrible,' I said.

'Yes. We must have some more.'

We had a waiter who was very quick.

'I was telling you about Stinker,' he said.

'Yes, tell me about Stinker.'

'Well, when we got to Egypt he wouldn't talk about anything except Smith. He used to walk around acting as though the dog was always with him. Damn fool walked around saying, "Come on, Smith, old boy, come on," and he kept looking down and talking to him as he walked along. Kept reaching down and patting the air and stroking this bloody dog that wasn't there.'

'Where was it?'

'Malta, I suppose. Must have been in Malta.'

'Isn't this awful whisky?'

'Terrible. We must have some more when we've finished this.'

'Cheers.'

'Cheers.'

'Waiter. Oh waiter. Yes; again.'

'So Smith was in Malta.'

'Yes,' he said. 'And this damn fool Stinker Sullivan went on like this right up to the time he was killed.'

'Must have been mad.'

'He was. Mad as a hatter. You know once he walked into the Sporting Club at Alexandria at drinking time.'

'That wasn't so mad.'

'He walked into the big lounge and as he went in he held the door open and started calling his dog. Then when he thought the dog had come in, he closed the door and started walking right down the length of the room, stopping every now and then and looking round and saying, "Come on, Smith, old boy, come on." He kept flipping his fingers. Once he got down under a table where two men and two women were drinking. He got on to his hands and knees and said, "Smith, come on out of there; come here at once," and he put out his hand and started dragging nothing at all from under the table. Then he apologized to the people at the table. "This is the hell of a dog," he said to them. You should have seen their faces. He went on like that all down the room and when he came to the other end he held the door open for the dog to go out and then went out after it.'

'Man was mad.'

'Mad as a hatter. And you should have seen their faces. It was full of people drinking and they didn't know whether it was them who were crazy or whether it was Stinker. They kept looking up at each other to make sure that they weren't the only ones who couldn't see the dog. One man dropped his drink.'

'That was awful.'

'Terrible.'

The waiter came and went. The room was full of people now, all sitting at little tables, talking and drinking and wearing their uniforms. The pilot poked the ice down into his glass with his finger.

'He used to jink too,' he said.

'Who?'

'Stinker. He used to talk about it.'

'Jinking isn't anything,' I said. 'It's like not touching the cracks on the pavement when you're walking along.'

'Balls. That's just personal. Doesn't affect anyone else.'

'Well, it's like car-waiting.'

'What's car-waiting?'

'I always do it,' I said.

'What is it?'

'Just as you're going to drive off, you sit back and count twenty, then you drive off.'

'You're mad too,' he said. 'You're like Stinker.'

'It's a wonderful way to avoid accidents. I've never had one in a car yet; at least, not a bad one.'

'You're drunk.'

'No, I always do it.'

'Why?'

'Because then if someone was going to have stepped off the kerb in front of your car, you won't hit them because you started later. You were delayed because you counted twenty, and the person who stepped off the kerb whom you would have hit – you missed him.'

'Why?'

'He stepped off the kerb long before you got there because you counted twenty.'

'That's a good idea.'

'I know it's a good idea.'

'It's a bloody marvellous idea.'

'I've saved lots of lives. And you can drive straight across intersections because the car you would have hit has already gone by. It went by just a little earlier because you delayed yourself by counting twenty.'

'Marvellous.'

'Isn't it?'

'But it's like jinking,' he said. 'You never really know what would have happened.'

'I always do it,' I said.

We kept right on drinking.

'Look at that woman,' I said.

'The one with the bosom?'

'Yes, marvellous bosom.'

He said slowly, 'I bet I've killed lots of women more beautiful than that one.'

'Not lots with bosoms like that.'

'I'll bet I have. Shall we have another drink?'

'Yes, one for the road.'

'There aren't any other women with bosoms like that,' I said. 'Not in Germany anyway.'

'Oh yes there are. I've killed lots of them.'

'All right. You've killed lots of women with wonderful bosoms.'

He leaned back and waved his hand around the room. 'See all the people in this room?' he said.

'Yes.'

'Wouldn't there be a bloody row if they were all suddenly dead; if they all suddenly fell off their chairs on to the floor dead?'

'What about it?'

'Wouldn't there be a bloody row?'

'Certainly there'd be a row.'

'If all the waiters got together and put stuff in all the drinks and everyone died.'

'There'd be a godalmighty row.'

'Well, I've done that hundreds of times. I've killed more people than there are in this room hundreds of times. So have you.'

'Lots more,' I said. 'But that's different.'

'Same sort of people. Men and women and waiters. All drinking in a pub.'

'That's different.'

'Like hell it is. Wouldn't there be a bloody row if it happened here?'

'Bloody awful row.'

'But we've done it. Lots of times.'

'Hundreds of times,' I said. 'This is nothing.'

'This is a lousy place.'

'Yes, it's lousy. Let's go somewhere else.'

'Finish our drinks.'

We finished our drinks and we both tried to pay the bill, so we tossed for it and I won. It came to sixteen dollars and twenty-five cents. He gave the waiter a two-dollar tip.

We got up and walked around the tables and over to the door.

'Taxi,' he said.

'Yes, must have a taxi.'

There wasn't a doorman. We stood out on the kerb

waiting for a taxi to come along and he said, 'This is a good town.'

'Wonderful town,' I said. I felt fine. It was dark outside, but there were a few street-lamps, and we could see the cars going by and the people walking on the other side of the street. There was a thin, quiet drizzle falling, and the wetness on the black street shone yellow under the lights of the cars and under the street-lamps. The tyres of the cars hissed on the wet surface.

'Let's go to a place which has lots of whisky,' he said. 'Lots of whisky and a man with egg on his beard serving it.'

'Fine.'

'Somewhere where there are no other people but just us and the man with egg on his beard. Either that.'

'Yes,' I said. 'Either that or what?'

'Or a place with a hundred thousand people in it.'

'Yes,' I said. 'OK.'

We stood there waiting and we could see the lights of the cars as they came round the bend over to the left, coming towards us with the tyres swishing on the wet surface and going past us up the road to the bridge which goes over the river. We could see the drizzle falling through the beams of their headlights and we stood there waiting for a taxi.

The Mildenhall Treasure

First published in *Saturday Evening Post* (September 1947)

Around seven o'clock in the morning, Gordon Butcher got out of bed and switched on the light. He walked barefoot to the window and drew back the curtains and looked out.

This was January and it was still dark, but he could tell there hadn't been any snow in the night.

'That wind,' he said aloud to his wife. 'Just listen to that wind.'

His wife was out of bed now, standing beside him near the window, and the two of them were silent, listening to the swish of the icy wind as it came sweeping in over the fens.

'It's a nor'easter,' he said.

'There'll be snow for certain before nightfall,' she told him. 'And plenty of it.'

She was dressed before him, and she went into the next room and leaned over the cot of her six-year-old daughter and gave her a kiss. She called out a good morning to the two other older children in the third room, then she went downstairs to make breakfast.

At a quarter to eight, Gordon Butcher put on his coat, his cap and his leather gloves, and walked out of the back door into the bitter early-morning winter weather. As he moved through the half-daylight over the yard to the shed where his bicycle stood, the wind was like a knife on his cheek. He wheeled out the bike and mounted and began to ride down the middle of the narrow road, right into the face of the gale.

Gordon Butcher was thirty-eight. He was not an ordinary farm labourer. He took orders from no man unless he wished. He owned his own tractor, and with this he ploughed other men's fields and gathered other men's harvests under contract. His thoughts were only for his wife, his son, his two daughters. His wealth was in his small brick house, his two cows, his tractor, his skill as a ploughman.

Gordon Butcher's head was very curiously shaped, the back of it protruding like the sharp end of an enormous egg, and his ears stuck out, and a front tooth was missing on the left side. But none of this seemed to matter very much when you met him face to face in the open air. He looked at you with steady blue eyes that were without any malice or cunning or greed. And the mouth didn't have those thin lines of bitterness around the edges which one so often sees on men who work the land and spend their days fighting the weather.

His only eccentricity, to which he would cheerfully admit if you asked him, was in talking aloud to himself when he was alone. This habit, he said, grew from the fact that the kind of work he did left him entirely by himself for ten hours a day, six days a week. 'It keeps me company,' he said, 'hearing me own voice now and again.'

He biked on down the road, pedalling hard against the brutal wind.

'All right,' he said, 'all right, why don't you blow a bit? Is that the best you can do? My goodness me, I hardly know you're there this morning!' The wind howled around him and snapped at his coat and squeezed its way through the pores of the heavy wool, through his jacket underneath, through his shirt and vest, and it touched his bare skin with an icy fingertip.

'Why,' he said, 'it's lukewarm you are today. You'll have to do a sight better than that if you're going to make *me* shiver.'

And now the darkness was diluting into a pale-grey morning light, and Gordon Butcher could see the cloudy roof of the sky very low above his head and flying with the wind. Grey-blue the clouds were, flecked here and there with black, a solid mass from horizon to horizon, the whole thing moving with the wind, sliding past above his head like a great grey sheet of metal unrolling. All around him lay the bleak and lonely fen-country of Suffolk, mile upon mile of it that went on for ever.

He pedalled on. He rode through the outskirts of the little town of Mildenhall and headed for the village of West Row where the man called Ford had his place.

He had left his tractor at Ford's the day before because his next job was to plough up four and a half acres on Thistley Green for Ford. It was not Ford's land. It is important to remember this, but Ford was the one who had asked him to do the work.

Actually, a farmer called Rolfe owned the four and a half acres.

Rolfe had asked Ford to get it ploughed because Ford, like Gordon Butcher, did ploughing jobs for other men.

The difference between Ford and Gordon Butcher was that Ford was somewhat grander. He was a fairly prosperous small-time agricultural engineer who had a nice house and a large yard full of sheds filled with farm implements and machinery. Gordon Butcher had only his one tractor.

On this occasion, however, when Rolfe had asked Ford to plough up his four and a half acres on Thistley Green, Ford was too busy to do the work so he hired Gordon Butcher to do it for him.

There was no one about in Ford's yard when Butcher rode in. He parked his bike, filled up his tractor with paraffin and petrol, warmed the engine, hitched the plough behind, mounted the high seat and drove out to Thistley Green.

The field was not half a mile away, and around eight thirty Butcher drove the tractor in through the gate on to the field itself. Thistley Green was maybe a hundred acres all told, with a low hedge running round it. And although it was actually one large field, different parts of it were owned by different men. These separate parts were easy to define because each was cultivated in its own way. Rolfe's plot of four and a half acres was over to one side near the southern boundary fence. Butcher knew where it was and he drove his tractor round the edge of the field, then inward until he was on the plot.

The plot was barley stubble now, covered with the short and rotting yellow stalks of barley harvested last autumn, and only recently had it been broad-sheared so that now it was ready for the plough.

'Deep-plough it,' Ford had said to Butcher the day

before. 'It's for sugar-beet. Rolfe's putting sugar-beet in there.'

They only plough about four inches down for barley, but for sugar-beet they plough deep, to ten or twelve inches. A horse-drawn plough can't plough as deep as that. It was only since motor-tractors came along that the farmers had been able to deep-plough properly. Rolfe's land had been deep-ploughed for sugar-beet some years before this, but it wasn't Butcher who had done the ploughing and no doubt the job had been skimped a bit and the ploughman had not gone quite as deep as he should. Had he done so, what was about to happen today would have happened then, and that would have been a different story.

Gordon Butcher began to plough. Up and down the field he went, lowering the plough deeper and deeper each trip until at last it was cutting twelve inches into the ground and turning up a smooth even wave of black earth as it went.

The wind was coming faster now, rushing in from the killer sea, sweeping over the flat Norfolk fields, past Saxthorpe and Reepham and Honingham and Swaffham and Larling and over the border to Suffolk, to Mildenhall and to Thistley Green where Gordon Butcher sat upright high on the seat of his tractor, driving back and forth over the plot of yellow barley stubble that belonged to Rolfe. Gordon Butcher could smell the sharp crisp smell of snow not far away, he could see the low roof of the sky – no longer flecked with black, but pale and whitish grey – sliding by overhead like a solid sheet of metal unrolling.

'Well,' he said, raising his voice above the clatter of the tractor, 'you are surely fashed at somebody today. What an almighty fuss it is now of blowin' and whistlin' and freezin'. Like a woman,' he added. 'Just like a woman does sometimes in the evening,' and he kept his eye upon the line of the furrow, and he smiled.

At noon he stopped the tractor, dismounted and fished in his pocket for his lunch. He found it and sat on the ground in the lee of one of the huge tractor-wheels. He ate large pieces of bread and very small pieces of cheese. He had nothing to drink, for his only Thermos had got smashed by the jolting of the tractor two weeks before, and in wartime, for this was in January 1942, you could not buy another anywhere. For about fifteen minutes he sat on the ground in the shelter of the wheel and ate his lunch. Then he got up and examined his peg.

Unlike many ploughmen, Butcher always hitched his plough to the tractor with a wooden peg so that if the plough fouled a root or a large stone, the peg would simply break at once, leaving the plough behind and saving the shares from serious damage. All over the black fen country, just below the surface, lie enormous trunks of ancient oak trees, and a wooden peg will save a ploughshare many times a week out there. Although Thistley Green was well-cultivated land, field-land, not fen-land, Butcher was taking no chances with his plough.

He examined the wooden peg, found it sound, mounted the tractor again, and went on with his ploughing.

The tractor nosed back and forth over the ground, leaving a smooth black wave of soil behind it. And still the wind blew colder but it did not snow.

Around three o'clock the thing happened.

There was a slight jolt, the wooden peg broke, and the tractor left the plough behind. Butcher stopped, dismounted and walked back to the plough to see what it had struck. It was surprising for this to have happened here, on field-land. There should be no oak trees underneath the soil in this place.

He knelt down beside the plough and began to scoop the soil away around the point of the ploughshare. The lower tip of the share was twelve inches down. There was a lot of soil to be scooped up. He dug his gloved fingers into the earth and scooped it out with both hands. Six inches down . . . eight inches . . . ten inches . . . twelve. He slid his fingers along the blade of the ploughshare until they reached the forward point of it. The soil was loose and crumbly, and it kept falling back into the hole he was digging. He could not therefore see the twelve-inch-deep point of the share. He could only feel it. And now he could feel that the point was indeed lodged against something solid. He scooped away more earth. He enlarged the hole. It was necessary to see clearly what sort of an obstacle he had struck. If it was fairly small, then perhaps he could dig it out with his hands and get on with the job. If it was a tree-trunk he would have to go back to Ford's and fetch a spade.

'Come on,' he said aloud. 'I'll have you out of there, you hidden demon, you rotten old thing.' And suddenly, as the gloved fingers scraped away a final handful of black earth, he caught sight of the curved rim of something flat, like the rim of a huge thick plate sticking up out of the soil. He rubbed the rim with his fingers and he rubbed again. Then all at once, the rim gave off a greenish glint, and Gordon Butcher bent his head closer and closer still, peering down into the little hole he had dug with his hands. For one last time, he rubbed the rim clean with his fingers, and in a flash of light, he saw clearly the unmistakable blue-green crust of ancient buried metal, and his heart stood still.

It should be explained here that farmers in this part of Suffolk, and particularly in the Mildenhall area, have for years been turning up ancient objects from the soil. Flint arrowheads from very long ago have been found in considerable numbers, but more interesting than that, Roman pottery and Roman implements have also been found. It is known that the Romans favoured this part of the country during their occupation of Britain, and all local farmers are therefore well aware of the possibility of finding something interesting during a day's work. And so there was a kind of permanent awareness among Mildenhall people of the presence of treasure underneath the earth of their land.

Gordon Butcher's reaction, as soon as he saw the rim of that enormous plate, was a curious one. He immediately drew away. Then he got to his feet and turned his back on what he had just seen. He paused only long enough to switch off the engine of his tractor before he walked off fast in the direction of the road.

He did not know precisely what impulse caused him to stop digging and walk away. He will tell you that the only thing he can remember about those first few seconds was the whiff of danger that came to him from that little patch of greenish blue. The moment he touched it with his fingers, something electric went through his body, and there came to him a powerful premonition that this was a thing that could destroy the peace and happiness of many people.

In the beginning, all he had wished was to be away from it, and to leave it behind him and be done with it for ever. But after he had gone a few hundred yards or so, he began to slow his pace. At the gate leading out from Thistley Green, he stopped.

'What in the world is the matter with you, Mr Gordon Butcher?' he said aloud to the howling wind. 'Are you frightened or something? No, I'm not frightened. But I'll tell you straight, I'm not keen to handle this alone.'

That was when he thought of Ford.

He thought of Ford at first because it was for him that he was working. He thought of him second because he knew that Ford was a kind of collector of old stuff, of all the old stones and arrowheads which people kept digging up from time to time in the district, which they brought to Ford and which Ford placed upon the mantel in his parlour. It was believed that Ford sold these things, but no one knew or cared how he did it.

Gordon Butcher turned towards Ford's place and walked fast out of the gate on to the narrow road, down the road around the sharp left-hand corner and so to the house. He found Ford in his large shed, bending over a damaged harrow, mending it. Butcher stood by the door and said, 'Mr Ford!'

Ford looked around without straightening his body.

'Well, Gordon,' he said, 'what is it?'

Ford was middle-aged or a little older, bald-headed,

long-nosed, with a clever foxy look about his face. His mouth was thin and sour, and when he looked at you, and when you saw the tightness of his mouth and the thin, sour line of his lips, you knew that this was a mouth that never smiled. His chin receded, his nose was long and sharp and he had the air about him of a sour old crafty fox from the woods.

'What is it?' he said, looking up from the harrow.

Gordon Butcher stood by the door, blue-cheeked with cold, a little out of breath, rubbing his hands slowly one against the other.

'The tractor left the plough behind,' he said quietly. 'There's metal down there. I saw it.'

Ford's head gave a jerk. 'What kind of metal?' he said sharply.

'Flat. Quite flat like a sort of huge plate.'

'You didn't dig it out?' Ford had straightened up now and there was a glint of eagles in his eyes.

Butcher said, 'No, I left it alone and came straight on here.'

Ford walked quickly over to the corner and took his coat off the nail. He found a cap and gloves, then he found a spade and went towards the door. There was something odd, he noticed, in Butcher's manner.

'You're sure it was metal?'

'Crusted up,' Butcher said. 'But it was metal all right.'

'How deep?'

'Twelve inches down. At least the top of it was twelve inches down. The rest is deeper.'

'How d'you know it was a plate?'

'I don't,' Butcher said. 'I only saw a little bit of the rim. But it looked like a plate to me. An enormous plate.'

Ford's foxy face went quite white with excitement. 'Come on,' he said. 'We'll go back and see.'

The two men walked out of the shed into the fierce, ever-mounting fury of the wind. Ford shivered.

'Curse this filthy weather,' he said. 'Curse and blast this filthy freezing weather,' and he sank his pointed foxy face deep into the collar of his coat and began to ponder upon the possibilities of Butcher's find.

One thing Ford knew which Butcher did not know. He knew that back in 1932 a man called Lethbridge, a lecturer in Anglo-Saxon Antiquities at Cambridge University, had been excavating in the district and that he had actually unearthed the foundations of a Roman villa on Thistley Green itself. Ford was not forgetting that, and he quickened his pace. Butcher walked beside him without speaking and soon they were there. They went through the gate and over the field to the plough, which lay about ten yards behind the tractor.

Ford knelt down beside the front of the plough and peered into the small hole Gordon Butcher had dug with his hands. He touched the rim of green-blue metal with a gloved finger. He scraped away a bit more earth. He leaned farther forward so that his pointed nose was right down the hole. He ran fingers over the rough green surface. Then he stood up and said, 'Let's get the plough out of the way and do some digging.' Although there were fireworks exploding in his head and shivers running all over his body, Ford kept his voice very soft and casual.

Between them they pulled the plough back a couple of yards.

'Give me the spade,' Ford said, and he began cautiously to dig the soil away in a circle about three feet in diameter around the exposed patch of metal. When the hole was two feet deep, he threw away the spade and used his hands. He knelt down and scraped the soil away, and gradually the little patch of metal grew and grew until at last there lay exposed before them the great round disc of an enormous plate. It was fully twenty-four inches in diameter. The lower point of the plough had just caught the raised centre rim of the plate, for one could see the dent.

Carefully Ford lifted it out of the hole. He got to his feet, and stood wiping the soil away from it, turning it over and over in his hands. There was nothing much to see, for the whole surface was crusted over with a thick layer of a hard greenish-blue substance. But he knew that it was an enormous plate or dish of great weight and thickness. It weighed about eighteen pounds!

Ford stood in the field of yellow barley stubble and gazed at the huge plate. His hands began to shake. A tremendous and almost unbearable excitement started boiling up inside him and it was not easy for him to hide it. But he did his best.

'Some sort of a dish,' he said.

Butcher was kneeling on the ground beside the hole. 'Must be pretty old,' he said.

'Could be old,' Ford said. 'But it's all rusted up and eaten away.'

'That don't look like rust to me,' Butcher said. 'That greenish stuff isn't rust. It's something else . . .'

'It's green rust,' Ford said rather superbly, and that ended the discussion.

Butcher, still on his knees, was poking about casually in the now three-feet-wide hole with his gloved hands. 'There's another one down here,' he said.

Instantly, Ford laid the great dish on the ground. He knelt beside Butcher, and within minutes they had unearthed a second large green-encrusted plate. This one was a shade smaller than the first, and deeper. More of a bowl than a dish.

Ford stood up and held the new find in his hands. Another heavy one. And now he knew for certain they were on to something absolutely tremendous. They were on to Roman Treasure, and almost without question it was pure silver. Two things pointed to its being pure silver. First the weight, and second, the particular type of green crust caused by oxidation.

How often is a piece of Roman silver discovered in the world?

Almost never any more. And had pieces as large as this *ever* been unearthed before?

Ford wasn't sure, but he very much doubted it.

Worth millions it must be.

Worth literally millions of pounds.

His breath, coming fast, was making little white clouds in the freezing atmosphere.

'There's still more down here, Mr Ford,' Butcher was

saying. 'I can feel bits of it all over the place. You'll need the spade again.'

The third piece they got out was another large plate, somewhat similar to the first. Ford placed it in the barley stubble with the other two.

When Butcher felt the first flake of snow upon his cheek he looked up and saw over to the northeast a great white curtain drawn across the sky, a solid wall of snow flying forward on the wings of the wind.

'Here she comes!' he said, and Ford looked round and saw the snow moving upon them and he said, 'It's a blizzard. It's a filthy stinking blizzard!'

The two men stared at the blizzard as it raced across the fens towards them. Then it was on them, and all around was snow and snowflakes in the eyes and ears and mouth and down the neck and all around. And when Butcher glanced down at the ground a few seconds later it was already white.

'That's all we want,' Ford said. 'A filthy rotten stinking blizzard,' and he shivered and sank his sharp and foxy face deeper into the collar of his coat. 'Come on,' he said. 'See if there's any more.'

Butcher knelt down again and poked around in the soil, then in the slow and casual manner of a man having a lucky dip in a barrel of sawdust, he pulled out another plate and held it out to Ford. Ford took it and placed it with the other three. Now Ford knelt down beside Butcher and began to dip into the soil with him.

For a whole hour the two men stayed out there digging and scratching in that little three-foot patch of soil. And during that hour they found and laid upon the ground beside them *no less than thirty-four separate pieces*! There were dishes, bowls, goblets, spoons, ladles and several other things, all of them crusted over but each one recognizable for what it was. And all the while the blizzard swirled around them and the snow gathered in little mounds upon their caps and on their shoulders and the flakes melted on their faces so that rivers of icy water trickled down their necks. A large globule of half-frozen liquid dangled continuously, like a snow drop, from the end of Ford's pointed nose.

They worked in silence. It was too cold to speak. And as one precious article after the other was unearthed, Ford laid them carefully on the ground in rows, pausing every now and then to wipe the snow away from a dish or a spoon which was in danger of being completely covered.

At last Ford said, 'That's the lot, I think.'

'Yes.'

Ford stood up and stamped his feet on the ground. 'Got a sack in the tractor?' he said, and while Butcher walked over to fetch the sack, he turned and gazed upon the four-and-thirty pieces lying in the snow at his feet. He counted them again. If they were silver, which they surely must be, and if they were Roman, which they undoubtedly were, then this was a discovery that would rock the world.

Butcher called to him from the tractor, 'It's only a dirty old sack.'

'It'll do.'

Butcher brought the sack over and held it open while Ford carefully put the articles into it. They all went in except one. The massive two-foot plate was too large for the neck of the sack.

The two men were really cold now. For over an hour they had knelt and scratched about out there in the open field with the blizzard swirling around them. Already, nearly six inches of snow had fallen. Butcher was half frozen. His cheeks were dead-white, blotched with blue, his feet were numb like wood, and when he moved his legs he could not feel the ground beneath his feet. He was much colder than Ford. His coat and clothes were not so thick, and ever since early morning he had been sitting high up on the seat of the tractor, exposed to the bitter wind. His blue-white face was tight and unmoving. All he wanted was to get home to his family and to the fire that he knew would be burning in the grate.

Ford, on the other hand, was not thinking about the cold. His mind was concentrated solely upon one thing – how to get possession for himself of this fabulous treasure. His position, as he knew very well, was not a strong one.

In England there is a very curious law about finding any kind of gold or silver treasure. This law goes back hundreds of years, and is still strictly enforced today. The law states that if a person digs up out of the ground, even out of his own garden, a piece of metal that is either *gold* or *silver*, it automatically becomes what is known as Treasure Trove and is the property of the Crown. The Crown doesn't in these days mean the actual King or Queen. It means the country or the government. The law also states that it is a criminal offence to conceal such a find. You are simply not allowed to hide the stuff and keep it for yourself. You must report it at once, preferably to the police. And if you do report it at once, you as the finder will be entitled to receive from the government in money the full amount of the market value of the article. You are not required to report the digging up of other metals. You are allowed to find as much valuable pewter, bronze, copper or even platinum as you wish, and you can keep it all, but not gold or silver.

The other curious part of this curious law is this: it is the person who *discovers* the treasure in the first place who gets the reward from the government. The owner of the land gets nothing – unless of course the finder is trespassing on the land when he makes the discovery. But if the finder of the treasure has been hired by the owner to do a job on his land, then he, the finder, gets all the reward.

In this case, the finder was Gordon Butcher. Farthermore, he was not trespassing. He was performing a job which he had been hired to do. This treasure therefore belonged to Butcher and to no one else. All he had to do was to take it and show it to an expert, who would immediately identify it as silver, then turn it in to the police. In time, he would receive from the government one hundred per cent of its value – perhaps a million pounds.

All this left Ford out in the cold and Ford knew it. He had no rights whatsoever to the treasure by law. Thus, as he must have told himself at the time, his only chance of getting hold of the stuff for himself lay in the fact that Butcher was an ignorant man who didn't know the law and who did not anyway have the faintest idea of the value of the find. The probability was that in a few days Butcher would forget all about it. He was too simple-minded a fellow, too artless, too trusting, too unselfish to give the matter much thought.

Now, out there in the desolate snow-swept field, Ford bent down and took hold of the huge dish with one hand. He raised it but he did not lift it. The lower rim remained resting on the snow. With his other hand, he grasped the top of the sack. He didn't lift that either. He just held it. And there he stooped amid the swirling snowflakes, both hands embracing, as it were, the treasure, but not actually taking it. It was a subtle and canny gesture. It managed somehow to signify ownership before ownership had been discussed. A child plays the same game when he reaches out and closes his fingers over the biggest chocolate éclair on the plate and then says, 'Can I have this one, Mummy?' He's already got it.

'Well, Gordon,' Ford said, stooping over, holding the sack and the great dish in his gloved fingers. 'I don't suppose you want any of this old stuff.'

It was not a question. It was a statement of fact framed as a question.

The blizzard was still raging. The snow was falling so densely the two men could hardly see one another.

'You ought to get along home and warm yourself up,' Ford went on. 'You look frozen to death.'

'I *feel* frozen to death,' Butcher said.

'Then you get on that tractor quick and hurry home,' said the thoughtful, kind-hearted Ford. 'Leave the plough here and leave your bike at my place. The important thing is to get back and warm yourself up before you catch pneumonia.'

'I think that's just what I will do, Mr Ford,' Butcher said. 'Can you manage all right with that sack? It's mighty heavy.'

'I might not even bother about it today,' Ford said casually. 'I just might leave it here and come back for it another time. Rusty old stuff.'

'So long then, Mr Ford.'

''Bye, Gordon.'

Gordon Butcher mounted the tractor and drove away into the blizzard.

Ford hoisted the sack on to his shoulder, and then, not without difficulty, he lifted the massive dish with his other hand and tucked it under his arm.

'I am carrying,' he told himself, as he trudged through the snow, 'I am now carrying what is probably the biggest treasure ever dug up in the whole history of England.'

When Gordon Butcher came stamping and blowing through the back door of his small brick house late that afternoon, his wife was ironing by the fire. She looked up and saw his blue-white face and snow-encrusted clothes.

'My goodness, Gordon, you look froze to death!' she cried.

'I am,' he said. 'Help me off with these clothes, love. My fingers aren't hardly working at all.'

She took off his gloves, his coat, his jacket, his wet shirt. She pulled off his boots and socks. She fetched a towel and rubbed his chest and shoulders vigorously all over to restore the circulation. She rubbed his feet.

'Sit down there by the fire,' she said, 'and I'll get you a hot cup of tea.'

Later, when he was settled comfortably in the warmth with dry clothes on his back and the mug of tea in his hand, he told her what had happened that afternoon.

'He's a foxy one, that Mr Ford,' she said, not looking up from her ironing. 'I never did like him.'

'He got pretty excited about it all, I can tell you that,' Gordon Butcher said. 'Jumpy as a jack-rabbit he was.'

'That may be,' she said. 'But you ought to have had more sense than to go crawling about on your hands and knees in a freezing blizzard just because Mr Ford said to do it.'

'I'm all right,' Gordon Butcher said, 'I'm warming up nicely now.'

And that, believe it or not, was about the last time the subject of the treasure was discussed in the Butcher household for some years.

The reader should be reminded that this was wartime, 1942. Britain was totally absorbed in the desperate war against Hitler and Mussolini. Germany was bombing England, and England was bombing Germany, and nearly every night Gordon Butcher heard the roar of motors from the big aerodrome at nearby Mildenhall as the bombers took off for Hamburg, Berlin, Kiel, Wilhelmshaven or Frankfurt. Sometimes he would wake in the early hours and hear them coming home, and sometimes the Germans flew over to bomb the aerodrome, and the Butcher house would shake with the *crumph* and crash of bombs not far away.

Butcher himself was exempt from military service. He was a farmer, a skilled ploughman, and they had told him when he volunteered for the Army in 1939 that he was not wanted. The island's food supplies must be kept going, they told him, and it was vital that men like him stay on their jobs and cultivate the land.

Ford, being in the same business, was also exempt. He was a bachelor, living alone, and he was thus able to live a secret life and to do secret things within the walls of his home.

And so, on that terrible snowy afternoon when they dug up the treasure, Ford carried it home and laid everything out on a table in the back room.

Thirty-four separate pieces! They covered the entire table. And by the look of it, they were in marvellous condition. Silver does not rust. The green crust of oxidation can even be protection for the surface of the metal underneath. And with care, it could all be removed.

Ford decided to use an ordinary domestic silver polish known as Silvo, and he bought a large stock of it from the ironmonger's shop in Mildenhall. Then he took first the great two-foot plate which weighed more than eighteen pounds. He worked on it in the evenings. He soaked it all over with Silvo. He rubbed and rubbed. He worked patiently on this single dish every night for more than sixteen weeks.

At last, one memorable evening, there showed beneath his rubbing a small area of shining silver, and on the silver, raised up and beautifully worked, there was a part of a man's head.

He kept at it, and gradually the little patch of shining metal spread and spread, the blue-green crust crept outwards to the edges of the plate, until finally the top surface of the great dish lay before him in its full glory, covered all over with a wondrous pattern of animals and men and many odd legendary things.

Ford was astounded by the beauty of the great plate. It was filled with life and movement. There was a fierce face with tangled hair, a dancing goat with a human head, there were men and women and animals of many kinds cavorting around the rim, and no doubt all of them told a story.

Next, he set about cleaning the reverse side of the plate. Weeks and weeks it took. And when the work was completed and the whole plate on both sides was shining like a star, he placed it safely in the lower cupboard of his big oak sideboard and locked the cupboard door.

One by one, he tackled the remaining thirty-three pieces. A mania had taken hold of him now, a fierce compulsion to make every item shine in all its silver brilliance. He wanted to see all thirty-four pieces laid out on the big table in a dazzling array of silver. He wanted that more than anything else, and he worked desperately hard to achieve his wish.

He cleaned the two smaller dishes next, then the large fluted bowl, then the five long-handled ladles, the goblets, the wine-cups, the spoons. Every single piece was cleaned with equal care and made to shine with equal brilliance, and when they were all done, two years had passed and it was 1944.

But no strangers were allowed to look. Ford discussed the matter with no man or woman, and Rolfe, the owner of the plot on Thistley Green where the treasure had been found, knew nothing except that Ford, or someone Ford had hired, had ploughed his land extremely well and very deep.

One can guess why Ford hid the treasure instead of reporting it to the police as Treasure Trove. Had he reported it, it would have been taken away and Gordon Butcher would have been rewarded as the finder. Rewarded with a fortune. So the only thing Ford could do was to hang on to it and hide it in the hope, presumably, of selling it quietly to some dealer or collector at a later date.

It is possible, of course, to take a more charitable view and assume that Ford kept the treasure solely because he loved beautiful things and wanted to have them around him. No one will ever know the true answer.

Another year went by.

The war against Hitler was won.

And then, in 1946, just after Easter, there was a knock on the door of Ford's house. Ford opened it.

'Why hello, Mr Ford. How are you after all these years?'

'Hello, Dr Fawcett,' Ford said. 'You been keeping all right?'

'I'm fine, thank you,' Dr Fawcett said. 'It's been a long time, hasn't it?'

'Yes,' Ford said. 'That old war kept us all pretty busy.'

'May I come in?' Dr Fawcett asked.

'Of course,' Ford said. 'Come on in.'

Dr Hugh Alderson Fawcett was a keen and learned

archaeologist who before the war had made a point of visiting Ford once a year in search of old stones or arrowheads. Ford had usually collected a batch of such items during the twelve months and he was always willing to sell them to Fawcett. They were seldom of great value, but now and again something quite good had turned up.

'Well,' said Fawcett, taking off his coat in the little hall. 'Well, well, well. It's been nearly seven years since I was here last.'

'Yes, it's been a long time,' Ford said.

Ford led him into the front room and showed him a box of flint arrowheads which had been picked up in the district. Some were good, others not so good. Fawcett picked through them, sorted them, and a deal was done.

'Nothing else?'

'No, I don't think so.'

Ford wished fervently that Dr Fawcett had never come. He wished even more fervently that he would go away.

It was at this point that Ford noticed something that made him sweat. He saw suddenly that he had left lying on the mantel over the fireplace the two most beautiful of the Roman spoons from the treasure hoard. These spoons had fascinated him because each was inscribed with the name of a Roman girl child to whom it had been given, presumably as a christening present, by Roman parents who had been converted to Christianity. One name was Pascentia, the other was Papittedo. Rather lovely names.

Ford, sweating with fear, tried to place himself between Dr Fawcett and the mantelpiece. He might even, he thought, be able to slip the spoons into his pocket if he got the chance.

He didn't get the chance.

Perhaps Ford had polished them so well that a little flash of reflected light from the silver caught the doctor's eye. Who knows? The fact remains that Fawcett saw them. The moment he saw them, he pounced like a tiger.

'Great heavens alive!' he cried. 'What are these?'

'Pewter,' Ford said, sweating more than ever. 'Just a couple of old pewter spoons.'

'Pewter?' cried Fawcett, turning one of the spoons over in his fingers. 'Pewter! You call this *pewter*?'

'That's right,' Ford said. 'It's pewter.'

'You know what this is?' Fawcett said, his voice going high with excitement. 'Shall I tell you what this *really* is?'

'You don't have to tell me,' Ford said, truculent. 'I know what it is. It's old pewter. And quite nice, too.'

Fawcett was reading the inscription in Roman letters on the scoop of the spoon. 'Papittedo!' he cried.

'What's that mean?' Ford asked him.

Fawcett picked up the other spoon. 'Pascentia,' he said. 'Beautiful! These are the names of Roman children! And these spoons, my friend, are made of solid silver! Solid Roman silver!'

'Not possible,' Ford said.

'They're magnificent!' Fawcett cried out, going into raptures. 'They're perfect! They're unbelievable! Where on earth did you find them? It's most important to know where you found them! Was there anything else?' Fawcett was hopping about all over the room.

'Well . . .' Ford said, licking dry lips.

'You must report them at once!' Fawcett cried. 'They're

Treasure Trove! The British Museum is going to want these and that's for certain! How long have you had them?'

'Just a little while,' Ford told him.

'And *who* found them?' Fawcett asked, looking straight at him. 'Did you find them yourself or did you get them from somebody else? This is vital! The finder will be able to tell us all about it!'

Ford felt the walls of the room closing in on him and he didn't quite know what to do.

'Come on, man! Surely you know where you got them! Every detail will have to come out when you hand them in. Promise me you'll go to the police with them at once?'

'Well . . .' Ford said.

'If you don't, then I'm afraid I shall be forced to report it myself,' Fawcett told him. 'It's my duty.'

The game was up now and Ford knew it. A thousand questions would be asked. How did you find it? When did you find it? What were you doing? Where was the exact spot? Whose land were you ploughing? And sooner or later, inevitably, the name of Gordon Butcher would have to come into it. It was unavoidable. And then, when Butcher was questioned, he would remember the size of the hoard and tell them all about it.

So the game was up. And the only thing to do at this point was to unlock the doors of the big sideboard and show the entire hoard to Dr Fawcett.

Ford's excuse for keeping it all and not turning it in would have to be that he thought it was pewter. So long as he stuck to that, he told himself, they couldn't do anything to him.

Dr Fawcett would probably have a heart attack when he saw what there was in that cupboard.

'There is actually quite a bit more of it,' Ford said.

'Where?' cried Fawcett, spinning round. 'Where, man, where? Lead me to it!'

'I really thought it was pewter,' Ford said, moving slowly and very reluctantly forward to the oak sideboard. 'Otherwise I would naturally have reported it at once.'

He bent down and unlocked the lower doors of the sideboard. He opened the doors.

And then Dr Hugh Alderson Fawcett very nearly did have a heart attack. He flung himself on his knees. He gasped. He choked. He began spluttering like an old kettle. He reached out for the great silver dish. He took it. He held it in shaking hands and his face went as white as snow. He didn't speak. He couldn't. He was literally and physically and mentally struck absolutely dumb by the sight of the treasure.

The interesting part of the story ends here. The rest is routine. Ford went to Mildenhall police station and made a report. The police came at once and collected all thirty-four pieces, and they were sent under guard to the British Museum for examination.

Then an urgent message from the Museum to the Mildenhall police. It was far and away the finest Roman silver ever found in the British Isles. It was of enormous value. The Museum (which is really a public governmental institution) wished to acquire it. In fact, they insisted upon acquiring it.

The wheels of the law began to turn. An official inquest and hearing was arranged at the nearest large town, Bury St Edmunds. The silver was moved there under special police guard. Ford was summoned to appear before the coroner and a jury of fourteen, while Gordon Butcher, that good and quiet man, was ordered also to present himself to give evidence.

On Monday, July the first, 1946, the hearing took place, and the coroner cross-questioned Ford closely.

'You thought it was pewter?'

'Yes.'

'Even after you had cleaned it?'

'Yes.'

'You took no steps to inform any experts of the find?'

'No.'

'What did you intend to do with the articles?'

'Nothing. Just keep them.'

And when he had concluded his evidence, Ford asked permission to go outside into the fresh air because he said he felt faint. Nobody was surprised.

Then Butcher was called, and in a few simple words he told of his part in the affair.

Dr Fawcett gave his evidence, so did several other learned archaeologists, all of whom testified to the extreme rarity of the treasure. They said that it was of the fourth century after Christ; that it was the table silver of a wealthy Roman family; that it had probably been buried by the owner's bailiff to save it from the Picts and Scots who swept down from the north in about AD 365–7 and laid waste many Roman settlements. The man who buried it had probably been liquidated either by a Pict or a Scot, and the treasure had remained concealed a foot below the soil ever since. The workmanship, said the experts, was magnificent. Some of it may have been executed in England, but more probably the articles were made in Italy or in Egypt. The great plate was of course the finest piece. The head in the centre was that of Neptune, the sea-god, with dolphins in his hair and seaweed in his beard. All around him, sea-nymphs and sea-monsters gambolled. On the broad rim of the plate stood Bacchus and his attendants. There was wine and revelry. Hercules was there, quite drunk, supported by two satyrs, his lion's skin fallen from his shoulders. Pan was there, too, dancing upon his goat-legs with his pipes in his hand. And everywhere there were maenads, female devotees of Bacchus, rather tipsy women.

The court was told also that several of the spoons bore the monogram of Christ (Chi-Rho), and that the two which were inscribed with the names Pascentia and Papittedo were undoubtedly christening presents.

The experts concluded their evidence and the court adjourned. Soon the jury returned, and their verdict was astonishing. No blame was attached to anyone for anything, although the finder of the treasure was no longer entitled to receive full compensation from the Crown because the find had not been declared at once.

Nevertheless, there would probably be a measure of compensation paid, and with this in view, the finders were declared to be jointly Ford and Butcher.

Not Butcher. Ford and Butcher.

There is no more to tell other than that the treasure was acquired by the British Museum, where it now stands proudly displayed in a large glass case for all to see. And already people have travelled great distances to go and look upon those lovely things which Gordon Butcher found beneath his plough on that cold and windy winter afternoon. One day, a book or two will be compiled about them, full of suppositions and abstruse conclusions, and men who move in archaeological circles will talk for ever about the Treasure of Mildenhall.

As a gesture, the Museum rewarded the co-finders with one thousand pounds each. Butcher, the true finder, was happy and surprised to receive so much money. He did not realize that had he been allowed to take the treasure home originally, he would almost certainly have revealed its existence and would thus have become eligible to receive one hundred per cent of its value, which could have been anything between half a million and a million pounds.

Nobody knows what Ford thought about it all. He must have been relieved and perhaps somewhat surprised when he heard that the court had believed his story about pewter. But above all he must have been shattered by the loss of his great treasure. For the rest of his life he would be kicking himself for leaving those two spoons on the mantel above the fireplace for Dr Fawcett to see.

Man from the South

First published in *Collier's* (4 September 1948)
as 'Collector's Item'; also known
as 'The Smoker'

It was getting on towards six o'clock so I thought I'd buy myself a beer and go out and sit in a deck-chair by the swimming-pool and have a little evening sun.

I went to the bar and got the beer and carried it outside and wandered down the garden towards the pool.

It was a fine garden with lawns and beds of azaleas and tall coconut palms, and the wind was blowing strongly through the tops of the palm trees, making the leaves hiss and crackle as though they were on fire. I could see the clusters of big brown nuts hanging down underneath the leaves.

There were plenty of deck-chairs around the swimming-pool and there were white tables and huge brightly coloured umbrellas and sunburned men and women sitting around in bathing suits. In the pool itself there were three or four girls and about a dozen boys, all splashing about and making a lot of noise and throwing a large rubber ball at one another.

I stood watching them. The girls were English girls from the hotel. The boys I didn't know about, but they sounded American and I thought they were probably naval cadets who'd come ashore from the US naval training vessel which had arrived in harbour that morning.

I went over and sat down under a yellow umbrella where there were four empty seats, and I poured my beer and settled back comfortably with a cigarette.

It was very pleasant sitting there in the sunshine with beer and cigarette. It was pleasant to sit and watch the bathers splashing about in the green water.

The American sailors were getting on nicely with the English girls. They'd reached the stage where they were diving under the water and tipping them up by their legs.

Just then I noticed a small, oldish man walking briskly around the edge of the pool. He was immaculately dressed in a white suit and he walked very quickly with little bouncing strides, pushing himself high up on to his toes with each step. He had on a large creamy Panama hat, and he came bouncing along the side of the pool, looking at the people and the chairs.

He stopped beside me and smiled, showing two rows of very small, uneven teeth, slightly tarnished. I smiled back.

'Excuse pleess, but may I sit here?'

'Certainly,' I said. 'Go ahead.'

He bobbed around to the back of the chair and inspected it for safety, then he sat down and crossed his legs. His white buckskin shoes had little holes punched all over them for ventilation.

'A fine evening,' he said. 'They are all evenings fine here in Jamaica.' I couldn't tell if the accent was Italian or Spanish, but I felt fairly sure he was some sort of a South American. And old too, when you saw him close. Probably around sixty-eight or seventy.

'Yes,' I said. 'It is wonderful here, isn't it?'

'And who, might I ask, are all dese? Dese is no hotel people.' He was pointing at the bathers in the pool.

'I think they're American sailors,' I told him. 'They're Americans who are learning to be sailors.'

'Of course dey are Americans. Who else in de world is going to make as much noise as dat? You are not American, no?'

'No,' I said. 'I am not.'

Suddenly one of the American cadets was standing in front of us. He was dripping wet from the pool and one of the English girls was standing there with him.

'Are these chairs taken?' he said.

'No,' I answered.

'Mind if I sit down?'

'Go ahead.'

'Thanks,' he said. He had a towel in his hand and when he sat down he unrolled it and produced a pack of cigarettes and a lighter. He offered the cigarettes to the girl and she refused; then he offered them to me and I took one. The little man said. 'Tank you, no, but I tink I have a cigar.' He pulled out a crocodile case and got himself a cigar, then he produced a knife which had a small scissors in it and he snipped the end off the cigar.

'Here, let me give you a light.' The American boy held up his lighter.

'Dat will not work in dis wind.'

'Sure, it'll work. It always works.'

The little man removed his unlighted cigar from his mouth, cocked his head on one side and looked at the boy.

'*All*-ways?' he said slowly.

'Sure, it never fails. Not with me anyway.'

The little man's head was still cocked over on one side and he was still watching the boy. 'Well, well. So you say dis famous lighter it never fails. Iss dat you say?'

'Sure,' the boy said. 'That's right.' He was about nineteen or twenty, with a long freckled face and a rather sharp birdlike nose. His chest was not very sunburned and there were freckles there too, and a few wisps of pale-reddish hair. He was holding the lighter in his right hand, ready to flip the wheel. 'It never fails,' he said, smiling now because he was purposely exaggerating his little boast. 'I promise you it never fails.'

'One momint, pleess.' The hand that held the cigar came up high, palm outward, as though it were stopping traffic. 'Now juss one momint.' He had a curiously soft, toneless voice and he kept looking at the boy all the time.

'Shall we not perhaps make a little bet on dat?' He smiled at the boy. 'Shall we not make a little bet on whether your lighter lights?'

'Sure, I'll bet,' the boy said. 'Why not?'

'You like to bet?'

'Sure, I'll always bet.'

The man paused and examined his cigar, and I must say I didn't much like the way he was behaving. It seemed he was already trying to make something out of this, and to embarrass the boy, and at the same time I had the feeling he was relishing a private little secret all his own.

He looked up again at the boy and said slowly, 'I like to

bet, too. Why we don't have a good bet on dis ting? A good big bet.'

'Now wait a minute,' the boy said. 'I can't do that. But I'll bet you a quarter. I'll even bet you a dollar, or whatever it is over here – some shillings, I guess.'

The little man waved his hand again. 'Listen to me. Now we have some fun. We make a bet. Den we go up to my room here in de hotel where iss no wind and I bet you you cannot light dis famous lighter of yours ten times running without missing once.'

'I'll bet I can,' the boy said.

'All right. Good. We make a bet, yes?'

'Sure. I'll bet you a buck.'

'No, no. I make you very good bet. I am rich man and I am sporting man also. Listen to me. Outside de hotel iss my car. Iss very fine car. American car from your country. Cadillac –'

'Hey, now. Wait a minute.' The boy leaned back in his deck-chair and he laughed. 'I can't put up that sort of property. This is crazy.'

'Not crazy at all. You strike lighter successfully ten times running and Cadillac is yours. You like to have dis Cadillac, yes?'

'Sure, I'd like to have a Cadillac.' The boy was still grinning.

'All right. Fine. We make a bet and I put up my Cadillac.'

'And what do I put up?'

The little man carefully removed the red band from his

still-unlighted cigar. 'I never ask you, my friend, to bet something you cannot afford. You understand?'

'Then what do I bet?'

'I make it very easy for you, yes?'

'OK. You make it easy.'

'Some small ting you can afford to give away, and if you did happen to lose it you would not feel too bad. Right?'

'Such as what?'

'Such as, perhaps, de little finger of your left hand.'

'My *what*!' The boy stopped grinning.

'Yes. Why not? You win, you take de car. You looss, I take de finger.'

'I don't get it. How d'you mean, you take the finger?'

'I chop it off.'

'Jumping jeepers! That's a crazy bet. I think I'll just make it a dollar.'

The little man leaned back, spread out his hands palms upward and gave a tiny contemptuous shrug of the shoulders. 'Well, well, well,' he said. 'I do not understand. You say it lights but you will not bet. Den we forget it, yes?'

The boy sat quite still, staring at the bathers in the pool. Then he remembered suddenly he hadn't lighted his cigarette. He put it between his lips, cupped his hands around the lighter and flipped the wheel. The wick lighted and burned with a small, steady, yellow flame and the way he held his hands the wind didn't get to it at all.

'Could I have a light, too?' I said.

'Gee, I'm sorry. I forgot you didn't have one.'

I held out my hand for the lighter, but he stood up and came over to do it for me.

'Thank you,' I said, and he returned to his seat.

'You having a good time?' I asked.

'Fine,' he answered. 'It's pretty nice here.'

There was silence then, and I could see that the little man had succeeded in disturbing the boy with his absurd proposal. He was sitting there very still, and it was obvious that a small tension was beginning to build up inside him. Then he started shifting about in his seat, and rubbing his chest, and stroking the back of his neck, and finally he placed both hands on his knees and began tap-tapping with his fingers against the knee-caps. Soon he was tapping with one of his feet as well.

'Now just let me check up on this bet of yours,' he said at last. 'You say we go up to your room and if I make this lighter light ten times running I win a Cadillac. If it misses just once then I forfeit the little finger of my left hand. Is that right?'

'Certainly. Dat is de bet. But I think you are afraid.'

'What do we do if I lose? Do I have to hold my finger out while you chop it off?'

'Oh no! Dat would be no good. And you might be tempted to refuse to hold it out. What I should do I should tie one of your hands to de table before we started and I should stand dere with a knife ready to go *chop* de momint your lighter missed.'

'What year is the Cadillac?' the boy asked.

'Excuse. I not understand.'

'What year – how old is the Cadillac?'

'Ah! How old? Yes. It is last year. Quite new car. But I see you are not betting man. Americans never are.'

The boy paused for just a moment and he glanced first at the English girl, then at me. 'Yes,' he said sharply. 'I'll bet you.'

'Good!' The little man clapped his hands together quietly, once. 'Fine,' he said. 'We do it now. And you, sir,' he turned to me, 'you would perhaps be good enough to, what you call it, to – to referee.' He had pale, almost colourless eyes with tiny bright black pupils.

'Well,' I said. 'I think it's a crazy bet. I don't think I like it very much.'

'Nor do I,' said the English girl. It was the first time she'd spoken. 'I think it's a stupid, ridiculous bet.'

'Are you serious about cutting off this boy's finger if he loses?' I said.

'Certainly I am. Also about giving him Cadillac if he win. Come now. We go to my room.'

He stood up. 'You like to put on some clothes first?' he said.

'No,' the boy answered. 'I'll come like this.' Then he turned to me. 'I'd consider it a favour if you'd come along and referee.'

'All right,' I said. 'I'll come along, but I don't like the bet.'

'You come too,' he said to the girl. 'You come and watch.'

The little man led the way back through the garden to the hotel. He was animated now, and excited, and that seemed to make him bounce up higher than ever on his toes as he walked along.

'I live in annexe,' he said. 'You like to see car first? Iss just here.'

He took us to where we could see the front driveway of

the hotel and he stopped and pointed to a sleek pale-green Cadillac parked close by.

'Dere she iss. De green one. You like?'

'Say, that's a nice car,' the boy said.

'All right. Now we go up and see if you can win her.'

We followed him into the annexe and up one flight of stairs. He unlocked his door and we all trooped into what was a large pleasant double bedroom. There was a woman's dressing-gown lying across the bottom of one of the beds.

'First,' he said, 'we 'ave a little Martini.'

The drinks were on a small table in the far corner, all ready to be mixed, and there was a shaker and ice and plenty of glasses. He began to make the Martini, but meanwhile he'd rung the bell and now there was a knock on the door and a coloured maid came in.

'Ah!' he said, putting down the bottle of gin, taking a wallet from his pocket and pulling out a pound note. 'You will do something for me now, pleess.' He gave the maid the pound.

'You keep dat,' he said. 'And now we are going to play a little game in here and I want you to go off and find for me two – no tree tings. I want some nails; I want a hammer, and I want a chopping knife, a butcher's chopping knife which you can borrow from de kitchen. You can get, yes?'

'A *chopping knife*!' The maid opened her eyes wide and clasped her hands in front of her. 'You mean a *real* chopping knife?'

'Yes, yes, of course. Come on now, pleess. You can find dose tings surely for me.'

'Yes, sir, I'll try, sir. Surely I'll try to get them.' And she went.

The little man handed round the Martinis. We stood there and sipped them, the boy with the long freckled face and the pointed nose, bare-bodied except for a pair of faded brown bathing shorts; the English girl, a large-boned, fair-haired girl wearing a pale-blue bathing suit, who watched the boy over the top of her glass all the time; the little man with the colourless eyes standing there in his immaculate white suit drinking his Martini and looking at the girl in her pale-blue bathing dress. I didn't know what to make of it all. The man seemed serious about the bet and he seemed serious about the business of cutting off the finger. But hell, what if the boy lost? Then we'd have to rush him to the hospital in the Cadillac that he hadn't won. That would be a fine thing. Now wouldn't that be a really fine thing? It would be a damn silly unnecessary thing so far as I could see.

'Don't you think this is rather a silly bet?' I said.

'I think it's a fine bet,' the boy answered. He had already downed one large Martini.

'I think it's a stupid, ridiculous bet,' the girl said. 'What'll happen if you lose?'

'It won't matter. Come to think of it, I can't remember ever in my life having had any use for the little finger on my left hand. Here he is.' The boy took hold of the finger. 'Here he is and he hasn't ever done a thing for me yet. So why shouldn't I bet him. I think it's a fine bet.'

The little man smiled and picked up the shaker and refilled our glasses.

'Before we begin,' he said, 'I will present to de – to de referee de key of de car.' He produced a car key from his pocket and gave it to me. 'De papers,' he said, 'de owning papers and insurance are in de pocket of de car.'

Then the coloured maid came in again. In one hand she carried a small chopper, the kind used by butchers for chopping meat bones, and in the other a hammer and a bag of nails.

'Good! You get dem all. Tank you, tank you. Now you can go.' He waited until the maid had closed the door, then he put the implements on one of the beds and said, 'Now we prepare ourselves, yes?' And to the boy, 'Help me, pleess, with dis table. We carry it out a little.'

It was the usual kind of hotel writing desk, just a plain rectangular table about four feet by three with a blotting pad, inks, pens and paper. They carried it out into the room away from the wall, and removed the writing things.

'And now,' he said, 'a chair.' He picked up a chair and placed it beside the table. He was very brisk and very animated, like a person organizing games at a children's party. 'And now de nails. I must put in de nails.' He fetched the nails and began to hammer them into the top of the table.

We stood there, the boy, the girl and I, holding Martinis in our hands, watching the little man at work. We watched him hammer two nails into the table, about six inches apart. He didn't hammer them right home; he allowed a small part of each one to stick up. Then he tested them for firmness with his fingers.

Anyone would think the son of a bitch had done this before, I told myself. He never hesitates. Table, nails, hammer, kitchen chopper. He knows exactly what he needs and how to arrange it.

'And now,' he said, 'all we want is some string.' He found some string. 'All right, at last we are ready. Will you pleess to sit here at de table,' he said to the boy.

The boy put his glass away and sat down.

'Now place de left hand between dese two nails. De nails are only so I can tie your hand in place. All right, good. Now I tie your hand secure to de table – so.'

He wound the string around the boy's wrist, then several times around the wide part of the hand, then he fastened it tight to the nails. He made a good job of it and when he'd finished there wasn't any question about the boy being able to draw his hand away. But he could move his fingers.

'Now pleess, clench de fist, all except for de little finger. You must leave de little finger out, lying on de table.

'*Ex*-cellent! *Ex*-cellent! Now we are ready. Wid your right hand you manipulate de lighter. But one momint, pleess.'

He skipped over to the bed and picked up the chopper. He came back and stood beside the table with the chopper in his hand.

'We are all ready?' he said. 'Mister referee, you must say to begin.'

The English girl was standing there in her pale-blue bathing costume right behind the boy's chair. She was just standing there, not saying anything. The boy was sitting quite still, holding the lighter in his right hand, looking at the chopper. The little man was looking at me.

'Are you ready?' I asked the boy.

'I'm ready.'

'And you?' to the little man.

'Quite ready,' he said and he lifted the chopper up in the air and held it there about two feet above the boy's finger, ready to chop. The boy watched it, but he didn't flinch and his mouth didn't move at all. He merely raised his eyebrows and frowned.

'All right,' I said. 'Go ahead.'

The boy said, 'Will you please count aloud the number of times I light it?'

'Yes,' I said. 'I'll do that.'

With his thumb he raised the top of the lighter, and again with the thumb he gave the wheel a sharp flick. The flint sparked and the wick caught fire and burned with a small yellow flame.

'One!' I called.

He didn't blow the flame out; he closed the top of the lighter on it and he waited for perhaps five seconds before opening it again.

He flicked the wheel very strongly and once more there was a small flame burning on the wick.

'Two!'

No one else said anything. The boy kept his eyes on the lighter. The little man held the chopper up in the air and he too was watching the lighter.

'Three!'

'Four!'

'Five!'

'Six!'

'Seven!' Obviously it was one of those lighters that worked. The flint gave a big spark and the wick was the right length. I watched the thumb snapping the top down on to the flame. Then a pause. Then the thumb raising the top once more. This was an all-thumb operation. The thumb did everything. I took a breath, ready to say eight. The thumb flicked the wheel. The flint sparked. The little flame appeared.

'Eight!' I said, and as I said it the door opened. We all turned and we saw a woman standing in the doorway, a small, black-haired woman, rather old, who stood there for about two seconds then rushed forward shouting, 'Carlos! Carlos!' She grabbed his wrist, took the chopper from him, threw it on the bed, took hold of the little man by the lapels of his white suit and began shaking him very vigorously, talking to him fast and loud and fiercely all the time in some Spanish-sounding language. She shook him so fast you couldn't see him any more. He became a faint, misty, quickly moving outline, like the spokes of a turning wheel.

Then she slowed down and the little man came into view again and she hauled him across the room and pushed him backwards on to one of the beds. He sat on the edge of it, blinking his eyes and testing his head to see if it would still turn on his neck.

'I am so sorry,' the woman said. 'I am so terribly sorry that this should happen.' She spoke almost perfect English.

'It is too bad,' she went on. 'I suppose it is really my fault. For ten minutes I leave him alone to go and have my hair washed and I come back and he is at it again.' She looked sorry and deeply concerned.

The boy was untying his hand from the table. The English girl and I stood there and said nothing.

'He is a menace,' the woman said. 'Down where we live at home he has taken altogether forty-seven fingers from different people, and he has lost eleven cars. In the end they threatened to have him put away somewhere. That's why I brought him up here.'

'We were only having a little bet,' mumbled the little man from the bed.

'I suppose he bet you a car,' the woman said.

'Yes,' the boy answered. 'A Cadillac.'

'He has no car. It's mine. And that makes it worse,' she said, 'that he should bet you when he has nothing to bet with. I am ashamed and very sorry about it all.' She seemed an awfully nice woman.

'Well,' I said, 'then here's the key of your car.' I put it on the table.

'We were only having a little bet,' mumbled the little man.

'He hasn't anything left to bet with,' the woman said. 'He hasn't a thing in the world. Not a thing. As a matter of fact I myself won it all from him a long while ago. It took time, a lot of time, and it was hard work, but I won it all in the end.' She looked up at the boy and she smiled, a slow sad smile, and she came over and put out a hand to take the key from the table.

I can see it now, that hand of hers; it had only one finger on it, and a thumb.

The Sound Machine

First published in *The New Yorker*
(17 September 1949)

It was a warm summer evening and Klausner walked quickly through the front gate and around the side of the house and into the garden at the back. He went on down the garden until he came to a wooden shed and he unlocked the door, went inside and closed the door behind him.

The interior of the shed was an unpainted room. Against one wall, on the left, there was a long wooden workbench, and on it, among a littering of wires and batteries and small sharp tools, there stood a black box about three feet long, the shape of a child's coffin.

Klausner moved across the room to the box. The top of the box was open, and he bent down and began to poke and peer inside it among a mass of different-coloured wires and silver tubes. He picked up a piece of paper that lay beside the box, studied it carefully, put it down, peered inside the box and started running his fingers along the wires, tugging gently at them to test the connections, glancing back at the paper, then into the box, then at the paper again, checking each wire. He did this for perhaps an hour.

Then he put a hand around to the front of the box where there were three dials, and he began to twiddle them, watching at the same time the movement of the mechanism inside the box. All the while he kept speaking softly to himself, nodding his head, smiling sometimes, his hands always moving, the fingers moving swiftly, deftly, inside the box, his mouth twisting into curious shapes when a thing was delicate or difficult to do, saying, 'Yes . . . Yes . . . And now this one . . . Yes . . . Yes . . . But is this right? Is it – where's my diagram? . . . Ah, yes . . . Of course . . . Yes, yes . . . That's right . . . And now . . . Good . . . Good . . . Yes . . . Yes, yes, yes.' His concentration was intense; his movements were quick; there was an air of urgency about the way he worked, of breathlessness, of strong suppressed excitement.

Suddenly he heard footsteps on the gravel path outside and he straightened and turned swiftly as the door opened and a tall man came in. It was Scott. It was only Scott, the doctor.

'Well, well, well,' the doctor said. 'So this is where you hide yourself in the evenings.'

'Hullo, Scott,' Klausner said.

'I happened to be passing,' the doctor told him, 'so I dropped in to see how you were. There was no one in the house, so I came on down here. How's that throat of yours been behaving?'

'It's all right. It's fine.'

'Now I'm here I might as well have a look at it.'

'Please don't trouble. I'm quite cured. I'm fine.'

The doctor began to feel the tension in the room. He looked at the black box on the bench; then he looked at the man. 'You've got your hat on,' he said.

'Oh, have I?' Klausner reached up, removed the hat and put it on the bench.

The doctor came up closer and bent down to look into the box. 'What's this?' he said. 'Making a radio?'

'No. Just fooling around.'

'It's got rather complicated-looking innards.'

'Yes.' Klausner seemed tense and distracted.

'What is it?' the doctor asked. 'It's rather a frightening-looking thing, isn't it?'

'It's just an idea.'

'Yes?'

'It has to do with sound, that's all.'

'Good heavens, man! Don't you get enough of that sort of thing all day in your work?'

'I like sound.'

'So it seems.' The doctor went to the door, turned, and said, 'Well, I won't disturb you. Glad your throat's not worrying you any more.' But he kept standing there, looking at the box, intrigued by the remarkable complexity of its inside, curious to know what this strange patient of his was up to. 'What's it really for?' he asked. 'You've made me inquisitive.'

Klausner looked down at the box, then at the doctor, and he reached up and began gently to scratch the lobe of his right ear. There was a pause. The doctor stood by the door, waiting, smiling.

'All right, I'll tell you, if you're interested.' There was another pause, and the doctor could see that Klausner was having trouble about how to begin.

He was shifting from one foot to the other, tugging at the lobe of his ear, looking at his feet, and then at last, slowly, he said, 'Well, it's like this . . . the theory is very simple, really. The human ear . . . You know that it can't hear everything. There are sounds that are so low-pitched or so high-pitched that it can't hear them.'

'Yes,' the doctor said. 'Yes.'

'Well, speaking very roughly, any note so high that it has more than fifteen thousand vibrations a second – we can't hear it. Dogs have better ears than us. You know you can buy a whistle whose note is so high-pitched that you can't hear it at all. But a dog can hear it.'

'Yes, I've seen one,' the doctor said.

'Of course you have. And up the scale, higher than the note of that whistle, there is another note – a vibration if you like, but I prefer to think of it as a note. You can't hear that one either. And above that there is another and another rising right up the scale for ever and ever and ever, an endless succession of notes . . . an infinity of notes . . . there is a note – if only our ears could hear it – so high that it vibrates a million times a second . . . and another a million times as high as that . . . and on and on, higher and higher, as far as numbers go, which is . . . infinity . . . eternity . . . beyond the stars.'

Klausner was becoming more animated every moment. He was a small frail man, nervous and twitchy, with always-moving hands. His large head inclined towards his left shoulder as though his neck were not quite strong enough to support it rigidly. His face was smooth and pale, almost white, and the pale-grey eyes that blinked and peered from behind a pair of steel spectacles were bewildered, unfocused, remote. He was a frail, nervous, twitchy little man, a moth of a man, dreamy and distracted; suddenly fluttering and animated; and now the doctor, looking at that strange pale face and those pale-grey eyes, felt that somehow there was about this little person a quality of distance, of immense, immeasurable distance, as though the mind were far away from where the body was.

The doctor waited for him to go on. Klausner sighed and clasped his hands tightly together. 'I believe,' he said, speaking more slowly now, 'that there is a whole world of sound about us all the time that we cannot hear. It is possible that up there in those high-pitched inaudible regions there is a new exciting music being made, with subtle harmonies and fierce grinding discords, a music so powerful that it would drive us mad if only our ears were tuned to hear the sound of it. There may be anything . . . for all we know there may –'

'Yes,' the doctor said. 'But it's not very probable.'

'Why not? Why not?' Klausner pointed to a fly sitting on a small roll of copper wire on the workbench. 'You see that fly? What sort of a noise is that fly making now? None – that one can hear. But for all we know the creature may be whistling like mad on a very high note, or barking or croaking or singing a song. It's got a mouth, hasn't it? It's got a throat!'

The doctor looked at the fly and he smiled. He was still standing by the door with his hand on the doorknob. 'Well,' he said. 'So you're going to check up on that?'

'Some time ago,' Klausner said, 'I made a simple instrument that proved to me the existence of many odd inaudible sounds. Often I have sat and watched the needle of my instrument recording the presence of sound vibrations in the air when I myself could hear nothing. And *those* are the sounds I want to listen to. I want to know where they come from and who or what is making them.'

'And that machine on the table there,' the doctor said, 'is that going to allow you to hear these noises?'

'It may. Who knows? So far, I've had no luck. But I've made some changes in it and tonight I'm ready for another trial. This machine,' he said, touching it with his hands, 'is designed to pick up sound vibrations that are too high-pitched for reception by the human ear, and to convert them to a scale of audible tones. I tune it in, almost like a radio.'

'How d' you mean?'

'It isn't complicated. Say I wish to listen to the squeak of a bat. That's a fairly high-pitched sound – about thirty thousand vibrations a second. The average human ear can't quite hear it. Now, if there were a bat flying around this room and I tuned in to thirty thousand on my machine, I would hear the squeaking of that bat very clearly. I would even hear the correct note – F sharp, or B flat, or whatever it might be – but merely at a much *lower pitch*. Don't you understand?'

The doctor looked at the long black coffin-box. 'And you're going to try it tonight?'

'Yes.'

'Well, I wish you luck.' He glanced at his watch. 'My goodness!' he said. 'I must fly. Good-bye, and thank you for telling me. I must call again some time and find out what happened.' The doctor went out and closed the door behind him.

For a while longer, Klausner fussed about with the wires in the black box; then he straightened up and in a soft excited whisper said, 'Now we'll try again . . . We'll take it out into the garden this time . . . and then perhaps . . . perhaps . . . the reception will be better. Lift it up now . . . carefully . . . Oh, my God, it's heavy!' He carried the box to the door, found that he couldn't open the door without putting it down, carried it back, put it on the bench, opened the door, and then carried it with some difficulty into the garden. He placed the box carefully on a small wooden table that stood on the lawn. He returned to the shed and fetched a pair of earphones. He plugged the wire connections from the earphones into the machine and put the earphones over his ears. The movements of his hands were quick and precise. He was excited, and breathed loudly and quickly through his mouth. He kept on talking to himself with little words of comfort and encouragement, as though he were afraid – afraid that the machine might not work and afraid also of what might happen if it did.

He stood there in the garden beside the wooden table, so pale, small and thin that he looked like an ancient, consumptive, bespectacled child. The sun had gone down. There was no wind, no sound at all. From where he stood, he could see over a low fence into the next garden, and there was a woman walking down the garden with a flower basket on her arm. He watched her for a while without thinking about her at all. Then he turned to the box on the table and pressed a switch on its front. He put his left hand on the volume control and his right on the knob that moved a needle across a large central dial, like the wavelength dial of a radio. The dial was marked with many numbers, in a series of bands, starting at fifteen thousand and going on up to one million.

And now he was bending forward over the machine. His head was cocked to one side in a tense listening attitude. His right hand was beginning to turn the knob. The needle was travelling slowly across the dial, so slowly he could hardly see it move, and in the earphones he could hear a faint, spasmodic crackling.

Behind this crackling sound he could hear a distant humming tone which was the noise of the machine itself, but that was all. As he listened, he became conscious of a curious sensation, a feeling that his ears were stretching out away from his head, that each ear was connected to his head by a thin stiff wire, like a tentacle, and that the wires were lengthening, that the ears were going up and up towards a secret and forbidden territory, a dangerous ultrasonic region where ears had never been before and had no right to be.

The little needle crept slowly across the dial, and suddenly he heard a shriek, a frightful piercing shriek, and he jumped and dropped his hands, catching hold of the edge of the table. He stared around him as if expecting to see the person who had shrieked. There was no one in sight except the woman in the garden next door, and it was certainly not she. She was bending down, cutting yellow roses and putting them in her basket.

Again it came – a throatless, inhuman shriek, sharp and short, very clear and cold. The note itself possessed a minor, metallic quality that he had never heard before. Klausner looked around him, searching instinctively for the source of the noise. The woman next door was the only living thing in sight. He saw her reach down, take a rose stem in the fingers of one hand and snip the stem with a pair of scissors. Again he heard the scream.

It came at the exact moment when the rose stem was cut.

At this point, the woman straightened up, put the scissors in the basket with the roses and turned to walk away.

'Mrs Saunders!' Klausner shouted, his voice shrill with excitement. 'Oh, Mrs Saunders!'

And looking round, the woman saw her neighbour standing on his lawn – a fantastic, arm-waving little person with a pair of earphones on his head – calling to her in a voice so high and loud that she became alarmed.

'Cut another one! Please cut another one quickly!'

She stood still, staring at him. 'Why, Mr Klausner,' she said, 'what's the matter?'

'Please do as I ask,' he said. 'Cut just one more rose!'

Mrs Saunders had always believed her neighbour to be a rather peculiar person; now it seemed that he had gone completely crazy. She wondered whether she should run into the house and fetch her husband. No, she thought. No, he's harmless. I'll just humour him. 'Certainly, Mr Klausner, if you like,' she said. She took her scissors from the basket, bent down and snipped another rose.

Again Klausner heard that frightful, throatless shriek in the earphones; again it came at the exact moment the rose stem was cut. He took off the earphones and ran to the fence that separated the two gardens. 'All right,' he said. 'That's enough. No more. Please, no more.'

The woman stood there, a yellow rose in one hand, clippers in the other, looking at him.

'I'm going to tell you something, Mrs Saunders,' he said, 'something that you won't believe.' He put his hands on top of the fence and peered at her intently through his thick spectacles. 'You have, this evening, cut a basketful of roses. You have with a sharp pair of scissors cut through the stems of living things, and each rose that you cut screamed in the most terrible way. Did you know that, Mrs Saunders?'

'No,' she said. 'I certainly didn't know that.'

'It happens to be true,' he said. He was breathing rather rapidly, but he was trying to control his excitement. 'I heard them shrieking. Each time you cut one, I heard the cry of pain. A very high-pitched sound, approximately one hundred and thirty-two thousand vibrations a second. You couldn't possibly have heard it yourself. But *I* heard it.'

'Did you really, Mr Klausner?' She decided she would make a dash for the house in about five seconds.

'You might say,' he went on, 'that a rosebush has no nervous system to feel with, no throat to cry with. You'd be right. It hasn't. Not like ours, anyway. But *how do you know, Mrs Saunders*' – and here he leaned far over the fence and spoke in a fierce whisper – '*how do you know* that a rosebush doesn't feel as much pain when someone cuts its stem in two as you would feel if someone cut your wrist off with a garden shears? *How do you know that?* It's *alive*, isn't it?'

'Yes, Mr Klausner. Oh yes – and good night.' Quickly she turned and ran up the garden to her house. Klausner went back to the table. He put on the earphones and stood for a while listening. He could still hear the faint crackling sound and the humming noise of the machine, but nothing more. He bent down and took hold of a small white daisy growing on the lawn. He took it between thumb and forefinger and slowly pulled it upwards and sideways until the stem broke.

From the moment that he started pulling to the moment when the stem broke, he heard – he distinctly heard in the earphones – a faint high-pitched cry, curiously inanimate. He took another daisy and did it again. Once more he heard the cry, but he wasn't so sure now that it expressed *pain*. No, it wasn't pain; it was surprise. Or was it? It didn't really express any of the feelings or emotions known to a human being. It was just a cry, a neutral, stony cry – a single emotionless note, expressing nothing. It had been the same with the roses. He had been wrong in calling it a cry of pain. A flower probably didn't feel pain. It felt something else which we didn't know about – something called toin or spurl or plinuckment, or anything you like.

He stood up and removed the earphones. It was getting dark and he could see pricks of light shining in the windows of the houses all around him. Carefully he picked up the black box from the table, carried it into the shed and put it on the workbench. Then he went out, locked the door behind him and walked up to the house.

The next morning Klausner was up as soon as it was light. He dressed and went straight to the shed. He picked up the machine and carried it outside, clasping it to his chest with both hands, walking unsteadily under its weight. He went past the house, out through the front gate, and across the road to the park. There he paused and looked around him; then he went on until he came to a large tree, a beech tree, and he placed the machine on the ground close to the trunk of the tree. Quickly he went back to the house and got an axe from the coal cellar and carried it across the road into the park. He put the axe on the ground beside the tree.

Then he looked around him again, peering nervously through his thick glasses in every direction. There was no one about. It was six in the morning.

He put the earphones on his head and switched on the machine. He listened for a moment to the faint familiar humming sound; then he picked up the axe, took a stance with his legs wide apart and swung the axe as hard as he could at the base of the tree-trunk. The blade cut deep into the wood and stuck there, and at the instant of impact he heard a most extraordinary noise in the earphones. It was a new noise, unlike any he had heard before – a harsh, noteless, enormous noise, a growling, low-pitched, screaming sound, not quick and short like the noise of the roses, but drawn out like a sob, lasting for fully a minute, loudest at the moment when the axe struck, fading gradually fainter and fainter until it was gone.

Klausner stared in horror at the place where the blade of the axe had sunk into the woodflesh of the tree; then gently he took the axe handle, worked the blade loose and threw the thing on the ground. With his fingers he touched the gash that the axe had made in the wood, touching the edges of the gash, trying to press them together to close the wound, and he kept saying, 'Tree . . . oh tree . . . I am sorry . . . I am so sorry . . . but it will heal . . . it will heal fine . . .'

For a while he stood there with his hands upon the trunk of the great tree; then suddenly he turned away and hurried off out of the park, across the road, through the front gate and back into his house. He went to the telephone, consulted the book, dialled a number and waited. He held the receiver tightly in his left hand and tapped the table impatiently with his right. He heard the telephone buzzing at the other end, and then the click of a lifted receiver and a man's voice, a sleepy voice, saying: 'Hullo. Yes.'

'Dr Scott?' he said.

'Yes. Speaking.'

'Dr Scott. You must come at once – quickly please.'

'Who is it speaking?'

'Klausner here, and you remember what I told you last night about my experiment with sound, and how I hoped I might –'

'Yes, yes, of course, but what's the matter? Are you ill?'

'No, I'm not ill, but –'

'It's half past six in the morning,' the doctor said, 'and you call me, but you are not ill.'

'Please come. Come quickly. I want someone to hear it. It's driving me mad! I can't believe it . . .'

The doctor heard the frantic, almost hysterical note in the man's voice, the same note he was used to hearing in the voices of the people who called up and said, 'There's been an accident. Come quickly.' He said slowly, 'You really want me to get out of bed and come over now?'

'Yes, now. At once please.'

'All right then, I'll come.'

Klausner sat down beside the telephone and waited. He tried to remember what the shriek of the tree had sounded like, but he couldn't. He could remember only that it had been enormous and frightful and that it had made him feel sick with horror. He tried to imagine what sort of a noise a human would make if he had to stand anchored to the ground while someone deliberately swung a small sharp thing at his leg so that the blade cut in deep and wedged itself in the cut. Same sort of noise perhaps? No. Quite different. The noise of the tree was worse than any known human noise because of that frightening, toneless, throatless quality. He began to wonder about other living things, and he thought immediately of a field of wheat, a field of wheat standing up straight and yellow and alive, with the mower going through it, cutting the stems, five hundred stems a second, every second. Oh, my God, what would *that* noise be like? Five hundred wheat plants screaming together, and every second another five hundred being cut and screaming and – no, he thought, I do not want to go to a wheat field with my machine. I would never eat bread after that. But what about potatoes and cabbages and carrots and onions? And what about apples? Ah, no. Apples are all right. They fall off naturally when they are ripe. Apples are all right if you let them fall off instead of tearing them from the tree branch. But not vegetables. Not a potato for example. A potato would surely shriek; so would a carrot and an onion and a cabbage . . .

He heard the click of the front-gate latch and he jumped up and went out and saw the tall doctor coming down the path, little black bag in hand.

'Well,' the doctor said. 'Well, what's all the trouble?'

'Come with me, Doctor. I want you to hear it. I called you because you're the only one I've told. It's over the road in the park. Will you come now?'

The doctor looked at him. He seemed calmer now. There was no sign of madness or hysteria; he was merely disturbed and excited.

They went across the road into the park and Klausner led the way to the great beech tree at the foot of which stood the long black coffin-box of the machine – and the axe.

'Why did you bring it out here?' the doctor asked.

'I wanted a tree. There aren't any big trees in the garden.'

'And why the axe?'

'You'll see in a moment. But now please put on these earphones and listen. Listen carefully and tell me afterwards precisely what you hear. I want to make quite sure . . .'

The doctor smiled and took the earphones and put them over his ears.

Klausner bent down and flicked the switch on the panel of the machine; then he picked up the axe and took his stance with his legs apart, ready to swing. For a moment he paused. 'Can you hear anything?' he said to the doctor.

'Can I what?'

'Can you *hear* anything?'

'Just a humming noise.'

Klausner stood there with the axe in his hands trying to bring himself to swing, but the thought of the noise that the tree would make made him pause again.

'What are you waiting for?' the doctor asked.

'Nothing,' Klausner answered, and then he lifted the axe and swung it at the tree; and as he swung, he thought he felt, he could swear he felt a movement of the ground on which he stood. He felt a slight shifting of the earth beneath his feet as though the roots of the tree were moving underneath the soil, but it was too late to check the blow and the axe blade struck the tree and wedged deep into the wood. At that moment, high overhead, there was the cracking sound of wood splintering and the swishing sound of leaves brushing against other leaves and they both looked up and the doctor cried, 'Watch out! Run, man! Quickly, run!'

The doctor had ripped off the earphones and was running away fast, but Klausner stood spellbound, staring up at the great branch, sixty feet long at least, that was bending slowly downwards, breaking and crackling and splintering at its thickest point, where it joined the main trunk of the tree. The branch came crashing down and Klausner leaped aside just in time. It fell upon the machine and smashed it into pieces.

'Great heavens!' shouted the doctor as he came running back. 'That was a near one! I thought it had got you!'

Klausner was staring at the tree. His large head was

leaning to one side and upon his smooth white face there was a tense, horrified expression. Slowly he walked up to the tree and gently he prised the blade loose from the trunk.

'Did you hear it?' he said, turning to the doctor. His voice was barely audible.

The doctor was still out of breath from the running and the excitement. 'Hear what?'

'In the earphones. Did you hear anything when the axe struck?'

The doctor began to rub the back of his neck. 'Well,' he said, 'as a matter of fact . . .' He paused and frowned and bit his lower lip. 'No, I'm not sure. I couldn't be sure. I don't suppose I had the earphones on for more than a second after the axe struck.'

'Yes, yes, but what did you hear?'

'I don't know,' the doctor said. 'I don't know what I heard. Probably the noise of the branch breaking.' He was speaking rapidly, rather irritably.

'What did it sound like?' Klausner leaned forward slightly, staring hard at the doctor. '*Exactly* what did it sound like?'

'Oh hell!' the doctor said. 'I really don't know. I was more interested in getting out of the way. Let's leave it.'

'Dr Scott, *what-did-it-sound-like*?'

'For God's sake, how could I tell, what with half the tree falling on me and having to run for my life?' The doctor certainly seemed nervous. Klausner had sensed it now. He stood quite still, staring at the doctor, and for fully half a minute he didn't speak. The doctor moved his feet, shrugged his shoulders and half turned to go. 'Well,' he said. 'We'd better get back.'

'Look,' said the little man, and now his smooth white face became suddenly suffused with colour. 'Look,' he said, 'you stitch this up.' He pointed to the last gash that the axe had made in the tree-trunk. 'You stitch this up quickly.'

'Don't be silly,' the doctor said.

'You do as I say. Stitch it up.' Klausner was gripping the axe handle and he spoke softly, in a curious, almost a threatening tone.

'Don't be silly,' the doctor said. 'I can't stitch through wood. Come on. Let's get back.'

'So you can't stitch through wood?'

'No, of course not.'

'Have you got any iodine in your bag?'

'What if I have?'

'Then paint the cut with iodine. It'll sting, but that can't be helped.'

'Now look,' the doctor said, and again he turned as if to go. 'Let's not be ridiculous. Let's get back to the house and then . . .'

'*Paint-the-cut-with-iodine*.'

The doctor hesitated. He saw Klausner's hands tightening on the handle of the axe. He decided that his only alternative was to run away fast, and he certainly wasn't going to do that.

'All right,' he said. 'I'll paint it with iodine.'

He got his black bag, which was lying on the grass about ten yards away, opened it and took out a bottle of iodine and some cotton-wool. He went up to the tree-trunk, uncorked the bottle, tipped some of the iodine on to the cotton-wool, bent down and began to dab it into the cut. He kept one eye on Klausner who was standing motionless with the axe in his hands, watching him.

'Make sure you get it right in.'

'Yes,' the doctor said.

'Now do the other one, the one just above it!'

The doctor did as he was told.

'There you are,' he said. 'It's done.'

He straightened up and surveyed his work in a very serious manner. 'That should do nicely.'

Klausner came closer and gravely examined the two wounds.

'Yes,' he said, nodding his huge head slowly up and down. 'Yes, that will do nicely.' He stepped back a pace. 'You'll come and look at them again tomorrow?'

'Oh yes,' the doctor said. 'Of course.'

'And put some more iodine on?'

'If necessary, yes.'

'Thank you, Doctor,' Klausner said, and he nodded his head again and dropped the axe and all at once he smiled, a wild excited smile, and quickly the doctor went over to him and gently he took him by the arm and he said, 'Come on, we must go now,' and suddenly they were walking away, the two of them, walking silently, rather hurriedly, across the park, over the road, back to the house.

Poison

First published in *Collier's* (June 1950)

It must have been around midnight when I drove home, and as I approached the gates of the bungalow I switched off the headlamps of the car so the beam wouldn't swing in through the window of the side bedroom and wake Harry Pope. But I needn't have bothered. Coming up the drive I noticed his light was still on, so he was awake anyway – unless perhaps he'd dropped off while reading.

I parked the car and went up the five steps to the balcony, counting each step carefully in the dark so I wouldn't take an extra one which wasn't there when I got to the top. I crossed the balcony, pushed through the screen doors into the house itself and switched on the light in the hall. I went across to the door of Harry's room, opened it quietly and looked in.

He was lying on the bed and I could see he was awake. But he didn't move. He didn't even turn his head towards me, but I heard him say, 'Timber, Timber, come here.'

He spoke slowly, whispering each word carefully, separately, and I pushed the door right open and started to go quickly across the room.

'Stop. Wait a moment, Timber.' I could hardly hear what he was saying. He seemed to be straining enormously to get the words out.

'What's the matter, Harry?'

'Sshhh!' he whispered. 'Sshhh! For God's sake, don't make a noise. Take your shoes off before you come nearer. *Please* do as I say, Timber.'

The way he was speaking reminded me of George Barling after he got shot in the stomach when he stood leaning against a crate containing a spare aeroplane engine, holding both hands on his stomach and saying things about the German pilot in just the same hoarse straining half-whisper Harry was using now.

'Quickly, Timber, but take your shoes off first.'

I couldn't understand about taking off the shoes but I figured that if he was as ill as he sounded I'd better humour him, so I bent down and removed the shoes and left them in the middle of the floor. Then I went over to his bed.

'Don't touch the bed! For God's sake, don't touch the bed!' He was still speaking like he'd been shot in the stomach and I could see him lying there on his back with a single sheet covering three-quarters of his body. He was wearing a pair of pyjamas with blue, brown and white stripes, and he was sweating terribly. It was a hot night and I was sweating a little myself, but not like Harry. His whole face was wet and the pillow around his head was sodden with moisture. It looked like a bad go of malaria to me.

'What is it, Harry?'

'A krait,' he said.

'A *krait*! Oh my God! Where'd it bite you? How long ago?'

'Shut up,' he whispered.

'Listen, Harry,' I said, and I leaned forward and touched his shoulder. 'We've got to be quick. Come on now, quickly, tell me where it bit you.' He was lying there very still and tense as though he was holding on to himself hard because of sharp pain.

'I haven't been bitten,' he whispered. 'Not yet. It's on my stomach. Lying there asleep.'

I took a quick pace backwards. I couldn't help it, and I stared at his stomach or rather at the sheet that covered it. The sheet was rumpled in several places and it was impossible to tell if there was anything underneath.

'You don't really mean there's a krait lying on your stomach now?'

'I swear it.'

'How did it get there?' I shouldn't have asked the question because it was easy to see he wasn't fooling. I should have told him to keep quiet.

'I was reading,' Harry said, and he spoke very slowly, taking each word in turn and speaking it carefully so as not to move the muscles of his stomach. 'Lying on my back reading and I felt something on my chest, behind the book. Sort of tickling. Then out of the corner of my eye saw this little krait sliding over my pyjamas. Small, about ten inches. Knew I mustn't move. Couldn't have anyway. Lay there watching it. Thought it would go over top of the sheet.' Harry paused and was silent for a few moments. His eyes looked down along his body towards the place where the sheet covered his stomach, and I could see he was watching to make sure his whispering wasn't disturbing the thing that lay there.

'There was a fold in the sheet,' he said, speaking more slowly than ever now and so softly I had to lean close to hear him. 'See it, it's still there. It went under that. I could feel it through my pyjamas, moving on my stomach. Then it stopped moving and now it's lying there in the warmth. Probably asleep. I've been waiting for you.' He raised his eyes and looked at me.

'How long ago?'

'Hours,' he whispered. 'Hours and bloody hours and hours. I can't keep still much longer. I've been wanting to cough.'

There was not much doubt about the truth of Harry's story. As a matter of fact, it wasn't a surprising thing for a krait to do. They hang around people's houses and they go for the warm places. The surprising thing was that Harry hadn't been bitten. The bite is quite deadly, except sometimes when you catch it at once and they kill a fair number of people each year in Bengal, mostly in the villages.

'All right, Harry,' I said, and now I was whispering too. 'Don't move and don't talk any more unless you have to. You know it won't bite unless it's frightened. We'll fix it in no time.'

I went softly out of the room in my stocking feet and fetched a small sharp knife from the kitchen. I put it in my trouser pocket ready to use instantly in case something went wrong while we were still thinking out a plan. If Harry coughed or moved or did something to frighten the krait and got bitten, I was going to be ready to cut the bitten place and try to suck the venom out. I came back to the bedroom and Harry was still lying there very quiet and sweating all over his face. His eyes followed me as I moved across the room to his bed and I could see he was wondering what I'd been up to. I stood beside him, trying to think of the best thing to do.

'Harry,' I said, and now when I spoke I put my mouth almost on his ear so I wouldn't have to raise my voice above the softest whisper, 'I think the best thing to do is for me to draw the sheet back very, very gently. Then we could have a look first. I think I could do that without disturbing it.'

'Don't be a damn fool.' There was no expression in his voice. He spoke each word too slowly, too carefully, and too softly for that. The expression was in the eyes and around the corners of the mouth.

'Why not?'

'The light would frighten him. It's dark under there now.'

'Then how about whipping the sheet back quick and brushing it off before it has time to strike?'

'Why don't you get a doctor?' Harry said. The way he looked at me told me I should have thought of that myself in the first place.

'A doctor. Of course. That's it. I'll get Ganderbai.'

I tiptoed out to the hall, looked up Ganderbai's number in the book, lifted the phone and told the operator to hurry.

'Dr Ganderbai,' I said. 'This is Timber Woods.'

'Hello, Mr Woods. You not in bed yet?'

'Look, could you come round at once? And bring serum – for a krait bite.'

'Who's been bitten?' The question came so sharply it was like a small explosion in my ear.

'No one. No one yet. But Harry Pope's in bed and he's got one lying on his stomach – asleep under the sheet on his stomach.'

For about three seconds there was silence on the line. Then speaking slowly, not like an explosion now but slowly, precisely, Ganderbai said, 'Tell him to keep quite still. He is not to move or to talk. Do you understand?'

'Of course.'

'I'll come at once!' He rang off and I went back to the bedroom. Harry's eyes watched me as I walked across to his bed.

'Ganderbai's coming. He said for you to lie still.'

'What in God's name does he think I'm doing!'

'Look, Harry, he said no talking. Absolutely no talking. Either of us.'

'Why don't you shut up then?' When he said this, one side of his mouth started twitching with rapid little downward movements that continued for a while after he finished speaking. I took out my handkerchief and very gently I wiped the sweat off his face and neck, and I could feel the slight twitching of the muscle – the one he used for smiling – as my fingers passed over it with the handkerchief.

I slipped out to the kitchen, got some ice from the icebox, rolled it up in a napkin, and began to crush it small. That business of the mouth, I didn't like that. Or the way he talked, either. I carried the ice pack back to the bedroom and laid it across Harry's forehead.

'Keep you cool.'

He screwed up his eyes and drew breath sharply

through his teeth. 'Take it away,' he whispered. 'Make me cough.' His smiling-muscle began to twitch again.

The beam of a headlamp shone through the window as Ganderbai's car swung around to the front of the bungalow. I went out to meet him, holding the ice pack with both hands.

'How is it?' Ganderbai asked, but he didn't stop to talk, he walked on past me across the balcony and through the screen doors into the hall. 'Where is he? Which room?'

He put his bag down on a chair in the hall and followed me into Harry's room. He was wearing soft-soled bedroom slippers and he walked across the floor noiselessly, delicately, like a careful cat. Harry watched him out of the sides of his eyes. When Ganderbai reached the bed he looked down at Harry and smiled, confident and reassuring, nodding his head to tell Harry it was a simple matter and he was not to worry but just to leave it to Dr Ganderbai. Then he turned and went back to the hall and I followed him.

'First thing is to try to get some serum into him,' he said, and he opened his bag and started to make preparations. 'Intravenously. But I must do it neatly. Don't want to make him flinch.'

We went into the kitchen and he sterilized a needle. He had a hypodermic syringe in one hand and a small bottle in the other and he stuck the needle through the rubber top of the bottle and began drawing a pale yellow liquid up into the syringe by pulling out the plunger. Then he handed the syringe to me.

'Hold that till I ask for it.'

He picked up the bag and together we returned to the room. Harry's eyes were bright now and wide open. Ganderbai bent over Harry and, very cautiously, like a man handling sixteenth-century lace, he rolled up the pyjama sleeve to the elbow without moving the arm. I noticed he stood well away from the bed.

He whispered, 'I'm going to give you an injection. Serum. Just a prick but try not to move. Don't tighten your stomach muscles. Let them go limp.'

Harry looked at the syringe.

Ganderbai took a piece of red rubber tubing from his bag and slid one end under and up and around Harry's biceps; then he tied the tubing tight with a knot. He sponged a small area of the bare forearm with alcohol, handed the swab to me and took the syringe from my hand. He held it up to the light, squinting at the calibrations, squinting out some of the yellow fluid. I stood still beside him, watching. Harry was watching too and sweating all over his face so it shone like it was smeared thick with face cream melting on his skin and running down on to the pillow.

I could see the blue vein on the inside of Harry's forearm, swollen now because of the tourniquet, and then I saw the needle above the vein, Ganderbai holding the syringe almost flat against the arm, sliding the needle in sideways through the skin into the blue vein, sliding it slowly but so firmly it went in smooth as into cheese. Harry looked at the ceiling and closed his eyes and opened them again, but he didn't move.

When it was finished Ganderbai leaned forward,

putting his mouth close to Harry's ear. 'Now you'll be all right even if you *are* bitten. But don't move. Please don't move. I'll be back in a moment.'

He picked up his bag and went out to the hall and I followed.

'Is he safe now?' I asked.

'No.'

'How safe is he?'

The little Indian doctor stood there in the hall rubbing his lower lip.

'It must give some protection, mustn't it?' I asked.

He turned away and walked to the screen doors that led on to the veranda. I thought he was going through them, but he stopped this side of the doors and stood looking out into the night.

'Isn't the serum very good?' I asked.

'Unfortunately not,' he answered, without turning round. 'It might save him. It might not. I am trying to think of something else to do.'

'Shall we draw the sheet back quick and brush it off before it has time to strike?'

'Never! We are not entitled to take a risk.' He spoke sharply and his voice was pitched a little higher than usual.

'We can't very well leave him lying there,' I said. 'He's getting nervous.'

'Please! Please!' he said, turning round, holding both hands up in the air. 'Not so fast, please. This is not a matter to rush into bald-headed.' He wiped his forehead with his handkerchief and stood there, frowning, nibbling his lip.

'You see,' he said at last. 'There is a way to do this. You

know what we must do – we must administer an anaesthetic to the creature where it lies.'

It was a splendid idea.

'It is not safe,' he continued, 'because a snake is cold-blooded and anaesthetic does not work so well or so quick with such animals, but it is better than any other thing to do. We could use ether . . . chloroform . . .' He was speaking slowly and trying to think the thing out while he talked.

'Which shall we use?'

'Chloroform,' he said suddenly. 'Ordinary chloroform. That is best. Now quick!' He took my arm and pulled me towards the balcony. 'Drive to my house! By the time you get there I will have waked up my boy on the telephone and he will show you my poisons cupboard. Here is the key of the cupboard. Take a bottle of chloroform. It has an orange label and the name is printed on it. I stay here in case anything happens. Be quick now, hurry! No, no, you don't need your shoes!'

I drove fast and in about fifteen minutes I was back with the bottle of chloroform. Ganderbai came out of Harry's room and met me in the hall. 'You got it?' he said. 'Good, good. I just been telling him what we are going to do. But now we must hurry. It is not easy for him in there like that all this time. I am afraid he might move.'

He went back to the bedroom and I followed, carrying the bottle carefully with both hands. Harry was lying on the bed in precisely the same position as before with the sweat pouring down his cheeks. His face was white and wet. He turned his eyes towards me and I smiled at him and nodded confidently. He continued to look at me. I raised my thumb, giving him the OK signal. He closed his eyes. Ganderbai was squatting down by the bed, and on the floor beside him was the hollow rubber tube that he had previously used as a tourniquet, and he'd got a small paper funnel fitted into one end of the tube.

He began to pull a little piece of the sheet out from under the mattress. He was working directly in line with Harry's stomach, about eighteen inches from it, and I watched his fingers as they tugged gently at the edge of the sheet. He worked so slowly it was almost impossible to discern any movement either in his fingers or in the sheet that was being pulled.

Finally he succeeded in making an opening under the sheet and he took the rubber tube and inserted one end of it in the opening so that it would slide under the sheet along the mattress towards Harry's body. I do not know how long it took him to slide that tube in a few inches. It may have been twenty minutes, it may have been forty. I never once saw the tube move. I knew it was going in because the visible part of it grew gradually shorter, but I doubted that the krait could have felt even the faintest vibration. Ganderbai himself was sweating now, large pearls of sweat standing out all over his forehead and along his upper lip. But his hands were steady and I noticed that his eyes were watching, not the tube in his hands, but the area of crumpled sheet above Harry's stomach.

Without looking up, he held out a hand to me for the chloroform. I twisted out the ground-glass stopper and put the bottle right into his hand, not letting go till I was sure he had a good hold on it. Then he jerked his head for me to come closer and he whispered, 'Tell him I'm going to soak the mattress and that it will be very cold under his body. He must be ready for that and he must not move. Tell him now.'

I bent over Harry and passed on the message.

'Why doesn't he get on with it?' Harry said.

'He's going to now, Harry. But it'll feel very cold, so be ready for it.'

'Oh God Almighty, get on, get on!' For the first time he raised his voice, and Ganderbai glanced up sharply, watched him for a few seconds, then went back to his business.

Ganderbai poured a few drops of chloroform into the paper funnel and waited while it ran down the tube. Then he poured some more. Then he waited again, and the heavy sickening smell of chloroform spread out over the room bringing with it faint unpleasant memories of white-coated nurses and white surgeons standing in a white room around a long white table. Ganderbai was pouring steadily now and I could see the heavy vapour of the chloroform swirling slowly like smoke above the paper funnel. He paused, held the bottle up to the light, poured one more funnelful and handed the bottle back to me. Slowly he drew out the rubber tube from under the sheet; then he stood up.

The strain of inserting the tube and pouring the chloroform must have been great, and I recollect that when Ganderbai turned and whispered to me, his voice was small and tired. 'We'll give it fifteen minutes. Just to be safe.'

I leaned over to tell Harry. 'We're going to give it fifteen minutes, just to be safe. But it's probably done for already.'

'Then why for God's sake don't you look and see!' Again he spoke loudly and Ganderbai sprang round, his small brown face suddenly very angry. He had almost pure-black eyes and he stared at Harry and Harry's smiling-muscle started to twitch. I took my handkerchief and wiped his wet face, trying to stroke his forehead a little for comfort as I did so.

Then we stood and waited beside the bed, Ganderbai watching Harry's face all the time in a curious intense manner. The little Indian was concentrating all his will-power on keeping Harry quiet. He never once took his eyes from the patient and although he made no sound, he seemed somehow to be shouting at him all the time, saying: Now listen, you've got to listen, you're not going to go spoiling this now, d'you hear me, and Harry lay there twitching his mouth, sweating, closing his eyes, opening them, looking at me, at the sheet, at the ceiling, at me again, but never at Ganderbai. Yet somehow Ganderbai was holding him. The smell of chloroform was oppressive and it made me feel sick, but I couldn't leave the room now. I had the feeling someone was blowing up a huge balloon and I could see it was going to burst, but I couldn't look away.

At length Ganderbai turned and nodded and I knew he was ready to proceed. 'You go over to the other side of the bed,' he said. 'We will each take one side of the sheet and draw it back together, but very slowly, please, and very quietly.'

'Keep still now, Harry,' I said and I went around to the other side of the bed and took hold of the sheet. Ganderbai stood opposite me, and together we began to draw back the sheet, lifting it up clear of Harry's body, taking it back very slowly, both of us standing well away but at the same time bending forward, trying to peer underneath it. The smell of chloroform was awful. I remember trying to hold my breath and when I couldn't do that any longer I tried to breathe shallow so the stuff wouldn't get into my lungs.

The whole of Harry's chest was visible now, or rather the striped pyjama top which covered it, and then I saw the white cord of his pyjama trousers, neatly tied in a bow. A little farther and I saw a button, a mother-of-pearl button, and that was something I had never had on my pyjamas, a fly button, let alone a mother-of-pearl one. This Harry, I thought, he is very refined. It is odd how one sometimes has frivolous thoughts at exciting moments, and I distinctly remember thinking about Harry being very refined when I saw that button.

Apart from the button there was nothing on his stomach.

We pulled the sheet back faster then, and when we had uncovered his legs and feet we let the sheet drop over the end of the bed on to the floor.

'Don't move,' Ganderbai said. 'Don't move, Mr Pope,' and he began to peer around along the side of Harry's body and under his legs.

'We must be careful,' he said. It may be anywhere. It could be up the leg of his pyjamas.'

When Ganderbai said this, Harry quickly raised his head from the pillow and looked down at his legs. It was the first time he had moved. Then suddenly he jumped up, stood on his bed and shook his legs one after the other violently in the air. At that moment we both thought he had been bitten and Ganderbai was already reaching down into his bag for a scalpel and a tourniquet when Harry ceased his caperings and stood still and looked at the mattress he was standing on and shouted, 'It's not there!'

Ganderbai straightened up and for a moment he too looked at the mattress; then he looked up at Harry. Harry was all right. He hadn't been bitten and now he wasn't going to get bitten and he wasn't going to be killed and everything was fine. But that didn't seem to make anyone feel any better.

'Mr Pope, you are of course *quite* sure you saw it in the first place?' There was a note of sarcasm in Ganderbai's voice that he would never have employed in ordinary circumstances. 'You don't think you might possibly have been dreaming, do you, Mr Pope?' The way Ganderbai was looking at Harry, I realized that the sarcasm was not seriously intended. He was only easing up a bit after the strain.

Harry stood on his bed in his striped pyjamas, glaring at Ganderbai, and the colour began to spread out over his cheeks.

'Are you telling me I'm a liar?' he shouted.

Ganderbai remained absolutely still, watching Harry. Harry took a pace forward on the bed and there was a shining look in his eyes.

'Why, you dirty little Hindu sewer rat!'

'Shut up, Harry!' I said.

'You dirty black –'

'Harry!' I called. 'Shut up, Harry!' It was terrible, the things he was saying.

Ganderbai went out of the room as though neither of us was there and I followed him and put my arm around his shoulder as he walked across the hall and out on to the balcony.

'Don't you listen to Harry,' I said. 'This thing's made him so he doesn't know what he's saying.'

We went down the steps from the balcony to the drive and across the drive in the darkness to where his old Morris car was parked. He opened the door and got in.

'You did a wonderful job,' I said. 'Thank you so very much for coming.'

'All he needs is a good holiday,' he said quietly, without looking at me, then he started the engine and drove off.

Taste

First published in *The New Yorker*
(December 1951)

There were six of us to dinner that night at Mike Schofield's house in London: Mike and his wife and daughter, my wife and I, and a man called Richard Pratt.

Richard Pratt was a famous gourmet. He was president of a small society known as the Epicures, and each month he circulated privately to its members a pamphlet on food and wines. He organized dinners where sumptuous dishes and rare wines were served. He refused to smoke for fear of harming his palate, and when discussing a wine, he had a curious, rather droll habit of referring to it as though it were a living being. 'A prudent wine,' he would say, 'rather diffident and evasive, but quite prudent.' Or, 'A good-humoured wine, benevolent and cheerful – slightly obscene, perhaps, but none the less good-humoured.'

I had been to dinner at Mike's twice before when Richard Pratt was there, and on each occasion Mike and his wife had gone out of their way to produce a special meal for the famous gourmet. And this one, clearly, was to be no exception. The moment we entered the dining-room, I could see that the table was laid for a feast. The tall candles, the yellow roses, the quantity of shining silver, the three wine glasses to each person, and above all, the faint scent of roasting meat from the kitchen brought the first warm oozings of saliva to my mouth.

As we sat down, I remembered that on both Richard Pratt's previous visits Mike had played a little betting game with him over the claret, challenging him to name its breed and its vintage. Pratt had replied that that should not be difficult provided it was one of the great years. Mike had then bet him a case of the wine in question that he could not do it. Pratt had accepted, and had won both times. Tonight I felt sure that the little game would be played over again, for Mike was quite willing to lose the bet in order to prove that his wine was good enough to be recognized, and Pratt, for his part, seemed to take a grave, restrained pleasure in displaying his knowledge.

The meal began with a plate of whitebait, fried very crisp in butter, and to go with it there was a Moselle. Mike got up and poured the wine himself, and when he sat down again, I could see that he was watching Richard Pratt. He had set the bottle in front of me so that I could read the label. It said, 'Geierslay Ohligsberg, 1945'. He leaned over and whispered to me that Geierslay was a tiny village in the Moselle, almost unknown outside Germany. He said that this wine we were drinking was something unusual, that the output of the vineyard was so small that it was almost impossible for a stranger to get any of it. He had visited Geierslay personally the previous summer in order to obtain the few dozen bottles that they had finally allowed him to have.

'I doubt anyone else in the country has any of it at the

moment,' he said. I saw him glance again at Richard Pratt. 'Great thing about Moselle,' he continued, raising his voice, 'it's the perfect wine to serve before a claret. A lot of people serve a Rhine wine instead, but that's because they don't know any better. A Rhine wine will kill a delicate claret, you know that? It's barbaric to serve a Rhine before a claret. But a Moselle – ah! – a Moselle is exactly right.'

Mike Schofield was an amiable, middle-aged man. But he was a stockbroker. To be precise, he was a jobber in the stock market, and like a number of his kind, he seemed to be somewhat embarrassed, almost ashamed, to find that he had made so much money with so slight a talent. In his heart he knew that he was not really much more than a bookmaker – an unctuous, infinitely respectable, secretly unscrupulous bookmaker – and he knew that his friends knew it, too. So he was seeking now to become a man of culture, to cultivate a literary and aesthetic taste, to collect paintings, music, books and all the rest of it. His little sermon about Rhine wine and Moselle was a part of this thing, this culture that he sought.

'A charming little wine, don't you think?' he said. He was still watching Richard Pratt. I could see him give a rapid furtive glance down the table each time he dropped his head to take a mouthful of whitebait. I could almost *feel* him waiting for the moment when Pratt would take his first sip, and look up from his glass with a smile of pleasure, of astonishment, perhaps even of wonder, and then there would be a discussion and Mike would tell him about the village of Geierslay.

But Richard Pratt did not taste his wine. He was completely engrossed in conversation with Mike's eighteen-year-old daughter, Louise. He was half turned towards her, smiling at her, telling her, so far as I could gather, some story about a chef in a Paris restaurant. As he spoke, he leaned closer and closer to her, seeming in his eagerness almost to impinge upon her, and the poor girl leaned as far as she could away from him, nodding politely, rather desperately, and looking not at his face but at the topmost button of his dinner-jacket.

We finished our fish, and the maid came around removing the plates. When she came to Pratt, she saw that he had not yet touched his food, so she hesitated, and Pratt noticed her. He waved her away, broke off his conversation and quickly began to eat, popping the little crisp brown fish quickly into his mouth with rapid jabbing movements of his fork. Then, when he had finished, he reached for his glass, and in two short swallows he tipped the wine down his throat and turned immediately to resume his conversation with Louise Schofield.

Mike saw it all. I was conscious of him sitting there, very still, containing himself, looking at his guest. His round jovial face seemed to loosen slightly and to sag, but he contained himself and was still and said nothing.

Soon the maid came forward with the second course. This was a large roast of beef. She placed it on the table in front of Mike, who stood up and carved it, cutting the slices very thin, laying them gently on the plates for the maid to take around. When he had served everyone, including himself, he put down the carving knife and leaned forward with both hands on the edge of the table.

'Now,' he said, speaking to all of us but looking at Richard Pratt. 'Now for the claret. I must go and fetch the claret, if you'll excuse me.'

'You go and fetch it, Mike?' I said. 'Where is it?'

'In my study, with the cork out – breathing.'

'Why the study?'

'Acquiring room temperature, of course. It's been there twenty-four hours.'

'But why the study?'

'It's the best place in the house. Richard helped me choose it last time he was here.'

At the sound of his name, Pratt looked around.

'That's right, isn't it?' Mike said.

'Yes,' Pratt answered, nodding gravely. 'That's right.'

'On top of the green filing cabinet in my study,' Mike said. 'That's the place we chose. A good draught-free spot in a room with an even temperature. Excuse me now, will you, while I fetch it.'

The thought of another wine to play with had restored his humour, and he hurried out the door, to return a minute later more slowly, walking softly, holding in both hands a wine basket in which a dark bottle lay. The label was out of sight, facing downwards. 'Now!' he cried as he came towards the table. 'What about this one, Richard? You'll never name this one!'

Richard Pratt turned slowly and looked up at Mike; then his eyes travelled down to the bottle nestling in its small wicker basket, and he raised his eyebrows, a slight, supercilious arching of the brows, and with it a pushing outwards of the wet lower lip, suddenly imperious and ugly.

'You'll never get it,' Mike said. 'Not in a hundred years.'

'A claret?' Richard Pratt asked, condescending.

'Of course.'

'I assume, then, that it's from one of the smaller vineyards?'

'Maybe it is. Richard. And then again, maybe it isn't.'

'But it's a good year? One of the great years?'

'Yes, I guarantee that.'

'Then it shouldn't be too difficult,' Richard Pratt said, drawling his words, looking exceedingly bored. Except that, to me, there was something strange about his drawling and his boredom: between the eyes a shadow of something evil, and in his bearing an intentness that gave me a faint sense of uneasiness as I watched him.

'This one is really rather difficult,' Mike said. 'I won't force you to bet on this one.'

'Indeed. And why not?' Again the slow arching of the brows, the cool, intent look.

'Because it's difficult.'

'That's not very complimentary to me, you know.'

'My dear man,' Mike said, 'I'll bet you with pleasure, if that's what you wish.'

'It shouldn't be too hard to name it.'

'You mean you want to bet?'

'I'm perfectly willing to bet,' Richard Pratt said.

'All right, then, we'll have the usual. A case of the wine itself.'

'You don't think I'll be able to name it, do you?'

'As a matter of fact, and with all due respect, I don't,' Mike said. He was making some effort to remain polite, but Pratt was not bothering overmuch to conceal his contempt for the whole proceeding. And yet, curiously, his next question seemed to betray a certain interest.

'You like to increase the bet?'

'No, Richard. A case is plenty.'

'Would you like to bet fifty cases?'

'That would be silly.'

Mike stood very still behind his chair at the head of the table, carefully holding the bottle in its ridiculous wicker basket. There was a trace of whiteness around his nostrils now, and his mouth was shut very tight.

Pratt was lolling back in his chair, looking up at him, the eyebrows raised, the eyes half closed, a little smile touching the corners of his lips. And again I saw, or thought I saw, something distinctly disturbing about the man's face, that shadow of intentness between the eyes, and in the eyes themselves, right in their centres where it was black, a small slow spark of shrewdness, hiding.

'So you don't want to increase the bet?'

'As far as I'm concerned, old man, I don't give a damn,' Mike said. 'I'll bet you anything you like.'

The three women and I sat quietly, watching the two men. Mike's wife was becoming annoyed; her mouth had gone sour and I felt that at any moment she was going to interrupt. Our roast beef lay before us on our plates, slowly steaming.

'So you'll bet me anything I like?'

'That's what I told you. I'll bet you anything you damn well please, if you want to make an issue out of it.'

'Even ten thousand pounds?'

'Certainly I will, if that's the way you want it.' Mike was more confident now. He knew quite well that he could call any sum Pratt cared to mention.

'So you say I can name the bet?' Pratt asked again.

'That's what I said.'

There was a pause while Pratt looked slowly around the table, first at me, then at the three women, each in turn. He appeared to be reminding us that we were witness to the offer.

'Mike!' Mrs Schofield said. 'Mike, why don't we stop this nonsense and eat our food. It's getting cold.'

'But it isn't nonsense,' Pratt told her evenly. 'We're making a little bet.'

I noticed the maid standing in the background holding a dish of vegetables, wondering whether to come forward with them or not.

'All right, then,' Pratt said. 'I'll tell you what I want you to bet.'

'Come on, then,' Mike said, rather reckless. 'I don't give a damn what it is – you're on.'

Pratt nodded, and again the little smile moved the corners of his lips, and then, quite slowly, looking at Mike all the time, he said, 'I want you to bet me the hand of your daughter in marriage.'

Louise Schofield gave a jump. 'Hey!' she cried. 'No! That's not funny! Look here, Daddy, that's not funny at all.'

'No, dear,' her mother said. 'They're only joking.'

'I'm not joking,' Richard Pratt said.

'It's ridiculous,' Mike said. He was off balance again now.

'You said you'd bet anything I liked.'

'I meant money.'

'You didn't *say* money.'

'That's what I meant.'

'Then it's a pity you didn't say it. But anyway, if you wish to go back on your offer, that's quite all right with me.'

'It's not a question of going back on my offer, old man. It's a no-bet anyway, because you can't match the stake. You yourself don't happen to have a daughter to put up against mine in case you lose. And if you had, I wouldn't want to marry her.'

'I'm glad of that, dear,' his wife said.

'I'll put up anything you like,' Pratt announced. 'My house, for example. How about my house?'

'Which one?' Mike asked, joking now.

'The country one.'

'Why not the other one as well?'

'All right then, if you wish it. Both my houses.'

At that point I saw Mike pause. He took a step forward and placed the bottle in its basket gently down on the table. He moved the salt-cellar to one side, then the pepper, and then he picked up his knife, studied the blade thoughtfully for a moment, and put it down again. His daughter, too, had seen him pause.

'Now, Daddy!' she cried. 'Don't be *absurd*! It's *too* silly for words. I refuse to be betted on like this.'

'Quite right, dear,' her mother said. 'Stop it at once, Mike, and sit down and eat your food.'

Mike ignored her. He looked over at his daughter and he smiled, a slow, fatherly, protective smile. But in his eyes, suddenly, there glimmered a little triumph. 'You know,' he said, smiling as he spoke. 'You know, Louise, we ought to think about this a bit.'

'Now, stop it, Daddy! I refuse even to listen to you! Why, I've never heard anything so ridiculous in my life!'

'No, seriously, my dear. Just wait a moment and hear what I have to say.'

'But I don't *want* to hear it.'

'Louise! Please! It's like this. Richard here has offered us a serious bet. He is the one who wants to make it, not me. And if he loses, he will have to hand over a considerable amount of property. Now, wait a minute, my dear, don't interrupt. The point is this. *He cannot possibly win.*'

'He seems to think he can.'

'Now listen to me, because I know what I'm talking about. The expert, when tasting a claret – so long as it is not one of the famous great wines like Lafite or Latour – can only get a certain way towards naming the vineyard. He can, of course, tell you the Bordeaux district from which the wine comes, whether it is from St Emilion, Pomerol, Graves, or Médoc. But then each district has several communes, little counties, and each county has many, many small vineyards. It is impossible for a man to differentiate between them all by taste and smell alone. I don't mind telling you that this one I've got here is a wine from a small vineyard that is surrounded by many other small vineyards, and he'll never get it. It's impossible.'

'You can't be sure of that,' his daughter said.

'I'm telling you I can. Though I say it myself, I understand quite a bit about this wine business, you know. And anyway, heavens alive, girl, I'm your father and you don't think I'd let you in for – for something you didn't want, do you? I'm trying to make you some money.'

'Mike!' his wife said sharply. 'Stop it now, Mike, please!'

Again he ignored her. 'If you will take this bet,' he said to his daughter, 'in ten minutes you will be the owner of two large houses.'

'But I don't want two large houses, Daddy.'

'Then sell them. Sell them back to him on the spot. I'll arrange all that for you. And then, just think of it, my dear, you'll be rich! You'll be independent for the rest of your life!'

'Oh, Daddy, I don't like it. I think it's silly.'

'So do I,' the mother said. She jerked her head briskly up and down as she spoke, like a hen. 'You ought to be ashamed of yourself, Michael, ever suggesting such a thing! Your own daughter, too!'

Mike didn't even look at her. 'Take it!' he said eagerly, staring hard at the girl. 'Take it, quick! I'll guarantee you won't lose.'

'But I don't like it, Daddy.'

'Come on, girl. Take it!'

Mike was pushing her hard. He was leaning towards her, fixing her with two hard bright eyes, and it was not easy for the daughter to resist him.

'But what if I lose?'

'I keep telling you, you can't lose. I'll guarantee it.'

'Oh, Daddy, must I?'

'I'm making you a fortune. So come on now. What do you say, Louise? All right?'

For the last time, she hesitated. Then she gave a helpless little shrug of the shoulders and said, 'Oh all right then. Just so long as you swear there's no danger of losing.'

'Good!' Mike cried. 'That's fine! Then it's a bet!'

'Yes,' Richard Pratt said, looking at the girl. 'It's a bet.'

Immediately, Mike picked up the wine, tipped the first thimbleful into his own glass, then skipped excitedly around the table filling up the others. Now everyone was watching Richard Pratt, watching his face as he reached slowly for his glass with his right hand and lifted it to his nose. The man was about fifty years old and he did not have a pleasant face. Somehow, it was all mouth – mouth and lips – the full, wet lips of the professional gourmet, the lower lip hanging downwards in the centre, a pendulous, permanently open taster's lip, shaped open to receive the rim of a glass or a morsel of food. Like a keyhole, I thought, watching it; his mouth is like a large wet keyhole.

Slowly he lifted the glass to his nose. The point of the nose entered the glass and moved over the surface of the wine, delicately sniffing. He swirled the wine gently around in the glass to receive the bouquet. His concentration was intense. He had closed his eyes, and now the whole top half of his body, the head and neck and chest, seemed to become a kind of huge sensitive smelling-machine, receiving, filtering, analysing the message from the sniffing nose.

Mike, I noticed, was lounging in his chair, apparently

unconcerned, but he was watching every move. Mrs Schofield, the wife, sat prim and upright at the other end of the table, looking straight ahead, her face tight with disapproval. The daughter, Louise, had shifted her chair away a little, and sidewise, facing the gourmet, and she, like her father, was watching closely.

For at least a minute, the smelling process continued; then, without opening his eyes or moving his head, Pratt lowered the glass to his mouth and tipped in almost half the contents. He paused, his mouth full of wine, getting the first taste; then he permitted some of it to trickle down his throat and I saw his Adam's apple move as it passed by. But most of it he retained in his mouth. And now, without swallowing again, he drew in through his lips a thin breath of air which mingled with the fumes of the wine in the mouth and passed on down into his lungs. He held the breath, blew it out through his nose, and finally began to roll the wine around under the tongue, and chewed it, actually chewed it with his teeth as though it were bread.

It was a solemn, impressive performance, and I must say he did it well.

'Um,' he said, putting down the glass, running a pink tongue over his lips. 'Um – yes. A very interesting little wine – gentle and gracious, almost feminine in the after taste.'

There was an excess of saliva in his mouth, and as he spoke he spat an occasional bright speck of it on to the table.

'Now we can start to eliminate,' he said. 'You will pardon me for doing this carefully, but there is much at stake.

Normally I would perhaps take a bit of a chance, leaping forward quickly and landing right in the middle of the vineyard of my choice. But this time – I must move cautiously this time, must I not?' He looked up at Mike and he smiled, a thick-lipped, wet-lipped smile. Mike did not smile back.

'First, then, which district in Bordeaux does this wine come from? That is not too difficult to guess. It is far too light in the body to be from either St Emilion or Graves. It is obviously a Médoc. There's no doubt about *that*.

'Now – from which commune in Médoc does it come? That also, by elimination, should not be too difficult to decide. Margaux? No. It cannot be Margaux. It has not the violent bouquet of a Margaux. Pauillac? It cannot be Pauillac, either. It is too tender, too gentle and wistful for a Pauillac. The wine of Pauillac has a character that is almost imperious in its taste. And also, to me, a Pauillac contains just a little pith, a curious, dusty, pithy flavour that the grape acquires from the soil of the district. No, no. This – this is a very gentle wine, demure and bashful in the first taste, emerging shyly but quite graciously in the second. A little arch, perhaps, in the second taste, and a little naughty also, teasing the tongue with a trace, just a trace, of tannin. Then, in the after taste, delightful – consoling and feminine, with a certain blithely generous quality that one associates only with the wines of the commune of St Julien. Unmistakably this is a St Julien.'

He leaned back in his chair, held his hands up level with his chest, and placed the fingertips carefully together. He was becoming ridiculously pompous, but I thought that some of it was deliberate, simply to mock his host. I found myself waiting rather tensely for him to go on. The girl Louise was lighting a cigarette. Pratt heard the match strike and he turned on her, flaring suddenly with real anger. 'Please!' he said. 'Please don't do that! It's a disgusting habit, to smoke at table.'

She looked up at him, still holding the burning match in one hand, the big slow eyes settling on his face, resting there a moment, moving away again, slow and contemptuous. She bent her head and blew out the match, but continued to hold the unlighted cigarette in her fingers.

'I'm sorry, my dear,' Pratt said, 'but I simply cannot have smoking at table.'

She didn't look at him again.

'Now, let me see – where were we?' he said. 'Ah, yes. This wine is from Bordeaux, from the commune of St Julien, in the district of Médoc. So far, so good. But now we come to the more difficult part – the name of the vineyard itself. For in St Julien there are many vineyards, and as our host so rightly remarked earlier on, there is often not much difference between the wine of one and the wine of another. But we shall see.'

He paused again, closing his eyes. 'I am trying to establish the "growth",' he said. 'If I can do that, it will be half the battle. Now, let me see. This wine is obviously not from a first-growth vineyard – nor even a second. It is not a great wine. The quality, the – the – what do you call it? – the radiance, the power, is lacking. But a third growth – that it could be. And yet I doubt it. We know it is a good year – our host has said so – and this is probably flattering it a little bit. I must be careful. I must be very careful here.'

He picked up his glass and took another small sip.

'Yes,' he said, sucking his lips, 'I was right. It is a fourth growth. Now I am sure of it. A fourth growth from a very good year – from a great year, in fact. And that's what made it taste for a moment like a third- or even a second-growth wine. Good! That's better! Now we are closing in! What are the fourth-growth vineyards in the commune of St Julien?'

Again he paused, took up his glass, and held the rim against that sagging pendulous lower lip of his. Then I saw the tongue shoot out, pink and narrow, the tip of it dipping into the wine, withdrawing swiftly again – a repulsive sight. When he lowered the glass, his eyes remained closed, the face concentrated, only the lips moving, sliding over each other like two pieces of wet, spongy rubber.

'There it is again!' he cried. 'Tannin in the middle taste, and the quick astringent squeeze upon the tongue. Yes, yes, of course! Now I have it! This wine comes from one of those small vineyards around Beychevelle. I remember now. The Beychevelle district, and the river and the little harbour that has silted up so the wine ships can no longer use it. Beychevelle . . . could it actually be a Beychevelle itself? No, I don't think so. Not quite. But it is somewhere very close. Château Talbot? Could it be Talbot? Yes, it could. Wait one moment.'

He sipped the wine again, and out of the side of my eye I noticed Mike Schofield and how he was leaning farther and farther forward over the table, his mouth slightly open, his small eyes fixed upon Richard Pratt.

'No. I was wrong. It was not a Talbot. A Talbot comes

forward to you just a little quicker than this one; the fruit is nearer to the surface. If it is a '34, which I believe it is, then it couldn't be Talbot. Well, well. Let me think. It is not a Beychevelle and it is not a Talbot, and yet – yet it is so close to both of them, so close, that the vineyard must be almost in between. Now, which could that be?'

He hesitated, and we waited, watching his face. Everyone, even Mike's wife, was watching him now. I heard the maid put down the dish of vegetables on the sideboard behind me, gently, so as not to disturb the silence.

'Ah!' he cried. 'I have it! Yes, I think I have it!'

For the last time, he sipped the wine. Then, still holding the glass up near his mouth, he turned to Mike and he smiled, a slow, silky smile, and he said, 'You know what this is? This is the little Château Branaire-Ducru.'

Mike sat tight, not moving.

'And the year, 1934.'

We all looked at Mike, waiting for him to turn the bottle round in its basket and show the label.

'Is that your final answer?' Mike said.

'Yes, I think so.'

'Well, is it or isn't it?'

'Yes, it is.'

'What was the name again?'

'Château Branaire-Ducru. Pretty little vineyard. Lovely old château. Know it quite well. Can't think why I didn't recognize it at once.'

'Come on, Daddy,' the girl said. 'Turn it round and let's have a peek. I want my two houses.'

'Just a minute,' Mike said. 'Wait just a minute.' He was

sitting very quiet, bewildered-looking, and his face was becoming puffy and pale, as though all the force was draining slowly out of him.

'Michael!' his wife called sharply from the other end of the table. 'What's the matter?'

'Keep out of this, Margaret, will you, please?'

Richard Pratt was looking at Mike, smiling with his mouth, his eyes small and bright. Mike was not looking at anyone.

'Daddy!' the daughter cried, agonized. 'But, Daddy, you don't mean to say he's guessed it right!'

'Now, stop worrying, my dear,' Mike said. 'There's nothing to worry about.'

I think it was more to get away from his family than anything else that Mike then turned to Richard Pratt and said, 'I'll tell you what, Richard. I think you and I better slip off into the next room and have a little chat?'

'I don't want a little chat,' Pratt said. 'All I want is to see the label on that bottle.' He knew he was a winner now; he had the bearing, the quiet arrogance of a winner, and I could see that he was prepared to become thoroughly nasty if there was any trouble. 'What are you waiting for?' he said to Mike. 'Go and turn it round.'

Then this happened: the maid, the tiny, erect figure of the maid in her white and black uniform, was standing beside Richard Pratt, holding something out in her hand. 'I believe these are yours, sir,' she said.

Pratt glanced around, saw the pair of thin horn-rimmed spectacles that she held out to him, and for a moment he hesitated. 'Are they? Perhaps they are. I don't know.'

'Yes, sir, they're yours.' The maid was an elderly woman – nearer seventy than sixty – a faithful family retainer of many years' standing. She put the spectacles down on the table beside him.

Without thanking her, Pratt took them up and slipped them into his top pocket, behind the white handkerchief.

But the maid didn't go away. She remained standing beside and slightly behind Richard Pratt, and there was something so unusual in her manner and in the way she stood there, small, motionless and erect, that I for one found myself watching her with a sudden apprehension. Her old grey face had a frosty, determined look, the lips were compressed, the little chin was out and the hands were clasped together tight before her. The curious cap on her head and the flash of white down the front of her uniform made her seem like some tiny, ruffled, white-breasted bird.

'You left them in Mr Schofield's study,' she said. Her voice was unnaturally, deliberately polite. 'On top of the green filing cabinet in his study, sir, when you happened to go in there by yourself before dinner.'

It took a few moments for the full meaning of her words to penetrate, and in the silence that followed I became aware of Mike and how he was slowly drawing himself up in his chair, and the colour coming to his face, and the eyes opening wide, and the curl of the mouth, and the dangerous little patch of whiteness beginning to spread around the area of the nostrils.

'Now, Michael!' his wife said. 'Keep calm now, Michael, dear! Keep calm!'

Dip in the Pool

First published in *The New Yorker*
(19 January 1952)

On the morning of the third day, the sea calmed. Even the most delicate passengers – those who had not been seen around the ship since sailing time – emerged from their cabins and crept up on to the sun deck, where the deck steward gave them chairs and tucked rugs around their legs and left them lying in rows, their faces upturned to the pale, almost heatless January sun.

It had been moderately rough the first two days, and this sudden calm and the sense of comfort that it brought created a more genial atmosphere over the whole ship. By the time evening came, the passengers, with twelve hours of good weather behind them, were beginning to feel confident, and at eight o'clock that night the main dining-room was filled with people eating and drinking with the assured, complacent air of seasoned sailors.

The meal was not half over when the passengers became aware, by a slight friction between their bodies and the seats of their chairs, that the big ship had actually started rolling again. It was very gentle at first, just a slow, lazy leaning to one side, then to the other, but it was enough to cause a subtle, immediate change of mood over the whole room. A few of the passengers glanced up from their food, hesitating, waiting, almost listening for the next roll, smiling nervously, little secret glimmers of apprehension in their eyes. Some were completely unruffled, some were openly smug, a number of the smug ones making jokes about food and weather in order to torture the few who were beginning to suffer. The movement of the ship then became rapidly more and more violent, and only five or six minutes after the first roll had been noticed, she was swinging heavily from side to side, the passengers bracing themselves in their chairs, leaning against the pull as in a car cornering.

At last the really bad roll came, and Mr William Botibol, sitting at the purser's table, saw his plate of poached turbot with hollandaise sauce sliding suddenly away from under his fork. There was a flutter of excitement, everybody reaching for plates and wine glasses. Mrs Renshaw, seated at the purser's right, gave a little scream and clutched that gentleman's arm.

'Going to be a dirty night,' the purser said, looking at Mrs Renshaw. 'I think it's blowing up a very dirty night.' There was just the faintest suggestion of relish in the way he said it.

A steward came hurrying up and sprinkled water on the tablecloth between the plates. The excitement subsided. Most of the passengers continued with their meal. A small number, including Mrs Renshaw, got carefully to their feet and threaded their ways with a kind of concealed haste between the tables and through the doorway.

'Well,' the purser said, 'there she goes.' He glanced around with approval at the remainder of his flock, who were sitting quiet, looking complacent, their faces reflecting openly that extraordinary pride that travellers seem to take in being recognized as 'good sailors'.

When the eating was finished and the coffee had been served, Mr Botibol, who had been unusually grave and thoughtful since the rolling started, suddenly stood up and carried his cup of coffee around to Mrs Renshaw's vacant place, next to the purser. He seated himself in her chair, then immediately leaned over and began to whisper urgently in the purser's ear. 'Excuse me,' he said, 'but could you tell me something, please?'

The purser, small and fat and red, bent forward to listen. 'What's the trouble. Mr Botibol?'

'What I want to know is this.' The man's face was anxious and the purser was watching it. 'What I want to know is will the captain already have made his estimate on the day's run – you know, for the auction pool? I mean, before it began to get rough like this?'

The purser, who had prepared himself to receive a personal confidence, smiled and leaned back in his seat to relax his full belly. 'I should say so – yes,' he answered. He didn't bother to whisper his reply, although automatically he lowered his voice, as one does when answering a whisperer.

'About how long ago do you think he did it?'

'Some time this afternoon. He usually does it in the afternoon.'

'About what time?'

'Oh, I don't know. Around four o'clock, I should guess.'

'Now tell me another thing. How does the captain

decide which number it shall be? Does he take a lot of trouble over that?'

The purser looked at the anxious frowning face of Mr Botibol and he smiled, knowing quite well what the man was driving at. 'Well, you see, the captain has a little conference with the navigating officer, and they study the weather and a lot of other things, and then they make their estimate.'

Mr Botibol nodded, pondering this answer for a moment. Then he said, 'Do you think the captain knew there was bad weather coming today?'

'I couldn't tell you,' the purser replied. He was looking into the small black eyes of the other man, seeing the two single little sparks of excitement dancing in their centres. 'I really couldn't tell you, Mr Botibol. I wouldn't know.'

'If this gets any worse it might be worth buying some of the low numbers. What do you think?' The whispering was more urgent, more anxious now.

'Perhaps it will,' the purser said. 'I doubt the old man allowed for a really rough night. It was pretty calm this afternoon when he made his estimate.'

The others at the table had become silent and were trying to hear, watching the purser with that intent, half-cocked, listening look that you can see also at the race track when they are trying to overhear a trainer talking about his chance: the slightly open lips, the upstretched eyebrows, the head forward and cocked a little to one side – that desperately straining, half-hypnotized, listening look that comes to all of them when they are hearing something straight from the horse's mouth.

'Now suppose *you* were allowed to buy a number, which one would *you* choose today?' Mr Botibol whispered.

'I don't know what the range is yet,' the purser patiently answered. 'They don't announce the range till the auction starts after dinner. And I'm really not very good at it anyway. I'm only the purser, you know.'

At that point Mr Botibol stood up. 'Excuse me, all,' he said, and he walked carefully away over the swaying floor between the other tables, and twice he had to catch hold of the back of a chair to steady himself against the ship's roll.

'The sun deck, please,' he said to the elevator man.

The wind caught him full in the face as he stepped out on to the open deck. He staggered and grabbed hold of the rail and held on tight with both hands, and he stood there looking out over the darkening sea, where the great waves were welling up high and white horses were riding against the wind with plumes of spray behind them as they went.

'Pretty bad out there, wasn't it, sir?' the elevator man said on the way down.

Mr Botibol was combing his hair back into place with a small red comb. 'Do you think we've slackened speed at all on account of the weather?' he asked.

'Oh my word yes, sir. We slackened off considerable since this started. You got to slacken off speed in weather like this or you'll be throwing the passengers all over the ship.'

Down in the smoking-room people were already gathering for the auction. They were grouping themselves politely around the various tables, the men a little stiff in their dinner-jackets, a little pink and overshaved and stiff beside their cool, white-armed women. Mr Botibol took a chair close to the auctioneer's table. He crossed his legs, folded his arms and settled himself in his seat with the rather desperate air of a man who has made a tremendous decision and refuses to be frightened.

The pool, he was telling himself, would probably be around seven thousand dollars. That was almost exactly what it had been the last two days with the numbers selling for between three and four hundred apiece. It being a British ship, they did it in pounds, but he liked to do his thinking in his own currency. Seven thousand dollars was plenty of money. My goodness yes! And what he would do, he would get them to pay him in hundred-dollar bills and he would take it ashore in the inside pocket of his jacket. No problem there. And right away, yes right away, he would buy a Lincoln convertible. He would pick it up on the way from the ship and drive it home just for the pleasure of seeing Ethel's face when she came out the front door and looked at it. Wouldn't that be something, to see Ethel's face when he glided up to the door in a brand-new pale-green Lincoln convertible! Hello, Ethel honey, he would say, speaking very casual. I just thought I'd get you a little present. I saw it in the window as I went by, so I thought of you and how you were always wanting one. You like it, honey? he would say. You like the colour? And then he would watch her face.

The auctioneer was standing up behind his table now. 'Ladies and gentlemen!' he shouted. 'The captain has estimated the day's run, ending midday tomorrow, at five hundred and fifteen miles. As usual we will take the ten numbers on either side of it to make up the range. That makes it five hundred and five to five hundred and twenty-five. And of course for those who think the true figure will be still farther away, there'll be "low field" and "high field" sold separately as well. Now, we'll draw the first number out of the hat . . . here we are . . . five hundred and twelve?'

The room became quiet. The people sat still in their chairs, all eyes watching the auctioneer. There was a certain tension in the air, and as the bids got higher, the tension grew. This wasn't a game or a joke; you could be sure of that by the way one man would look across at another who had raised his bid – smiling perhaps, but only the lips smiling, the eyes bright and absolutely cold.

Number five hundred and twelve was knocked down for one hundred and ten pounds. The next three or four numbers fetched roughly the same amount.

The ship was rolling heavily, and each time she went over, the wooden panelling on the walls creaked as if it were going to split. The passengers held on to the arms of their chairs, concentrating upon the auction.

'Low field!' the auctioneer called out. 'The next number is low field.'

Mr Botibol sat up very straight and tense. He would wait, he had decided, until the others had finished bidding, then he would jump in and make the last bid. He had figured that there must be at least five hundred dollars in his account at the bank at home, probably nearer six. That was about two hundred pounds – over two hundred. This ticket wouldn't fetch more than that.

'As you all know,' the auctioneer was saying, 'low field covers every number *below* the smallest number in the range, in this case every number below five hundred and five. So, if you think this ship is going to cover less than five hundred and five miles in the twenty-four hours ending at noon tomorrow, you better get in and buy this number. So what am I bid?'

It went clear up to one hundred and thirty pounds. Others besides Mr Botibol seemed to have noticed that the weather was rough. One hundred and forty . . . fifty . . . There it stopped. The auctioneer raised his hammer.

'Going at one hundred and fifty . . .'

'Sixty!' Mr Botibol called, and every face in the room turned and looked at him.

'Seventy!'

'Eighty!' Mr Botibol called.

'Ninety!'

'Two hundred!' Mr Botibol called. He wasn't stopping now – for anyone.

There was a pause.

'Any advance on two hundred pounds?'

Sit still, he told himself. Sit absolutely still and don't look up. Hold your breath. No one's going to bid you up so long as you hold your breath.

'Going for two hundred pounds . . .' The auctioneer

had a pink bald head and there were little beads of sweat sparkling on top of it. 'Going . . .' Mr Botibol held his breath. 'Going . . . Gone!' The man banged the hammer on the table. Mr Botibol wrote out a cheque and handed it to the auctioneer's assistant, then he settled back in his chair to wait for the finish. He did not want to go to bed before he knew how much there was in the pool.

They added it up after the last number had been sold and it came to twenty-one hundred-odd pounds. That was around six thousand dollars. Ninety per cent to go to the winner, ten per cent to seamen's charities. Ninety per cent of six thousand was five thousand four hundred. Well – that was enough. He could buy the Lincoln convertible and there would be something left over, too. With this gratifying thought, he went off, happy and excited, to his cabin.

When Mr Botibol awoke the next morning he lay quite still for several minutes with his eyes shut, listening for the sound of the gale, waiting for the roll of the ship. There was no sound of any gale and the ship was not rolling. He jumped up and peered out of the porthole. The sea – Oh Jesus God – was smooth as glass, the great ship was moving through it fast, obviously making up for time lost during the night. Mr Botibol turned away and sat slowly down on the edge of his bunk. A fine electricity of fear was beginning to prickle under the skin of his stomach. He hadn't a hope now. One of the higher numbers was certain to win it after this.

'Oh my God,' he said aloud. 'What shall I do?'

What, for example, would Ethel say? It was simply not possible to tell her that he had spent almost all of their two years' savings on a ticket in the ship's pool. Nor was it possible to keep the matter secret. To do that he would have to tell her to stop drawing cheques. And what about the monthly instalments on the television set and the Encyclopaedia Britannica? Already he could see the anger and contempt in the woman's eyes, the blue becoming grey and the eyes themselves narrowing as they always did when there was anger in them.

'Oh my God. What *shall* I do?'

There was no point in pretending that he had the slightest chance now – not unless the goddam ship started to go backwards. They'd have to put her in reverse and go full speed astern and keep right on going if he was to have any chance of winning it now. Well, maybe he should ask the captain to do just that. Offer him ten per cent of the profits. Offer him more if he wanted it. Mr Botibol started to giggle. Then very suddenly he stopped, his eyes and mouth both opening wide in a kind of shocked surprise. For it was at this moment that the idea came. It hit him hard and quick, and he jumped up from his bed, terribly excited, ran over to the porthole and looked out again. Well, he thought, why not? Why ever not? The sea was calm and he wouldn't have any trouble keeping afloat until they picked him up. He had a vague feeling that someone had done this thing before, but that didn't prevent him from doing it again. The ship would have to stop and lower a boat, and the boat would have to go back maybe half a mile to get him, and then it would have to return to the ship and be hoisted back on board. It would take at least an hour, the whole thing. An hour was about thirty miles. It would knock thirty miles off the day's run. That would do it. 'Low field' would be sure to win it then. Just so long as he made certain someone saw him falling over; but that would be simple to arrange. And he'd better wear light clothes, something easy to swim in. Sports clothes, that was it. He would dress as though he were going up to play some deck tennis – just a shirt and a pair of shorts and tennis shoes. And leave his watch behind. What was the time? Nine fifteen. The sooner the better, then. Do it now and get it over with. Have to do it soon, because the time limit was midday.

Mr Botibol was both frightened and excited when he stepped out on to the sun deck in his sports clothes. His small body was wide at the hips, tapering upward to extremely narrow sloping shoulders, so that it resembled, in shape at any rate, a bollard. His white skinny legs were covered with black hairs, and he came cautiously out on deck, treading softly in his tennis shoes. Nervously he looked around him. There was only one other person in sight, an elderly woman with very thick ankles and immense buttocks, who was leaning over the rail staring at the sea. She was wearing a coat of Persian lamb and the collar was turned up so Mr Botibol couldn't see her face.

He stood still, examining her carefully from a distance. Yes, he told himself, she would probably do. She would probably give the alarm just as quickly as anyone else. But wait one minute, take your time, William Botibol, take your time. Remember what you told yourself a few minutes ago in the cabin when you were changing? You remember that?

The thought of leaping off a ship into the ocean a thousand miles from the nearest land had made Mr Botibol – a cautious man at the best of times – unusually advertent. He was by no means satisfied yet that this woman he saw before him was *absolutely certain* to give the alarm when he made his jump. In his opinion there were two possible reasons why she might fail him. Firstly, she might be deaf and blind. It was not very probable, but on the other hand it *might* be so, and why take a chance? All he had to do was check it by talking to her for a moment beforehand. Secondly – and this will demonstrate how suspicious the mind of a man can become when it is working through self-preservation and fear – secondly, it had occurred to him that the woman might herself be the owner of one of the high numbers in the pool and as such would have a sound financial reason for not wishing to stop the ship. Mr Botibol recalled that people had killed their fellows for far less than six thousand dollars. It was happening every day in the newspapers. So why take a chance on that either? Check on it first. Be sure of your facts. Find out about it by a little polite conversation. Then, provided that the woman appeared also to be a pleasant, kindly human being, the thing was a cinch and he could leap overboard with a light heart.

Mr Botibol advanced casually towards the woman and took up a position beside her, leaning on the rail. 'Hullo,' he said pleasantly.

She turned and smiled at him, a surprisingly lovely, almost a beautiful smile, although the face itself was very plain. 'Hullo,' she answered him.

Check, Mr Botibol told himself, on the first question. She is neither blind nor deaf. 'Tell me,' he said, coming straight to the point, 'what did you think of the auction last night?'

'Auction?' she asked, frowning. 'Auction? What auction?'

'You know, that silly old thing they have in the lounge after dinner, selling numbers on the ship's daily run. I just wondered what you thought about it.'

She shook her head, and again she smiled, a sweet and pleasant smile that had in it perhaps the trace of an apology. 'I'm very lazy,' she said. 'I always go to bed early. I have my dinner in bed. It's so restful to have dinner in bed.'

Mr Botibol smiled back at her and began to edge away. 'Got to go and get my exercise now,' he said. 'Never miss my exercise in the morning. It was nice seeing you. Very nice seeing you . . .' He retreated about ten paces, and the woman let him go without looking around.

Everything was now in order. The sea was calm, he was lightly dressed for swimming, there were almost certainly no man-eating sharks in this part of the Atlantic, and there was this pleasant kindly old woman to give the alarm. It was a question now only of whether the ship would be delayed long enough to swing the balance in his favour. Almost certainly it would. In any event, he could do a little to help in that direction himself. He could make a few difficulties about getting hauled up into the lifeboat. Swim around a bit, back away from them surreptitiously as they tried to come up close to fish him out. Every minute, every second gained would help him win. He began to move forward again to the rail, but now a new fear assailed him. Would he get caught in the propeller? He had heard about that happening to persons falling off the sides of big ships. But then, he wasn't going to fall, he was going to jump, and that was a very different thing. Provided he jumped out far enough he would be sure to clear the propeller.

Mr Botibol advanced slowly to a position at the rail about twenty yards away from the woman. She wasn't looking at him now. So much the better. He didn't want her watching him as he jumped off. So long as no one was watching he would be able to say afterwards that he had slipped and fallen by accident. He peered over the side of the ship. It was a long, long drop. Come to think of it now, he might easily hurt himself badly if he hit the water flat. Wasn't there someone who once split his stomach open that way, doing a belly flop from a high dive? He must jump straight and land feet first. Go in like a knife. Yes, sir. The water seemed cold and deep and grey and it made him shiver to look at it. But it was now or never. Be a man, William Botibol, be a man. All right then . . . now . . . here goes . . .

He climbed up on to the wide wooden toprail, stood there poised, balancing for three terrifying seconds, then he leaped – he leaped up and out as far as he could go and at the same time he shouted, '*Help!*'

'*Help! Help!*' he shouted as he fell. Then he hit the water and went under.

When the first shout for help sounded, the woman who was leaning on the rail started up and gave a little jump of surprise. She looked around quickly and saw sailing past her through the air this small man dressed in white shorts and tennis shoes, spread-eagled and shouting as he went. For a moment she looked as though she weren't quite sure what she ought to do: throw a life belt, run away and give the alarm, or simply turn and yell. She drew back a pace from the rail and swung half round facing up to the bridge, and for this brief moment she remained motionless, tense, undecided. Then almost at once she seemed to relax, and she leaned forward far over the rail, staring at the water, where it was turbulent in the ship's wake. Soon a tiny round black head appeared in the foam, an arm was raised about it, once, twice, vigorously waving, and a small faraway voice was heard calling something that was difficult to understand. The woman leaned still farther over the rail, trying to keep the little bobbing black speck in sight, but soon, so very soon, it was such a long way away that she couldn't even be sure it was there at all.

After a while another woman came out on deck. This one was bony and angular, and she wore horn-rimmed spectacles. She spotted the first woman and walked over to her, treading the deck in the deliberate, military fashion of all spinsters.

'So *there* you are,' she said.

The woman with the fat ankles turned and looked at her, but said nothing.

'I've been searching for you,' the bony one continued. 'Searching all over.'

'It's very odd,' the woman with the fat ankles said. 'A man dived overboard just now, with his clothes on.'

'Nonsense!'

'Oh yes. He said he wanted to get some exercise and he dived in and didn't even bother to take his clothes off.'

'You better come down now,' the bony woman said. Her mouth had suddenly become firm, her whole face sharp and alert, and she spoke less kindly than before. 'And don't you ever go wandering about on deck alone like this again. You know quite well you're meant to wait for me.'

'Yes, Maggie,' the woman with the fat ankles answered, and again she smiled, a tender, trusting smile, and she took the hand of the other one and allowed herself to be led away across the deck.

'Such a nice man,' she said. 'He waved to me.'

Skin

First published in *The New Yorker* (17 May 1952)

That year – 1946 – winter was a long time going. Although it was April, a freezing wind blew through the streets of the city, and overhead the snow clouds moved across the sky.

The old man who was called Drioli shuffled painfully along the sidewalk of the Rue de Rivoli. He was cold and miserable, huddled up like a hedgehog in a filthy black coat, only his eyes and the top of his head visible above the turned-up collar.

The door of a café opened and the faint whiff of roasting chicken brought a pain of yearning to the top of his stomach. He moved on, glancing without any interest at the things in the shop windows – perfume, silk ties and shirts, diamonds, porcelain, antique furniture, finely bound books. Then a picture gallery. He had always liked picture galleries. This one had a single canvas on display in the window. He stopped to look at it. He turned to go on. He checked, looked back; and now, suddenly, there came to him a slight uneasiness, a movement of the memory, a distant recollection of something, somewhere, he had seen before. He looked again. It was a landscape, a clump of trees leaning madly over to one side as if blown by a tremendous wind, the sky swirling and twisting all around.

Attached to the frame there was a little plaque, and on this it said: CHAÏM SOUTINE (1894–1943).

Drioli stared at the picture, wondering vaguely what there was about it that seemed familiar. Crazy painting, he thought. Very strange and crazy – but I like it . . . Chaïm Soutine . . . Soutine . . . 'By God!' he cried suddenly. 'My little Kalmuck, that's who it is! My little Kalmuck with a picture in the finest shop in Paris! Just imagine that!'

The old man pressed his face closer to the window. He could remember the boy – yes, quite clearly he could remember him. But when? When? The rest of it was not so easy to recollect. It was so long ago. How long? Twenty – no, more like thirty years, wasn't it? Wait a minute. Yes – it was the year before the war, the first war, 1913. That was it. And this Soutine, this ugly little Kalmuck, a sullen brooding boy whom he had liked – almost loved – for no reason at all that he could think of except that he could paint.

And how he could paint! It was coming back more clearly now – the street, the line of refuse cans along the length of it, the rotten smell, the brown cats walking delicately over the refuse, and then the women, moist fat women sitting on the doorsteps with their feet upon the cobblestones of the street. Which street? Where was it the boy had lived?

The Cité Falguière, that was it! The old man nodded his head several times, pleased to have remembered the name. Then there was the studio with the single chair in it, and the filthy red couch that the boy had used for sleeping; the drunken parties, the cheap white wine, the furious quarrels, and always, always the bitter sullen face of the boy brooding over his work.

It was odd, Drioli thought, how easily it all came back to him now, how each single small remembered fact seemed instantly to remind him of another.

There was that nonsense with the tattoo, for instance. Now, *that* was a mad thing if ever there was one. How had it started? Ah, yes – he had got rich one day, that was it, and he had bought lots of wine. He could see himself now as he entered the studio with the parcel of bottles under his arm – the boy sitting before the easel, and his (Drioli's) own wife standing in the centre of the room, posing for her picture.

'Tonight we shall celebrate,' he said. 'We shall have a little celebration, us three.'

'What is it that we celebrate?' the boy asked without looking up. 'Is it that you have decided to divorce your wife so she can marry me?'

'No,' Drioli said. 'We celebrate because today I have made a great sum of money with my work.'

'And I have made nothing. We can celebrate that also.'

'If you like.' Drioli was standing by the table unwrapping the parcel. He felt tired and he wanted to get at the wine. Nine clients in one day was all very nice, but it could play hell with a man's eyes. He had never done as many as nine before. Nine boozy soldiers – and the remarkable thing was that no fewer than seven of them had been able to pay in cash. This had made him extremely rich. But the work was terrible on the eyes. Drioli's eyes were half closed from fatigue, the whites streaked with little connecting lines of red; and about an inch behind each eyeball there was a small concentration of pain. But it was evening now and he was wealthy as a pig, and in the parcel there were three bottles – one for his wife, one for his friend and one for him. He had found the corkscrew and was drawing the corks from the bottles, each making a small plop as it came out.

The boy put down his brush. 'Oh Christ,' he said. 'How can one work with all this going on?'

The girl came across the room to look at the painting. Drioli came over also, holding a bottle in one hand, a glass in the other.

'No!' the boy shouted, blazing up suddenly. 'Please – no!' He snatched the canvas from the easel and stood it against the wall. But Drioli had seen it.

'I like it.'

'It's terrible.'

'It's marvellous. Like all the others that you do, it's marvellous. I love them all.'

'The trouble is,' the boy said, scowling, 'that in themselves they are not nourishing. I cannot eat them.'

'But still they are marvellous.' Drioli handed him a tumblerful of the pale-yellow wine. 'Drink it,' he said. 'It will make you happy.'

Never, he thought, had he known a more unhappy person, or one with a gloomier face. He had spotted him in a café some seven months before, drinking alone, and because he had looked like a Russian or some sort of an Asiatic, Drioli had sat down at his table and talked.

'You are a Russian?'

'Yes.'

'Where from?'

'Minsk.'

Drioli had jumped up and embraced him, crying that he too had been born in that city.

'It wasn't actually Minsk,' the boy had said. 'But quite near.'

'Where?'

'Smilovichi, about twelve miles away.'

'Smilovichi!' Drioli had shouted, embracing him again. 'I walked there several times when I was a boy.' Then he had sat down again, staring affectionately at the other's face. 'You know,' he had said, 'you don't look like a western Russian. You're like a Tartar, or a Kalmuck. You look exactly like a Kalmuck.'

Now, standing in the studio, Drioli looked again at the boy as he took the glass of wine and tipped it down his throat in one swallow. Yes, he did have a face like a Kalmuck – very broad and high-cheeked, with a wide coarse nose. This broadness of the cheeks was accentuated by the ears, which stood out sharply from the head. And then he had the narrow eyes, the black hair, the thick sullen mouth of a Kalmuck; but the hands – the hands were always a surprise, so small and white like a lady's, with tiny thin fingers.

'Give me some more,' the boy said. 'If we are to celebrate, then let us do it properly.'

Drioli distributed the wine and sat himself on a chair.

The boy sat on the old couch with Drioli's wife. The three bottles were placed on the floor between them.

'Tonight we shall drink as much as we possibly can,' Drioli said. 'I am exceptionally rich. I think perhaps I should go out now and buy some more bottles. How many shall I get?'

'Six more,' the boy said. 'Two for each.'

'Good. I shall go now and fetch them.'

'And I will help you.'

In the nearest café Drioli bought six bottles of white wine, and they carried them back to the studio. They placed them on the floor in two rows, and Drioli fetched the corkscrew and pulled the corks, all six of them; then they sat down again and continued to drink.

'It is only the very wealthy,' Drioli said, 'who can afford to celebrate in this manner.'

'That is true,' the boy said. 'Isn't that true, Josie?'

'Of course.'

'How do you feel, Josie?'

'Fine.'

'Will you leave Drioli and marry me?'

'No.'

'Beautiful wine,' Drioli said. 'It is a privilege to drink it.'

Slowly, methodically, they set about getting themselves drunk. The process was routine, but all the same there was a certain ceremony to be observed, and a gravity to be maintained, and a great number of things to be said, then said again – and the wine must be praised, and the slowness was important too, so that there would be time to savour the three delicious stages of transition, especially (for Drioli) the one when he began to float and his feet did not really belong to him. That was the best period of them all – when he could look down at his feet and they were so far away that he would wonder what crazy person they might belong to and why they were lying around on the floor like that, in the distance.

After a while, he got up to switch on the light. He was surprised to see that the feet came with him when he did this, especially because he couldn't feel them touching the ground. It gave him a pleasant sensation of walking on air. Then he began wandering around the room, peeking slyly at the canvases stacked against the walls.

'Listen,' he said at length. 'I have an idea.' He came across and stood before the couch, swaying gently. 'Listen, my little Kalmuck.'

'What?'

'I have a tremendous idea. Are you listening?'

'I'm listening to Josie.'

'Listen to me, *please*. You are my friend – my ugly little Kalmuck from Minsk – and to me you are such an artist that I would like to have a picture, a lovely picture –'

'Have them all. Take all you can find, but do not interrupt me when I am talking with your wife.'

'No, no. Now listen. I mean a picture that I can have with me always . . . forever . . . wherever I go . . . whatever happens . . . but always with me . . . a picture by you.' He reached forward and shook the boy's knee. 'Now listen to me, *please*.'

'Listen to him,' the girl said.

'It is this. I want you to paint a picture on my skin, on my back. Then I want you to tattoo over what you have painted so that it will be there always.'

'You have crazy ideas.'

'I will teach you how to use the tattoo. It is easy. A child could do it.'

'I am not a child.'

'*Please* . . .'

'You are quite mad. What is it you want?' The painter looked up into the slow, dark, wine-bright eyes of the other man. 'What in heaven's name is it you want?'

'You could do it easily! You could! You could!'

'You mean with the tattoo?'

'Yes, with the tattoo! I will teach you in two minutes!'

'Impossible!'

'Are you saying I don't know what I'm talking about?'

No, the boy could not possibly be saying that because if anyone knew about the tattoo it was he – Drioli. Had he not, only last month, covered a man's whole belly with the most wonderful and delicate design composed entirely of flowers? What about the client who had had so much hair upon his chest that he had done him a picture of a grizzly bear so designed that the hair on the chest became the furry coat of the bear? Could he not draw the likeness of a lady and position it with such subtlety upon a man's arm that when the muscle of the arm was flexed the lady came to life and performed some astonishing contortions?

'All I am saying,' the boy told him, 'is that you are drunk and this is a drunken idea.'

'We could have Josie for a model. A study of Josie upon

my back. Am I not entitled to a picture of my wife upon my back?'

'Of Josie?'

'Yes.' Drioli knew he only had to mention his wife and the boy's thick brown lips would loosen and begin to quiver.

'No,' the girl said.

'Darling Josie, *please*. Take this bottle and finish it, then you will feel more generous. It is an enormous idea. Never in my life have I had such an idea before.'

'What idea?'

'That he should make a picture of you upon my back. Am I not entitled to that?'

'A picture of me?'

'A nude study,' the boy said. 'It is an agreeable idea.'

'Not nude,' the girl said.

'It is an enormous idea,' Drioli said.

'It's a damn crazy idea,' the girl said.

'It is in any event an idea,' the boy said. 'It is an idea that calls for a celebration.'

They emptied another bottle among them. Then the boy said, 'It is no good. I could not possibly manage the tattoo. Instead, I will paint this picture on your back and you will have it with you so long as you do not take a bath and wash it off. If you never take a bath again in your life then you will have it always, as long as you live.'

'No,' Drioli said.

'Yes – and on the day that you decide to take a bath I will know that you do not any longer value my picture. It will be a test of your admiration for my art.'

'I do not like the idea,' the girl said. 'His admiration for your art is so great that he would be unclean for many years. Let us have the tattoo. But not nude.'

'Then just the head,' Drioli said.

'I could not manage it.'

'It is immensely simple. I will undertake to teach you in two minutes. You will see. I shall go now and fetch the instruments. The needles and the inks. I have inks of many different colours – as many different colours as you have paints, and far more beautiful . . .'

'It is impossible.'

'I have many inks. Have I not many different colours of inks, Josie?'

'Yes.'

'You will see,' Drioli said. 'I will go now and fetch them.' He got up from his chair and walked unsteadily, but with determination, out of the room.

In half an hour Drioli was back. 'I have brought everything,' he cried, waving a brown suitcase. 'All the necessities of the tattooist are here in this bag.'

He placed the bag on the table, opened it, and laid out the electric needles and the small bottles of coloured inks. He plugged in the electric needle, then he took the instrument in his hand and pressed a switch. It made a buzzing sound and the quarter inch of needle that projected from the end of it began to vibrate swiftly up and down. He threw off his jacket and rolled up his left sleeve. 'Now look. Watch me and I will show you how easy it is. I will make a design on my arm, here.'

His forearm was already covered with blue markings,

but he selected a small clear patch of skin upon which to demonstrate.

'First, I choose my ink – let us use ordinary blue – and I dip the point of my needle in the ink . . . so . . . and I hold the needle up straight and I run it lightly over the surface of the skin . . . like this . . . and with the little motor and the electricity, the needle jumps up and down and punctures the skin and the ink goes in and there you are . . . See how easy it is . . . see how I draw a picture of a greyhound here upon my arm . . .'

The boy was intrigued. 'Now let *me* practise a little – on your arm.'

With the buzzing needle he began to draw blue lines upon Drioli's arm. 'It is simple,' he said. 'It is like drawing with pen and ink. There is no difference except that it is slower.'

'There is nothing to it. Are you ready? Shall we begin?'

'At once.'

'The model!' cried Drioli. 'Come on, Josie!' He was in a bustle of enthusiasm now, tottering around the room arranging everything, like a child preparing for some exciting game. 'Where will you have her? Where shall she stand?'

'Let her be standing there, by my dressing-table. Let her be brushing her hair. I will paint her with her hair down over her shoulders and her brushing it.'

'Tremendous. You are a genius.'

Reluctantly, the girl walked over and stood by the dressing-table, carrying her glass of wine with her.

Drioli pulled off his shirt and stepped out of his trousers. He retained only his underpants and his socks and shoes, and he stood there, swaying gently from side to side, his small body firm, white-skinned, almost hairless. 'Now,' he said, 'I am the canvas. Where will you place your canvas?'

'As always, upon the easel.'

'Don't be crazy. I am the canvas.'

'Then place yourself upon the easel. That is where you belong.'

'How can I?'

'Are you the canvas or are you not the canvas?'

'I am the canvas. Already I begin to feel like a canvas.'

'Then place yourself upon the easel. There should be no difficulty.'

'Truly, it is not possible.'

'Then sit on the chair. Sit back to front, then you can lean your drunken head against the back of it. Hurry now, for I am about to commence.'

'I am ready. I am waiting.'

'First,' the boy said, 'I shall make an ordinary painting. Then, if it pleases me, I shall tattoo over it.' With a wide brush he began to paint upon the naked skin of the man's back.

'Ayee! Ayee!' Drioli screamed. 'A monstrous centipede is marching down my spine!'

'Be still now! Be still!' The boy worked rapidly, applying the paint only in a thin blue wash so that it would not afterwards interfere with the process of tattooing. His concentration, as soon as he began to paint, was so great that it appeared somehow to supersede his drunkenness. He applied the brush strokes with quick short jabs of the arm, holding the wrist stiff, and in less than half an hour it was finished.

'All right. That's all,' he said to the girl, who immediately returned to the couch, lay down and fell asleep.

Drioli remained awake. He watched the boy take up the needle and dip it in the ink; then he felt the sharp tickling sting as it touched the skin of his back. The pain, which was unpleasant but never extreme, kept him from going to sleep. By following the track of the needle and by watching the different colours of ink that the boy was using, Drioli amused himself trying to visualize what was going on behind him. The boy worked with an astonishing intensity. He appeared to have become completely absorbed in the little machine and in the unusual effects it was able to produce.

Far into the small hours of the morning the machine buzzed and the boy worked. Drioli could remember that when the artist finally stepped back and said, 'It is finished,' there was daylight outside and the sound of people walking in the street.

'I want to see it,' Drioli said. The boy held up a mirror, at an angle, and Drioli craned his neck to look.

'Good God!' he cried. It was a startling sight. The whole of his back, from the top of the shoulders to the base of the spine, was a blaze of colour – gold and green and blue and black and scarlet. The tattoo was applied so heavily it looked almost like an impasto. The boy had followed as closely as possible the original brush strokes, filling them in solid, and it was marvellous the way he had made use of the spine and the protrusion of the shoulder blades so that they became part of the composition. What is more, he had somehow managed to achieve – even with this slow process – a certain spontaneity. The portrait was quite alive; it contained much of that twisted, tortured quality so characteristic of Soutine's other work. It was not a good likeness. It was a mood rather than a likeness, the model's face vague and tipsy, the background swirling around her head in a mass of dark-green curling strokes.

'It's tremendous!'

'I rather like it myself.' The boy stood back, examining it critically. 'You know,' he added, 'I think it's good enough for me to sign.' And taking up the buzzer again, he inscribed his name in red ink on the right-hand side, over the place where Drioli's kidney was.

The old man who was called Drioli was standing in a sort of trance, staring at the painting in the window of the picture-dealer's shop. It had been so long ago, all that – almost as though it had happened in another life.

And the boy? What had become of him? He could remember now that after returning from the war – the first war – he had missed him and had questioned Josie.

'Where is my little Kalmuck?'

'He is gone,' she had answered. 'I do not know where, but I heard it said that a dealer had taken him up and sent him away to Céret to make more paintings.'

'Perhaps he will return.'

'Perhaps he will. Who knows?'

That was the last time they had mentioned him. Shortly afterwards they had moved to Le Havre, where there were more sailors and business was better. The old man smiled as he remembered Le Havre. Those were the pleasant years, the years between the wars, with the small shop near the docks and the comfortable rooms and always enough work, with every day three, four, five sailors coming and wanting pictures on their arms. Those were truly the pleasant years.

Then had come the second war, and Josie being killed, and the Germans arriving, and that was the finish of his business. No one had wanted pictures on their arms any more after that. And by that time he was too old for any other kind of work. In desperation he had made his way back to Paris, hoping vaguely that things would be easier in the big city. But they were not.

And now, after the war was over, he possessed neither the means nor the energy to start up his small business again. It wasn't very easy for an old man to know what to do, especially when one did not like to beg. Yet how else could he keep alive?

Well, he thought, still staring at the picture. So that is my little Kalmuck. And how quickly the sight of one small object such as this can stir the memory. Up to a few moments ago he had even forgotten that he had a tattoo on his back. It had been ages since he had thought about it. He put his face closer to the window and looked into the gallery. On the walls he could see many other pictures and all seemed to be the work of the same artist. There were a great number of people strolling around. Obviously it was a special exhibition.

On a sudden impulse, Drioli turned, pushed open the door of the gallery and went in.

It was a long room with a thick wine-coloured carpet, and by God how beautiful and warm it was! There were all these people strolling about looking at the pictures, well-washed, dignified people, each of whom held a catalogue in the hand. Drioli stood just inside the door, nervously glancing around, wondering whether he dared go forward and mingle with this crowd. But before he had had time to gather his courage, he heard a voice beside him saying, 'What is it you want?'

The speaker wore a black morning coat. He was plump and short and had a very white face. It was a flabby face with so much flesh upon it that the cheeks hung down on either side of the mouth in two fleshy collops, spaniel-wise. He came up close to Drioli and said again, 'What is it you want?'

Drioli stood still.

'If you please,' the man was saying, 'take yourself out of my gallery.'

'Am I not permitted to look at the pictures?'

'I have asked you to leave.'

Drioli stood his ground. He felt suddenly, overwhelmingly outraged.

'Let us not have trouble,' the man was saying. 'Come on now, this way.' He put a fat white paw on Drioli's arm and began to push him firmly to the door.

That did it. 'Take your goddam hands off me!' Drioli shouted. His voice rang clear down the long gallery and all the heads jerked around as one – all the startled faces stared down the length of the room at the person who had made this noise. A flunkey came running over to help, and the two men tried to hustle Drioli through the door. The people stood still, watching the struggle. Their faces expressed only a mild interest, and seemed to be saying, 'It's all right. There's no danger to us. It's being taken care of.'

'I, too!' Drioli was shouting. 'I, too, have a picture by this painter! He was my friend and I have a picture which he gave me!'

'He's mad.'

'A lunatic. A raving lunatic.'

'Someone should call the police.'

With a rapid twist of the body Drioli suddenly jumped clear of the two men, and before anyone could stop him he was running down the gallery shouting. 'I'll show you! I'll show you! I'll show you!' He flung off his overcoat, then his jacket and shirt, and he turned so that his naked back was towards the people.

'There!' he cried, breathing quickly. 'You see? There it is!'

There was a sudden absolute silence in the room, each person arrested in what he was doing, standing motionless in a kind of shocked, uneasy bewilderment. They were staring at the tattooed picture. It was still there, the colours as bright as ever, but the old man's back was thinner now, the shoulder blades protruded more sharply, and the effect, though not great, was to give the picture a curiously wrinkled, squashed appearance.

Somebody said, 'My God, but it is!'

Then came the excitement and the noise of voices as the people surged forward to crowd round the old man.

'It is unmistakable!'

'His early manner, yes?'

'It is fantastic, fantastic!'

'And look, it is signed!'

'Bend your shoulders forward, my friend, so that the picture stretches out flat.'

'Old one, when was this done?'

'In 1913,' Drioli said, without turning around. 'In the autumn of 1913.'

'Who taught Soutine to tattoo?'

'I taught him.'

'And the woman?'

'She was my wife.'

The gallery owner was pushing through the crowd towards Drioli. He was calm now, deadly serious, making a smile with his mouth. 'Monsieur,' he said, 'I will buy it.' Drioli could see the loose fat upon the face vibrating as he moved his jaw. 'I said I will buy it, Monsieur.'

'How can you buy it?' Drioli asked softly.

'I will give two hundred thousand francs for it.' The dealer's eyes were small and dark, the wings of his broad nose-base were beginning to quiver.

'Don't do it!' someone murmured in the crowd. 'It is worth twenty times as much.'

Drioli opened his mouth to speak. No words came, so he shut it; then he opened it again and said slowly, 'But how can I sell it?' He lifted his hands, let them drop loosely to his sides. 'Monsieur, how can I possibly sell it?' All the sadness in the world was in his voice.

'Yes!' they were saying in the crowd. 'How can he sell it? It is a part of himself!'

'Listen,' the dealer said, coming up close. 'I will help

you. I will make you rich. Together we shall make some private arrangement over this picture, no?'

Drioli watched him with slow, apprehensive eyes. 'But how can you buy it, Monsieur? What will you do with it when you have bought it? Where will you keep it? Where will you keep it tonight? And where tomorrow?'

'Ah, where will I keep it? Yes, where will I keep it? Now, where will I keep it? Well, now . . .' The dealer stroked the bridge of his nose with a fat white finger. 'It would seem,' he said, 'that if I take the picture, I take you also. That is a disadvantage.' He paused and stroked his nose again. 'The picture itself is of no value until you are dead. How old are you, my friend?'

'Sixty-one.'

'But you are perhaps not very robust, no?' The dealer lowered the hand from his nose and looked Drioli up and down, slowly, like a farmer appraising an old horse.

'I do not like this,' Drioli said, edging away. 'Quite honestly, Monsieur, I do not like it.' He edged straight into the arms of a tall man, who put out his hands and caught him gently by the shoulders. Drioli glanced around and apologized. The man smiled down at him, patting one of the old fellow's naked shoulders reassuringly with a hand encased in a canary-coloured glove.

'Listen, my friend,' the stranger said, still smiling. 'Do you like to swim and bask yourself in the sun?'

Drioli looked up at him, rather startled.

'Do you like fine food and red wine from the great châteaux of Bordeaux?' The man was still smiling, showing strong white teeth with a flash of gold among them. He spoke in a soft coaxing manner, one gloved hand still resting on Drioli's shoulder. 'Do you like such things?'

'Well – yes,' Drioli answered, still greatly perplexed. 'Of course.'

'And the company of beautiful women?'

'Why not?'

'And a cupboard full of suits and shirts made to your own personal measurements? It would seem that you are a little lacking for clothes.'

Drioli watched this suave man, waiting for the rest of the proposition.

'Have you ever had a shoe constructed especially for your own foot?'

'No.'

'You would like that?'

'Well . . .'

'And a man who will shave you in the mornings and trim your hair?'

Drioli simply stood and gaped.

'And a plump attractive girl to manicure the nails of your fingers?'

Someone in the crowd giggled.

'And a bell beside your bed to summon a maid to bring your breakfast in the morning? Would you like these things, my friend? Do they appeal to you?'

Drioli stood still and looked at him.

'You see, I am the owner of the Hotel Bristol in Cannes. I now invite you to come down there and live as my guest for the rest of your life in luxury and comfort.' The man paused, allowing his listener time to savour this cheerful prospect.

'Your only duty – shall I call it your pleasure – will be to spend your time on my beach in bathing trunks, walking among my guests, sunning yourself, swimming, drinking cocktails. You would like that?'

There was no answer.

'Don't you see – all the guests will thus be able to observe this fascinating picture by Soutine. You will become famous, and men will say, "Look, there is the fellow with ten million francs upon his back." You like this idea, Monsieur? It pleases you?'

Drioli looked up at the tall man in the canary gloves, still wondering whether this was some sort of a joke. 'It is a comical idea,' he said slowly. 'But do you really mean it?'

'Of course I mean it.'

'Wait,' the dealer interrupted. 'See here, old one. Here is the answer to our problem. I will buy the picture, and I will arrange with a surgeon to remove the skin from your back, and then you will be able to go off on your own and enjoy the great sum of money I shall give you for it.'

'With no skin on my back?'

'No, no, please! You misunderstand. This surgeon will put a new piece of skin in the place of the old one. It is simple.'

'Could he do that?'

'There is nothing to it.'

'Impossible!' said the man with the canary gloves. 'He's too old for such a major skin-grafting operation. It would kill him. It would kill you, my friend.'

'It would kill me?'

'Naturally. You would never survive. Only the picture would come through.'

'In the name of God!' Drioli cried. He looked around aghast at the faces of the people watching him, and in the silence that followed, another man's voice, speaking quietly from the back of the group, could be heard saying, 'Perhaps, if one were to offer this old man enough money, he might consent to kill himself on the spot. Who knows?' A few people sniggered. The dealer moved his feet uneasily on the carpet.

Then the hand in the canary glove was tapping Drioli again upon the shoulder. 'Come on,' the man was saying, smiling his broad white smile. 'You and I will go and have a good dinner and we can talk about it some more while we eat. How's that? Are you hungry?'

Drioli watched him, frowning. He didn't like the man's long flexible neck, or the way he craned it forward at you when he spoke, like a snake.

'Roast duck and Chambertin,' the man was saying. He put a rich succulent accent on the words, splashing them out with his tongue. 'And perhaps a *soufflé aux marrons*, light and frothy.'

Drioli's eyes turned up towards the ceiling, his lips became loose and wet. One could see the poor old fellow beginning literally to drool at the mouth.

'How do you like your duck?' the man went on. 'Do you like it very brown and crisp outside, or shall it be . . .'

'I am coming,' Drioli said quickly. Already he had picked up his shirt and was pulling it frantically over his head. 'Wait for me, Monsieur. I am coming.' And within a minute he had disappeared out of the gallery with his new patron.

It wasn't more than a few weeks later that a picture by Soutine, of a woman's head, painted in an unusual manner, nicely framed and heavily varnished, turned up for sale in Buenos Aires. That – and the fact that there is no hotel in Cannes called Bristol – causes one to wonder a little, and to pray for the old man's health, and to hope fervently that wherever he may be at this moment, there is a plump attractive girl to manicure the nails of his fingers, and a maid to bring him his breakfast in bed in the mornings.

My Lady Love, My Dove

First published in *The New Yorker* (21 June 1952)

It has been my habit for many years to take a nap after lunch. I settle myself in a chair in the living-room with a cushion behind my head and my feet up on a small square leather stool, and I read until I drop off.

On this Friday afternoon, I was in my chair and feeling as comfortable as ever with a book in my hands – an old favourite, Doubleday and Westwood's *The Genera of Diurnal Lepidoptera* – when my wife, who has never been a silent lady, began to talk to me from the sofa opposite. 'These two people,' she said, 'what time are they coming?'

I made no answer, so she repeated the question, louder this time.

I told her politely that I didn't know.

'I don't think I like them very much,' she said. 'Especially him.'

'No, dear, all right.'

'Arthur. I said I don't think I like them very much.'

I lowered my book and looked across at her lying with her feet up on the sofa, flipping over the pages of some fashion magazine. 'We've only met them once,' I said.

'A dreadful man, really. Never stopped telling jokes, or stories, or something.'

'I'm sure you'll manage them very well, dear.'

'And she's pretty frightful, too. When do you think they'll arrive?'

Somewhere around six o'clock, I guessed.

'But don't *you* think they're awful?' she asked, pointing at me with her finger.

'Well . . .'

'They're *too* awful, they really are.'

'We can hardly put them off now, Pamela.'

'They're absolutely the end,' she said.

'Then why did you ask them?' The question slipped out before I could stop myself and I regretted it at once, for it is a rule with me never to provoke my wife if I can help it. There was a pause, and I watched her face, waiting for the answer – the big white face that to me was something so strange and fascinating there were occasions when I could hardly bring myself to look away from it. In the evenings sometimes – working on her embroidery, or painting those small intricate flower pictures – the face would tighten and glimmer with a subtle inward strength that was beautiful beyond words, and I would sit and stare at it minute after minute while pretending to read. Even now, at this moment, with that compressed acid look, the frowning forehead, the petulant curl of the nose, I had to admit that there was a majestic quality about this woman, something splendid, almost stately; and so tall she was, far taller than I – although today, in her fifty-first year, I think one would have to call her big rather than tall.

'You know very well why I asked them,' she answered sharply. 'For bridge, that's all. They play an absolutely first-class game, and for a decent stake.' She glanced up and saw me watching her. 'Well,' she said, 'that's about the way you feel too, isn't it?'

'Well, of course, I . . .'

'Don't be a fool, Arthur.'

'The only time I met them I must say they did seem quite nice.'

'So is the butcher.'

'Now Pamela, dear – please. We don't want any of that.'

'Listen,' she said, slapping down the magazine on her lap, 'you saw the sort of people they were as well as I did. A pair of stupid climbers who think they can go anywhere just because they play good bridge.'

'I'm sure you're right, dear, but what I don't honestly understand is why –'

'I keep telling you – so that for once we can get a decent game. I'm sick and tired of playing with rabbits. But I really can't see why I should have these awful people in the house.'

'Of course not, my dear, but isn't it a little late now –'

'Arthur?'

'Yes?'

'Why for God's sake do you always argue with me? You *know* you disliked them as much as I did.'

'I really don't think you need worry, Pamela. After all, they seemed quite a nice well-mannered young couple.'

'Arthur, don't be pompous.' She was looking at me hard with those wide grey eyes of hers, and to avoid them – they sometimes made me quite uncomfortable – I got up and walked over to the French windows that led into the garden.

The big sloping lawn out in front of the house was newly mown, striped with pale and dark ribbons of green. On the far side, the two laburnums were in full flower at last, the long golden chains making a blaze of colour against the darker trees beyond. The roses were out too, and the scarlet begonias, and in the long herbaceous border all my lovely hybrid lupins, columbine, delphinium, sweet-william, and the huge, pale, scented iris. One of the gardeners was coming up the drive from his lunch. I could see the roof of his cottage through the trees and beyond it to one side, the place where the drive went out through the iron gates on the Canterbury road.

My wife's house. Her garden. How beautiful it all was! How peaceful! Now, if only Pamela would try to be a little less solicitous of my welfare, less prone to coax me into doing things for my own good rather than for my own pleasure, then everything would be heaven. Mind you, I don't want to give the impression that I do not love her – I worship the very air she breathes – or that I can't manage her, or that I am not the captain of my ship. All I am trying to say is that she can be a trifle irritating at times, the way she carries on. For example, those little mannerisms of hers – I do wish she would drop them all, especially the way she has of pointing a finger at me to emphasize a phrase. You must remember that I am a man who is built rather small, and a gesture like this, when used to excess by a person like my wife, is apt to intimidate. I sometimes find it difficult to convince myself that she is not an overbearing woman.

'Arthur!' she called. 'Come here.'

'What?'

'I've just had a most marvellous idea. Come here.'

I turned and went over to where she was lying on the sofa.

'Look,' she said, 'do you want to have some fun?'

'What sort of fun?'

'With the Snapes.'

'Who are the Snapes?'

'Come on,' she said. 'Wake up. Henry and Sally Snape. Our week-end guests.'

'Well?'

'Now listen. I was lying here thinking how awful they really are . . . the way they behave . . . him with his jokes and her like a sort of love-crazed sparrow . . .' She hesitated, smiling slyly, and for some reason, I got the impression she was about to say a shocking thing. 'Well – if that's the way they behave when they're in front of us, then what on earth must they be like when they're alone together?'

'Now wait a minute, Pamela –'

'Don't be an ass, Arthur. Let's have some fun – some real fun for once – tonight.' She had half raised herself up off the sofa, her face bright with a kind of sudden recklessness, the mouth slightly open, and she was looking at me with two round grey eyes, a spark dancing slowly in each.

'Why shouldn't we?'

'What do you want to do?'

'Why, it's obvious. Can't you see?'

'No, I can't.'

'All we've got to do is put a microphone in their room.' I admit I was expecting something pretty bad, but when she said this I was so shocked I didn't know what to answer.

'That's exactly what we'll do,' she said.

'Here!' I cried. 'No. Wait a minute. You can't do that.'

'Why not?'

'That's about the nastiest trick I ever heard of. It's like – why, it's like listening at keyholes, or reading letters, only far far worse. You don't mean this seriously, do you?'

'Of course I do.'

I knew how much she disliked being contradicted but there were times when I felt it necessary to assert myself, even at considerable risk. 'Pamela,' I said, snapping the words out sharply, 'I forbid you to do it!'

She took her feet down from the sofa and sat up straight. 'What in God's name are you trying to pretend to be, Arthur? I simply don't understand you.'

'That shouldn't be too difficult.'

'Tommyrot! I've known you do lots of worse things than this before now.'

'Never!'

'Oh yes I have. What makes you suddenly think you're a so much nicer person than I am?'

'I've never done things like that.'

'All right, my boy,' she said, pointing her finger at me like a pistol. 'What about the time at the Milfords' last Christmas? Remember? You nearly laughed your head off and I had to put my hand over your mouth to stop them hearing us. What about that for one?'

'That was different,' I said. 'It wasn't our house. And they weren't our guests.'

'It doesn't make any difference at all.' She was sitting very upright, staring at me with those round grey eyes, and the chin was beginning to come up high in a peculiarly contemptuous manner. 'Don't be such a pompous hypocrite,' she said. 'What on earth's come over you?'

'I really think it's a pretty nasty thing, you know, Pamela. I honestly do.'

'But listen, Arthur. I'm a *nasty* person. And so are you – in a secret sort of way. That's why we get along together.'

'I never heard such nonsense.'

'Mind you, if you've suddenly decided to change your character completely, that's another story.'

'You've got to stop talking this way, Pamela.'

'You see,' she said, 'if you really *have* decided to reform, then what on earth am I going to do?'

'You don't know what you're saying.'

'Arthur, how could a nice person like you want to associate with a stinker?'

I sat myself down slowly in the chair opposite her, and she was watching me all the time. You understand, she was a big woman, with a big white face, and when she looked at me hard, as she was doing now, I became – how shall I say it – surrounded, almost enveloped by her, as though she were a great tub of cream and I had fallen in.

'You don't honestly want to do this microphone thing, do you?'

'But of course I do. It's time we had a bit of fun around here. Come on, Arthur. Don't be so stuffy.'

'It's not right, Pamela.'

'It's just as right' – up came the finger again – 'just as

right as when you found those letters of Mary Probert's in her purse and you read them through from beginning to end.'

'We should never have done that.'

'*We!*'

'You read them afterwards, Pamela.'

'It didn't harm anyone at all. You said so yourself at the time. And this one's no worse.'

'How would *you* like it if someone did it to *you*?'

'How could I *mind* if I didn't know it was being done? Come on, Arthur. Don't be so flabby.'

'I'll have to think about it.'

'Maybe the great radio engineer doesn't know how to connect the mike to the speaker?'

'That's the easiest part.'

'Well, go on then. Go on and do it.'

'I'll think about it and let you know later.'

'There's no time for that. They might arrive any moment.'

'Then I won't do it. I'm not going to be caught red-handed.'

'If they come before you're through, I'll simply keep them down here. No danger. What's the time, anyway?'

It was nearly three o'clock.

'They're driving down from London,' she said, 'and they certainly won't leave till after lunch. That gives you plenty of time.'

'Which room are you putting them in?'

'The big yellow room at the end of the corridor. That's not too far away, is it?'

'I suppose it could be done.'

'And by the by,' she said, 'where are you going to have the speaker?'

'I haven't said I'm going to do it yet.'

'My God!' she cried, 'I'd like to see someone try and stop you now. You ought to see your face. It's all pink and excited at the very prospect. Put the speaker in our bedroom, why not? But go on – and hurry.'

I hesitated. It was something I made a point of doing whenever she tried to order me about, instead of asking nicely. 'I don't like it, Pamela.'

She didn't say any more after that; she just sat there, absolutely still, watching me, a resigned, waiting expression on her face, as though she were in a long queue. This, I knew from experience, was a danger signal. She was like one of those bomb things with the pin pulled out, and it was only a matter of time before – bang! and she would explode. In the silence that followed, I could almost hear her ticking.

So I got up quietly and went out to the workshop and collected a mike and a hundred and fifty feet of wire. Now that I was away from her, I am ashamed to admit that I began to feel a bit of excitement myself, a tiny warm prickling sensation under the skin, near the tips of my fingers. It was nothing much, mind you – really nothing at all. Good heavens, I experience the same thing every morning of my life when I open the paper to check the closing prices on two or three of my wife's larger stockholdings. So I wasn't going to get carried away by a silly joke like this. At the same time, I couldn't help being amused.

I took the stairs two at a time and entered the yellow

room at the end of the passage. It had the clean, unlived-in appearance of all guest rooms, with its twin beds, yellow satin bedspreads, pale-yellow walls and golden-coloured curtains. I began to look around for a good place to hide the mike. This was the most important part of all, for whatever happened, it must not be discovered. I thought first of the basket of logs by the fireplace. Put it under the logs. No – not safe enough. Behind the radiator? Or on top of the wardrobe? Under the desk? None of these seemed very professional to me. All might be subject to chance inspection because of a dropped collar stud or something like that. Finally, with considerable cunning, I decided to put it inside the springing of the sofa. The sofa was against the wall, near the edge of the carpet, and my lead wire could go straight under the carpet over to the door.

I tipped up the sofa and slit the material underneath. Then I tied the microphone securely up among the springs, making sure that it faced the room. After that, I led the wire under the carpet to the door. I was calm and cautious in everything I did. Where the wire had to emerge from under the carpet and pass out of the door, I made a little groove in the wood so that it was almost invisible.

All this, of course, took time, and when I suddenly heard the crunch of wheels on the gravel of the drive outside, and then the slamming of car doors and the voices of our guests, I was still only halfway down the corridor, tacking the wire along the skirting. I stopped and straightened up, hammer in hand, and I must confess that I felt afraid. You have no idea how unnerving that noise was to me. I experienced the same sudden stomachy feeling of fright as when a bomb once dropped the other side of the village during the war, one afternoon, while I was working quietly in the library with my butterflies.

Don't worry, I told myself. Pamela will take care of these people. She won't let them come up here.

Rather frantically, I set about finishing the job, and soon I had the wire tacked all along the corridor and through into our bedroom. Here, concealment was not so important, although I still did not permit myself to get careless, because of the servants. So I laid the wire under the carpet and brought it up unobtrusively into the back of the radio. Making the final connections was an elementary technical matter and took me no time at all.

Well – I had done it. I stepped back and glanced at the little radio. Somehow, now, it looked different – no longer a silly box for making noises but an evil little creature that crouched on the table top with a part of its own body reaching out secretly into a forbidden place far away. I switched it on. It hummed faintly but made no other sound. I took my bedside clock, which had a loud tick, and carried it along to the yellow room and placed it on the floor by the sofa. When I returned, sure enough the radio creature was ticking away as loudly as if the clock were in the room – even louder.

I fetched back the clock. Then I tidied myself up in the bathroom, returned my tools to the workshop and prepared to meet the guests. But first, to compose myself, and so that I would not have to appear in front of them with the blood, as it were, still wet on my hands, I spent five minutes in the library with my collection. I concentrated on a tray of the lovely *Vanessa cardui* – the 'painted lady' – and made a few notes for a paper I was preparing entitled 'The Relation between Colour Pattern and Framework of Wings', which I intended to read at the next meeting of our society in Canterbury. In this way I soon regained my normal grave, attentive manner.

When I entered the living-room, our two guests, whose names I could never remember, were seated on the sofa. My wife was mixing drinks.

'Oh, *there* you are, Arthur,' she said. 'Where *have* you been?'

I thought this was an unnecessary remark. 'I'm so sorry,' I said to the guests as we shook hands. 'I was busy and forgot the time.'

'We all know what *you've* been doing,' the girl said, smiling wisely. 'But we'll forgive him, won't we, dearest?'

'I think we should,' the husband answered.

I had a frightful, fantastic vision of my wife telling them, amidst roars of laughter, precisely what I had been doing upstairs. She *couldn't* – she *couldn't* have done that! I looked round at her and she too was smiling as she measured out the gin.

'I'm sorry we disturbed you,' the girl said.

I decided that if this was going to be a joke then I'd better join in quickly, so I forced myself to smile with her.

'You must let us see it,' the girl continued.

'See what?'

'Your collection. Your wife says that they are absolutely beautiful.'

I lowered myself slowly into a chair and relaxed. It was

ridiculous to be so nervous and jumpy. 'Are you interested in butterflies?' I asked her.

'I'd love to see yours, Mr Beauchamp.'

The Martinis were distributed and we settled down to a couple of hours of talk and drink before dinner. It was from then on that I began to form the impression that our guests were a charming couple. My wife, coming from a titled family, is apt to be conscious of her class and breeding, and is often hasty in her judgement of strangers who are friendly towards her – particularly tall men. She is frequently right, but in this case I felt that she might be making a mistake. As a rule, I myself do not like tall men either; they are apt to be supercilious and omniscient. But Henry Snape – my wife had whispered his name – struck me as being an amiable simple young man with good manners whose main preoccupation, very properly, was Mrs Snape. He was handsome in a long-faced, horsy sort of way, with dark-brown eyes that seemed to be gentle and sympathetic. I envied him his fine mop of black hair, and caught myself wondering what lotion he used to keep it looking so healthy. He did tell us one or two jokes, but they were on a high level and no one could have objected.

'At school,' he said, 'they used to call me Scervix. Do you know why?'

'I haven't the least idea,' my wife answered.

'Because cervix is Latin for nape.'

This was rather deep and it took me a while to work out.

'What school was that, Mr Snape?' my wife asked.

'Eton,' he said, and my wife gave a quick little nod of

approval. Now she will talk to him, I thought, so I turned my attention to the other one, Sally Snape. She was an attractive girl with a bosom. Had I met her fifteen years earlier I might well have got myself into some sort of trouble. As it was, I had a pleasant enough time telling her all about my beautiful butterflies. I was observing her closely as I talked, and after a while I began to get the impression that she was not, in fact, quite so merry and smiling a girl as I had been led to believe at first. She seemed to be coiled in herself, as though with a secret she was jealously guarding. The deep-blue eyes moved too quickly about the room, never settling or resting on one thing for more than a moment; and over all her face, though so faint that they might not even have been there, those small downward lines of sorrow.

'I'm so looking forward to our game of bridge,' I said, finally changing the subject.

'Us too,' she answered. 'You know, we play almost every night, we love it so.'

'You are extremely expert, both of you. How did you get to be so good?'

'It's practice,' she said. 'That's all. Practice, practice, practice.'

'Have you played in any championships?'

'Not yet, but Henry wants very much for us to do that. It's hard work, you know, to reach that standard. Terribly hard work.' Was there not here, I wondered, a hint of resignation in her voice? Yes, that was probably it; he was pushing her too hard, making her take it too seriously, and the poor girl was tired of it all.

At eight o'clock, without changing, we moved in to dinner. The meal went well, with Henry Snape telling us some very droll stories. He also praised my Richebourg '34 in a most knowledgeable fashion, which pleased me greatly. By the time coffee came, I realized that I had grown to like these two youngsters immensely, and as a result I began to feel uncomfortable about this microphone business. It would have been all right if they had been horrid people, but to play this trick on two such charming young persons as these filled me with a strong sense of guilt. Don't misunderstand me. I was not getting cold feet. It didn't seem necessary to stop the operation. But I refused to relish the prospect openly as my wife seemed now to be doing, with covert smiles and winks and secret little noddings of the head.

Around nine thirty, feeling comfortable and well fed, we returned to the large living-room to start our bridge. We were playing for a fair stake – ten shillings a hundred – so we decided not to split families, and I partnered my wife the whole time. We all four of us took the game seriously, which is the only way to take it, and we played silently, intently, hardly speaking at all except to bid. It was not the money we played for. Heaven knows, my wife had enough of that, and so apparently did the Snapes. But among experts it is almost traditional that they play for a reasonable stake.

That night the cards were evenly divided, but for once my wife played badly, so we got the worst of it. I could see that she wasn't concentrating fully, and as we came along towards midnight she began not even to care. She kept glancing up at me with those large grey eyes of hers, the eyebrows raised, the nostrils curiously open, a little gloating smile around the corner of her mouth.

Our opponents played a fine game. Their bidding was masterly, and all through the evening they made only one mistake. That was when the girl badly overestimated her partner's hand and bid six spades. I doubled and they went three down, vulnerable, which cost them eight hundred points. It was just a momentary lapse, but I remember that Sally Snape was very put out by it, even though her husband forgave her at once, kissing her hand across the table and telling her not to worry.

Around twelve thirty my wife announced that she wanted to go to bed.

'Just one more rubber?' Henry Snape said.

'No, Mr Snape. I'm tired tonight. Arthur's tired, too. I can see it. Let's all go to bed.'

She herded us out of the room and we went upstairs, the four of us together. On the way up, there was the usual talk about breakfast and what they wanted and how they were to call the maid. 'I think you'll like your room,' my wife said. 'It has a view right across the valley, and the sun comes to you in the morning around ten o'clock.'

We were in the passage now, standing outside our own bedroom door, and I could see the wire I had put down that afternoon and how it ran along the top of the skirting down to their room. Although it was nearly the same colour as the paint, it looked very conspicuous to me. 'Sleep well,' my wife said. 'Sleep well, Mrs Snape. Good night, Mr Snape.' I followed her into our room and shut the door.

'Quick!' she cried. 'Turn it on!' My wife was always like that, frightened that she was going to miss something. She had a reputation, when she went hunting – I never go myself – of always being right up with the hounds whatever the cost to herself or her horse for fear that she might miss a kill. I could see she had no intention of missing this one.

The little radio warmed up just in time to catch the noise of their door opening and closing again.

'There!' my wife said. 'They've gone in.' She was standing in the centre of the room in her blue dress, her hands clasped before her, her head craned forward, intently listening, and the whole of the big white face seemed somehow to have gathered itself together, tight like a wineskin.

Almost at once the voice of Henry Snape came out of the radio, strong and clear. 'You're just a goddam little fool,' he was saying, and this voice was so different from the one I remembered, so harsh and unpleasant, it made me jump. 'The whole bloody evening wasted! Eight hundred points – that's eight pounds between us!'

'I got mixed up,' the girl answered. 'I won't do it again, I promise.'

'What's *this*!' my wife said. 'What's going on?' Her mouth was wide open now, the eyebrows stretched up high, and she came quickly over to the radio and leaned forward, ear to the speaker. I must say I felt rather excited myself.

'I promise, I promise I won't do it again,' the girl was saying.

'We're not taking any chances,' the man answered grimly. 'We're going to have another practice right now.'

'Oh no, please! I couldn't stand it!'

'Look,' the man said, 'all the way out here to take money off this rich bitch and you have to go and mess it up.'

My wife's turn to jump.

'The second time this week,' he went on.

'I promise I won't do it again.'

'Sit down. I'll sing them out and you answer.'

'No, Henry, *please*! Not all five hundred of them. It'll take three hours.'

'All right, then. We'll leave out the finger positions. I think you're sure of those. We'll just do the basic bids showing honour tricks.'

'Oh Henry, must we? I'm so tired.'

'It's absolutely essential you get them perfect,' he said. 'We have a game every day next week, you know that. And we've got to eat.'

'What is this?' my wife whispered. 'What on earth is it?'

'Shhh!' I said. 'Listen!'

'All right,' the man's voice was saying. 'Now we'll start from the beginning. Ready?'

'Oh Henry, *please*!' She sounded very near to tears.

'Come on, Sally. Pull yourself together.'

Then, in a quite different voice, the one we had been used to hearing in the living-room, Henry Snape said, '*One* club.' I noticed that there was a curious lilting emphasis on the word 'one', the first part of the word drawn out long.

'Ace queen of clubs,' the girl replied wearily. 'King jack of spades. No hearts, and ace jack of diamonds.'

'And how many cards to each suit? Watch my finger positions carefully.'

'You said we could miss those.'

'Well – if you're quite sure you know them?'

'Yes, I know them.'

A pause, then 'A *club*.'

'King jack of clubs,' the girl recited. 'Ace of spades. Queen jack of hearts, and ace queen of diamonds.'

Another pause, then 'I'll say *one* club.'

'Ace king of clubs . . .'

'My heavens alive!' I cried. 'It's a bidding code! They show every card in the hand!'

'Arthur, it couldn't be!'

'It's like those men who go into the audience and borrow something from you and there's a girl blindfolded on the stage and from the way he phrases the question she can tell him exactly what it is – even a railway ticket, and what station it's from.'

'It's impossible!'

'Not at all. But it's tremendous hard work to learn. Listen to them.'

'I'll go *one heart*,' the man's voice was saying.

'King queen ten of hearts. Ace jack of spades. No diamonds. Queen jack of clubs . . .'

'And you see,' I said, 'he tells her the *number* of cards he has in each suit by the position of his fingers.'

'How?'

'I don't know. You heard him saying about it.'

'My *God*, Arthur! Are you sure that's what they're doing?'

'I'm afraid so.' I watched her as she walked quickly over to the side of the bed to fetch a cigarette. She lit it with her back to me and then swung round, blowing the smoke up at the ceiling in a thin stream. I knew we were going to have to do something about this, but I wasn't quite sure what because we couldn't possibly accuse them without revealing the source of our information. I waited for my wife's decision.

'Why, Arthur,' she said slowly, blowing out clouds of smoke. 'Why, this is a *mar-vellous* idea. D'you think *we* could learn to do it?'

'What!'

'Of course. Why not?'

'Here! No! Wait a minute, Pamela . . .' but she came swiftly across the room, right up close to me where I was standing, and she dropped her head and looked down at me – the old look of a smile that wasn't a smile, at the corners of the mouth, and the curl of the nose, and the big full grey eyes staring at me with their bright black centres, and then they were grey, and all the rest was white-flecked, with hundreds of tiny red veins – and when she looked at me like this, hard and close, I swear to you it made me feel as though I were drowning.

'Yes,' she said. 'Why not?'

'But Pamela . . . Good heavens . . . No . . . After all . . .'

'Arthur, I do wish you wouldn't *argue* with me all the time. That's exactly what we'll do. Now, go fetch a deck of cards; we'll start right away.'

Lamb to the Slaughter

First published in *Harper's* (September 1953)

The room was warm and clean, the curtains drawn, the two table lamps alight – hers and the one by the empty chair opposite. On the sideboard behind her, two tall glasses, soda water, whisky. Fresh ice cubes in the Thermos bucket.

Mary Maloney was waiting for her husband to come home from work.

Now and again she would glance up at the clock, but without anxiety, merely to please herself with the thought that each minute gone by made it nearer the time when he would come. There was a slow smiling air about her, and about everything she did. The drop of the head as she bent over her sewing was curiously tranquil. Her skin – for this was her sixth month with child – had acquired a wonderful translucent quality, the mouth was soft, and the eyes, with their new placid look, seemed larger, darker than before.

When the clock said ten minutes to five, she began to listen, and a few moments later, punctually as always, she heard the tyres on the gravel outside, and the car door slamming, the footsteps passing the window, the key turning in the lock. She laid aside her sewing, stood up and went forward to kiss him as he came in.

'Hullo darling,' she said.

'Hullo,' he answered.

She took his coat and hung it in the closet. Then she walked over and made the drinks, a strongish one for him, a weak one for herself; and soon she was back again in her chair with the sewing, and he in the other, opposite, holding the tall glass with both his hands, rocking it so the ice cubes tinkled against the side.

For her, this was always a blissful time of day. She knew he didn't want to speak much until the first drink was finished, and she, on her side, was content to sit quietly, enjoying his company after the long hours alone in the house. She loved to luxuriate in the presence of this man, and to feel – almost as a sunbather feels the sun – that warm male glow that came out of him to her when they were alone together. She loved him for the way he sat loosely in a chair, for the way he came in a door, or moved slowly across the room with long strides. She loved the intent, far look in his eyes when they rested on her, the funny shape of the mouth, and especially the way he remained silent about his tiredness, sitting still with himself until the whisky had taken some of it away.

'Tired, darling?'

'Yes,' he said. 'I'm tired.' And as he spoke, he did an unusual thing. He lifted his glass and drained it in one swallow although there was still half of it, at least half of it, left. She wasn't really watching him, but she knew what he had done because she heard the ice cubes falling back against the bottom of the empty glass when he lowered his arm. He paused a moment, leaning forward in the chair, then he got up and went slowly over to fetch himself another.

'I'll get it!' she cried, jumping up.

'Sit down,' he said.

When he came back, she noticed that the new drink was dark amber with the quantity of whisky in it.

'Darling, shall I get your slippers?'

'No.'

She watched him as he began to sip the dark-yellow drink, and she could see little oily swirls in the liquid because it was so strong.

'I think it's a shame,' she said, 'that when a policeman gets to be as senior as you, they keep him walking about on his feet all day long.'

He didn't answer, so she bent her head again and went on with her sewing; but each time he lifted the drink to his lips, she heard the ice cubes clinking against the side of the glass.

'Darling,' she said. 'Would you like me to get you some cheese? I haven't made any supper because it's Thursday.'

'No,' he said.

'If you're too tired to eat out,' she went on, 'it's still not too late. There's plenty of meat and stuff in the freezer, and you can have it right here and not even move out of the chair.'

Her eyes waited on him for an answer, a smile, a little nod, but he made no sign.

'Anyway,' she went on, 'I'll get you some cheese and crackers first.'

'I don't want it,' he said.

She moved uneasily in her chair, the large eyes still watching his face. 'But you *must* have supper. I can easily do it here. I'd like to do it. We can have lamb chops. Or pork. Anything you want. Everything's in the freezer.'

'Forget it,' he said.

'But darling, you *must* eat! I'll fix it anyway, and then you can have it or not, as you like.'

She stood up and placed her sewing on the table by the lamp.

'Sit down,' he said. 'Just for a minute, sit down.'

It wasn't till then that she began to get frightened.

'Go on,' he said. 'Sit down.'

She lowered herself back slowly into the chair, watching him all the time with those large, bewildered eyes. He had finished the second drink and was staring down into the glass, frowning.

'Listen,' he said. 'I've got something to tell you.'

'What is it, darling? What's the matter?'

He had now become absolutely motionless, and he kept his head down so that the light from the lamp beside him fell across the upper part of his face, leaving the chin and mouth in shadow. She noticed there was a little muscle moving near the corner of his left eye.

'This is going to be a bit of a shock to you, I'm afraid,' he said. 'But I've thought about it a good deal and I've decided the only thing to do is tell you right away. I hope you won't blame me too much.'

And he told her. It didn't take long, four or five minutes at most, and she sat very still through it all, watching him with a kind of dazed horror as he went farther and farther away from her with each word.

'So there it is,' he added. 'And I know it's kind of a bad time to be telling you, but there simply wasn't any other way. Of course I'll give you money and see you're looked after. But there needn't really be any fuss. I hope not anyway. It wouldn't be very good for my job.'

Her first instinct was not to believe any of it, to reject it all. It occurred to her that perhaps he hadn't even spoken, that she herself had imagined the whole thing. Maybe, if she went about her business and acted as though she hadn't been listening, then later, when she sort of woke up again, she might find none of it had ever happened.

'I'll get the supper,' she managed to whisper, and this time he didn't stop her.

When she walked across the room she couldn't feel her feet touching the floor. She couldn't feel anything at all – except a slight nausea and a desire to vomit. Everything was automatic now – down the steps to the cellar, the light switch, the deep-freeze, the hand inside the cabinet taking hold of the first object it met. She lifted it out, and looked at it. It was wrapped in paper, so she took off the paper and looked at it again.

A leg of lamb.

All right then, they would have lamb for supper. She carried it upstairs, holding the thin bone-end of it with both her hands, and as she went through the living-room, she saw him standing over by the window with his back to her, and she stopped.

'For God's sake,' he said, hearing her, but not turning round. 'Don't make supper for me. I'm going out.'

At that point, Mary Maloney simply walked up behind him and without any pause she swung the big frozen leg of lamb high in the air and brought it down as hard as she could on the back of his head.

She might just as well have hit him with a steel club.

She stepped back a pace, waiting, and the funny thing was that he remained standing there for at least four or five seconds, gently swaying. Then he crashed to the carpet.

The violence of the crash, the noise, the small table overturning, helped bring her out of the shock. She came out slowly, feeling cold and surprised, and she stood for a while blinking at the body, still holding the ridiculous piece of meat tight with both hands.

All right, she told herself. So I've killed him.

It was extraordinary, now, how clear her mind became all of a sudden. She began thinking very fast. As the wife of a detective, she knew quite well what the penalty would be. That was fine. It made no difference to her. In fact, it would be a relief. On the other hand, what about the child? What were the laws about murderers with unborn children? Did they kill them both – mother and child? Or did they wait until the tenth month? What did they do?

Mary Maloney didn't know. And she certainly wasn't prepared to take a chance.

She carried the meat into the kitchen, placed it in a pan, turned the oven on high, and shoved it inside. Then she washed her hands and ran upstairs to the bedroom. She sat down before the mirror, tidied her hair, touched up her lips and face. She tried a smile. It came out rather peculiar. She tried again.

'Hullo, Sam,' she said brightly, aloud.

The voice sounded peculiar too.

'I want some potatoes please, Sam. Yes, and I think a can of peas.'

That was better. Both the smile and the voice were coming out better now. She rehearsed it several times more. Then she ran downstairs, took her coat, went out the back door, down the garden, into the street.

It wasn't six o'clock yet and the lights were still on in the grocery shop.

'Hullo, Sam,' she said brightly, smiling at the man behind the counter.

'Why, good evening, Mrs Maloney. How're *you*?'

'I want some potatoes please, Sam. Yes, and I think a can of peas.'

The man turned and reached up behind him on the shelf for the peas.

'Patrick's decided he's tired and doesn't want to eat out tonight,' she told him. 'We usually go out Thursdays, you know, and now he's caught me without any vegetables in the house.'

'Then how about meat, Mrs Maloney?'

'No, I've got meat, thanks. I got a nice leg of lamb from the freezer.'

'Oh.'

'I don't much like cooking it frozen, Sam, but I'm taking a chance on it this time. You think it'll be all right?'

'Personally,' the grocer said, 'I don't believe it makes any difference. You want these Idaho potatoes?'

'Oh yes, that'll be fine. Two of those.'

'Anything else?' The grocer cocked his head on one side, looking at her pleasantly. 'How about afterwards? What you going to give him for afterwards?'

'Well – what would you suggest, Sam?'

The man glanced around his shop. 'How about a nice big slice of cheesecake? I know he likes that.'

'Perfect,' she said. 'He loves it.'

And when it was all wrapped and she had paid, she put on her brightest smile and said, 'Thank you, Sam. Good night.'

'Good night, Mrs Maloney. And thank *you*.'

And now, she told herself as she hurried back, all she was doing now, she was returning home to her husband and he was waiting for his supper; and she must cook it good, and make it as tasty as possible because the poor man was tired; and if, when she entered the house, she happened to find anything unusual, or tragic, or terrible, then naturally it would be a shock and she'd become frantic with grief and horror. Mind you, she wasn't *expecting* to find anything. She was just going home with the vegetables. Mrs Patrick Maloney going home with the vegetables on Thursday evening to cook supper for her husband.

That's the way, she told herself. Do everything right and natural. Keep things absolutely natural and there'll be no need for any acting at all.

Therefore, when she entered the kitchen by the back door, she was humming a little tune to herself and smiling.

'Patrick!' she called. 'How are you, darling?'

She put the parcel down on the table and went through into the living-room; and when she saw him lying there on the floor with his legs doubled up and one arm twisted back underneath his body, it really was rather a shock. All the old love and longing for him welled up inside her, and she ran over to him, knelt down beside him, and began to cry her heart out. It was easy. No acting was necessary.

A few minutes later she got up and went to the phone. She knew the number of the police station, and when the man at the other end answered, she cried to him, 'Quick! Come quick! Patrick's dead!'

'Who's speaking?'

'Mrs Maloney. Mrs Patrick Maloney.'

'You mean Patrick Maloney's dead?'

'I think so,' she sobbed. 'He's lying on the floor and I think he's dead.'

'Be right over,' the man said.

The car came very quickly, and when she opened the front door, two policemen walked in. She knew them both – she knew nearly all the men at that precinct – and she fell right into Jack Noonan's arms, weeping hysterically. He put her gently in a chair, then went over to join the other one, who was called O'Malley, kneeling by the body.

'Is he dead?' she cried.

'I'm afraid he is. What happened?'

Briefly, she told her story about going out to the grocer's and coming back to find him on the floor. While she was talking, crying and talking, Noonan discovered a small patch of congealed blood on the dead man's head. He showed it to O'Malley, who got up at once and hurried to the phone.

Soon, other men began to come into the house. First a doctor, then two detectives, one of whom she knew by name. Later, a police photographer arrived and took pictures, and a man who knew about fingerprints. There was a great deal of whispering and muttering beside the corpse, and the detectives kept asking her a lot of questions. But they always treated her kindly. She told her story again, this time right from the beginning, when Patrick had come in, and she was sewing, and he was tired, so tired he hadn't wanted to go out for supper. She told how she'd put the meat in the oven – 'It's there now, cooking' – and how she'd slipped out to the grocer's for vegetables, and come back to find him lying on the floor.

'Which grocer?' one of the detectives asked.

She told him, and he turned and whispered something to the other detective, who immediately went outside into the street.

In fifteen minutes he was back with a page of notes, and there was more whispering, and through her sobbing she heard a few of the whispered phrases – '. . . acted quite normal . . . very cheerful . . . wanted to give him a good supper . . . peas . . . cheesecake . . . impossible that she . . .'

After a while, the photographer and the doctor departed and two other men came in and took the corpse away on a stretcher. Then the fingerprint man went away.

The two detectives remained, and so did the two policemen. They were exceptionally nice to her and Jack Noonan asked if she wouldn't rather go somewhere else, to her sister's house perhaps, or to his own wife, who would take care of her and put her up for the night.

No, she said. She didn't feel she could move even a yard at the moment. Would they mind awfully if she stayed just where she was until she felt better? She didn't feel too good at the moment, she really didn't.

Then hadn't she better lie down on the bed? Jack Noonan asked.

No, she said. She'd like to stay right where she was, in this chair. A little later perhaps, when she felt better, she would move.

So they left her there while they went about their business, searching the house. Occasionally one of the detectives asked her another question. Sometimes Jack Noonan spoke at her gently as he passed by. Her husband, he told her, had been killed by a blow on the back of the head administered with a heavy blunt instrument, almost certainly a large piece of metal. They were looking for the weapon. The murderer may have taken it with him, but on the other hand he may've thrown it away or hidden it somewhere on the premises.

'It's the old story,' he said. 'Get the weapon, and you've got the man.'

Later, one of the detectives came up and sat beside her. Did she know, he asked, of anything in the house that could've been used as the weapon? Would she mind having a look around to see if anything was missing – a very big spanner, for example, or a heavy metal vase.

They didn't have any heavy metal vases, she said.

Or a big spanner?

She didn't think they had a big spanner. But there might be some things like that in the garage.

The search went on. She knew that there were other policemen in the garden all around the house. She could hear their footsteps on the gravel outside, and sometimes she saw the flash of a torch through a chink in the curtains. It began to get late, nearly nine, she noticed, by the clock on the mantel. The four men searching the rooms seemed to be growing weary, a trifle exasperated.

'Jack,' she said, the next time Sergeant Noonan went by. 'Would you mind giving me a drink?'

'Sure I'll give you a drink. You mean this whisky?'

'Yes, please. But just a small one. It might make me feel better.'

He handed her the glass.

'Why don't you have one yourself?' she said. 'You must be awfully tired. Please do. You've been very good to me.'

'Well,' he answered. 'It's not strictly allowed, but I might take just a drop to keep me going.'

One by one the others came in and were persuaded to take a little nip of whisky. They stood around rather awkwardly with the drinks in their hands, uncomfortable in her presence, trying to say consoling things to her. Sergeant Noonan wandered into the kitchen, came out quickly and said, 'Look, Mrs Maloney. You know that oven of yours is still on, and the meat still inside.'

'Oh *dear* me!' she cried. 'So it is!'

'I better turn it off for you, hadn't I?'

'Will you do that, Jack? Thank you so much.'

When the sergeant returned the second time, she looked at him with her large, dark, tearful eyes. 'Jack Noonan,' she said.

'Yes?'

'Would you do me a small favour – you and these others?'

'We can try, Mrs Maloney.'

'Well,' she said. 'Here you all are, and good friends of dear Patrick's too, and helping to catch the man who killed him. You must be terribly hungry by now because it's long past your suppertime, and I know Patrick would never forgive me, God bless his soul, if I allowed you to remain in his house without offering you decent hospitality. Why don't you eat up that lamb that's in the oven. It'll be cooked just right by now.'

'Wouldn't dream of it,' Sergeant Noonan said.

'Please,' she begged. 'Please eat it. Personally, I couldn't touch a thing, certainly not what's been in the house when he was here. But it's all right for you. It'd be a favour to me if you'd eat it up. Then you can go on with your work again afterwards.'

There was a good deal of hesitating among the four policemen, but they were clearly hungry, and in the end they were persuaded to go into the kitchen and help themselves. The woman stayed where she was, listening to them through the open door, and she could hear them speaking among themselves, their voices thick and sloppy because their mouths were full of meat.

'Have some more, Charlie?'

'No. Better not finish it.'

'She *wants* us to finish it. She said so. Be doing her a favour.'

'OK then. Give me some more.'

'That's a hell of a big club the guy must've used to hit poor Patrick,' one of them was saying. 'The doc says his skull was smashed all to pieces just like from a sledge-hammer.'

'That's why it ought to be easy to find.'

'Exactly what I say.'

'Whoever done it, they're not going to be carrying a thing like that around with them longer than they need.'

One of them belched.

'Personally, I think it's right here on the premises.'

'Probably right under our very noses. What you think, Jack?'

And in the other room, Mary Maloney began to giggle.

Nunc Dimittis

First published in *Collier's* (4 September 1953)
as 'The Devious Bachelor'; also known as
'A Connoisseur's Revenge'

It is nearly midnight, and I can see that if I don't make a start with writing this story now, I never shall. All the evening I have been sitting here trying to force myself to begin, but the more I have thought about it, the more appalled and ashamed and distressed I have become by the whole thing.

My idea – and I believe it was a good one – was to try, by a process of confession and analysis, to discover a reason or at any rate some justification for my outrageous behaviour towards Janet de Pelagia. I wanted, essentially, to address myself to an imaginary and sympathetic listener, a kind of mythical *you*, someone gentle and understanding to whom I might tell unashamedly every detail of this unfortunate episode. I can only hope that I am not too upset to make a go of it.

If I am to be quite honest with myself, I suppose I shall have to admit that what is disturbing me most is not so much the sense of my own shame, or even the hurt that I have inflicted upon poor Janet; it is the knowledge that I have made a monstrous fool of myself and that all my friends – if I can still call them that – all those warm and lovable people who used to come so often to my house, must now be regarding me as nothing but a vicious, vengeful old man. Yes, that surely hurts. When I say to you that my friends were my whole life – everything, absolutely everything in it – then perhaps you will begin to understand.

Will you? I doubt it – unless I digress for a minute to tell you roughly the sort of person I am.

Well – let me see. Now that I come to think of it, I suppose I am, after all, a type; a rare one, mark you, but nevertheless a quite definite type – the wealthy, leisurely, middle-aged man of culture, adored (I choose the word carefully) by his many friends for his charm, his money, his air of scholarship, his generosity, and I sincerely hope for himself also. You will find him (this type) only in the big capitals – London, Paris, New York; of that I am certain. The money he has was earned by his dead father, whose memory he is inclined to despise. This is not his fault, for there is something in his make-up that compels him secretly to look down upon all people who never had the wit to learn the difference between Rockingham and Spode, Waterford and Venetian, Sheraton and Chippendale, Monet and Manet, or even Pommard and Montrachet.

He is, therefore, a connoisseur, possessing above all things an exquisite taste. His Constables, Boningtons, Lautrecs, Redons, Vuillards, Matthew Smiths are as fine as anything in the Tate; and because they are so fabulous and beautiful they create an atmosphere of suspense around him in the home, something tantalizing, breathtaking, faintly frightening – frightening to think that he has the power and the right, if he feels inclined, to slash, tear, plunge his fist through a superb Dedham Vale, a Mont

Saint-Victoire, an Arles cornfield, a Tahiti maiden, a portrait of Madame Cézanne. And from the walls on which these wonders hang there issues a little golden glow of splendour, a subtle emanation of grandeur in which he lives and moves and entertains with a sly nonchalance that is not entirely unpractised.

He is invariably a bachelor, yet he never appears to get entangled with the women who surround him, who love him so dearly. It is just possible – and this you may or may not have noticed – that there is a frustration, a discontent, a regret somewhere inside him. Even a slight aberration.

I don't think I need say any more. I have been very frank. You should know me well enough by now to judge me fairly – and dare I hope it? – to sympathize with me when you hear my story. You may even decide that much of the blame for what has happened should be placed, not upon me, but upon a lady called Gladys Ponsonby. After all, she was the one who started it. Had I not escorted Gladys Ponsonby back to her house that night nearly six months ago, and had she not spoken so freely to me about certain people, and certain things, then this tragic business could never have taken place.

It was last December, if I remember rightly, and I had been dining with the Ashendens in that lovely house of theirs that overlooks the southern fringe of Regent's Park. There were a fair number of people there, but Gladys Ponsonby was the only one beside myself who had come alone. So when it was time for us to leave, I naturally offered to see her safely back to her house. She accepted and we left together in my car; but unfortunately, when we arrived at her place she insisted that I come in and have 'one for the road', as she put it. I didn't wish to seem stuffy, so I told the chauffeur to wait and followed her in.

Gladys Ponsonby is an unusually short woman, certainly not more than four feet nine or ten, maybe even less than that – one of those tiny persons who gives me, when I am beside her, the comical, rather wobbly feeling that I am standing on a chair. She is a widow, a few years younger than me – maybe fifty-three or four, and it is possible that thirty years ago she was quite a fetching little thing. But now the face is loose and puckered with nothing distinctive about it whatsoever. The individual features, the eyes, the nose, the mouth, the chin, are buried in the folds of fat around the puckered little face and one does not notice them. Except perhaps the mouth, which reminds me – I cannot help it – of a salmon.

In the living-room, as she gave me my brandy, I noticed that her hand was a trifle unsteady. The lady is tired, I told myself, so I mustn't stay long. We sat down together on the sofa and for a while discussed the Ashendens' party and the people who were there. Finally I got up to go.

'Sit down, Lionel,' she said. 'Have another brandy.'

'No, really, I must go.'

'Sit down and don't be so stuffy. *I'm* having another one, and the least you can do is keep me company while I drink it.'

I watched her as she walked over to the sideboard, this tiny woman, faintly swaying, holding her glass out in front of her with both hands as though it were an offering; and the sight of her walking like that, so incredibly short and squat and stiff, suddenly gave me the ludicrous notion that she had no legs at all above the knees.

'Lionel, what are you chuckling about?' She half turned to look at me as she poured the drink, and some of it slopped over the side of the glass.

'Nothing, my dear. Nothing at all.'

'Well, stop it, and tell me what you think of my new portrait.' She indicated a large canvas hanging over the fireplace that I had been trying to avoid with my eye ever since I entered the room. It was a hideous thing, painted, as I well knew, by a man who was now all the rage in London, a very mediocre painter called John Royden. It was a full-length portrait of Gladys, Lady Ponsonby, painted with a certain technical cunning that made her out to be a tall and quite alluring creature.

'Charming,' I said.

'Isn't it, though! I'm so glad you like it.'

'Quite charming.'

'I think John Royden is a genius. Don't you think he's a genius, Lionel?'

'Well – that might be going a bit far.'

'You mean it's a little early to say for sure?'

'Exactly.'

'But listen, Lionel – and I think this will surprise you. John Royden is so sought after now that he won't even *consider* painting anyone for less than a thousand guineas!'

'Really?'

'Oh, yes! And everyone's queueing up, simply *queueing up* to get themselves done.'

'Most interesting.'

'Now take your Mr Cézanne or whatever his name is. I'll bet *he* never got that sort of money in *his* lifetime.'

'Never.'

'And you say *he* was a genius?'

'Sort of – yes.'

'Then so is Royden,' she said, settling herself again on the sofa. 'The money proves it.'

She sat silent for a while, sipping her brandy, and I couldn't help noticing how the unsteadiness of her hand was causing the rim of the glass to jog against her lower lip. She knew I was watching her, and without turning her head she swivelled her eyes and glanced at me cautiously out of the corners of them. 'A penny for your thoughts?'

Now, if there is one phrase in the world I cannot abide, it is this. It gives me an actual physical pain in the chest and I began to cough.

'Come on, Lionel. A penny for them.'

I shook my head, quite unable to answer. She turned away abruptly and placed the brandy glass on a small table to her left; and the manner in which she did this seemed to suggest – I don't know why – that she felt rebuffed and was now clearing the decks for action. I waited, rather uncomfortable in the silence that followed, and because I had no conversation left in me, I made a great play about smoking my cigar, studying the ash intently and blowing the smoke up slowly towards the ceiling. But she made no move. There was beginning to be something about this lady I did not much like, a mischievous brooding air that made me want to get up quickly and go away. When she looked around again, she was smiling at me slyly with those little buried eyes of hers, but the mouth – oh, just like a salmon's – was absolutely rigid.

'Lionel, I think I'll tell you a secret.'

'Really, Gladys, I simply must get home.'

'Don't be frightened, Lionel. I won't embarrass you. You look so frightened all of a sudden.'

'I'm not very good at secrets.'

'I've been thinking,' she said, 'you're such a great expert on pictures, this ought to interest you.' She sat quite still except for her fingers, which were moving all the time. She kept them perpetually twisting and twisting around each other, and they were like a bunch of small white snakes wriggling in her lap.

'Don't you want to hear my secret, Lionel?'

'It isn't that, you know. It's just that it's so awfully late . . .'

'This is probably the best-kept secret in London. A woman's secret. I suppose it's known to about – let me see – about thirty or forty women altogether. And not a single man. Except him, of course – John Royden.'

I didn't wish to encourage her, so I said nothing.

'But first of all, promise – *promise* you won't tell a soul?'

'Dear me!'

'You *promise*, Lionel?'

'Yes, Gladys, all right, I promise.'

'Good! Now listen.' She reached for the brandy glass and settled back comfortably in the far corner of the sofa. 'I suppose you know John Royden paints only women?'

'I didn't.'

'And they're always full-length portraits, either standing or sitting – like mine there. Now take a good look at it, Lionel. Do you see how beautifully the dress is painted?'

'Well . . .'

'Go over and look carefully, please.'

I got up reluctantly and went over and examined the painting. To my surprise I noticed that the paint of the dress was laid on so heavily it was actually raised out from the rest of the picture. It was a trick, quite effective in its way, but neither difficult to do nor entirely original.

'You see?' she said. 'It's thick, isn't it, where the dress is?'

'Yes.'

'But there's a bit more to it than that, you know, Lionel. I think the best way is to describe what happened the very first time I went along for a sitting.'

Oh, what a bore this woman is, I thought, and how can I get away?

'That was about a year ago, and I remember how excited I was to be going into the studio of the great painter. I dressed myself up in a wonderful new thing I'd just got from Norman Hartnell, and a special little red hat, and off I went. Mr Royden met me at the door, and of course I was fascinated by him at once. He had a small pointed beard and thrilling blue eyes, and he wore a black velvet jacket. The studio was huge, with red velvet sofas and velvet chairs – he loves velvet – and velvet curtains and even a velvet carpet on the floor. He sat me down, gave me a drink and came straight to the point. He told me about how he painted quite differently from other artists. In his opinion, he said, there was only one method of attaining perfection when painting a woman's body and I mustn't be shocked when I heard what it was.

'"I don't think I'll be shocked, Mr Royden," I told him.

'"I'm sure you won't either," he said. He had the most marvellous white teeth and they sort of shone through his beard when he smiled. "You see, it's like this," he went on. "You examine any painting you like of a woman – I don't care who it's by – and you'll see that although the dress may be well painted, there is an effect of artificiality, of flatness about the whole thing, as though the dress were draped over a log of wood. And you know why?"

'"No, Mr Royden, I don't."

'"Because the painters themselves didn't really know what was underneath!"'

Gladys Ponsonby paused to take a few more sips of brandy. 'Don't look so startled, Lionel,' she said to me. 'There's nothing wrong about this. Keep quiet and let me finish. So then Mr Royden said, "That's why I insist on painting my subjects first of all in the nude."

'"Good Heavens, Mr Royden!" I exclaimed.

'"If you object to that, I don't mind making a slight concession, Lady Ponsonby," he said. "But I prefer it the other way."

'"Really, Mr Royden, I don't know."

'"And when I've done you like that," he went on, "we'll have to wait a few weeks for the paint to dry. Then you come back and I paint on your underclothing. And when that's dry, I paint on the dress. You see, it's quite simple."'

'The man's an absolute bounder!' I cried.

'No, Lionel, no! You're quite wrong. If only you could

have heard him, so charming about it all, so genuine and sincere. Anyone could see he really *felt* what he was saying.'

'I tell you, Gladys, the man's a bounder!'

'Don't be so silly, Lionel. And anyway, let me finish. The first thing I told him was that my husband (who was alive then) would never agree.

' "Your husband need never know," he answered. "Why trouble him? No one knows my secret except the women I've painted."

'And when I protested a bit more, I remember he said, "My dear Lady Ponsonby, there's nothing immoral about this. Art is only immoral when practised by amateurs. It's the same with medicine. You wouldn't refuse to undress before your doctor, would you?"

'I told him I would if I'd gone to him for ear-ache. That made him laugh. But he kept on at me about it and I must say he was very convincing, so after a while I gave in and that was that. So now, Lionel, my sweet, you know the secret.' She got up and went over to fetch herself some more brandy.

'Gladys, is this really true?'

'Of course it's true.'

'You mean to say that's the way he paints all his subjects?'

'Yes. And the joke is the husbands never know anything about it. All they see is a nice fully clothed portrait of their wives. Of course, there's nothing wrong with being painted in the nude; artists do it all the time. But our silly husbands have a way of objecting to that sort of thing.'

'By gad, the fellow's got a nerve!'

'I think he's a genius.'

'I'll bet he got the idea from Goya.'

'Nonsense, Lionel.'

'Of course he did. But listen, Gladys. I want you to tell me something. Did you by any chance know about this . . . this peculiar technique of Royden's before you went to him?'

When I asked the question she was in the act of pouring the brandy, and she hesitated and turned her head to look at me, a little silky smile moving the corners of her mouth, 'Damn you, Lionel,' she said. 'You're far too clever. You never let me get away with a single thing.'

'So you knew?'

'Of course. Hermione Girdlestone told me.'

'Exactly as I thought!'

'There's still nothing wrong.'

'Nothing,' I said. 'Absolutely nothing.' I could see it all quite clearly now. This Royden was indeed a bounder, practising as neat a piece of psychological trickery as ever I'd seen. The man knew only too well that there was a whole set of wealthy indolent women in the city who got up at noon and spent the rest of the day trying to relieve their boredom with bridge and canasta and shopping until the cocktail hour came along. All they craved was a little excitement, something out of the ordinary, and the more expensive the better. Why – the news of an entertainment like this would spread through their ranks like smallpox. I could just see the great plump Hermione Girdlestone leaning over the canasta table and telling them about it . . . 'But my dear, it's *simp*-ly fascinating . . . I can't *tell* you how intriguing it is . . . *much* more fun than going to your doctor . . .'

'You won't tell anyone, Lionel, will you? You promised.'

'No, of course not. But now I must go, Gladys, I really must.'

'Don't be so silly. I'm just beginning to enjoy myself. Stay till I've finished this drink, anyway.'

I sat patiently on the sofa while she went on with her interminable brandy sipping. The little buried eyes were still watching me out of their corners in that mischievous, canny way, and I had a strong feeling that the woman was now hatching out some farther unpleasantness or scandal. There was the look of serpents in those eyes and a queer curl around the mouth; and in the air – although maybe I only imagined it – the faint smell of danger.

Then suddenly, so suddenly that I jumped, she said, 'Lionel, what's this I hear about you and Janet de Pelagia?'

'Now, Gladys, please . . .'

'Lionel, you're blushing!'

'Nonsense.'

'Don't tell me the old bachelor has really taken a tumble at last?'

'Gladys, this is too absurd.' I began making movements to go, but she put a hand on my knee and stopped me.

'Don't you know by now, Lionel, that there *are* no secrets?'

'Janet is a fine girl.'

'You can hardly call her a *girl*.' Gladys Ponsonby paused, staring down into the large brandy glass that she held cupped in both hands. 'But of course, I agree with you, Lionel, she's a wonderful person in every way. Except,' and now she spoke very slowly, 'except that she *does* say some rather peculiar things occasionally.'

'What sort of things?'

'Just things, you know – things about people. About you.'

'What did she say about me?'

'Nothing at all, Lionel. It wouldn't interest you.'

'What did she say about me?'

'It's not even worth repeating, honestly it isn't. It's only that it struck me as being rather odd at the time.'

'Gladys – what did she say?' While I waited for her to answer, I could feel the sweat breaking out all over my body.

'Well now, let me see. Of course, she was only joking or I couldn't dream of telling you, but I suppose she *did* say how it was all a wee bit of a bore.'

'What was?'

'Sort of going out to dinner with you nearly every night – that kind of thing.'

'She said it was a bore?'

'Yes.' Gladys Ponsonby drained the brandy glass with one last big gulp, and sat up straight. 'If you really want to know, she said it was a crashing bore. And then . . .'

'What did she say then?'

'Now look, Lionel – there's no need to get excited. I'm only telling you this for your own good.'

'Then please hurry up and tell it.'

'It's just that I happened to be playing canasta with Janet this afternoon and I asked her if she was free to dine with me tomorrow. She said no, she wasn't.'

'Go on.'

'Well – actually what she said was "I'm dining with that crashing old bore Lionel Lampson."'

'Janet said that?'

'Yes, Lionel dear.'

'What else?'

'Now, that's enough. I don't think I should tell the rest.'

'Finish it, please!'

'Why, Lionel, don't keep shouting at me like that. Of course I'll tell you if you insist. As a matter of fact, I wouldn't consider myself a true friend if I didn't. Don't you think it's the sign of true friendship when two people like us . . .'

'Gladys! *Please* hurry.'

'Good heavens, you must give me time to *think*. Let me see now – so far as I can remember, what she *actually* said was this . . .' – and Gladys Ponsonby, sitting upright on the sofa with her feet not quite touching the floor, her eyes away from me now, looking at the wall, began cleverly to mimic the deep tone of that voice I knew so well – '"Such a bore, my dear, because with Lionel one can *always* tell exactly what will happen *right* from beginning to end. For dinner we'll go to the Savoy Grill – it's *always* the Savoy Grill – and for two hours I'll have to listen to the pompous old . . . I mean I'll have to listen to him droning away about pictures and porcelain – *always* pictures and porcelain. Then in the taxi going home he'll reach out for my hand, and he'll lean closer, and I'll get a whiff of stale cigar smoke and brandy, and he'll start burbling about how he wished – oh, how he wished he was just twenty years younger. And I will say, 'Could you open a window, do you mind?' And when we arrive at my house I'll tell him to keep the taxi, but he'll pretend he hasn't heard and pay it off quickly. And then at the front door, while I fish for my key, he'll stand beside me with a sort of silly spaniel look in his eyes, and I'll slowly put the key in the lock, and slowly turn it, and then – very quickly, before he has time to move – I'll say good night and skip inside and shut the door behind me . . ." Why, Lionel! What's the matter, dear? You look positively ill . . .'

At that point, mercifully, I must have swooned clear away. I can remember practically nothing of the rest of that terrible night except for a vague and disturbing suspicion that when I regained consciousness I broke down completely and permitted Gladys Ponsonby to comfort me in a variety of different ways. Later, I believe I walked out of the house and was driven home, but I remained more or less unconscious of everything about me until I woke up in my bed the next morning.

I awoke feeling weak and shaken. I lay still with my eyes closed, trying to piece together the events of the night before – Gladys Ponsonby's living-room, Gladys on the sofa sipping brandy, the little puckered face, the mouth that was like a salmon's mouth, the things she had said . . . What was it she had said? Ah, yes. About me. My God, yes! About Janet and me! Those outrageous, unbelievable remarks! Could Janet really have made them? Could she?

I can remember with what terrifying swiftness my hatred of Janet de Pelagia now began to grow. It all happened in a few minutes – a sudden, violent welling up of a hatred that filled me till I thought I was going to burst. I tried to dismiss it, but it was on me like a fever, and in no time at all I was hunting around, as would some filthy gangster, for a method of revenge.

A curious way to behave, you may say, for a man such as me; to which I would answer – no, not really, if you consider the circumstances. To my mind, this was the sort of thing that could drive a man to murder. As a matter of fact, had it not been for a small sadistic streak that caused me to seek a more subtle and painful punishment for my victim, I might well have become a murderer myself. But mere killing, I decided, was too good for this woman, and far too crude for my taste. So I began looking for a superior alternative.

I am not normally a scheming person; I consider it an odious business and have had no practice in it whatsoever. But fury and hate can concentrate a man's mind to an astonishing degree, and in no time at all a plot was forming and unfolding in my head – a plot so superior and exciting that I began to be quite carried away at the idea of it. By the time I had filled in the details and overcome one or two minor objections, my brooding vengeful mood had changed to one of extreme elation, and I remember how I started bouncing up and down absurdly on my bed and clapping my hands. The next thing I knew I had the telephone directory on my lap and was searching eagerly for a name. I found it, picked up the phone and dialled the number.

'Hello,' I said. 'Mr Royden? Mr John Royden?'

'Speaking.'

Well – it wasn't difficult to persuade the man to call around and see me for a moment. I had never met him, but of course he knew my name, both as an important collector of paintings and as a person of some consequence in society. I was a big fish for him to catch.

'Let me see now, Mr Lampson,' he said, 'I think I ought to be free in about a couple of hours. Will that be all right?'

I told him it would be fine, gave my address and rang off.

I jumped out of bed. It was really remarkable how exhilarated I felt all of a sudden. One moment I had been in an agony of despair, contemplating murder and suicide and I don't know what, the next, I was whistling an aria from Puccini in my bath. Every now and again I caught myself rubbing my hands together in a devilish fashion, and once, during my exercises, when I overbalanced doing a double knee-bend, I sat on the floor and giggled like a schoolboy.

At the appointed time Mr John Royden was shown into my library and I got up to meet him. He was a small neat man with a slightly ginger goatee beard. He wore a black velvet jacket, a rust-brown tie, a red pullover and black suède shoes. I shook his small neat hand.

'Good of you to come along so quickly, Mr Royden.'

'Not at all, sir.' The man's lips – like the lips of nearly all bearded men – looked wet and naked, a trifle indecent, shining pink in among all that hair. After telling him again how much I admired his work, I got straight down to business.

'Mr Royden,' I said. 'I have a rather unusual request to make of you, something quite personal in its way.'

'Yes, Mr Lampson?' He was sitting in the chair opposite me and he cocked his head over to one side, quick and perky like a bird.

'Of course, I know I can trust you to be discreet about anything I say.'

'Absolutely, Mr Lampson.'

'All right. Now my proposition is this: there is a certain lady in town here whose portrait I would like you to paint. I very much want to possess a fine painting of her. But there are certain complications. For example, I have my own reasons for not wishing her to know that it is I who am commissioning the portrait.'

'You mean . . .'

'Exactly, Mr Royden. That is exactly what I mean. As a man of the world I'm sure you will understand.'

He smiled, a crooked little smile that only just came through his beard, and he nodded his head knowingly up and down.

'Is it not possible,' I said, 'that a man might be – how shall I put it? – extremely fond of a lady and at the same time have his own good reasons for not wishing her to know about it yet?'

'More than possible, Mr Lampson.'

'Sometimes a man has to stalk his quarry with great caution, waiting patiently for the right moment to reveal himself.'

'Precisely, Mr Lampson.'

'There are better ways of catching a bird than by chasing it through the woods.'

'Yes, indeed, Mr Lampson.'

'Putting salt on its tail, for instance.'

'Ha-ha!'

'All right, Mr Royden. I think you understand. Now – do you happen by any chance to know a lady called Janet de Pelagia?'

'Janet de Pelagia? Let me see now – yes. At least, what I mean is, I've heard of her. I couldn't exactly say I know her.'

'That's a pity. It makes it a little more difficult. Do you think you could get to meet her – perhaps at a cocktail party or something like that?'

'Shouldn't be too tricky, Mr Lampson.'

'Good, because what I suggest is this: that you go up to her and tell her she's the sort of model you've been searching for for years – just the right face, the right figure, the right coloured eyes. You know the sort of thing. Then ask her if she'd mind sitting for you free of charge. Say you'd like to do a picture of her for next year's Academy. I feel sure she'd be delighted to help you, and honoured too, if I may say so. Then you will paint her and exhibit the picture and deliver it to me after the show is over. No one but you need know that I have bought it.'

The small round eyes of Mr John Royden were watching me shrewdly, I thought, and the head was again cocked over to one side. He was sitting on the edge of his chair, and in this position, with the pullover making a flash of red down his front, he reminded me of a robin on a twig listening for a suspicious noise.

'There's really nothing wrong about it at all,' I said. 'Just call it – if you like – a harmless little conspiracy being perpetrated by a . . . well . . . by a rather romantic old man.'

'I know, Mr Lampson, I know . . .' He still seemed to be hesitating, so I said quickly, 'I'll be glad to pay you double your usual fee.'

That did it. The man actually licked his lips. 'Well, Mr Lampson, I must say this sort of thing's not really in my line, you know. But all the same, it'd be a very heartless man who refused such a – shall I say, such a romantic assignment?'

'I should like a full-length portrait, Mr Royden, please. A large canvas – let me see – about twice the size of that Manet on the wall there.'

'About sixty by thirty-six?'

'Yes. And I should like her to be standing. That to my mind is her most graceful attitude.'

'I quite understand, Mr Lampson. And it'll be a pleasure to paint such a lovely lady.'

I expect it will, I told myself. The way you go about it, my boy, I'm quite sure it will. But I said, 'All right, Mr Royden, then I'll leave it all to you. And don't forget, please – this is a little secret between ourselves.'

When he had gone I forced myself to sit still and take twenty-five deep breaths. Nothing else would have restrained me from jumping up and shouting for joy like an idiot. I have never in my life felt so exhilarated. My plan was working! The most difficult part was already accomplished. There would be a wait now, a long wait. The way this man painted, it would take him several months to finish the picture. Well, I would just have to be patient, that's all.

I now decided, on the spur of the moment, that it would be best if I were to go abroad in the interim; and the very next morning, after sending a message to Janet (with whom, you will remember, I was due to dine that night) telling her I had been called away, I left for Italy.

There, as always, I had a delightful time, marred only by a constant nervous excitement caused by the thought of returning to the scene of action.

I eventually arrived back, four months later, in July, on the day after the opening of the Royal Academy, and I found to my relief that everything had gone according to plan during my absence. The picture of Janet de Pelagia had been painted and hung in the Exhibition, and it was already the subject of much favourable comment both by the critics and the public. I myself refrained from going to see it, but Royden told me on the telephone that there had been several inquiries by persons who wished to buy it, all of whom had been informed that it was not for sale. When the show was over, Royden delivered the picture to my house and received his money.

I immediately had it carried up to my workroom, and with mounting excitement I began to examine it closely. The man had painted her standing up in a black evening dress and there was a red plush sofa in the background. Her left hand was resting on the back of a heavy chair, also of red plush, and there was a huge crystal chandelier hanging from the ceiling.

My God, I thought, what a hideous thing! The portrait

itself wasn't so bad. He had caught the woman's expression – the forward drop of the head, the wide blue eyes, the large, ugly-beautiful mouth with the trace of a smile in one corner. He had flattered her, of course. There wasn't a wrinkle on her face or the slightest suggestion of fat under her chin. I bent forward to examine the painting of the dress. Yes – here the paint was thicker, much thicker. At this point, unable to wait another moment, I threw off my coat and prepared to go to work.

I should mention here that I am myself an expert cleaner and restorer of paintings. The cleaning, particularly, is a comparatively simple process, provided one has patience and a gentle touch, and those professionals who make such a secret of their trade and charge such shocking prices get no business from me. Where my own pictures are concerned I always do the job myself.

I poured out the turpentine and added a few drops of alcohol. I dipped a small wad of cotton-wool in the mixture, squeezed it out, and then gently, with a circular motion, I began to work upon the black paint of the dress. I could only hope that Royden had allowed each layer to dry thoroughly before applying the next, otherwise the two would merge and the process I had in mind would be impossible. Soon I would know. I was working on one square inch of black dress somewhere around the lady's stomach and I took plenty of time, cautiously testing and teasing the paint, adding a drop or two more alcohol to my mixture, testing again, adding another drop until finally it was just strong enough to loosen the pigment.

For perhaps a whole hour I worked away on this little

square of black, proceeding more and more gently as I came closer to the layer below. Then, a tiny pink spot appeared, and gradually it spread and spread until the whole of my square inch was a clear shining patch of pink. Quickly I neutralized with pure turps.

So far so good. I knew now that the black paint could be removed without disturbing what was underneath. So long as I was patient and industrious I would easily be able to take it all off. Also, I had discovered the right mixture to use and just how hard I could safely rub, so things should go much quicker now.

I must say it was rather an amusing business. I worked first from the middle of her body downward, and as the lower half of her dress came away bit by bit on to my little wads of cotton, a queer pink undergarment began to reveal itself. I didn't for the life of me know what the thing was called, but it was a formidable apparatus constructed of what appeared to be a strong thick elastic material, and its purpose was apparently to contain and to compress the woman's bulging figure into a neat streamlined shape, giving a quite false impression of slimness. As I travelled lower and lower down, I came upon a striking arrangement of suspenders, also pink, which were attached to this elastic armour and hung downwards four or five inches to grip the tops of the stockings.

Quite fantastic the whole thing seemed to me as I stepped back a pace to survey it. It gave me a strong sense of having somehow been cheated; for had I not, during all these past months, been admiring the sylph-like figure of this lady? She was a faker. No question about it. But do many other females practise this sort of deception, I wondered. I knew, of course, that in the days of stays and corsets it was usual for ladies to strap themselves up; yet for some reason I was under the impression that nowadays all they had to do was diet.

When the whole of the lower half of the dress had come away, I immediately turned my attention to the upper portion, working my way slowly upward from the lady's middle. Here, around the midriff, there was an area of naked flesh; then higher up upon the bosom itself and actually containing it, I came upon a contrivance made of some heavy black material edged with frilly lace. This, I knew very well, was the brassière – another formidable appliance upheld by an arrangement of black straps as skilfully and scientifically rigged as the supporting cables of a suspension bridge.

Dear me, I thought. One lives and learns.

But now at last the job was finished, and I stepped back again to take a final look at the picture. It was truly an astonishing sight! This woman, Janet de Pelagia, almost life size, standing there in her underwear – in a sort of drawing-room, I suppose it was – with a great chandelier above her head and a red plush chair by her side; and she herself – this was the most disturbing part of all – looking so completely unconcerned, with the wide placid blue eyes, the faintly smiling, ugly-beautiful mouth. Also I noticed, with something of a shock, that she was exceedingly bow-legged, like a jockey. I tell you frankly, the whole thing embarrassed me. I felt as though I had no right to be in the room, certainly no right to stare. So after a while I went out and shut the door behind me. It seemed like the only decent thing to do.

Now, for the next and final step! And do not imagine simply because I have not mentioned it lately that my thirst for revenge had in any way diminished during the last few months. On the contrary, it had if anything increased; and with the last act about to be performed, I can tell you I found it hard to contain myself. That night, for example, I didn't even go to bed.

You see, I couldn't wait to get the invitations out. I sat up all night preparing them and addressing the envelopes. There were twenty-two of them in all, and I wanted each to be a personal note. 'I'm having a little dinner on Friday night, the twenty-second, at eight. I do hope you can come along . . . I'm so looking forward to seeing you again . . .'

The first, the most carefully phrased, was to Janet de Pelagia. In it I regretted not having seen her for so long . . . I had been abroad . . . It was time we got together again, etc., etc. The next was to Gladys Ponsonby. Then one to Lady Hermione Girdlestone, another to Princess Bicheno, Mrs Cudbird, Sir Hubert Kaul, Mrs Galbally, Peter Euan-Thomas, James Pisker, Sir Eustace Piegrome, Peter van Santen, Elizabeth Moynihan, Lord Mulherrin, Bertram Sturt, Philip Cornelius, Jack Hill, Lady Akeman, Mrs Icely, Humphrey King-Howard, Johnny O'Coffey, Mrs Uvary and the Dowager Countess of Waxworth.

It was a carefully selected list, containing as it did the most distinguished men, the most brilliant and influential women in the top crust of our society.

I was well aware that a dinner at my house was regarded

as quite an occasion; everybody liked to come. And now, as I watched the point of my pen moving swiftly over the paper, I could almost see the ladies in their pleasure picking up their bedside telephones the morning the invitations arrived, shrill voices calling to shriller voices over the wires . . . 'Lionel's giving a party . . . he's asked you too? My dear, how nice . . . his food is always *so* good . . . and *such* a lovely man, isn't he though, yes . . .'

Is that really what they would say? It suddenly occurred to me that it might not be like that at all. More like this perhaps: 'I agree, my dear, yes, not a bad old man . . . but a bit of a bore, don't you think? . . . What did you say? . . . dull? But desperately, my dear. You've hit the nail right on the head . . . did you ever hear what Janet de Pelagia once said about him? . . . Ah yes, I thought you'd heard that one . . . screamingly funny, don't you think? . . . poor Janet . . . how she stood it as long as she did I don't know . . .'

Anyway, I got the invitations off, and within a couple of days everybody with the exception of Mrs Cudburd and Sir Hubert Kaul, who were away, had accepted with pleasure.

At eight thirty on the evening of the twenty-second, my large drawing-room was filled with people. They stood about the room, admiring the pictures, drinking their Martinis, talking with loud voices. The women smelled strongly of scent, the men were pink-faced and carefully buttoned up in their dinner-jackets. Janet de Pelagia was wearing the same black dress she had used for the portrait, and every time I caught sight of her, a kind of huge bubble-vision – as in those absurd cartoons – would float up above my head, and in it I would see Janet in her underclothes, the black brassière, the pink elastic belt, the suspenders, the jockey's legs.

I moved from group to group, chatting amiably with them all, listening to their talk. Behind me I could hear Mrs Galbally telling Sir Eustace Piegrome and James Pisker how the man at the next table to hers at Claridges the night before had had red lipstick on his white moustache. 'Simply *plastered* with it,' she kept on saying, 'and the old boy was ninety if he was a day . . .' On the other side, Lady Girdlestone was telling somebody where one could get truffles cooked in brandy, and I could see Mrs Icely whispering something to Lord Mulherrin while his Lordship kept shaking his head slowly from side to side like an old and dispirited metronome.

Dinner was announced, and we all moved out.

'My goodness!' they cried as they entered the dining-room. 'How dark and sinister!'

'I can hardly see a thing!'

'What divine little candles!'

'But Lionel, how romantic!'

There were six very thin candles set about two feet apart from each other down the centre of the long table. Their small flames made a little glow of light around the table itself, but left the rest of the room in darkness. It was an amusing arrangement and apart from the fact that it suited my purpose well, it made a pleasant change. The guests soon settled themselves in their right places and the meal began.

They all seemed to enjoy the candlelight and things went famously, though for some reason the darkness caused them to speak much louder than usual. Janet de Pelagia's voice struck me as being particularly strident. She was sitting next to Lord Mulherrin, and I could hear her telling him about the boring time she had had at Cap Ferrat the week before. 'Nothing but Frenchmen,' she kept saying. 'Nothing but Frenchmen in the whole place . . .'

For my part, I was watching the candles. They were so thin that I knew it would not be long before they burned down to their bases. Also I was mighty nervous – I will admit that – but at the same time intensely exhilarated, almost to the point of drunkenness. Every time I heard Janet's voice or caught sight of her face shadowed in the light of the candles, a little ball of excitement exploded inside me and I felt the fire of it running under my skin.

They were eating their strawberries when at last I decided the time had come. I took a deep breath and in a loud voice I said, 'I'm afraid we'll have to have the lights on now. The candles are nearly finished. Mary,' I called. 'Oh, Mary, switch on the lights, will you please?'

There was a moment of silence after my announcement. I heard the maid walking over to the door, then the gentle click of the switch and the room was flooded with a blaze of light. They all screwed up their eyes, opened them again, gazed about them.

At that point I got up from my chair and slid quietly from the room, but as I went I saw a sight that I shall never forget as long as I live. It was Janet, with both hands in mid-air, stopped, frozen rigid, caught in the act of gesticulating towards someone across the table. Her mouth had dropped open two inches and she wore the surprised, not-quite-understanding look of a person who precisely one second before has been shot dead, right through the heart.

In the hall outside I paused and listened to the beginning of the uproar, the shrill cries of the ladies and the outraged unbelieving exclamations of the men; and soon there was a great hum of noise with everybody talking or shouting at the same time. Then – and this was the sweetest moment of all – I heard Lord Mulherrin's voice, roaring above the rest, 'Here! Someone! Hurry! Give her some water quick!'

Out in the street the chauffeur helped me into my car, and soon we were away from London and bowling merrily along the Great North Road towards this, my other house, which is only ninety-five miles from Town anyway.

The next two days I spent in gloating. I mooned around in a dream of ecstasy, half drowned in my own complacency and filled with a sense of pleasure so great that it constantly gave me pins and needles all along the lower parts of my legs. It wasn't until this morning when Gladys Ponsonby called me on the phone that I suddenly came to my senses and realized I was not a hero at all but an outcast. She informed me – with what I thought was just a trace of relish – that everybody was up in arms, that all of them, all my old and loving friends, were saying the most terrible things about me and had sworn never never to speak to me again. Except her, she kept saying. Everybody except her. And didn't I think it would be rather cosy, she asked, if she were to come down and stay with me a few days to cheer me up?

I'm afraid I was too upset by that time even to answer her politely. I put the phone down and went away to weep.

Then at noon today came the final crushing blow. The post arrived, and with it – I can hardly bring myself to write about it, I am so ashamed – came a letter, the sweetest, most tender little note imaginable from none other than Janet de Pelagia herself. She forgave me completely, she wrote, for everything I had done. She knew it was only a joke and I must not listen to the horrid things other people were saying about me. She loved me as she always had and always would to her dying day.

Oh, what a cad, what a brute I felt when I read this! The more so when I found that she had actually sent me by the same post a small present as an added sign of her affection – a half-pound jar of my favourite food of all, fresh caviare.

I can never under any circumstances resist good caviare. It is perhaps my greatest weakness. So although I naturally had no appetite whatsoever for food at dinnertime this evening, I must confess I took a few spoonfuls of the stuff in an effort to console myself in my misery. It is even possible that I took a shade too much, because I haven't been feeling any too chipper this last hour or so. Perhaps I ought to go up right away and get myself some bicarbonate of soda. I can easily come back and finish this later, when I'm in better trim.

You know – now I come to think of it, I really do feel rather ill all of a sudden.

Edward the Conqueror

First published in *The New Yorker*
(31 October 1953)

Louisa, holding a dishcloth in her hand, stepped out the kitchen door at the back of the house into the cool October sunshine.

'Edward!' she called. '*Ed-ward!* Lunch is ready!'

She paused a moment, listening; then she strolled out on to the lawn and continued across it – a little shadow attending her – skirting the rose bed and touching the sundial lightly with one finger as she went by. She moved rather gracefully for a woman who was small and plump, with a lilt in her walk and a gentle swinging of the shoulders and the arms. She passed under the mulberry tree on to the brick path, then went all the way along the path until she came to the place where she could look down into the dip at the end of this large garden.

'*Edward!* Lunch!'

She could see him now, about eighty yards away, down in the dip on the edge of the wood – the tallish narrow figure in khaki slacks and dark-green sweater, working beside a big bonfire with a fork in his hands, pitching brambles on to the top of the fire. It was blazing fiercely, with orange flames and clouds of milky smoke, and the smoke was drifting back over the garden with a wonderful scent of autumn and burning leaves.

Louisa went down the slope towards her husband. Had she wanted, she could easily have called again and made herself heard, but there was something about a first-class bonfire that impelled her towards it, right up close so she could feel the heat and listen to it burn.

'Lunch,' she said, approaching.

'Oh, hello. All right – yes. I'm coming.'

'*What* a good fire.'

'I've decided to clear this place right out,' her husband said. 'I'm sick and tired of all these brambles.' His long face was wet with perspiration. There were small beads of it clinging all over his moustache like dew, and two little rivers were running down his throat on to the turtleneck of the sweater.

'You better be careful you don't overdo it, Edward.'

'Louisa, I do wish you'd stop treating me as though I were eighty. A bit of exercise never did anyone any harm.'

'Yes, dear, I know. Oh, Edward! Look! Look!'

The man turned and looked at Louisa, who was pointing now to the far side of the bonfire.

'Look, Edward! The cat!'

Sitting on the ground, so close to the fire that the flames sometimes seemed actually to be touching it, was a large cat of a most unusual colour. It stayed quite still, with its head on one side and its nose in the air, watching the man and woman with a cool yellow eye.

'It'll get burned!' Louisa cried, and she dropped the dishcloth and darted swiftly in and grabbed it with both hands, whisking it away and putting it on the grass well clear of the flames.

'You crazy cat,' she said, dusting off her hands. 'What's the matter with you?'

'Cats know what they're doing,' the husband said. 'You'll never find a cat doing something it doesn't want. Not cats.'

'Whose is it? You ever seen it before?'

'No, I never have. Damn peculiar colour.'

The cat had seated itself on the grass and was regarding them with a sidewise look. There was a veiled inward expression about the eyes, something curiously omniscient and pensive, and around the nose a most delicate air of contempt, as though the sight of these two middle-aged persons – the one small, plump and rosy, the other lean and extremely sweaty – were a matter of some surprise but very little importance. For a cat, it certainly had an unusual colour – a pure silvery grey with no blue in it at all – and the hair was very long and silky.

Louisa bent down and stroked its head. 'You must go home,' she said. 'Be a good cat now and go on home to where you belong.'

The man and wife started to stroll back up the hill towards the house. The cat got up and followed, at a distance at first, but edging closer and closer as they went along. Soon it was alongside them, then it was ahead, leading the way across the lawn to the house, and walking as though it owned the whole place, holding its tail straight up in the air, like a mast.

'Go home,' the man said. 'Go on home. We don't want you.'

But when they reached the house, it came in with them,

and Louisa gave it some milk in the kitchen. During lunch, it hopped up on to the spare chair between them and sat through the meal with its head just above the level of the table, watching the proceedings with those dark-yellow eyes which kept moving slowly from the woman to the man and back again.

'I don't like this cat,' Edward said.

'Oh, I think it's a beautiful cat. I do hope it stays a little while.'

'Now, listen to me, Louisa. The creature can't possibly stay here. It belongs to someone else. It's lost. And if it's still trying to hang around this afternoon, you'd better take it to the police. They'll see it gets home.'

After lunch, Edward returned to his gardening. Louisa, as usual, went to the piano. She was a competent pianist and a genuine music-lover, and almost every afternoon she spent an hour or so playing for herself. The cat was now lying on the sofa, and she paused to stroke it as she went by. It opened its eyes, looked at her a moment, then closed them again and went back to sleep.

'You're an awfully nice cat,' she said. 'And such a beautiful colour. I wish I could keep you.' Then her fingers, moving over the fur on the cat's head, came into contact with a small lump, a little growth just above the right eye.

'Poor cat,' she said. 'You've got bumps on your beautiful face. You must be getting old.'

She went over and sat down on the long piano bench, but she didn't immediately start to play. One of her special little pleasures was to make every day a kind of concert day, with a carefully arranged programme which she worked out in detail before she began. She never liked to break her enjoyment by having to stop while she wondered what to play next. All she wanted was a brief pause after each piece while the audience clapped enthusiastically and called for more. It was so much nicer to imagine an audience, and now and again while she was playing – on the lucky days, that is – the room would begin to swim and fade and darken, and she would see nothing but row upon row of seats and a sea of white faces upturned towards her, listening with a rapt and adoring concentration.

Sometimes she played from memory, sometimes from music. Today she would play from memory; that was the way she felt. And what should the programme be? She sat before the piano with her small hands clasped on her lap, a plump rosy little person with a round and still quite pretty face, her hair done up in a neat bun at the back of her head. By looking slightly to the right, she could see the cat curled up asleep on the sofa, and its silvery-grey coat was beautiful against the purple of the cushion. How about some Bach to begin with? Or, better still, Vivaldi. The Bach adaptation for organ of the D minor *Concerto Grosso*. Yes – that first. Then perhaps a little Schumann. *Carnaval*? That would be fun. And after that – well, a touch of Liszt for a change. One of the *Petrarch Sonnets*. The second one – that was the loveliest – the E major. Then another Schumann, another of his gay ones – *Kinderszenen*. And lastly, for the encore, a Brahms waltz, or maybe two of them if she felt like it.

Vivaldi, Schumann, Liszt, Schumann, Brahms. A very nice programme, one that she could play easily without the music. She moved herself a little closer to the piano and paused a moment while someone in the audience – already she could feel that this was one of the lucky days – while someone in the audience had his last cough; then, with the slow grace that accompanied nearly all her movements, she lifted her hands to the keyboard and began to play.

She wasn't, at that particular moment, watching the cat at all – as a matter of fact she had forgotten its presence – but as the first deep notes of the Vivaldi sounded softly in the room, she became aware, out of the corner of one eye, of a sudden flurry, a flash of movement on the sofa to her right. She stopped playing at once. 'What is it?' she said, turning to the cat. 'What's the matter?'

The animal, who a few seconds before had been sleeping peacefully, was now sitting bolt upright on the sofa, very tense, the whole body aquiver, ears up and eyes wide open, staring at the piano.

'Did I frighten you?' she asked gently. 'Perhaps you've never heard music before.'

No, she told herself. I don't think that's what it is. On second thoughts, it seemed to her that the cat's attitude was not one of fear. There was no shrinking or backing away. If anything, there was a leaning forward, a kind of eagerness about the creature, and the face – well, there was rather an odd expression on the face, something of a mixture between surprise and shock. Of course, the face of a cat is a small and fairly expressionless thing, but if you watch carefully the eyes and ears working together, and particularly that little area of mobile skin below the ears and slightly to one side, you can occasionally see the reflection of very powerful emotions. Louisa was watching the face closely now, and because she was curious to see what would happen a second time, she reached out her hands to the keyboard and began again to play the Vivaldi.

This time the cat was ready for it, and all that happened to begin with was a small extra tensing of the body. But as the music swelled and quickened into that first exciting rhythm of the introduction to the fugue, a strange look that amounted almost to ecstasy began to settle upon the creature's face. The ears, which up to then had been pricked up straight, were gradually drawn back, the eyelids drooped, the head went over to one side, and at that moment Louisa could have sworn that the animal was actually *appreciating* the work.

What she saw (or thought she saw) was something she had noticed many times on the faces of people listening very closely to a piece of music. When the sound takes complete hold of them and drowns them in itself, a peculiar, intensely ecstatic look comes over them that you can recognize as easily as a smile. So far as Louisa could see, the cat was now wearing almost exactly this kind of look.

Louisa finished the fugue, then played the siciliana, and all the way through she kept watching the cat on the sofa. The final proof for her that the animal was listening came at the end, when the music stopped. It blinked, stirred itself a little, stretched a leg, settled into a more comfortable position, took a quick glance round the room, then looked expectantly in her direction. It was precisely the way a concert-goer reacts when the music momentarily releases him in the pause between two movements of a symphony. The behaviour was so thoroughly human it gave her a queer agitated feeling in the chest.

'You like that?' she asked. 'You like Vivaldi?'

The moment she'd spoken, she felt ridiculous, but not – and this to her was a trifle sinister – not quite so ridiculous as she knew she should have felt.

Well, there was nothing for it now except to go straight ahead with the next number on the programme, which was *Carnaval*. As soon as she began to play, the cat again stiffened and sat up straighter; then, as it became slowly and blissfully saturated with the sound, it relapsed into that queer melting mood of ecstasy that seemed to have something to do with drowning and with dreaming. It was really an extravagant sight – quite a comical one, too – to see this silvery cat sitting on the sofa and being carried away like this. And what made it more screwy than ever, Louisa thought, was the fact that this music, which the animal seemed to be enjoying so much, was manifestly too *difficult*, too *classical*, to be appreciated by the majority of humans in the world.

Maybe, she thought, the creature's not really enjoying it at all. Maybe it's a sort of hypnotic reaction, like with snakes. After all, if you can charm a snake with music, then why not a cat? Except that millions of cats hear the stuff every day of their lives, on radio and gramophone and piano, and, as far as she knew, there'd never yet been a case of one behaving like this. This one was acting as though it were following every single note. It was certainly a fantastic thing.

But was it not also a wonderful thing? Indeed it was. In fact, unless she was much mistaken, it was a kind of miracle, one of those animal miracles that happen about once every hundred years.

'I could see you *loved* that one,' she said when the piece was over. 'Although I'm sorry I didn't play it any too well today. Which did you like best – the Vivaldi or the Schumann?'

The cat made no reply, so Louisa, fearing she might lose the attention of her listener, went straight into the next part of the programme – Liszt's second *Petrarch Sonnet*.

And now an extraordinary thing happened. She hadn't played more than three or four bars when the animal's whiskers began perceptibly to twitch. Slowly it drew itself up to an extra height, laid its head on one side, then on the other, and stared into space with a kind of frowning concentrated look that seemed to say, What's this? Don't tell me. I know it so well, but just for the moment I don't seem to be able to place it. Louisa was fascinated, and with her little mouth half open and half smiling, she continued to play, waiting to see what on earth was going to happen next.

The cat stood up, walked to one end of the sofa, sat down again, listened some more; then all at once it bounded to the floor and leaped up on to the piano bench beside her. There it sat, listening intently to the lovely sonnet, not dreamily this time, but very erect, the large yellow eyes fixed upon Louisa's fingers.

'Well!' she said as she struck the last chord. 'So you came up to sit beside me, did you? You like this better than the sofa? All right, I'll let you stay, but you must keep still and not jump about.' She put out a hand and stroked the cat softly along the back, from head to tail. 'That was Liszt,' she went on. 'Mind you, he can sometimes be quite horribly vulgar, but in things like this he's really charming.'

She was beginning to enjoy this odd animal pantomime, so she went straight on into the next item on the programme, Schumann's *Kinderszenen*.

She hadn't been playing for more than a minute or two when she realized that the cat had again moved, and was now back in its old place on the sofa. She'd been watching her hands at the time, and presumably that was why she hadn't even noticed its going; all the same, it must have been an extremely swift and silent move. The cat was still staring at her, still apparently attending closely to the music, and yet it seemed to Louisa that there was not now the same rapturous enthusiasm there'd been during the previous piece, the Liszt. In addition, the act of leaving the stool and returning to the sofa appeared in itself to be a mild but positive gesture of disappointment.

'What's the matter?' she asked when it was over. 'What's wrong with Schumann? What's so marvellous about Liszt?' The cat looked straight back at her with those yellow eyes that had small jet-black bars lying vertically in their centres.

This, she told herself, is really beginning to get interesting – a trifle spooky, too, when she came to think of it. But one look at the cat sitting there on the sofa, so bright and attentive, so obviously waiting for more music, quickly reassured her.

'All right,' she said. 'I'll tell you what I'm going to do. I'm going to alter my programme specially for you. You seem to like Liszt so much, I'll give you another.'

She hesitated, searching her memory for a good Liszt; then softly she began to play one of the twelve little pieces from *Der Weihnachtsbaum*. She was now watching the cat very closely, and the first thing she noticed was that the whiskers again began to twitch. It jumped down to the carpet, stood still a moment, inclining its head, quivering with excitement, and then, with a slow, silky stride, it walked round the piano, hopped up on the bench, and sat down beside her.

They were in the middle of all this when Edward came in from the garden.

'Edward!' Louisa cried, jumping up. 'Oh, Edward, darling! Listen to this! Listen what's happened!'

'What is it now?' he said. 'I'd like some tea.' He had one of those narrow, sharp-nosed, faintly magenta faces, and the sweat was making it shine as though it were a long wet grape.

'It's the cat!' Louisa cried, pointing to it sitting quietly on the piano bench. 'Just *wait* till you hear what's happened!'

'I thought I told you to take it to the police.'

'But, Edward, *listen* to me. This is *terribly* exciting. This is a *musical* cat.'

'Oh yes?'

'This cat can appreciate music, and it can understand it too.'

'Now stop this nonsense, Louisa, and let's for God's sake have some tea. I'm hot and tired from cutting brambles and building bonfires.' He sat down in an armchair, took a cigarette from a box beside him and lit it with an immense patent lighter that stood near the box.

'What you don't understand,' Louisa said, 'is that something extremely exciting has been happening here in our own house while you were out, something that may even be . . . well . . . almost momentous.'

'I'm quite sure of that.'

'Edward, *please*!'

Louisa was standing by the piano, her little pink face pinker than ever, a scarlet rose high up on each cheek. 'If you want to know,' she said, 'I'll tell you what I think.'

'I'm listening, dear.'

'I think it might be possible that we are at this moment sitting in the presence of –' She stopped, as though suddenly sensing the absurdity of the thought.

'Yes?'

'You may think it silly, Edward, but it's honestly what I think.'

'In the presence of who, for heaven's sake?'

'Of Franz Liszt himself!'

Her husband took a long slow pull at his cigarette and blew the smoke up at the ceiling. He had the tight-skinned, concave cheeks of a man who has worn a full set of dentures for many years, and every time he sucked at a cigarette, the cheeks went in even more, and the bones of his face stood out like a skeleton's. 'I don't get you,' he said.

'Edward, listen to me. From what I've seen this afternoon with my own eyes, it really looks as though this might actually be some sort of a reincarnation.'

'You mean this lousy cat?'

'Don't talk like that, dear, please.'

'You're not ill, are you, Louisa?'

'I'm perfectly all right, thank you very much. I'm a bit confused – I don't mind admitting it, but who wouldn't be after what's just happened? Edward, I swear to you –'

'What *did* happen, if I may ask?'

Louisa told him, and all the while she was speaking, her husband lay sprawled in the chair with his legs stretched out in front of him, sucking at his cigarette and blowing the smoke up at the ceiling. There was a thin cynical smile on his mouth.

'I don't see anything very unusual about that,' he said when it was over. 'All it is – it's a trick cat. It's been taught tricks, that's all.'

'Don't be silly, Edward. Every time I play Liszt, he gets all excited and comes running over to sit on the stool beside me. But only for Liszt, and nobody can teach a cat the difference between Liszt and Schumann. You don't even know it yourself. But this one can do it every single time. Quite obscure Liszt, too.'

'Twice,' the husband said. 'He's only done it twice.'

'Twice is enough.'

'Let's see him do it again. Come on.'

'No,' Louisa said. 'Definitely not. Because if this *is* Liszt, as I believe it is, or anyway the soul of Liszt or whatever it is that comes back, then it's certainly not right or even very kind to put him through a lot of silly undignified tests.'

'My dear woman! This is a *cat* – a rather stupid grey cat

that nearly got its coat singed by the bonfire, this morning in the garden. And, anyway, what do you know about reincarnation?'

'If his soul is there, that's enough for me,' Louisa said firmly. 'That's all that counts.'

'Come on, then. Let's see him perform. Let's see him tell the difference between his own stuff and someone else's.'

'No, Edward. I've told you before. I refuse to put him through any more silly circus tests. He's had quite enough of that for one day. But I'll tell you what I *will* do. I'll play him a little more of his own music.'

'A fat lot that'll prove.'

'You watch. And one thing is certain – as soon as he recognizes it, he'll refuse to budge off that bench where he's sitting now.'

Louisa went to the music shelf, took down a book of Liszt, thumbed through it quickly, and chose another of his finger compositions – the B minor sonata. She had meant to play only the first part of the work, but once she got started and saw how the cat was sitting there literally quivering with pleasure and watching her hands with that rapturous concentrated look, she didn't have the heart to stop. She played it all the way through. When it was finished, she glanced up at her husband and smiled. 'There you are,' she said. 'You can't tell me he wasn't absolutely *loving* it.'

'He just likes the noise, that's all.'

'He was *loving* it. Weren't you, darling?' she said, lifting the cat in her arms. 'Oh my goodness, if only he could talk. Just think of it, dear – he met Beethoven in his youth! He knew Schubert and Mendelssohn and Schumann and Berlioz and Grieg and Delacroix and Ingres and Heine and Balzac. And let me see . . . My heavens, he was Wagner's father-in-law! I'm holding Wagner's father-in-law in my arms!'

'Louisa!' her husband said sharply, sitting up straight. 'Pull yourself together.' There was a new edge to his voice now, and he spoke louder.

Louisa glanced up quickly. 'Edward, I do believe you're jealous!'

'Oh sure, sure I'm jealous – of a lousy grey cat!'

'Then don't be so grumpy and cynical about it all. If you're going to behave like this, the best thing you can do is to go back to your gardening and leave the two of us together in peace. That will be best for all of us, won't it, darling?' she said, addressing the cat, stroking its head. 'And later on this evening, we shall have some more music together, you and I, some more of your own work. Oh yes,' she said, kissing the creature several times on the neck, 'and we might have a little Chopin, too. You needn't tell me – I happen to know you adore Chopin. You used to be great friends with him, didn't you, darling? As a matter of fact – if I remember rightly – it was in Chopin's apartment that you met the great love of your life, Madame Something-or-other. Had three illegitimate children by her, too, didn't you? Yes, you did, you naughty thing, and don't go trying to deny it. So you shall have some Chopin,' she said, kissing the cat again, 'and that'll probably bring back all sorts of lovely memories to you, won't it?'

'Louisa, stop this at once!'

'Oh, don't be so stuffy, Edward.'

'You're behaving like a perfect idiot, woman. And anyway, you forget we're going out this evening, to Bill and Betty's for canasta.'

'Oh, but I couldn't *possibly* go out now. There's no question of that.'

Edward got up slowly from his chair, then bent down and stubbed his cigarette hard into the ashtray. 'Tell me something,' he said quietly. 'You don't really believe this – this twaddle you're talking, do you?'

'But of *course* I do. I don't think there's any question about it now. And, what's more, I consider that it puts a tremendous responsibility upon us, Edward – upon both of us. You as well.'

'You know what I think,' he said. 'I think you ought to see a doctor. And damn quick too.'

With that, he turned and stalked out of the room, through the French windows, back into the garden.

Louisa watched him striding across the lawn towards his bonfire and his brambles, and she waited until he was out of sight before she turned and ran to the front door, still carrying the cat.

Soon she was in the car, driving to town.

She parked in front of the library, locked the cat in the car, hurried up the steps into the building and headed straight for the reference room. There she began searching the cards for books on two subjects – REINCARNATION and LISZT.

Under REINCARNATION she found something called *Recurring Earth-Lives – How and Why*, by a man called F. Milton Willis, published in 1921. Under LISZT she found two biographical volumes. She took out all three books, returned to the car and drove home.

Back in the house, she placed the cat on the sofa, sat herself down beside it with her three books and prepared to do some serious reading. She would begin, she decided, with Mr F. Milton Willis's work. The volume was thin and a trifle soiled, but it had a good heavy feel to it, and the author's name had an authoritative ring.

The doctrine of reincarnation, she read, states that spiritual souls pass from higher to higher forms of animals. 'A man can, for instance, no more be reborn as an animal than an adult can re-become a child.'

She read this again. But how did he know? How could he be so sure? He couldn't. No one could possibly be certain about a thing like that. At the same time, the statement took a great deal of the wind out of her sails.

'Around the centre of consciousness of each of us, there are, besides the dense outer body, four other bodies, invisible to the eye of flesh, but perfectly visible to people whose faculties of perception of superphysical things have undergone the requisite development . . .'

She didn't understand that one at all, but she read on, and soon she came to an interesting passage that told how long a soul usually stayed away from the earth before returning in someone else's body. The time varied according to type, and Mr Willis gave the following breakdown:

Drunkards and the unemployable	40/50	YEARS
Unskilled labourers	60/100	"
Skilled workers	100/200	"
The bourgeoisie	200/300	"
The upper-middle classes	500	"
The highest class of gentleman farmers	600/1,000	"
Those in the Path of Initiation	1,500/2,000	"

Quickly she referred to one of the other books, to find out how long Liszt had been dead. It said he died in Bayreuth in 1886. That was sixty-seven years ago. Therefore, according to Mr Willis, he'd have to have been an unskilled labourer to come back so soon. That didn't seem to fit at all. On the other hand, she didn't think much of the author's methods of grading. According to him, 'the highest class of gentleman farmer' was just about the most superior being on the earth. Red jackets and stirrup cups and the bloody, sadistic murder of the fox. No, she thought, that isn't right. It was a pleasure to find herself beginning to doubt Mr Willis.

Later in the book, she came upon a list of some of the more famous reincarnations. Epictetus, she was told, returned to earth as Ralph Waldo Emerson. Cicero came back as Gladstone, Alfred the Great as Queen Victoria, William the Conqueror as Lord Kitchener. Ashoka Vardhana, King of India in 272 BC, came back as Colonel

Henry Steel Olcott, an esteemed American lawyer. Pythagoras returned as Master Koot Hoomi, the gentleman who founded the Theosophical Society with Mme Blavatsky and Colonel H. S. Olcott (the esteemed American lawyer, alias Ashoka Vardhana, King of India). It didn't say who Mme Blavatsky had been. But 'Theodore Roosevelt,' it said.

> has for numbers of incarnations played great parts as a leader of men . . . From him descended the royal line of ancient Chaldea, he having been, about 30,000 BC, appointed Governor of Chaldea by the Ego we know as Caesar who was then ruler of Persia . . . Roosevelt and Caesar have been together time after time as military and administrative leaders; at one time, many thousands of years ago, they were husband and wife . . .

That was enough for Louisa. Mr F. Milton Willis was clearly nothing but a guesser. She was not impressed by his dogmatic assertions. The fellow was probably on the right track, but his pronouncements were extravagant, especially the first one of all, about animals. Soon she hoped to be able to confound the whole Theosophical Society with her proof that man could indeed reappear as a lower animal. Also that he did not have to be an unskilled labourer to come back within a hundred years.

She now turned to one of the Liszt biographies, and she was glancing through it casually when her husband came in again from the garden.

'What are you doing now?' he asked.

'Oh – just checking up a little here and there. Listen, my dear, did you know that Theodore Roosevelt once was Caesar's wife?'

'Louisa,' he said, 'look – why don't we stop this nonsense? I don't like to see you making a fool of yourself like this. Just give me that goddam cat and I'll take it to the police station myself.'

Louisa didn't seem to hear him. She was staring open-mouthed at a picture of Liszt in the book that lay on her lap. 'My God!' she cried. 'Edward, look!'

'What?'

'Look! The warts on his face! I forgot all about them! He had these great warts on his face and it was a famous thing. Even his students used to cultivate little tufts of hair on their own faces in the same spots, just to be like him.'

'What's that got to do with it?'

'Nothing. I mean, not the students. But the warts have.'

'Oh Christ,' the man said. 'Oh Christ God Almighty.'

'The cat has them, too! Look, I'll show you.'

She took the animal on to her lap and began examining its face. 'There! There's one! And there's another! Wait a minute! I do believe they're in the same places! Where's that picture?'

It was a famous portrait of the musician in his old age, showing the fine powerful face framed in a mass of long grey hair that covered his ears and came halfway down his neck. On the face itself, each large wart had been faithfully reproduced, and there were five of them in all.

'Now, in the picture there's *one* above the right eyebrow.'

She looked above the right eyebrow of the cat. 'Yes! It's there! In exactly the same place! And another on the left, at the top of the nose. That one's there, too! And one just below it on the cheek. And two fairly close together under the chin on the right side. Edward! Edward! Come and look! They're exactly the same.'

'It doesn't prove a thing.'

She looked up at her husband, who was standing in the centre of the room in his green sweater and khaki slacks, still perspiring freely. 'You're scared, aren't you, Edward? Scared of losing your precious dignity and having people think you might be making a fool of yourself just for once.'

'I refuse to get hysterical about it, that's all.'

Louisa turned back to the book and began reading some more. 'This is interesting,' she said. 'It says here that Liszt loved all of Chopin's works except one – the scherzo in B flat minor. Apparently he hated that. He called it the "Governess Scherzo", and said that it ought to be reserved solely for people in that profession.'

'So what?'

'Edward, listen. As you insist on being so horrid about all this, I'll tell you what I'm going to do. I'm going to play this scherzo right now and you can stay here and see what happens.'

'And then maybe you will deign to get us some supper.'

Louisa got up and took from the shelf a large green volume containing all of Chopin's works. 'Here it is. Oh yes, I remember it. It *is* rather awful. Now, listen – or, rather, watch. Watch to see what he does.'

She placed the music on the piano and sat down. Her husband remained standing. He had his hands in his pockets and a cigarette in his mouth, and in spite of himself he was watching the cat, which was now dozing on the sofa. When Louisa began to play, the first effect was as dramatic as ever. The animal jumped up as though it had been stung, and it stood motionless for at least a minute, the ears pricked up, the whole body quivering. Then it became restless and began to walk back and forth along the length of the sofa. Finally, it hopped down on to the floor, and with its nose and tail held high in the air, it marched slowly, majestically, from the room.

'There!' Louisa cried, jumping up and running after it. 'That does it! That really proves it!' She came back, carrying the cat, which she put down again on the sofa. Her whole face was shining with excitement now, her fists were clenched white, and the little bun on top of her head was loosening and going over to one side. 'What about it, Edward? What d'you think?' She was laughing nervously as she spoke.

'I must say it was quite amusing.'

'*Amusing!* My dear Edward, it's the most wonderful thing that's ever happened! Oh, goodness me!' she cried, picking up the cat again and hugging it to her bosom. 'Isn't it marvellous to think we've got Franz Liszt staying in the house?'

'Now, Louisa. Don't let's get hysterical.'

'I can't help it, I simply can't. And to *imagine* that he's actually going to live with us for always!'

'I beg your pardon?'

'Oh, Edward! I can hardly talk from excitement. And d'you know what I'm going to do next? Every musician in the whole world is going to want to meet him, that's a fact, and ask him about the people he knew – about Beethoven and Chopin and Schubert –'

'He can't talk,' her husband said.

'Well – all right. But they're going to want to meet him anyway, just to see him and touch him and to play their music to him, modern music he's never heard before.'

'He wasn't that great. Now, if it had been Bach or Beethoven . . .'

'Don't interrupt, Edward, please. So what I'm going to do is to notify all the important living composers everywhere. It's my duty. I'll tell them Liszt is here, and invite them to visit him. And you know what? They'll come flying in from every corner of the earth!'

'To see a grey cat?'

'Darling, it's the same thing. It's *him*. No one cares what he *looks* like. Oh, Edward, it'll be the most exciting thing there ever was!'

'They'll think you're mad.'

'You wait and see.' She was holding the cat in her arms and petting it tenderly but looking across at her husband, who now walked over to the French windows and stood there staring out into the garden. The evening was beginning, and the lawn was turning slowly from green to black, and in the distance he could see the smoke from his bonfire rising straight up in a white column.

'No,' he said, without turning round, 'I'm not having it. Not in this house. It'll make us both look perfect fools.'

'Edward, what do you mean?'

'Just what I say. I absolutely refuse to have you stirring up a lot of publicity about a foolish thing like this. You happen to have found a trick cat. OK – that's fine. Keep it, if it pleases you. I don't mind. But I don't wish you to go any farther than that. Do you understand me, Louisa?'

'Farther than what?'

'I don't want to hear any more of this crazy talk. You're acting like a lunatic.'

Louisa put the cat slowly down on the sofa. Then slowly she raised herself to her full small height and took one pace forward. '*Damn* you, Edward!' she shouted, stamping her foot. 'For the first time in our lives something really exciting comes along and you're scared to death of having anything to do with it because someone may laugh at you! That's right, isn't it? You can't deny it, can you?'

'Louisa,' her husband said. 'That's quite enough of that. Pull yourself together now and stop this at once.' He walked over and took a cigarette from the box on the table, then lit it with the enormous patent lighter. His wife stood watching him, and now the tears were beginning to trickle out of the inside corners of her eyes, making two little shiny rivers where they ran through the powder on her cheeks.

'We've been having too many of these scenes just lately, Louisa,' he was saying. 'No no, don't interrupt. Listen to me. I make full allowance for the fact that this may be an awkward time of life for you, and that –'

'Oh my God! You idiot! You pompous idiot! Can't you see that this is different, this is – this is something miraculous? Can't you see *that*?'

At that point, he came across the room and took her firmly by the shoulders. He had the freshly lit cigarette between his lips, and she could see faint contours on his skin where the heavy perspiration had dried in patches. 'Listen,' he said. 'I'm hungry. I've given up my golf and I've been working all day in the garden, and I'm tired and hungry and I want some supper. So do you. Off you go now to the kitchen and get us both something good to eat.'

Louisa stepped back and put both hands to her mouth. 'My heavens!' she cried. 'I forgot all about it. He must be absolutely famished. Except for some milk, I haven't given him a thing to eat since he arrived.'

'Who?'

'Why, *him*, of course. I must go at once and cook something really special. I wish I knew what his favourite dishes used to be. What do you think he would like best, Edward?'

'*Goddam* it, Louisa!'

'Now, Edward, please. I'm going to handle this *my* way just for once. You stay here,' she said, bending down and touching the cat gently with her fingers. 'I won't be long.'

Louisa went into the kitchen and stood for a moment, wondering what special dish she might prepare. How about a soufflé? A nice cheese soufflé? Yes, that would be rather special. Of course, Edward didn't much care for them, but that couldn't be helped.

She was only a fair cook, and she couldn't be sure of always having a soufflé come out well, but she took extra trouble this time and waited a long while to make certain the oven had heated fully to the correct temperature. While the soufflé was baking and she was searching around for something to go with it, it occurred to her that Liszt had probably never in his life tasted either avocado pears or grapefruit, so she decided to give him both of them at once in a salad. It would be fun to watch his reaction. It really would.

When it was all ready, she put it on a tray and carried it into the living-room. At the exact moment she entered, she saw her husband coming in through the French windows from the garden.

'Here's his supper,' she said, putting it on the table and turning towards the sofa. 'Where is he?'

Her husband closed the garden door behind him and walked across the room to get himself a cigarette.

'Edward, where is he?'

'Who?'

'You know who.'

'Ah, yes. Yes, that's right. Well – I'll tell you.' He was bending forward to light the cigarette, and his hands were cupped around the enormous patent lighter. He glanced up and saw Louisa looking at him – at his shoes and the bottoms of his khaki slacks, which were damp from walking in the long grass.

'I just went to see how the bonfire was going,' he said.

Her eyes travelled slowly upwards and rested on his hands.

'It's still burning fine,' he went on. 'I think it'll keep going all night.'

But the way she was staring made him uncomfortable.

'What is it?' he said, lowering the lighter. Then he looked down and noticed for the first time the long thin scratch that ran diagonally clear across the back of one hand, from the knuckle to the wrist.

'*Edward!*'

'Yes,' he said, 'I know. Those brambles are terrible. They tear you to pieces. Now, just a minute, Louisa. What's the matter?'

'*Edward!*'

'Oh, for God's sake, woman, sit down and keep calm. There's nothing to get worked up about. Louisa! Louisa, *sit down*!'

Galloping Foxley

First published in *Town & Country*
(November 1953)

Five days a week, for thirty-six years, I have travelled on the eight-twelve train to the City. It is never unduly crowded, and it takes me right into Cannon Street Station, only an eleven and a half minute walk from the door of my office in Austin Friars.

I have always liked the process of commuting; every phase of the little journey is a pleasure to me. There is a regularity about it that is agreeable and comforting to a person of habit, and in addition, it serves as a sort of slipway along which I am gently but firmly launched into the waters of daily business routine.

Ours is a smallish country station and only nineteen or twenty people gather there to catch the eight twelve. We are a group that rarely changes, and when occasionally a new face appears on the platform it causes a certain disclamatory, protestant ripple, like a new bird in a cage of canaries.

But normally, when I arrive in the morning with my usual four minutes to spare, there they all are, these good, solid, steadfast people, standing in their right places with their right umbrellas and hats and ties and faces and their newspapers under their arms, as unchanged and unchangeable through the years as the furniture in my own living-room. I like that.

I like also my corner seat by the window and reading *The Times* to the noise and motion of the train. This part of it lasts thirty-two minutes and it seems to soothe both my brain and my fretful old body like a good long massage. Believe me, there's nothing like routine and regularity for preserving one's peace of mind. I have now made this morning journey nearly ten thousand times in all, and I enjoy it more and more every day. Also (irrelevant, but interesting), I have become a sort of clock. I can tell at once if we are running two, three or four minutes late, and I never have to look up to know which station we are stopped at.

The walk at the other end from Cannon Street to my office is neither too long nor too short – a healthy little perambulation along streets crowded with fellow commuters all proceeding to their places of work on the same orderly schedule as myself. It gives me a sense of assurance to be moving among these dependable, dignified people who stick to their jobs and don't go gadding about all over the world. Their lives, like my own, are regulated nicely by the minute hand of an accurate watch, and very often our paths cross at the same times and places on the street each day.

For example, as I turn the corner into St Swithin's Lane, I invariably come head-on with a genteel middle-aged lady who wears silver pince-nez and carries a black briefcase in her hand – a first-rate accountant, I should say, or possibly an executive in the textile industry. When I cross over Threadneedle Street by the traffic lights, nine times out of ten I pass a gentleman who wears a different garden flower in his button-hole each day. He dresses in black trousers and grey spats and is clearly a punctual and meticulous person, probably a banker, or perhaps a solicitor like myself; and several times in the last twenty-five years, as we have hurried past one another across the street, our eyes have met in a fleeting glance of mutual approval and respect.

At least half the faces I pass on this little walk are now familiar to me. And good faces they are too, my kind of faces, my kind of people – sound, sedulous, businesslike folk with none of that restlessness and glittering eye about them that you see in all these so-called clever types who want to tip the world upside down with their Labour Governments and socialized medicines and all the rest of it.

So you can see that I am, in every sense of the words, a contented commuter. Or would it be more accurate to say that I *was* a contented commuter? At the time when I wrote the little autobiographical sketch you have just read – intending to circulate it among the staff of my office as an exhortation and an example – I was giving a perfectly true account of my feelings. But that was a whole week ago, and since then something rather peculiar has happened. As a matter of fact, it started to happen last Tuesday, the very morning that I was carrying the rough draft up to Town in my pocket; and this, to me, was so timely and coincidental that I can only believe it to have been the work of God. God had read my little essay and he had said to himself, 'This man Perkins is becoming over-complacent. It is high time I taught him a lesson.' I honestly believe that's what happened.

As I say, it was last Tuesday, the Tuesday after Easter, a warm yellow spring morning, and I was striding on to the platform of our small country station with *The Times* tucked under my arm and the draft of 'The Contented Commuter' in my pocket, when I immediately became aware that something was wrong. I could actually *feel* that curious little ripple of protest running along the ranks of my fellow commuters. I stopped and glanced around.

The stranger was standing plumb in the middle of the platform, feet apart and arms folded, looking for all the world as though he owned the place. He was a biggish, thickset man, and even from behind he somehow managed to convey a powerful impression of arrogance and oil. Very definitely, he was not one of us. He carried a cane instead of an umbrella, his shoes were brown instead of black, the grey hat was cocked at a ridiculous angle, and in one way and another there seemed to be an excess of silk and polish about his person. More than this I did not care to observe. I walked straight past him with my face to the sky, adding, I sincerely hope, a touch of real frost to an atmosphere that was already cool.

The train came in. And now, try if you can to imagine my horror when the new man actually followed me into *my own* compartment! Nobody has done this to me for fifteen years. My colleagues always respect my seniority. One of my special little pleasures is to have the place to myself for at least one, sometimes two or even three stations. But here, if you please, was this fellow, this stranger, straddling the seat opposite and blowing his nose and rustling the *Daily Mail* and lighting a disgusting pipe.

I lowered my *Times* and stole a glance at his face. I suppose he was about the same age as me – sixty-two or three – but he had one of those unpleasantly handsome, brown, leathery countenances that you see nowadays in advertisements for men's shirts – the lion shooter and the polo player and the Everest climber and the tropical explorer and the racing yachtsman all rolled into one; dark eyebrows, steely eyes, strong white teeth clamping the stem of a pipe. Personally, I mistrust all handsome men. The superficial pleasures of this life come too easily to them, and they seem to walk the world as though they themselves were personally responsible for their own good looks. I don't mind a *woman* being pretty. That's different. But in a man, I'm sorry, but somehow or other I find it downright offensive. Anyway, here was this one sitting right opposite me in the carriage, and I was looking at him over the top of my *Times* when suddenly he glanced up and our eyes met.

'D'you mind the pipe?' he asked, holding it up in his fingers. That was all he said. But the sound of his voice had a sudden and extraordinary effect upon me. In fact, I think I jumped. Then I sort of froze up and sat staring at him for at least a minute before I got a hold of myself and made an answer.

'This is a smoker,' I said, 'so you may do as you please.'

'I just thought I'd ask.'

There it was again, that curiously crisp, familiar voice, clipping its words and spitting them out very hard and small like a little quick-firing gun shooting out raspberry seeds. Where had I heard it before? And why did every word seem to strike upon some tiny tender spot far back in my memory? Good heavens, I thought. Pull yourself together. What sort of nonsense is this?

The stranger returned to his paper. I pretended to do the same. But by this time I was properly put out and I couldn't concentrate at all. Instead, I kept stealing glances at him over the top of the editorial page. It was really an intolerable face, vulgarly, almost lasciviously handsome, with an oily salacious sheen all over the skin. But had I or had I not seen it before sometime in my life? I began to think I had, because now, even when I looked at it I felt a peculiar kind of discomfort that I cannot quite describe – something to do with pain and with violence, perhaps even with fear.

We spoke no more during the journey, but you can well imagine that by then my whole routine had been thoroughly upset. My day was ruined; and more than one of my clerks at the office felt the sharper edge of my tongue, particularly after luncheon, when my digestion started acting up on me as well.

The next morning, there he was again standing in the middle of the platform with his cane and his pipe and his silk scarf and his nauseatingly handsome face. I walked past him and approached a certain Mr Grummitt, a stockbroker who has been commuting with me for over twenty-eight years. I can't say I've ever had an actual conversation with him before – we are rather a reserved lot on our station – but a crisis like this will usually break the ice.

'Grummitt,' I whispered. 'Who's the bounder?'

'Search me,' Grummitt said.

'Pretty unpleasant.'

'Very.'

'Not going to be a regular, I trust.'

'Oh God,' Grummitt said.

Then the train came in.

This time, to my great relief, the man got into another compartment.

But the following morning I had him with me again.

'Well,' he said, settling back in the seat directly opposite. 'It's a *topping* day.' And once again I felt that slow uneasy stirring of the memory, stronger than ever this time, closer to the surface but not yet quite within my reach.

Then came Friday, the last day of the week. I remember it had rained as I drove to the station, but it was one of those warm sparkling April showers that last only five or six minutes, and when I walked on to the platform, all the umbrellas were rolled up and the sun was shining and there were big white clouds floating in the sky. In spite of this, I felt depressed. There was no pleasure in this journey for me any longer. I knew the stranger would be there. And sure enough, he was, standing with his legs apart just as though he owned the place and this time swinging his cane casually back and forth through the air.

The cane! That did it! I stopped like I'd been shot.

'It's Foxley!' I cried under my breath. 'Galloping Foxley! And still swinging his cane!'

I stepped closer to get a better look. I tell you I've never had such a shock in all my life. It was Foxley all right. Bruce Foxley, or Galloping Foxley as we used to call him. And the last time I'd seen him, let me see – it was at school and I was no more than twelve or thirteen years old.

At that point the train came in, and heaven help me if he didn't get into my compartment once again. He put his hat and cane up on the rack, then turned and sat down and began lighting his pipe. He glanced up at me through the smoke with those rather small cold eyes and he said, '*Ripping* day, isn't it. Just like summer.'

There was no mistaking the voice now. It hadn't changed at all. Except that the things I had been used to hearing it say were different.

'All right, Perkins,' it used to say. 'All right, you nasty little boy. I am about to beat you again.'

How long ago was that? It must be nearly fifty years. Extraordinary, though, how little the features had altered. Still the same arrogant tilt of the chin, the flaring nostrils, the contemptuous staring eyes that were too small and a shade too close together for comfort; still the same habit of thrusting his face forward at you, impinging on you, pushing you into a corner, and even the hair I could remember – coarse and slightly wavy, with just a trace of oil all over it, like a well-tossed salad. He used to keep a bottle of green hair mixture on the side table in his study – when you have to dust a room you get to know and to hate all the objects in it – and this bottle had the Royal coat of arms on the label and the name of a shop in Bond Street, and under that, in small print, it said 'By

Appointment – Hairdressers To His Majesty King Edward VII'. I remember that particularly because it seemed so funny that a shop should want to boast about being hairdresser to someone who was practically bald – even a monarch.

And now I watched Foxley settle back in his seat and begin reading his paper. It was a curious sensation, sitting only a yard away from this man who fifty years before had made me so miserable that I had once contemplated suicide. He hadn't recognized *me*; there wasn't much danger of that because of my moustache. I felt fairly sure I was safe and could sit there and watch him all I wanted.

Looking back on it, there seems little doubt that I suffered very badly at the hands of Bruce Foxley my first year in school, and strangely enough, the unwitting cause of it all was my father. I was twelve and a half when I first went off to this fine old public school. That was, let me see, in 1907. My father, who wore a silk topper and morning coat, escorted me to the station, and I can remember how we were standing on the platform among piles of wooden tuck-boxes and trunks and what seemed like thousands of very large boys milling about and talking and shouting at one another, when suddenly somebody who was wanting to get by us gave my father a great push from behind and nearly knocked him off his feet.

My father, who was a small, courteous, dignified person, turned round with surprising speed and seized the culprit by the wrist.

'Don't they teach you better manners than that at this school, young man?' he said.

The boy, at least a head taller than my father, looked down at him with a cold, arrogant-laughing glare, and said nothing.

'It seems to me,' my father said, staring back at him, 'that an apology would be in order.'

But the boy just kept on looking down his nose at my father with this funny little arrogant smile at the corners of his mouth, and his chin kept coming farther and farther out.

'You strike me as being an impudent and ill-mannered boy,' my father went on. 'And I can only pray that you are an exception in your school. I would not wish for any son of mine to pick up such habits.'

At this point, the big boy inclined his head slightly in my direction, and a pair of small, cold, rather close-together eyes looked down into mine. I was not particularly frightened at the time; I knew nothing about the power of senior boys over junior boys at public schools; and I can remember that I looked straight back at him in support of my father, whom I adored and respected.

When my father started to say something more, the boy simply turned away and sauntered slowly down the platform into the crowd.

Bruce Foxley never forgot this episode; and of course the really unlucky thing about it for me was that when I arrived at school I found myself in the same 'house' as him. Even worse than that – I was in his study. He was doing his last year, and he was a prefect – a 'boazer', we called it – and as such he was officially permitted to beat any of the fags in the house. But being in his study, I automatically became his own particular, personal slave. I was his valet and cook and maid and errand-boy, and it was my duty to see that he never lifted a finger for himself unless absolutely necessary. In no society that I know of in the world is a servant imposed upon to the extent that we wretched little fags were imposed upon by the boazers at school. In frosty or snowy weather I even had to sit on the seat of the lavatory (which was in an unheated outhouse) every morning after breakfast to warm it before Foxley came along.

I could remember how he used to saunter across the room in his loose-jointed, elegant way, and if a chair were in his path he would knock it aside and I would have to run over and pick it up. He wore silk shirts and always had a silk handkerchief tucked up his sleeve, and his shoes were made by someone called Lobb (who also had a Royal crest). They were pointed shoes, and it was my duty to rub the leather with a bone for fifteen minutes each day to make it shine.

But the worst memories of all had to do with the changing-room.

I could see myself now, a small pale shrimp of a boy standing just inside the door of this huge room in my pyjamas and bedroom slippers and brown camel-hair dressing-gown. A single bright electric bulb was hanging on a flex from the ceiling, and all around the walls the black and yellow football shirts with their sweaty smell filling the room, and the voice, the clipped, pip-spitting voice, was saying, 'So which is it to be this time? Six with the dressing-gown on – or four with it off?'

I never could bring myself to answer this question. I would simply stand there staring down at the dirty floor-planks, dizzy with fear and unable to think of anything except that this other larger boy would soon start smashing away at me with his long, thin, white stick, slowly, scientifically, skilfully, legally and with apparent relish, and I would bleed. Five hours earlier, I had failed to get the fire to light in his study. I had spent my pocket money on a box of special firelighters and I had held a newspaper across the chimney opening to make a draught and I had knelt down in front of it and blown my guts out into the bottom of the grate; but the coals would not burn.

'If you're too obstinate to answer,' the voice was saying, 'then I'll have to decide for you.'

I wanted desperately to answer because I knew which one I had to choose. It's the first thing you learn when you arrive. Always keep the dressing-gown *on* and take the extra strokes. Otherwise you're almost certain to get cut. Even three with it on is better than one with it off.

'Take it off then and get into the far corner and touch your toes. I'm going to give you four.'

Slowly I would take it off and lay it on the ledge above the boot-lockers. And slowly I would walk over to the far corner, cold and naked now in my cotton pyjamas, treading softly and seeing everything around me suddenly very bright and flat and far away, like a magic-lantern picture, and very big, and very unreal, and sort of swimming through the water in my eyes.

'Go on and touch your toes. Tighter – much tighter than that.'

Then he would walk down to the far end of the changing-room and I would be watching him upside down between my legs, and he would disappear through a doorway that led down two steps into what we called 'the basin-passage'. This was a stone-floored corridor with wash-basins along one wall, and beyond it was the bathroom. When Foxley disappeared I knew he was walking down to the far end of the basin-passage. Foxley always did that. Then, in the distance, but echoing loud among the basins and the tiles, I would hear the noise of his shoes on the stone floor as he started galloping forward, and through my legs I would see him leaping up the two steps into the changing-room and come bounding towards me with his face thrust forward and the cane held high in the air. This was the moment when I shut my eyes and waited for the crack and told myself that whatever happened I must not straighten up.

Anyone who has been properly beaten will tell you that the real pain does not come until about eight or ten seconds after the stroke. The stroke itself is merely a loud crack and a sort of blunt thud against your backside, numbing you completely. (I'm told a bullet wound does the same.) But later on, oh my heavens, it feels like someone is laying a red-hot poker right across your naked buttocks and it is absolutely impossible to prevent yourself from reaching back and clutching it with your fingers.

Foxley knew all about this time lag, and the slow walk back over a distance that must altogether have been fifteen yards gave each stroke plenty of time to reach the peak of its pain before the next one was delivered.

On the fourth stroke I would invariably straighten up. I couldn't help it. It was an automatic defence reaction from a body that had had as much as it could stand.

'You flinched,' Foxley would say. 'That one doesn't count. Go on – down you get.'

The next time I would remember to grip my ankles.

Afterwards, he would watch me as I walked over – very stiff now and holding my backside – to put on my dressing-gown, but I would always try to keep turned away from him so he couldn't see my face. And when I went out, it would be, 'Hey you! Come back!'

I was in the passage then, and I would stop and turn and stand in the doorway, waiting.

'Come here. Come on, come back here. Now – haven't you forgotten something?'

All I could think of at that moment was the excruciating burning pain in my behind.

'You strike me as being an impudent and ill-mannered boy,' he would say, imitating my father's voice. 'Don't they teach you better manners than that at this school?'

'Thank . . . you,' I would stammer. 'Thank . . . you . . . for the beating.'

And then back up the dark stairs to the dormitory and it became much better then because it was all over and the pain was going and the others were clustering round and treating me with a certain rough sympathy born of having gone through the same thing themselves, many times.

'Hey Perkins, let's have a look.'

'How many d'you get?'

'Five, wasn't it? We heard them easily from here.'

'Come on, man. Let's see the marks.'

I would take down my pyjamas and stand there while this group of experts solemnly examined the damage.

'Rather far apart, aren't they? Not quite up to Foxley's usual standard.'

'Two of them are close. Actually touching. Look – these two are beauties!'

'That low one was a rotten shot.'

'Did he go right down the basin-passage to start his run?'

'You got an extra one for flinching, didn't you?'

'By golly, old Foxley's really got it in for *you*, Perkins.'

'Bleeding a bit too. Better wash it, you know.'

Then the door would open and Foxley would be there, and everyone would scatter and pretend to be doing his teeth or saying his prayers while I was left standing in the centre of the room with my pants down.

'What's going on here?' Foxley would say, taking a quick look at his own handiwork. 'You – Perkins! Put your pyjamas on properly and get into bed.'

And that was the end of a day.

Through the week, I never had a moment of time to myself. If Foxley saw me in the study taking up a novel or perhaps opening my stamp album, he would immediately find something for me to do. One of his favourites, especially when it was raining outside, was, 'Oh Perkins, I think a bunch of wild irises would look rather nice on my desk, don't you?'

Wild irises grew only around Orange Ponds. Orange Ponds was two miles down the road and half a mile across the fields. I would get up from my chair, put on my raincoat and my straw hat, take my umbrella – my brolly – and set off on this long and lonely trek. The straw hat had to be worn at all times outdoors, but it was easily destroyed by rain; therefore the brolly was necessary to protect the hat. On the other hand, you can't keep a brolly over your head while scrambling about on a woody bank looking for irises, so to save my hat from ruin I would put it on the ground under my brolly while I searched for the flowers. In this way, I caught many colds.

But the most dreaded day was Sunday. Sunday was for cleaning the study, and how well I can remember the terror of those mornings, the frantic dusting and scrubbing, and then the waiting for Foxley to come in to inspect.

'Finished?' he would ask.

'I . . . I think so.'

Then he would stroll over to the drawer of his desk and take out a single white glove, fitting it slowly on to his right hand, pushing each finger well home, and I would stand there watching and trembling as he moved around the room running his white-gloved forefinger along the picture tops, the skirting, the shelves, the window sills, the lampshades. I never took my eyes off that finger. For me it was an instrument of doom. Nearly always, it managed to discover some tiny crack that I had overlooked or perhaps hadn't even thought about; and when this happened Foxley would turn slowly around, smiling that dangerous little smile that wasn't a smile, holding up the white finger so that I should see for myself the thin smudge of dust that lay along the side of it.

'Well,' he would say. 'So you're a lazy little boy. Aren't you?'

No answer.

'Aren't you?'

'I thought I dusted it all.'

'Are you or are you not a nasty, lazy little boy?'

'Y-yes.'

'But your father wouldn't want you to grow up like that, would he? Your father is very particular about manners, is he not?'

No answer.

'I asked you, is your father particular about manners?'

'Perhaps – yes.'

'Therefore I will be doing him a favour if I punish you, won't I?'

'I don't know.'

'Won't I?'

'Y-yes.'

'We will meet later then, after prayers, in the changing-room.'

The rest of the day would be spent in an agony of waiting for the evening to come.

Oh my goodness, how it was all coming back to me now. Sunday was also letter-writing time.

Dear Mummy and Daddy – thank you very much for your letter. I hope you are both well. I am, except I have got a cold because I got caught in the rain but it will soon be over. Yesterday we played Shrewsbury and beat them 4–2. I watched and Foxley who you know is the head of our house scored one of our goals. Thank you very much for the cake. With love from William.

I usually went to the lavatory to write my letter, or to the boot-hole, or the bathroom – any place out of Foxley's way. But I had to watch the time. Tea was at four thirty and Foxley's toast had to be ready. Every day I had to make toast for Foxley, and on weekdays there were no fires allowed in the studies so all the fags, each making toast for his own study-holder, would have to crowd round the one small fire in the library, jockeying for position with his toasting-fork. Under these conditions, I still had to see that Foxley's toast was (1) very crisp (2) not burned at all (3) hot and ready exactly on time. To fail in any one of these requirements was a 'beatable offence'.

'Hey you! What's this?'

'It's toast.'

'Is this really your idea of toast?'

'Well . . .'

'You're too idle to make it right, aren't you?'

'I try to make it.'

'You know what they do to an idle horse, Perkins?'

'No.'

'Are you a horse?'

'No.'

'Well – anyway you're an ass – ha, ha – so I think you qualify. I'll be seeing you later.'

Oh, the agony of those days. To burn Foxley's toast was a 'beatable offence'. So was forgetting to take the mud off Foxley's football boots. So was failing to hang up

Foxley's football clothes. So was rolling up Foxley's brolly the wrong way round. So was banging the study door when Foxley was working. So was filling Foxley's bath too hot for him. So was not cleaning the buttons properly on Foxley's OTC uniform. So was making those blue metal-polish smudges on the uniform itself. So was failing to shine the *soles* of Foxley's shoes. So was leaving Foxley's study untidy at any time. In fact, so far as Foxley was concerned, I was practically a beatable offence myself.

I glanced out the window. My goodness, we were nearly there. I must have been dreaming away like this for quite a while, and I hadn't even opened my *Times*. Foxley was still leaning back in the corner seat opposite me reading his *Daily Mail*, and through a cloud of blue smoke from his pipe I could see the top half of his face over the newspaper, the small bright eyes, the corrugated forehead, the wavy, slightly oily hair.

Looking at him now, after all that time, was a peculiar and rather exciting experience. I knew he was no longer dangerous, but the old memories were still there and I didn't feel altogether comfortable in his presence. It was something like being inside the cage with a tame tiger.

What nonsense is this? I asked myself. Don't be so stupid. My heavens, if you wanted to you could go ahead and tell him exactly what you thought of him and he couldn't touch you. Hey – that was an idea!

Except that – well – after all, was it worth it? I was too old for that sort of thing now, and I wasn't sure that I really felt much anger towards him anyway.

So what should I do? I couldn't sit there staring at him like an idiot.

At that point, a little impish fancy began to take a hold of me. What I would like to do, I told myself, would be to lean across and tap him lightly on the knee and tell him who I was. Then I would watch his face. After that, I would begin talking about our schooldays together, making it just loud enough for the other people in the carriage to hear. I would remind him playfully of some of the things he used to do to me, and perhaps even describe the changing-room beatings so as to embarrass him a trifle. A bit of teasing and discomfort wouldn't do him any harm. And it would do *me* an awful lot of good.

Suddenly he glanced up and caught me staring at him. It was the second time this had happened, and I noticed a flicker of irritation in his eyes.

All right, I told myself. Here we go. But keep it pleasant and sociable and polite. It'll be much more effective that way, more embarrassing for him.

So I smiled at him and gave him a courteous little nod. Then, raising my voice, I said, 'I do hope you'll excuse me. I'd like to introduce myself.' I was leaning forward, watching him closely so as not to miss the reaction. 'My name is Perkins – William Perkins – and I was at Repton in 1907.'

The others in the carriage were sitting very still, and I could sense that they were all listening and waiting to see what would happen next.

'I'm glad to meet you,' he said, lowering the paper to his lap. 'Mine's Fortescue – Jocelyn Fortescue, Eton, 1916.'

Neck

First published in *Someone Like You* (1953)

When, about eight years ago, old Sir William Turton died and his son Basil inherited *The Turton Press* (as well as the title), I can remember how they started laying bets around Fleet Street as to just how long it would be before some nice young woman managed to persuade the little fellow that she must look after him. That is to say, him and his money.

The new Sir Basil Turton was maybe forty years old at the time, a bachelor, a man of mild and simple character who up to then had shown no interest in anything at all except his collection of modern paintings and sculpture. No woman had disturbed him; no scandal or gossip had ever touched his name. But now that he had become the proprietor of quite a large newspaper and magazine empire, it was necessary for him to emerge from the calm of his father's country house and come up to London.

Naturally, the vultures started gathering at once, and I believe that not only Fleet Street but very nearly the whole of the city was looking on eagerly as they scrambled for the body. It was slow motion, of course, deliberate and deadly slow motion, and therefore not so much like vultures as a bunch of agile crabs clawing for a piece of horsemeat under water.

But to everyone's surprise the little chap proved to be

remarkably elusive, and the chase dragged on right through the spring and early summer of that year. I did not know Sir Basil personally, nor did I have any reason to feel friendly towards him, but I couldn't help taking the side of my own sex and found myself cheering loudly every time he managed to get himself off the hook.

Then, round about the beginning of August, apparently at some secret female signal, the girls declared a sort of truce among themselves while they went abroad, and rested, and regrouped, and made fresh plans for the winter kill. This was a mistake because precisely at that moment a dazzling creature called Natalia something or other, whom nobody had heard of before, swept in from the Continent, took Sir Basil firmly by the wrist and led him off in a kind of swoon to the Registry Office at Caxton Hall, where she married him before anyone else, least of all the bridegroom, realized what was happening.

You can imagine that the London ladies were indignant, and naturally they started disseminating a vast amount of fruity gossip about the new Lady Turton ('That dirty poacher,' they called her). But we don't have to go into that. In fact, for the purposes of this story we can skip the next six years, which brings us right up to the present, to an occasion exactly one week ago today when I myself had the pleasure of meeting her ladyship for the first time. By now, as you must have guessed, she was not only running the whole of *The Turton Press*, but as a result had become a considerable political force in the country. I realize that other women have done this sort of thing before, but what made her particular case unusual was the fact that she was a foreigner and that nobody seemed to know precisely what country she came from – Yugoslavia, Bulgaria or Russia.

So last Thursday I went to this small dinner party at a friend's in London, and while we were standing around in the drawing-room before the meal, sipping good Martinis and talking about the atom bomb and Mr Bevan, the maid popped her head in to announce the last guest.

'Lady Turton,' she said.

Nobody stopped talking; we were too well-mannered for that. No heads were turned. Only our eyes swung round to the door, waiting for the entrance.

She came in fast – tall and slim in a red-gold dress with sparkles on it – the mouth smiling, the hand outstretched towards her hostess, and my heavens, I must say she was a beauty.

'Mildred, good evening!'

'My dear Lady Turton! How nice!'

I believe we *did* stop talking then, and we turned and stared and stood waiting quite meekly to be introduced, just like she might have been the Queen or a famous film star. But she was better looking than either of those. The hair was black, and to go with it she had one of those pale, oval, innocent fifteenth-century Flemish faces, almost exactly a Madonna by Memling or Van Eyck. At least that was the first impression. Later, when my turn came to shake hands, I got a closer look and saw that except for the outline and colouring it wasn't really a Madonna at all – far, far from it.

The nostrils for example were very odd, somehow

more open, more flaring, than any I had seen before, and excessively arched. This gave the whole nose a kind of open, snorting look that had something of the wild animal about it – the mustang.

And the eyes, when I saw them close, were not wide and round the way the Madonna painters used to make them, but long and half closed, half smiling, half sullen, and slightly vulgar, so that in one way and another they gave her a most delicately dissipated air. What's more, they didn't look at you directly. They came to you slowly from over on one side with a curious sliding motion that made me nervous. I tried to see their colour, thought it was pale grey, but couldn't be sure.

Then she was led away across the room to meet other people. I stood watching her. She was clearly conscious of her success and of the way these Londoners were deferring to her. 'Here am I,' she seemed to be saying, 'and I only came over a few years ago, but already I am richer and more powerful than any of you.' There was a little prance of triumph in her walk.

A few minutes later we went in to dinner, and to my surprise I found myself seated on her ladyship's right. I presumed that our hostess had done this as a kindness to me, thinking I might pick up some material for the special column I write each day in the evening paper. I settled myself down, ready for an interesting meal. But the famous lady took no notice of me at all; she spent her time talking to the man on her left, the host. Until at last, just as I was finishing my ice-cream, she suddenly turned, reached over, picked up my place card and read the name.

Then, with that queer sliding motion of the eyes, she looked into my face. I smiled and made a little bow. She didn't smile back, but started shooting questions at me, rather personal questions – job, age, family, things like that – in a peculiar lapping voice, and I found myself answering as best I could.

During this inquisition it came out among other things that I was a lover of painting and sculpture.

'Then you should come down to the country some time and see my husband's collection.' She said it casually, merely as a form of conversation, but you must realize that in my job I cannot afford to lose an opportunity like this.

'How kind of you, Lady Turton. But I'd simply love to. When shall I come?'

Her head went up and she hesitated, frowned, shrugged her shoulders, and then said, 'Oh, I don't care. Any time.'

'How about this next week-end? Would that be all right?'

The slow narrow eyes rested a moment on mine, then travelled away. 'I suppose so, if you wish. I don't care.'

And that was how on the following Saturday afternoon I came to be driving down to Wooton with my suitcase in the back of the car. You may think that perhaps I forced the invitation a bit, but I couldn't have got it any other way. And apart from the professional aspect, I personally wanted very much to see the house. As you know, Wooton is one of the truly great stone houses of the Early English Renaissance. Like its sisters, Longleat, Wollaton and Montacute, it was built in the latter half of the sixteenth century, when for the first time a great man's house could be designed as a comfortable dwelling, not as a castle, and when a new group of architects such as John Thorpe and the Smithsons were starting to do marvellous things all over the country. It lies south of Oxford, near a small town called Princes Risborough – not a long trip from London – and as I swung in through the main gates the sky was closing overhead and the early winter evening was beginning.

I went slowly up the long drive, trying to see as much of the grounds as possible, especially the famous topiary which I had heard such a lot about. And I must say it was an impressive sight. On all sides there were massive yew trees, trimmed and clipped into many different comical shapes – hens, pigeons, bottles, boots, armchairs, castles, egg-cups, lanterns, old women with flaring petticoats, tall pillars, some crowned with a ball, others with big rounded roofs and stemless mushroom finials – and in the half-darkness the greens had turned to black so that each figure, each tree, took on a dark, smooth, sculptural quality. At one point I saw a lawn covered with gigantic chessmen, each a live yew tree, marvellously fashioned. I stopped the car, got out and walked among them, and they were twice as tall as me. What's more, the set was complete, kings, queens, bishops, knights, rooks and pawns standing in position as for the start of a game.

Around the next bend I saw the great grey house itself, and in front of it the large entrance forecourt enclosed by a high balustraded wall with small pillared pavilions at its outer angles. The piers of the balustrades were surmounted by stone obelisks – the Italian influence on the Tudor mind – and a flight of steps at least a hundred feet wide led up to the house.

As I drove into the forecourt I noticed with rather a shock that the fountain basin in the middle supported a large statue by Epstein. A lovely thing, mind you, but surely not quite in sympathy with its surroundings. Then, looking back as I climbed the stairway to the front door, I saw that on all the little lawns and terraces round about there were other modern statues and many kinds of curious sculpture. In the distance, I thought I recognized Gaudier Brzeska, Brancusi, Saint-Gaudens, Henry Moore and Epstein again.

The door was opened by a young footman who led me up to a bedroom on the first floor. Her ladyship, he explained, was resting, so were the other guests, but they would all be down in the main drawing-room in an hour or so, dressed for dinner.

Now in my job it is necessary to do a lot of week-ending. I suppose I spend around fifty Saturdays and Sundays a year in other people's houses, and as a result I have become fairly sensitive to unfamiliar atmosphere. I can tell good or bad almost by sniffing with my nose the moment I get in the front door; and this one I was in now I did not like. The place smelled wrong. There was the faint, desiccated whiff of something troublesome in the air; I was conscious of it even as I lay steaming luxuriously in my great marble bath; and I couldn't help hoping that no unpleasant things were going to happen before Monday came.

The first of them – though more of a surprise than an

unpleasantness – occurred ten minutes later. I was sitting on the bed putting on my socks when softly the door opened, and an ancient lop-sided gnome in black tails slid into the room. He was the butler, he explained, and his name was Jelks, and he did so hope I was comfortable and had everything I wanted.

I told him I was and had.

He said he would do all he could to make my week-end agreeable. I thanked him and waited for him to go. He hesitated, and then, in a voice dripping with unction, he begged permission to mention a rather delicate matter. I told him to go ahead.

To be quite frank, he said, it was about tipping. The whole business of tipping made him acutely miserable.

Oh? And why was that?

Well, if I really wanted to know, he didn't like the idea that his guests felt under an obligation to tip him when they left the house – as indeed they did. It was an undignified proceeding both for the tipper and the tipped. Moreover, he was well aware of the anguish that was often created in the minds of guests such as myself, if I would pardon the liberty, who might feel compelled by convention to give more than they could really afford.

He paused, and two small crafty eyes watched my face for a sign. I murmured that he needn't worry himself about such things so far as I was concerned.

On the contrary, he said, he hoped sincerely that I would agree from the beginning to give him no tip at all.

'Well,' I said. 'Let's not fuss about it now, and when the time comes we'll see how we feel.'

'No, sir!' he cried. 'Please, I really must insist.'

So I agreed.

He thanked me, and shuffled a step or two closer. Then, laying his head on one side and clasping his hands before him like a priest, he gave a tiny apologetic shrug of the shoulders. The small sharp eyes were still watching me, and I waited, one sock on, the other in my hands, trying to guess what was coming next.

All that he would ask, he said softly, so softly now that his voice was like music heard faintly in the street outside a great concert hall, all that he would ask was that instead of a tip I should give him thirty-three and a third per cent of my winnings at cards over the week-end. If I lost, there would be nothing to pay.

It was all so soft and smooth and sudden that I was not even surprised.

'Do they play a lot of cards, Jelks?'

'Yes, sir, a great deal.'

'Isn't thirty-three and a third a bit steep?'

'I don't think so, sir.'

'I'll give you ten per cent.'

'No, sir, I couldn't do that.' He was now examining the fingernails of his left hand, and patiently frowning.

'Then we'll make it fifteen. All right?'

'Thirty-three and a third, sir. It's very reasonable. After all, sir, seeing that I don't even know if you are a good player, what I'm actually doing, not meaning to be personal, is backing a horse and I've never even seen it run.'

No doubt you think that I should never have started bargaining with the butler in the first place, and perhaps you are right. But being a liberal-minded person, I always try my best to be affable with the lower classes. Apart from that, the more I thought about it, the more I had to admit to myself that it was an offer no sportsman had the right to reject.

'All right then, Jelks. As you wish.'

'Thank you, sir.' He moved towards the door, walking slowly sideways like a crab; but once more he hesitated, a hand on the knob. 'If I may give you a little advice, sir – may I?'

'Yes?'

'It's simply that her ladyship tends to overbid her hand.'

Now this *was* going too far. I was so startled I dropped my sock. After all, it's one thing to have a harmless little sporting arrangement with the butler about tipping, but when he begins conniving with you to take money away from the hostess then it's time to call a halt.

'All right, Jelks. Now that'll do.'

'No offence, sir, I hope. All I mean is you're bound to be playing against her ladyship. She always partners Major Haddock.'

'Major Haddock? You mean Major Jack Haddock?'

'Yes, sir.'

I noticed there was the trace of a sneer around the corners of Jelks's nose when he spoke about this man. And it was worse with Lady Turton. Each time he said 'her ladyship' he spoke the words with the outsides of his lips as though he were nibbling a lemon, and there was a subtle, mocking inflexion in his voice.

'You'll excuse me now, sir. *Her ladyship* will be down at

seven o'clock. So will *Major Haddock* and the others.' He slipped out of the door, leaving behind him a certain dampness in the room and a faint smell of embrocation.

Shortly after seven, I found my way to the main drawing-room, and Lady Turton, as beautiful as ever, got up to greet me.

'I wasn't even sure you were coming,' she said in that peculiar lilting voice. 'What's your name again?'

'I'm afraid I took you at your word, Lady Turton. I hope it's all right.'

'Why not?' she said. 'There're forty-seven bedrooms in the house. This is my husband.'

A small man came around the back of her and said, 'You know, I'm so glad you were able to come.' He had a lovely warm smile and when he took my hand I felt instantly a touch of friendship in his fingers.

'And Carmen La Rosa,' Lady Turton said.

This was a powerfully built woman who looked as though she might have something to do with horses. She nodded at me, and although my hand was already halfway out she didn't give me hers, thus forcing me to convert the movement into a noseblow.

'You have a cold?' she said. 'I'm sorry.'

I did not like Miss Carmen La Rosa.

'And this is Jack Haddock.'

I knew this man slightly. He was a director of companies (whatever that may mean), and a well-known member of society. I had used his name a few times in my column, but I had never liked him, and this I think was mainly because I have a deep suspicion of all people who carry their military titles back with them into private life – especially majors and colonels. Standing there in his dinner-jacket with his full-blooded animal face and black eyebrows and large white teeth, he looked so handsome there was almost something indecent about it. He had a way of raising his upper lip when he smiled, baring the teeth, and he was smiling now as he gave me a hairy brown hand.

'I hope you're going to say some nice things about us in your column.'

'He better had,' Lady Turton said, 'or I'll say some nasty ones about him on my front page.'

I laughed, but the three of them, Lady Turton, Major Haddock and Carmen La Rosa, had already turned away and were settling themselves back on the sofa. Jelks gave me a drink, and Sir Basil drew me gently aside for a quiet chat at the other end of the room. Every now and again Lady Turton would call her husband to fetch her something – another Martini, a cigarette, an ashtray, a handkerchief – and he, half rising from his chair, would be forestalled by the watchful Jelks, who fetched it for him.

Clearly, Jelks loved his master; and just as clearly he hated the wife. Each time he did something for her he made a little sneer with his nose and drew his lips together so they puckered like a turkey's bottom.

At dinner, our hostess sat her two friends, Haddock and La Rosa, on either side of her. This unconventional arrangement left Sir Basil and me at the other end of the table, where we were able to continue our pleasant talk about painting and sculpture. Of course it was obvious to me by now that the major was infatuated with her ladyship. And again, although I hate to say it, it seemed as though the La Rosa woman was hunting the same bird.

All this foolishness appeared to delight the hostess. But it did not delight her husband. I could see that he was conscious of the little scene all the time we were talking; and often his mind would wander from our subject and he would stop short in mid-sentence, his eyes travelling down to the other end of the table to settle pathetically for a moment on that lovely head with the black hair and the curiously flaring nostrils. He must have noticed then how exhilarated she was, how the hand that gestured as she spoke rested every now and again on the major's arm, and how the other woman, the one who perhaps had something to do with horses, kept saying, 'Nata-*li*-a! Now Nata-*li*-a, listen to me!'

'Tomorrow,' I said, 'you must take me round and show me the sculptures you've put up in the garden.'

'Of course,' he said, 'with pleasure.' He glanced again at the wife, and his eyes had a sort of supplicating look that was piteous beyond words. He was so mild and passive a man in every way that even now I could see there was no anger in him, no danger, no chance of an explosion.

After dinner I was ordered straight to the card table to partner Miss Carmen La Rosa against Major Haddock and Lady Turton. Sir Basil sat quietly on the sofa with a book.

There was nothing unusual about the game itself; it was routine and rather dull. But Jelks was a nuisance. All evening he prowled around us, emptying ashtrays and asking about drinks and peering at our hands. He was obviously short-sighted and I doubt whether he saw much of what was going on because, as you may or may not know, here in England no butler has ever been permitted to wear spectacles – nor, for that matter, a moustache. This is the golden, unbreakable rule, and a very sensible one it is too, although I'm not quite sure what lies behind it. I presume that a moustache would make him look too much like a gentleman, and spectacles too much like an American, and where would we be then I should like to know? In any event, Jelks was a nuisance all evening; and so was Lady Turton, who was constantly being called to the phone on newspaper business.

At eleven o'clock she looked up from her cards and said, 'Basil, it's time you went to bed.'

'Yes, my dear, perhaps it is.' He closed the book, got up, and stood for a minute watching the play. 'Are you having a good game?' he asked.

The others didn't answer him, so I said, 'It's a nice game.'

'I'm so glad. And Jelks will look after you and get anything you want.'

'Jelks can go to bed too,' the wife said.

I could hear Major Haddock breathing through his nose beside me, and the soft drop of the cards one by one on to the table, and then the sound of Jelks's feet shuffling over the carpet towards us.

'You wouldn't prefer me to stay, m'lady?'

'No. Go to bed. You too, Basil.'

'Yes, my dear. Good night. Good night all.'

Jelks opened the door for him, and he went slowly out, followed by the butler.

As soon as the next rubber was over, I said that I too wanted to go to bed.

'All right,' Lady Turton said. 'Good night.'

I went up to my room, locked the door, took a pill and went to sleep.

The next morning, Sunday, I got up and dressed around ten o'clock and went down to the breakfast-room. Sir Basil was there before me, and Jelks was serving him with grilled kidneys and bacon and fried tomatoes. He was delighted to see me and suggested that as soon as we had finished eating we should take a long walk around the grounds. I told him nothing would give me more pleasure.

Half an hour later we started out, and you've no idea what a relief it was to get away from that house and into the open air. It was one of those warm shining days that come occasionally in mid-winter after a night of heavy rain, with a bright surprising sun and no breath of wind. Bare trees seemed beautiful in the sunlight, water still dripping from the branches, and wet places all around were sparkling with diamonds. The sky had small faint clouds.

'*What* a lovely day!'

'Yes – isn't it a lovely day!'

We spoke hardly another word during the walk; it wasn't necessary. But he took me everywhere and I saw it all – the huge chessmen and all the rest of the topiary. The elaborate garden houses, the pools, the fountains, the children's maze whose hedges were hornbeam and lime so that it was only good in summer when the leaves were out, and the parterres, the rockeries, the greenhouses with their vines and nectarine trees. And of course, the sculpture. Most of the contemporary European sculptors were there, in bronze, granite, limestone and wood; and although it was a pleasure to see them warming and glowing in the sun, to me they still looked a trifle out of place in these vast formal surroundings.

'Shall we rest here now a little while?' Sir Basil said after we had walked for more than an hour. So we sat down on a white bench beside a water-lily pond full of carp and goldfish, and lit cigarettes. We were some way from the house, on a piece of ground that was raised above its surroundings, and from where we sat the gardens were spread out below us like a drawing in one of those old books on garden architecture, with the hedges and lawns and terraces and fountains making a pretty pattern of squares and rings.

'My father bought this place just before I was born,' Sir Basil said. 'I've lived here ever since, and I know every inch of it. Each day I grow to love it more.'

'It must be wonderful in summer.'

'Oh, but it is. You should come down and see it in May and June. Will you promise to do that?'

'Of course,' I said. 'I'd love to come,' and as I spoke I was watching the figure of a woman dressed in red moving among the flowerbeds in the far distance. I saw her cross over a wide expanse of lawn, and there was a lilt in her walk, a little shadow attending her, and when she was over the lawn, she turned left and went along one side of a high wall of clipped yew until she came to another smaller lawn that was circular and had in its centre a piece of sculpture.

'This garden is younger than the house,' Sir Basil said. 'It was laid out early in the eighteenth century by a Frenchman called Beaumont, the same fellow who did Levens, in Westmorland. For at least a year he had two hundred and fifty men working on it.'

The woman in the red dress had been joined now by a man, and they were standing face to face, about a yard apart, in the very centre of the whole garden panorama, on this little circular patch of lawn, apparently conversing. The man had some small black object in his hand.

'If you're interested, I'll show you the bills that Beaumont put in to the old Duke while he was making it.'

'I'd like very much to see them. They must be fascinating.'

'He paid his labourers a shilling a day and they worked ten hours.'

In the clear sunlight it was not difficult to follow the movements and gestures of the two figures on the lawn. They had turned now towards the piece of sculpture, and were pointing at it in a sort of mocking way, apparently laughing and making jokes about its shape. I recognized it as being one of the Henry Moores, done in wood, a thin smooth object of singular beauty that had two or three holes in it and a number of strange limbs protruding.

'When Beaumont planted the yew trees for the chessmen and the other things, he knew they wouldn't amount to much for at least a hundred years. We don't seem to possess that sort of patience in our planning these days, do we? What do you think?'

'No,' I said. 'We don't.'

The black object in the man's hand turned out to be a camera, and now he had stepped back and was taking pictures of the woman beside the Henry Moore. She was striking a number of different poses, all of them, so far as I could see, ludicrous and meant to be amusing. Once she put her arms around one of the protruding wooden limbs and hugged it, and another time she climbed up and sat side-saddle on the thing, holding imaginary reins in her hands. A great wall of yew hid these two people from the house, and indeed from all the rest of the garden except the little hill on which we sat. They had every right to believe that they were not overlooked, and even if they had happened to glance our way – which was into the sun – I doubt whether they would have noticed the two small motionless figures sitting on the bench beside the pond.

'You know, I love these yews,' Sir Basil said. 'The colour of them is so wonderful in a garden because it rests the eye. And in the summer it breaks up the areas of brilliance into little patches and makes them more comfortable to admire. Have you noticed the different shades of green on the planes and facets of each clipped tree?'

'It's lovely, isn't it?'

The man now seemed to be explaining something to the woman, and pointing at the Henry Moore, and I could tell by the way they threw back their heads that they were laughing again. The man continued to point, and then the woman walked around the back of the wood carving, bent down and poked her head through one of its holes. The thing was about the size, shall I say, of a small horse, but thinner than that, and from where I sat I could see both sides of it – to the left, the woman's body, to the right, her head protruding through. It was very much like one of those jokes at the seaside where you put your head through a hole in a board and get photographed as a fat lady. The man was photographing her now.

'There's another thing about yews,' Sir Basil said. 'In the early summer when the young shoots come out . . .' At that moment he paused and sat up straighter and leaned slightly forward, and I could sense his whole body suddenly stiffening.

'Yes,' I said, 'when the young shoots come out?'

The man had taken the photograph, but the woman still had her head through the hole, and now I saw him put both hands (as well as the camera) behind his back and advance towards her. Then he bent forward so his face was close to hers, touching it, and he held it there while he gave her, I suppose, a few kisses or something like that. In the stillness that followed, I fancied I heard a faint faraway tinkle of female laughter coming to us through the sunlight across the garden.

'Shall we go back to the house?' I asked.

'Back to the house?'

'Yes, shall we go back and have a drink before lunch?'

'A drink? Yes, we'll have a drink.' But he didn't move. He sat very still, gone far away from me now, staring intently at the two figures. I also was staring at them. I couldn't take my eyes away; I *had* to look. It was like seeing a dangerous little ballet in miniature from a great distance, and you knew the dancers and the music but not the end of the story, nor the choreography, nor what they were going to do next, and you were fascinated, and you *had* to look.

'Gaudier Brzeska,' I said. 'How great do you think he might've become if he hadn't died so young?'

'Who?'

'Gaudier Brzeska.'

'Yes,' he said. 'Of course.'

I noticed now that something queer was happening. The woman still had her head through the hole, but she was beginning to wriggle her body from side to side in a slow unusual manner, and the man was standing motionless, a pace or so away, watching her. He seemed suddenly uneasy the way he stood there, and I could tell by the drop of the head and by the stiff intent set of the body that there was no laughter in him any more. For a while he remained still, then I saw him place his camera on the ground and go forward to the woman, taking her head in his hands; and all at once it was more like a puppet show than a ballet, with tiny wooden figures performing tiny jerky movements, crazy and unreal, on a faraway sunlit stage.

We sat quietly together on the white bench, and we watched while the tiny puppet man began to manipulate the woman's head with his hands. He was doing it gently, there was no doubt about that, slowly and gently, stepping back every now and then to think about it some more, and several times crouching down to survey the situation from another angle. Whenever he left her alone the woman would again start to wriggle her body, and the peculiar way she did it reminded me of a dog that feels a collar round its neck for the first time.

'She's stuck,' Sir Basil said.

And now the man was walking to the other side of the carving, the side where the woman's body was, and he put out his hands and began trying to do something with her neck. Then, as though suddenly exasperated, he gave the neck two or three quick jerky pulls, and this time the sound of the woman's voice, raised high in anger, or pain, or both, came back to us small and clear through the sunlight.

Out of the corner of one eye I could see Sir Basil nodding his head quietly up and down. 'I got my fist caught in a jar of boiled sweets once,' he said, 'and I couldn't get it out.'

The man had retreated a few yards, and was standing with hands on hips, head up, looking furious and sullen. The woman, from her uncomfortable position, appeared to be talking to him, or rather shouting at him, and although the body itself was pretty firmly fixed and could only wriggle, the legs were free and did a good deal of moving and stamping.

'I broke the jar with a hammer and told my mother I'd knocked it off the shelf by mistake.' He seemed calmer now, not tense at all, although his voice was curiously flat. 'I suppose we'd better go down and see if we can help.'

'Perhaps we should.'

But still he didn't move. He took out a cigarette and lit it, putting the used match carefully back in the box.

'I'm sorry,' he said. 'Will you have one?'

'Thanks, I think I will.' He made a little ceremony of giving me the cigarette and lighting it for me, and again he put the used match back in the box. Then we got up and walked slowly down the grass slope.

We came upon them silently, through an archway in the yew hedge, and it was naturally quite a surprise.

'What's the matter here?' Sir Basil asked. He spoke softly, with a dangerous softness that I'm sure his wife had never heard before.

'She's gone and put her head through the hole and now she can't get it out,' Major Haddock said. 'Just for a lark, you know.'

'For a what?'

'Basil!' Lady Turton shouted. 'Don't be such a damn fool! Do something, can't you!' She may not have been able to move much, but she could still talk.

'Pretty obvious we're going to have to break up this lump of wood,' the major said. There was a small smudge of red on his grey moustache, and this, like the single extra touch of colour that ruins a perfect painting, managed somehow to destroy all his manly looks. It made him comic.

'You mean break the Henry Moore?'

'My dear sir, there's no other way of setting the lady free. God knows how she managed to squeeze it in, but I know for a fact that she can't pull it out. It's the ears get in the way.'

'Oh dear,' Sir Basil said. 'What a terrible pity. My beautiful Henry Moore.'

At this stage Lady Turton began abusing her husband

in a most unpleasant manner, and there's no knowing how long it would have gone on had not Jelks suddenly appeared out of the shadows. He came sidling silently on to the lawn and stationed himself at a respectful distance from Sir Basil, as though awaiting instructions. His black clothes looked perfectly ridiculous in the morning sunlight, and with his ancient pink-white face and white hands he was like some small crabby animal that has lived all its life in a hole under the ground.

'Is there anything I can do, Sir Basil?' He kept his voice level, but I didn't think his face was quite straight. When he looked at Lady Turton there was a little exulting glimmer in his eyes.

'Yes, Jelks, there is. Go back and get me a saw or something so I can cut out a section of this wood.'

'Shall I call one of the men, Sir Basil? William is a good carpenter.'

'No, I'll do it myself. Just get the tools – and hurry.'

While they were waiting for Jelks, I strolled away because I didn't want to hear any more of the things that Lady Turton was saying to her husband. But I was back in time to see the butler returning, followed now by the other woman, Carmen La Rosa, who made a rush for the hostess.

'Nata-*li*-a! My dear Nata-*li*-a! What *have* they done to you?'

'Oh shut up,' the hostess said. 'And get out of the way, will you?'

Sir Basil took up a position close to his lady's head, waiting for Jelks. Jelks advanced slowly, carrying a saw in one hand, an axe in the other, and he stopped maybe a yard away. He then held out both implements in front of him so his master could choose, and there was a brief moment – no more than two or three seconds – of silence, and of waiting, and it just happened that I was watching Jelks at this time. I saw the hand that was carrying the axe come forward an extra fraction of an inch towards Sir Basil. It was so slight a movement it was barely noticeable – a tiny pushing forward of the hand, slow and secret, a little offer, a little coaxing offer that was accompanied perhaps by an infinitesimal lift of the eyebrows.

I'm not sure whether Sir Basil saw it, but he hesitated, and again the hand that held the axe came edging forward, and it was almost exactly like that card trick where the man says, 'Take one, whichever one you want,' and you always get the one he means you to have. Sir Basil got the axe. I saw him reach out in a dreamy sort of way, accepting it from Jelks, and then, the instant he felt the handle in his grasp he seemed to realize what was required of him and he sprang to life.

For me, after that, it was like the awful moment when you see a child running out into the road and a car is coming and all you can do is shut your eyes tight and wait until the noise tells you it has happened. The moment of waiting becomes a long lucid period of time with yellow and red spots dancing on a black field, and even if you open your eyes again and find that nobody has been killed or hurt, it makes no difference because so far as you and your stomach were concerned you saw it all.

I saw this one all right, every detail of it, and I didn't

open my eyes again until I heard Sir Basil's voice, even softer than usual, calling in gentle protest to the butler.

'Jelks,' he was saying, and I looked and saw him standing there as calm as you please, still holding the axe. Lady Turton's head was there too, still sticking through the hole, but her face had turned a terrible ashy grey, and the mouth was opening and shutting and making a kind of gurgling sound.

'Look here, Jelks,' Sir Basil was saying. 'What on earth are you thinking about? This thing's much too dangerous. Give me the saw.' And as he exchanged implements I noticed for the first time two little warm roses of colour appearing on his cheeks, and above them, all around the corners of his eyes, the twinkling tiny wrinkles of a smile.

The Wish

First published in *Someone Like You* (1953)

Under the palm of one hand the child became aware of the scab of an old cut on his knee-cap. He bent forward to examine it closely. A scab was always a fascinating thing; it presented a special challenge he was never able to resist.

Yes, he thought, I will pick it off, even if it isn't ready, even if the middle of it sticks, even if it hurts like anything.

With a fingernail he began to explore cautiously around the edges of the scab. He got the nail underneath it, and when he raised it, but ever so slightly, it suddenly came off, the whole hard brown scab came off beautifully, leaving an interesting little circle of smooth red skin.

Nice. Very nice indeed. He rubbed the circle and it didn't hurt. He picked up the scab, put it on his thigh and flipped it with a finger so that it flew away and landed on the edge of the carpet, the enormous red and black and yellow carpet that stretched the whole length of the hall from the stairs on which he sat to the front door in the distance. A tremendous carpet. Bigger than the tennis lawn. Much bigger than that. He regarded it gravely, settling his eyes upon it with mild pleasure. He had never really noticed it before, but now, all of a sudden, the colours seemed to brighten mysteriously and spring out at him in a most dazzling way.

You see, he told himself, I know how it is. The red parts of the carpet are red-hot lumps of coal. What I must do is this: I must walk all the way along it to the front door without touching them. If I touch the red I will be burned. As a matter of fact, I will be burned up completely. And the black parts of the carpet . . . yes, the black parts are snakes, poisonous snakes, adders mostly, and cobras, thick like tree-trunks round the middle, and if I touch one of *them*, I'll be bitten and I'll die before teatime. And if I get across safely, without being burned and without being bitten, I will be given a puppy for my birthday tomorrow.

He got to his feet and climbed higher up the stairs to obtain a better view of this vast tapestry of colour and death. Was it possible? Was there enough yellow? Yellow was the only colour he was allowed to walk on. Could it be done? This was not a journey to be undertaken lightly; the risks were too great for that. The child's face – a fringe of white-gold hair, two large blue eyes, a small pointed chin – peered down anxiously over the banisters. The yellow was a bit thin in places and there were one or two widish gaps, but it did seem to go all the way along to the other end. For someone who had only yesterday triumphantly travelled the whole length of the brick path from the stables to the summer-house without touching the cracks, this carpet thing should not be too difficult. Except for the snakes. The mere thought of snakes sent a fine electricity of fear running like pins down the backs of his legs and under the soles of his feet.

He came slowly down the stairs and advanced to the edge of the carpet. He extended one small sandalled foot and placed it cautiously upon a patch of yellow. Then he brought the other foot up, and there was just enough room for him to stand with the two feet together. There! He had started! His bright oval face was curiously intent, a shade whiter perhaps than before, and he was holding his arms out sideways to assist his balance. He took another step, lifting his foot high over a patch of black, aiming carefully with his toe for a narrow channel of yellow on the other side. When he had completed the second step he paused to rest, standing very stiff and still. The narrow channel of yellow ran forward unbroken for at least five yards and he advanced gingerly along it, bit by bit, as though walking a tightrope. Where it finally curled off sideways, he had to take another long stride, this time over a vicious-looking mixture of black and red. Halfway across he began to wobble. He waved his arms around wildly, windmill fashion, to keep his balance, and he got across safely and rested again on the other side. He was quite breathless now, and so tense he stood high on his toes all the time, arms out sideways, fists clenched. He was on a big safe island of yellow. There was lots of room on it, he couldn't possibly fall off, and he stood there resting, hesitating, waiting, wishing he could stay for ever on this big safe yellow island. But the fear of not getting the puppy compelled him to go on.

Step by step, he edged farther ahead, and between each one he paused to decide exactly where next he should put his foot. Once, he had a choice of ways, either to left or right, and he chose the left because although it seemed the more difficult, there was not so much black in that direction. The black was what made him nervous. He glanced quickly over his shoulder to see how far he had come. Nearly halfway. There could be no turning back now. He was in the middle and he couldn't turn back and he couldn't jump off sideways either because it was too far, and when he looked at all the red and all the black that lay ahead of him, he felt that old sudden sickening surge of panic in his chest – like last Easter-time, that afternoon when he got lost all alone in the darkest part of Piper's Wood.

He took another step, placing his foot carefully upon the only little piece of yellow within reach, and this time the point of the foot came within a centimetre of some black. It wasn't touching the black, he could see it wasn't touching, he could see the small line of yellow separating the toe of his sandal from the black; but the snake stirred as though sensing the nearness, and raised its head and gazed at the foot with bright beady eyes, watching to see if it was going to touch.

'*I'm not touching you! You mustn't bite me! You know I'm not touching you!*'

Another snake slid up noiselessly beside the first, raised its head, two heads now, two pairs of eyes staring at the foot, gazing at a little naked place just below the sandal strap where the skin showed through. The child went high up on his toes and stayed there, frozen stiff with terror. It was minutes before he dared to move again.

The next step would have to be a really long one. There was this deep curling river of black that ran clear across the width of the carpet, and he was forced by this position to cross it at its widest part. He thought first of trying to jump it, but decided he couldn't be sure of landing accurately on the narrow band of yellow the other side. He took a deep breath, lifted one foot, and inch by inch he pushed it out in front of him, far far out, then down and down until at last the tip of his sandal was across and resting safely on the edge of the yellow. He leaned forward, transferring his weight to his front foot. Then he tried to bring the back foot up as well. He strained and pulled and jerked his body, but the legs were too wide apart and he couldn't make it. He tried to get back again. He couldn't do that either. He was doing the splits and he was properly stuck. He glanced down and saw this deep curling river of black underneath him. Parts of it were stirring now, and uncoiling and sliding and beginning to shine with a dreadfully oily glister. He wobbled, waved his arms frantically to keep his balance, but that seemed to make it worse. He was starting to go over. He was going over to the right, quite slowly he was going over, then faster and faster, and at the last moment, instinctively he put out a hand to break the fall and the next thing he saw was this bare hand of his going right into the middle of a great glistening mass of black and he gave one piercing cry of terror as it touched.

Outside in the sunshine, far away behind the house, the mother was looking for her son.

The Soldier

First published in *Someone Like You* (1953)

It was one of those nights that made him feel he knew what it was like to be a blind man: not the shadow of an image for his eyes to discern, not even the forms of the trees visible against the sky.

Out of the darkness he became aware of small rustling noises in the hedge, the breathing of a horse some distance away in the field, the soft thud of a hoof as it moved its foot; and once he heard the rush of a bird flying past him low overhead.

'Jock,' he said, speaking loud. 'We'll go home now.' And he turned and began to walk back up the slope of the lane, the dog pulling ahead, showing the way in the dark.

It must be nearly midnight, he thought. That meant that soon it would be tomorrow. Tomorrow was worse than today. Tomorrow was the worst of all because it was going to become today – and today was now.

Today had not been very nice, especially that business with the splinter.

Stop it, he told himself. There isn't any sense thinking about it. It doesn't do anyone any good thinking about things like that. Think about something else for a change. You can kick out a dangerous thought, you know, if you put another in its place. Go right back as far as you can go.

Let's have some memories of sweet days. The seaside holidays in the summer, wet sand and red buckets and shrimping nets and the slippery seaweedy rocks and the small clear pools and sea anemones and snails and mussels and sometimes one grey translucent shrimp hovering deep down in the beautiful green water.

But how *could* that splinter have got into the sole of his foot without him feeling it?

It is not important. Do you remember hunting for cowries along the margin of the tide, each one so fine and perfect it became a precious jewel to be held in the hand all the way home; and the little orange-coloured scallops, the pearly oyster shells, the tiny bits of emerald glass, a live hermit crab, a cockle, the spine of a skate, and once, but never to be forgotten, the dry seawashed jawbone of a human being with teeth in it, white and wonderful among the shells and pebbles. Oh Mummy, look what I've found! Look, Mummy, look!

But to go back to the splinter. She had really been rather unpleasant about that.

'What do you mean, you didn't notice?' she had asked, scornful.

'I just didn't notice, that's all.'

'I suppose you're going to tell me if I stick a pin into your foot you won't feel it?'

'I didn't say that.'

And then she had jabbed him suddenly in the ankle with the pin she had been using to take out the splinter, and he hadn't been watching so he didn't know about it till she had cried out in a kind of horror. And when he had looked down, the pin was sticking into the flesh all by itself behind the anklebone, almost half of it buried.

'Take it out,' he had said. 'You can poison someone like that.'

'You mean you can't *feel* it?'

'Take it out, will you?'

'You mean it doesn't hurt?'

'The pain is terrible. Take it out.'

'What's the *matter* with you?'

'I said the pain is terrible. Didn't you hear me?'

Why did they *do* things like that to him?

When I was down beside the sea, a wooden spade they gave to me, to dig the sandy shore. My holes were empty as a cup, and every time the sea came up, till it could come no more.

A year ago the doctor had said, 'Shut your eyes. Now tell me whether I'm pushing this toe up or down.'

'Up,' he had said.

'And now?'

'Down. No, up. I think it's up.'

It was peculiar that a neurosurgeon should want to play with his toes.

'Did I get them all right, doctor?'

'You did very well.'

But that was a year ago. He had felt pretty good a year ago. The sort of things that happened now never used to happen then. Take, for example, just one item – the bathroom tap.

Why was the hot tap in the bathroom on a different side this morning? That was a new one.

It is not of the least importance, you understand, but it would be interesting to know why.

Do you think she could have changed it over, taken a spanner and a pipe-wrench and sneaked in during the night and changed it over?

Do you? Well – if you really want to know – yes. The way she'd been acting lately, she'd be quite capable of doing that.

A strange and difficult woman, that's what she was. Mind you, she used not to be, but there's no doubt at all that right now she was as strange and difficult as they come. Especially at night.

Yes, at night. That was the worst time of all – the night.

Why, when he put out his right hand in bed at night, could his fingers not feel what they were touching? He had knocked over the lamp and she had woken up and then sat up suddenly while he was feeling for it on the floor in the dark.

'What are you doing now?'

'I knocked over the lamp. I'm sorry.'

'Oh Christ,' she had said. 'Yesterday it was the glass of water. What's the *matter* with you?'

Once, the doctor had stroked the back of his hand with a feather, and he hadn't been able to feel that either. But he had felt it when the man scratched him with a pin.

'Shut your eyes. No – you mustn't look. Shut them tight. Now tell me if this is hot or cold.'

'Hot.'

'And this?'

'Cold.'

'And this?'

'Cold. I mean hot. Yes, it's hot, isn't it?'

'That's right,' the doctor had said. 'You did very well.'

But that was a year ago.

Why were the switches on the walls, just lately, always a few inches away from the well-remembered places when he felt for them in the dark?

Don't think about it, he told himself. The only thing is not to think about it.

And while we're on the subject, why did the walls of the living-room take on a slightly different shade of colour each day?

Green and blue-green and blue; and sometimes – sometimes slowly swimming like colours seen through the heat-haze of a brazier.

One by one, neatly, like index cards out of a machine, the little questions dropped.

Whose face appeared for one second at the window during dinner? Whose eyes?

'What are you staring at?'

'Nothing,' he had answered. 'But it would be nice if we could draw the curtains, don't you think?'

'Robert, what were you staring at?'

'Nothing.'

'Why were you staring at the window like that?'

'It would be nice if we could draw the curtains, don't you think?' he had answered.

He was going past the place where he had heard the horse in the field and now he could hear it again: the breathing, the soft hoof thuds, and the crunch of grass-cropping that was like the noise of a man munching celery.

'Hello, old horse,' he said, calling loud into the darkness. 'Hello, old horse over there.'

Suddenly he heard the footsteps behind him, slow, long-striding footsteps close behind, and he stopped. The footsteps stopped. He turned around, searching the darkness.

'Good evening,' he said. 'You here again?'

In the quiet that followed he could hear the wind moving the leaves in the hedge.

'Are you going my way?' he said.

Then he turned and walked on, the dog still pulling ahead, and the footsteps started after him again, but more softly now, as though the person were walking on toes.

He stopped and turned again.

'I can't see you,' he said, 'because it's so dark. Are you someone I know?'

Again the silence, and the cool summer wind on his cheeks, and the dog tugging on the leash to get home.

'All right,' he called. 'You don't have to answer if you don't want to. But remember I know you're there.'

Someone trying to be clever.

Far away in the night, over to the west and very high, he heard the faint hum of an aeroplane. He stopped again, head up, listening.

'Miles away,' he said. 'Won't come near here.'

But why, when one of them flew over the house, did everything inside him come to a stop, and his talking and what he was doing, while he sat or stood in a sort of paralysis waiting for the whistle-shriek of the bomb. That one after dinner this evening.

'Why did you duck like that?' she had asked.

'Duck?'

'Why did you duck? What are you ducking for?'

'Duck?' he had said again. 'I don't know what you mean.'

'I'll say you don't,' she had answered, staring at him hard with those hard, blue-white eyes, the lids dropping slightly, as always when there was contempt. The drop of her eyelids was something beautiful to him, the half-closed eyes and the way the lids dropped and the eyes became hooded when her contempt was extreme.

Yesterday, lying in bed in the early morning, when the noise of gunfire was just beginning far away down the valley, he had reached out with his left hand and touched her body for a little comfort.

'What on earth are you doing?'

'Nothing, dear.'

'You woke me up.'

'I'm sorry.'

It would be a help if she would only let him lie closer to her in the early mornings when he began to hear the noise of gunfire.

He would soon be home now. Around the last bend of the lane he could see a light glowing pink through the curtain of the living-room window, and he hurried forward to the gate and through it and up the path to the front door, the dog still pulling ahead.

He stood on the porch, feeling around for the doorknob in the dark.

It was on the right when he went out. He distinctly remembered it being on the right-hand side when he shut the door half an hour ago and went out.

It couldn't be that she had changed *that* over too? Just to fox him? Taken a bag of tools and quickly changed it over to the other side while he was out walking the dog?

He moved his hand over to the left – and the moment the fingers touched the knob, something small but violent exploded inside his head and with it a surge of fury and outrage and fear. He opened the door, shut it quickly behind him and shouted, 'Edna, are you there?'

There was no answer so he shouted again, and this time she heard him.

'What do you want now? You woke me up.'

'Come down here a moment, will you. I want to talk to you.'

'Oh for heaven's sake,' she answered. 'Be quiet and come on up.'

'Come here!' he shouted. 'Come here at once!'

'I'll be damned if I will. You come here.'

The man paused, head back, looking up the stairs into the dark of the second floor. He could see where the stair-rail curved to the left and went on up out of sight in the black towards the landing and if you went straight on across the landing you came to the bedroom, and it would be black in there too.

'Edna!' he shouted. 'Edna!'

'Oh go to hell.'

He began to move slowly up the stairs, treading quietly, touching the stair-rail for guidance, up and around the left-hand curve into the dark above. At the top he took an extra step that wasn't there; but he was ready for it and there was no noise. He paused awhile then, listening, and he wasn't sure, but he thought he could hear the guns starting up again far away down the valley, heavy stuff mostly, seventy-fives and maybe a couple of mortars somewhere in the background.

Across the landing now and through the open doorway – which was easy in the dark because he knew it so well – through on to the bedroom carpet that was thick and soft and pale grey although he could not feel or see it.

In the centre of the room he waited, listening for sounds. She had gone back to sleep and was breathing rather loud, making the slightest little whistle with the air between her teeth each time she exhaled. The curtain flapped gently against the open window, the alarm-clock tick-tick-ticked beside the bed.

Now that his eyes were becoming accustomed to the dark he could just make out the end of the bed, the white blanket tucked in under the mattress, the bulge of her feet under the bedclothes; and then, as though aware of the presence of the man in the room, the woman stirred. He heard her turn, and turn again. The sound of her breathing stopped. There was a succession of little movement-noises and once the bedsprings creaked, loud as a shout in the dark.

'Is that you, Robert?'

He made no move, no sound.

'Robert, are you there?'

The voice was strange and rather unpleasant to him.

'Robert!' She was wide awake now. 'Where are you?'

Where had he heard that voice before? It had a quality of stridence, dissonance, like two single high notes struck together hard in discord. Also there was an inability to pronounce the R of Robert. Who was it that used to say Wobert to him?

'Wobert,' she said again. 'What are you doing?'

Was it that nurse in the hospital, the tall one with fair hair? No, it was farther back. Such an awful voice as that he ought to remember. Give him a little time and he would get the name.

At that moment he heard the snap of the switch of the bedside lamp and in the flood of light he saw the woman half-sitting up in bed, dressed in some sort of a pink nightdress. There was a surprised, wide-eyed expression on her face. Her cheeks and chin were oily with cold cream.

'You better put that thing down,' she was saying, 'before you cut yourself.'

'Where's Edna?' He was staring at her hard.

The woman, half-sitting up in bed, watched him carefully. He was standing at the foot of the bed, a huge, broad man, standing motionless, erect, with heels together, almost at attention, dressed in his dark-brown, woolly, heavy suit.

'Go on,' she ordered. 'Put it down.'

'Where's Edna?'

'What's the matter with you, Wobert?'

'There's nothing the matter with me. I'm just asking you where's my wife?'

The woman was easing herself up gradually into an erect sitting position and sliding her legs towards the edge of the bed. 'Well,' she said at length, the voice changing, the hard blue-white eyes secret and cunning, 'if you really want to know, Edna's gone. She left just now while you were out.'

'Where did she go?'

'She didn't say.'

'And who are you?'

'I'm just a friend of hers.'

'You don't have to shout at me,' he said. 'What's all the excitement?'

'I simply want you to know I'm not Edna.'

The man considered this a moment, then he said, 'How did you know my name?'

'Edna told me.'

Again he paused, studying her closely, still slightly puzzled, but much calmer now, his eyes calm, perhaps even a little amused the way they looked at her.

'I think I prefer Edna.'

In the silence that followed they neither of them moved. The woman was very tense, sitting up straight with her arms tense on either side of her and slightly bent at the elbows, the hands pressing palms downward on the mattress.

'I love Edna, you know. Did she ever tell you I love her?'

The woman didn't answer.

'I think she's a bitch. But it's a funny thing I love her just the same.'

The woman was not looking at the man's face; she was watching his right hand.

'Awful cruel little bitch, Edna.'

And a long silence now, the man standing erect, motionless, the woman sitting motionless in the bed, and it was so quiet suddenly that through the open window they could hear the water in the millstream going over the dam far down the valley on the next farm.

Then the man again, speaking calmly, slowly, quite impersonally: 'As a matter of fact, I don't think she even likes me any more.'

The woman shifted closer to the edge of the bed. 'Put that knife down,' she said, 'before you cut yourself.'

'Don't shout, please. Can't you talk nicely?' Now, suddenly, the man leaned forward, staring intently into the woman's face, and he raised his eyebrows. 'That's strange,' he said. 'That's very strange.'

He took a step forward, his knees touching the bed.

'You look a bit like Edna yourself.'

'Edna's gone out. I told you that.'

He continued to stare at her and the woman kept quite still, the palms of her hands pressing deep into the mattress.

'Well,' he said. 'I wonder.'

'I told you Edna's gone out. I'm a friend of hers. My name is Mary.'

'My wife,' the man said, 'has a funny little brown mole just behind her left ear. You don't have that, do you?'

'I certainly don't.'

'Turn your head and let me look.'

'I told you I didn't have it.'

'Just the same, I'd like to make sure.'

The man came slowly around the end of the bed. 'Stay where you are,' he said. 'Please don't move.' And he came towards her slowly, watching her all the time, a little smile touching the corners of his mouth.

The woman waited until he was within reach, and then, with a quick right hand, so quick he never even saw it coming, she smacked him hard across the front of the face. And when he sat down on the bed and began to cry, she took the knife from his hand and went swiftly out of the room, down the stairs to the hall, where the telephone was.

The Great Automatic Grammatizator

First published in *Someone Like You* (1953)

'Well, Knipe, my boy. Now that it's all finished, I just called you in to tell you I think you've done a fine job.'

Adolph Knipe stood still in front of Mr Bohlen's desk. There seemed to be no enthusiasm in him at all.

'Aren't you pleased?'

'Oh yes, Mr Bohlen.'

'Did you see what the papers said this morning?'

'No, sir, I didn't.'

The man behind the desk pulled a folded newspaper towards him, and began to read: 'The building of the great automatic computing engine, ordered by the government some time ago, is now complete. It is probably the fastest electronic calculating machine in the world today. Its function is to satisfy the ever-increasing need of science, industry and administration for rapid mathematical calculation which, in the past, by traditional methods, would have been physically impossible, or would have required more time than the problems justified. The speed with which the new engine works, said Mr John Bohlen, head of the firm of electrical engineers mainly responsible for its construction, may be grasped by the fact that it can provide the correct answer in five seconds to a problem that would occupy a mathematician for a month. In three minutes, it can produce a calculation that by hand (if it were possible) would fill half a million sheets of foolscap paper. The automatic computing engine uses pulses of electricity, generated at the rate of a million a second, to solve all calculations that resolve themselves into addition, subtraction, multiplication and division. For practical purposes there is no limit to what it can do . . .'

Mr Bohlen glanced up at the long, melancholy face of the younger man. 'Aren't you proud, Knipe? Aren't you pleased?'

'Of course, Mr Bohlen.'

'I don't think I have to remind you that your own contribution, especially to the original plans, was an important one. In fact, I might go so far as to say that without you and some of your ideas, this project might still be on the drawing-boards today.'

Adolph Knipe moved his feet on the carpet, and he watched the two small white hands of his chief, the nervous fingers playing with a paper-clip, unbending it, straightening out the hairpin curves. He didn't like the man's hands. He didn't like his face either, with the tiny mouth and the narrow purple-coloured lips. It was unpleasant the way only the lower lip moved when he talked.

'Is anything bothering you, Knipe? Anything on your mind?'

'Oh no, Mr Bohlen. No.'

'How would you like to take a week's holiday? Do you good. You've earned it.'

'Oh, I don't know, sir.'

The older man waited, watching this tall, thin person who stood so sloppily before him. He was a difficult boy.

Why couldn't he stand up straight? Always drooping and untidy, with spots on his jacket, and hair falling all over his face.

'I'd like you to take a holiday, Knipe. You need it.'

'All right, sir. If you wish.'

'Take a week. Two weeks if you like. Go somewhere warm. Get some sunshine. Swim. Relax. Sleep. Then come back, and we'll have another talk about the future.'

Adolph Knipe went home by bus to his two-room apartment. He threw his coat on the sofa, poured himself a drink of whisky, and sat down in front of the typewriter that was on the table. Mr Bohlen was right. Of course he was right. Except that he didn't know the half of it. He probably thought it was a woman. Whenever a young man gets depressed, everybody thinks it's a woman.

He leaned forward and began to read through the half-finished sheet of typing still in the machine. It was headed 'A Narrow Escape', and it began: '*The night was dark and stormy, the wind whistled in the trees, the rain poured down like cats and dogs . . .*'

Adolph Knipe took a sip of whisky, tasting the malty-bitter flavour, feeling the trickle of cold liquid as it travelled down his throat and settled in the top of his stomach, cool at first, then spreading and becoming warm, making a little area of warmness in the gut. To hell with Mr John Bohlen anyway. And to hell with the great electrical computing machine. To hell with . . .

At exactly that moment, his eyes and mouth began slowly to open, in a sort of wonder, and slowly he raised his head and became still, absolutely motionless, gazing at the wall opposite with this look that was more perhaps of astonishment than of wonder, but quite fixed now, unmoving, and remaining thus for forty, fifty, sixty seconds. Then gradually (the head still motionless), a subtle change spreading over the face, astonishment becoming pleasure, very slight at first, only around the corners of the mouth, increasing gradually, spreading out until at last the whole face was open wide and shining with extreme delight. It was the first time Adolph Knipe had smiled in many, many months.

'Of course,' he said, speaking aloud, 'it's completely ridiculous.' Again he smiled, raising his upper lip and baring his teeth in a queerly sensual manner.

'It's a delicious idea, but so impracticable it doesn't really bear thinking about at all.'

From then on, Adolph Knipe began to think about nothing else. The idea fascinated him enormously, at first because it gave him a promise – however remote – of revenging himself in a most devilish manner upon his greatest enemies. From this angle alone, he toyed idly with it for perhaps ten or fifteen minutes; then all at once he found himself examining it quite seriously as a practical possibility. He took paper and made some preliminary notes. But he didn't get far. He found himself, almost immediately, up against the old truth that a machine, however ingenious, is incapable of original thought. It can handle no problems except those that resolve themselves into mathematical terms – problems that contain one, and only one, correct answer.

This was a stumper. There didn't seem any way around

it. A machine cannot have a brain. On the other hand, it *can* have a memory, can it not? Their own electronic calculator had a marvellous memory. Simply by converting electric pulses, through a column of mercury, into supersonic waves, it could store away at least a thousand numbers at a time, extracting any one of them at the precise moment it was needed. Would it not be possible, therefore, on this principle, to build a memory section of almost unlimited size?

Now what about that?

Then suddenly, he was struck by a powerful but simple little truth, and it was this: *That English grammar is governed by rules that are almost mathematical in their strictness!* Given the words, and given the sense of what is to be said, then there is only one correct order in which those words can be arranged.

No, he thought, that isn't quite accurate. In many sentences there are several alternative positions for words and phrases, all of which may be grammatically correct. But what the hell. The theory itself is basically true. Therefore, it stands to reason that an engine built along the lines of the electric computer could be adjusted to arrange words (instead of numbers) in their right order according to the rules of grammar. Give it the verbs, the nouns, the adjectives, the pronouns, store them in the memory section as a vocabulary, and arrange for them to be extracted as required. Then feed it with plots and leave it to write the sentences.

There was no stopping Knipe now. He went to work immediately, and there followed during the next few days a period of intense labour. The living-room became littered with sheets of paper: formulae and calculations; lists of words, thousands and thousands of words; the plots of stories, curiously broken up and subdivided; huge extracts from *Roget's Thesaurus*; pages filled with the first names of men and women; hundreds of surnames taken from the telephone directory; intricate drawings of wires and circuits and switches and thermionic valves; drawings of machines that could punch holes of different shapes in little cards, and of a strange electric typewriter that could type ten thousands words a minute. Also a kind of control panel with a series of small push-buttons, each one labelled with the name of a famous American magazine.

He was working in a mood of exultation, prowling around the room amidst this littering of paper, rubbing his hands together, talking out loud to himself; and sometimes, with a sly curl of the nose he would mutter a series of murderous imprecations in which the word 'editor' seemed always to be present. On the fifteenth day of continuous work, he collected the papers into two large folders which he carried – almost at a run – to the offices of John Bohlen Inc., electrical engineers.

Mr Bohlen was pleased to see him back.

'Well, Knipe, good gracious me, you look a hundred per cent better. You have a good holiday? Where'd you go?'

He's just as ugly and untidy as ever, Mr Bohlen thought. Why doesn't he stand up straight? He looks like a bent stick. 'You look a hundred per cent better, my boy.' I wonder what he's grinning about. Every time I see him, his ears seem to have got larger.

Adolph Knipe placed the folders on the desk. 'Look, Mr Bohlen!' he cried. 'Look at these!'

Then he poured out his story. He opened the folders and pushed the plans in front of the astonished little man. He talked for over an hour, explaining everything, and when he had finished, he stepped back, breathless, flushed, waiting for the verdict.

'You know what I think, Knipe? I think you're nuts.' Careful now, Mr Bohlen told himself. Treat him carefully. He's valuable, this one is. If only he didn't look so awful, with that long horse face and the big teeth. The fellow had ears as big as rhubarb leaves.

'But Mr Bohlen! It'll work! I've proved to you it'll work! You can't deny that!'

'Take it easy now, Knipe. Take it easy, and listen to me.'

Adolph Knipe watched his man, disliking him more every second.

'This idea,' Mr Bohlen's lower lip was saying, 'is very ingenious – I might almost say brilliant – and it only goes to confirm my opinion of your abilities, Knipe. But don't take it too seriously. After all, my boy, what possible use can it be to us? Who on earth wants a machine for writing stories? And where's the money in it, anyway? Just tell me that.'

'May I sit down, sir?'

'Sure, take a seat.'

Adolph Knipe seated himself on the edge of a chair. The older man watched him with alert brown eyes, wondering what was coming now.

'I would like to explain something, Mr Bohlen, if I may, about how I came to do all this.'

'Go right ahead, Knipe.' He would have to be humoured a little now, Mr Bohlen told himself. The boy was really valuable – a sort of genius, almost – worth his weight in gold to the firm. Just look at these papers here. Darndest thing you ever saw. Astonishing piece of work. Quite useless, of course. No commercial value. But it proved again the boy's ability.

'It's a sort of confession, I suppose, Mr Bohlen. I think it explains why I've always been so . . . so kind of worried.'

'You tell me anything you want, Knipe. I'm here to help you – you know that.'

The young man clasped his hands together tight on his lap, hugging himself with his elbows. It seemed as though suddenly he was feeling very cold.

'You see, Mr Bohlen, to tell the honest truth, I don't really care much for my work here. I know I'm good at it and all that sort of thing, but my heart's not in it. It's not what I want to do most.'

Up went Mr Bohlen's eyebrows, quick like a spring. His whole body became very still.

'You see, sir, all my life I've wanted to be a writer.'

'A writer!'

'Yes, Mr Bohlen. You may not believe it, but every bit of spare time I've had, I've spent writing stories. In the last ten years I've written hundreds, literally hundreds of short stories. Five hundred and sixty-six, to be precise. Approximately one a week.'

'Good heavens, man! What on earth did you do that for?'

'All I know, sir, is I have the urge.'

'What sort of urge?'

'The creative urge, Mr Bohlen.' Every time he looked up he saw Mr Bohlen's lips. They were growing thinner and thinner, more and more purple.

'And may I ask you what you do with these stories, Knipe?'

'Well, sir, that's the trouble. No one will buy them. Each time I finish one, I send it out on the rounds. It goes to one magazine after another. That's all that happens, Mr Bohlen, and they simply send them back. It's very depressing.'

Mr Bohlen relaxed. 'I can see quite well how you feel, my boy.' His voice was dripping with sympathy. 'We all go through it one time or another in our lives. But now – now that you've had proof – positive proof – from the experts themselves, from the editors, that your stories are – what shall I say – rather unsuccessful, it's time to leave off. Forget it, my boy. Just forget all about it.'

'No, Mr Bohlen! No! That's not true! I *know* my stories are good. My heavens, when you compare them with the stuff some of those magazines print – oh my word, Mr Bohlen! – the sloppy, boring stuff that you see in the magazines week after week – why, it drives me mad!'

'Now wait a minute, my boy . . .'

'Do you ever read the magazines, Mr Bohlen?'

'You'll pardon me, Knipe, but what's all this got to do with your machine?'

'Everything, Mr Bohlen, absolutely everything! What I want to tell you is, I've made a study of magazines, and it seems that each one tends to have its own particular type of story. The writers – the successful ones – know this, and they write accordingly.'

'Just a minute, my boy. Calm yourself down, will you. I don't think all this is getting us anywhere.'

'*Please*, Mr Bohlen, hear me through. It's all terribly important.' He paused to catch his breath. He was properly worked up now, throwing his hands around as he talked. The long, toothy face, with the big ears on either side, simply shone with enthusiasm, and there was an excess of saliva in his mouth which caused him to speak his words wet. 'So you see, on my machine, by having an adjustable co-ordinator between the "plot-memory" section and the "word-memory" section I am able to produce any type of story I desire simply by pressing the required button.'

'Yes, I know, Knipe, I know. This is all very interesting, but what's the point of it?'

'Just this, Mr Bohlen. The market is limited. We've got to be able to produce the right stuff, at the right time, whenever we want it. It's a matter of business, that's all. I'm looking at it from *your* point of view now – as a commercial proposition.'

'My dear boy, it can't possibly be a commercial proposition – ever. You know as well as I do what it costs to build one of these machines.'

'Yes, sir, I do. But with due respect, I don't believe you know what the magazines pay writers for stories.'

'What do they pay?'

'Anything up to twenty-five hundred dollars. It probably averages around a thousand.'

Mr Bohlen jumped.

'Yes, *sir*, it's true.'

'Absolutely impossible, Knipe! Ridiculous!'

'No, sir, it's true.'

'You mean to sit there and tell me that these magazines pay out money like that to a man for . . . just for scribbling off a story! Good heavens, Knipe! Whatever next! Writers must all be millionaires!'

'That's exactly it, Mr Bohlen! That's where the machine comes in. Listen a minute, sir, while I tell you some more. I've got it all worked out. The big magazines are carrying approximately three fiction stories in each issue. Now, take the fifteen most important magazines – the ones paying the most money. A few of them are monthlies, but most of them come out every week. All right. That makes, let us say, around forty big stories being bought each week. That's forty thousand dollars. So with our machine – when we get it working properly – we can collar nearly the whole of this market!'

'My dear boy, you're mad!'

'No, sir, honestly, it's true what I say. Don't you see that with volume alone we'll completely overwhelm them! This machine can produce a five-thousand word story, all typed and ready for dispatch, in thirty seconds. How can the writers compete with that? I ask you, Mr Bohlen, *how*?'

At that point, Adolph Knipe noticed a slight change in the man's expression, an extra brightness in the eyes, the nostrils distending, the whole face becoming still, almost rigid. Quickly, he continued. 'Nowadays, Mr Bohlen, the hand-made article hasn't a hope. It can't possibly compete with mass-production, especially in this country – you know that. Carpets . . . chairs . . . shoes . . . bricks . . . crockery . . . anything you like to mention – they're all made by machinery now. The quality may be inferior, but that doesn't matter. It's the cost of production that counts. And stories – well – they're just another product, like carpets and chairs, and no one cares how you produce them so long as you deliver the goods. We'll sell them wholesale, Mr Bohlen! We'll undercut every writer in the country! We'll corner the market!'

Mr Bohlen edged up straighter in his chair. He was leaning forward now, both elbows on the desk, the face alert, the small brown eyes resting on the speaker.

'I still think it's impracticable, Knipe.'

'Forty thousand a week!' cried Adolph Knipe. 'And if we halve the price, making it twenty thousand a week, that's still a million a year!' And softly he added, 'You didn't get any million a year for building the old electronic calculator, did you, Mr Bohlen?'

'But seriously now, Knipe. D'you really think they'd buy them?'

'Listen, Mr Bohlen. Who on earth is going to want custom-made stories when they can get the other kind at half the price? It stands to reason, doesn't it?'

'And how will you sell them? Who will you say has written them?'

'We'll set up our own literary agency, and we'll distribute them through that. And we'll invent all the names we want for the writers.'

'I don't like it, Knipe. To me, that smacks of trickery, does it not?'

'And another thing, Mr Bohlen. There's all manner of valuable by-products once you've got started. Take advertising, for example. Beer manufacturers and people like that are willing to pay good money these days if famous writers will lend their names to their products. Why, my heavens, Mr Bohlen! This isn't any children's plaything we're talking about. It's big business.'

'Don't get too ambitious, my boy.'

'And another thing. There isn't any reason why we shouldn't put *your* name, Mr Bohlen, on some of the better stories, if you wished it.'

'My goodness, Knipe. What should I want that for?'

'I don't know, sir, except that some writers get to be very much respected – like Mr Erle Gardner or Kathleen Norris, for example. We've got to have names, and I was certainly thinking of using my own on one or two stories, just to help out.'

'A writer, eh?' Mr Bohlen said, musing. 'Well, it would surely surprise them over at the club when they saw my name in the magazines – the good magazines.'

'That's right, Mr Bohlen.'

For a moment, a dreamy, faraway look came into Mr Bohlen's eyes, and he smiled. Then he stirred himself and began leafing through the plans that lay before him.

'One thing I don't quite understand, Knipe. Where do the plots come from? The machine can't possibly invent plots.'

'We feed those in, sir. That's no problem at all. Everyone has plots. There's three or four hundred of them written down in that folder there on your left. Feed them straight into the "plot-memory" section of the machine.'

'Go on.'

'There are many other little refinements too, Mr Bohlen. You'll see them all when you study the plans carefully. For example, there's a trick that nearly every writer uses, of inserting at least one long, obscure word into each story. This makes the reader think that the man is very wise and clever. So I have the machine do the same thing. There'll be a whole stack of long words stored away just for this purpose.'

'Where?'

'In the "word-memory" section,' he said, epexegetically.

Through most of that day the two men discussed the possibilities of the new engine. In the end, Mr Bohlen said he would have to think about it some more. The next morning, he was quietly enthusiastic. Within a week, he was completely sold on the idea.

'What we'll have to do, Knipe, is to say that we're merely building another mathematical calculator, but of a new type. That'll keep the secret.'

'Exactly, Mr Bohlen.'

And in six months the machine was completed. It was housed in a separate brick building at the back of the premises, and now that it was ready for action, no one was allowed near it excepting Mr Bohlen and Adolph Knipe.

It was an exciting moment when the two men – the one,

short, plump, breviped – the other tall, thin and toothy – stood in the corridor before the control panel and got ready to run off the first story. All around them were walls dividing up into many small corridors, and the walls were covered with wiring and plugs and switches and huge glass valves. They were both nervous, Mr Bohlen hopping from one foot to the other, quite unable to keep still.

'Which button?' Adolph Knipe asked, eyeing a row of small white discs that resembled the keys of a typewriter. 'You choose, Mr Bohlen. Lots of magazines to pick from – *Saturday Evening Post*, *Collier's*, *Ladies' Home Journal* – any one you like.'

'Goodness me, boy! How do I know?' He was jumping up and down like a man with hives.

'Mr Bohlen,' Adolph Knipe said gravely, 'do you realize that at this moment, with your little finger alone, you have it in your power to become the most versatile writer on this continent?'

'Listen, Knipe, just get on with it, will you please – and cut out the preliminaries.'

'OK, Mr Bohlen. Then we'll make it . . . let me see – this one. How's that?' He extended one finger and pressed down a button with the name TODAY'S WOMAN printed across it in diminutive black type. There was a sharp click, and when he took his finger away, the button remained down, below the level of the others.

'So much for the selection,' he said. 'Now – here we go!' He reached up and pulled a switch on the panel. Immediately, the room was filled with a loud humming noise, and a crackling of electric sparks, and the jingle of many, tiny, quickly moving levers; and almost in the same instant, sheets of quarto paper began sliding out from a slot to the right of the control panel and dropping into a basket below. They came out quick, one sheet a second, and in less than half a minute it was all over. The sheets stopped coming.

'That's it!' Adolph Knipe cried. 'There's your story!'

They grabbed the sheets and began to read. The first one they picked up started as follows: 'Aifkjmbsaoeg weztpplnvoqudskigt&,fuhpekanvbertyuiolkjhgfdsazxcvb nm,peruitrehdjkgmvnb,wmsuy . . .' They looked at the others. The style was roughly similar in all of them. Mr Bohlen began to shout. The younger man tried to calm him down.

'It's all right, sir. Really it is. It only needs a little adjustment. We've got a connection wrong somewhere, that's all. You must remember, Mr Bohlen, there's over a million feet of wiring in this room. You can't expect everything to be right first time.'

'It'll never work,' Mr Bohlen said.

'Be patient, sir. Be patient.'

Adolph Knipe set out to discover the fault, and in four days' time he announced that all was ready for the next try.

'It'll never work,' Mr Bohlen said. 'I know it'll never work.'

Knipe smiled and pressed the selector button marked *Reader's Digest*. Then he pulled the switch, and again the strange, exciting, humming sound filled the room. One page of typescript flew out of the slot into the basket.

'Where's the rest?' Mr Bohlen cried. 'It's stopped! It's gone wrong!'

'No, sir, it hasn't. It's exactly right. It's for the *Digest*, don't you see?'

This time it began: 'Fewpeopleyetknowthatarevolu tionarynewcurehasbeendiscoveredwhichmaywellbringper manentrelieftosufferersofthemostdreadeddiseaseofour time . . .' And so on.

'It's gibberish!' Mr Bohlen shouted.

'No, sir, it's fine. Can't you see? It's simply that she's not breaking up the words. That's an easy adjustment. But the story's there. Look, Mr Bohlen, look! It's all there except that the words are joined together.'

And indeed it was.

On the next try a few days later, everything was perfect, even the punctuation. The first story they ran off, for a famous women's magazine, was a solid, plotty story of a boy who wanted to better himself with his rich employer. This boy arranged, so the story went, for a friend to hold up the rich man's daughter on a dark night when she was driving home. Then the boy himself, happening by, knocked the gun out of his friend's hand and rescued the girl. The girl was grateful. But the father was suspicious. He questioned the boy sharply. The boy broke down and confessed. Then the father, instead of kicking him out of the house, said that he admired the boy's resourcefulness. The girl admired his honesty – and his looks. The father promised him to be head of the Accounts Department. The girl married him.

'It's tremendous, Mr Bohlen! It's exactly right!'

'Seems a bit sloppy to me, my boy.'

'No, sir, it's a seller, a real seller!'

In his excitement, Adolph Knipe promptly ran off six more stories in as many minutes. All of them – except one, which for some reason came out a trifle lewd – seemed entirely satisfactory.

Mr Bohlen was now mollified. He agreed to set up a literary agency in an office downtown, and to put Knipe in charge. In a couple of weeks, this was accomplished. Then Knipe mailed out the first dozen stories. He put his own name to four of them, Mr Bohlen's to one, and for the others he simply invented names.

Five of these stories were promptly accepted. The one with Mr Bohlen's name on it was turned down with a letter from the fiction editor saying, 'This is a skilful job, but in our opinion it doesn't quite come off. We would like to see more of this writer's work . . .' Adolph Knipe took a cab out to the factory and ran off another story for the same magazine. He again put Mr Bohlen's name to it, and mailed it immediately. That one they bought.

The money started pouring in. Knipe slowly and carefully stepped up the output, and in six months' time he was delivering thirty stories a week, and selling about half.

He began to make a name for himself in literary circles as a prolific and successful writer. So did Mr Bohlen; but not quite such a good name, although he didn't know it. At the same time, Knipe was building up a dozen or more fictitious persons as promising young authors. Everything was going fine.

At this point it was decided to adapt the machine for

writing novels as well as stories. Mr Bohlen, thirsting now for greater honours in the literary world, insisted that Knipe go to work at once on this prodigious task.

'I want to do a novel,' he kept saying. 'I want to do a novel.'

'And so you will, sir. And so you will. But please be patient. This is a very complicated adjustment I have to make.'

'Everyone tells me I ought to do a novel,' Mr Bohlen cried. 'All sorts of publishers are chasing after me day and night begging me to stop fooling around with stories and do something really important instead. A novel's the only thing that counts – that's what they say.'

'We're going to do novels,' Knipe told him. 'Just as many as we want. But please be patient.'

'Now listen to me, Knipe. What I'm going to do is a *serious* novel, something that'll make 'em sit up and take notice. I've been getting rather tired of the sort of stories you've been putting my name to lately. As a matter of fact, I'm none too sure you haven't been trying to make a monkey out of me.'

'A monkey, Mr Bohlen?'

'Keeping all the best ones for yourself, that's what you've been doing.'

'Oh no, Mr Bohlen! No!'

'So this time I'm going to make damn sure I write a high-class intelligent book. You understand that.'

'Look, Mr Bohlen. With the sort of switchboard I'm rigging up, you'll be able to write any sort of book you want.'

And this was true, for within another couple of months, the genius of Adolph Knipe had not only adapted the machine for novel writing, but had constructed a marvellous new control system which enabled the author to pre-select literally any type of plot and any style of writing he desired. There were so many dials and levers on the thing, it looked like the instrument panel of some enormous aeroplane.

First, by depressing one of a series of master buttons, the writer made his primary decision: historical, satirical, philosophical, political, romantic, erotic, humorous or straight. Then, from the second row (the basic buttons), he chose his theme: army life, pioneer days, civil war, world war, racial problem, wild west, country life, childhood memories, seafaring, the sea bottom and many, many more. The third row of buttons gave a choice of literary style: classical, whimsical, racy, Hemingway, Faulkner, Joyce, feminine, etc. The fourth row was for characters, the fifth for wordage – and so on and so on – ten long rows of pre-selector buttons.

But that wasn't all. Control had also to be exercised during the actual writing process (which took about fifteen minutes per novel), and to do this the author had to sit, as it were, in the driver's seat, and pull (or push) a battery of labelled stops, as on an organ. By so doing, he was able continually to modulate or merge fifty different and variable qualities such as tension, surprise, humour, pathos and mystery. Numerous dials and gauges on the dashboard itself told him throughout exactly how far along he was with his work.

Finally, there was the question of 'passion'. From a careful study of the books at the top of the best-seller lists for the past year, Adolph Knipe had decided that this was the most important ingredient of all – a magical catalyst that somehow or other could transform the dullest novel into a howling success – at any rate financially. But Knipe also knew that passion was powerful, heady stuff, and must be prudently dispensed – the right proportions at the right moments; and to ensure this, he had devised an independent control consisting of two sensitive sliding adjustors operated by foot-pedals, similar to the throttle and brake in a car. One pedal governed the percentage of passion to be injected, the other regulated its intensity. There was no doubt, of course – and this was the only drawback – that the writing of a novel by the Knipe methods was going to be rather like flying a plane and driving a car and playing an organ all at the same time, but this did not trouble the inventor. When all was ready, he proudly escorted Mr Bohlen into the machine house and began to explain the operating procedure for the new wonder.

'Good God, Knipe! I'll never be able to do all that! Dammit, man, it'd be easier to write the thing by hand!'

'You'll soon get used to it, Mr Bohlen, I promise you. In a week or two, you'll be doing it without hardly thinking. It's just like learning to drive.'

Well, it wasn't quite as easy at that, but after many hours of practice, Mr Bohlen began to get the hang of it, and finally, late one evening, he told Knipe to make ready for running off the first novel. It was a tense moment, with the fat little man crouching nervously in the driver's seat, and the tall toothy Knipe fussing excitedly around him.

'I intend to write an important novel, Knipe.'

'I'm sure you will, sir. I'm sure you will.'

With one finger, Mr Bohlen carefully pressed the necessary pre-selector buttons:

Master button – *satirical*

Subject – *racial problem*

Style – *classical*

Characters – *six men, four women, one infant*

Length – *fifteen chapters*

At the same time he had his eye particularly upon three organ stops marked *power*, *mystery*, *profundity*.

'Are you ready, sir?'

'Yes, yes, I'm ready.'

Knipe pulled the switch. The great engine hummed. There was a deep whirring sound from the oiled movement of fifty thousand cogs and rods and levers; then came the drumming of the rapid electrical typewriter, setting up a shrill, almost intolerable clatter. Out into the basket flew the typewritten pages – one every two seconds. But what with the noise and the excitement, and having to play upon the stops, and watch the chapter-counter and the pace-indicator and the passion-gauge, Mr Bohlen began to panic. He reacted in precisely the way a learner driver does in a car – by pressing both feet hard down on the pedals and keeping them there until the thing stopped.

'Congratulations on your first novel,' Knipe said, picking up the great bundle of typed pages from the basket.

Little pearls of sweat were oozing out all over Mr Bohlen's face. 'It sure was hard work, my boy.'

'But you got it done, sir. You got it done.'

'Let me see it, Knipe. How does it read?'

He started to go through the first chapter, passing each finished page to the younger man.

'Good heavens, Knipe! What's this!' Mr Bohlen's thin purple fish-lip was moving slightly as it mouthed the words, his cheeks were beginning slowly to inflate.

'But look here, Knipe! This is outrageous!'

'I must say it's a bit fruity, sir.'

'*Fruity!* It's perfectly revolting! I can't possibly put my name to this!'

'Quite right, sir. Quite right.'

'Knipe! Is this some nasty trick you've been playing on me?'

'Oh no, sir! No!'

'It certainly looks like it.'

'You don't think, Mr Bohlen, that you mightn't have been pressing a little hard on the passion-control pedals, do you?'

'My dear boy, how should *I* know.'

'Why don't you try another?'

So Mr Bohlen ran off a second novel, and this time it went according to plan.

Within a week, the manuscript had been read and accepted by an enthusiastic publisher. Knipe followed with one in his own name, then made a dozen more for good measure. In no time at all, Adolph Knipe's Literary Agency had become famous for its large stable of promising young novelists. And once again the money started rolling in.

It was at this stage that young Knipe began to display a real talent for big business.

'See here, Mr Bohlen,' he said. 'We still got too much competition. Why don't we just absorb all the other writers in the country?'

Mr Bohlen, who now sported a bottle-green velvet jacket and allowed his hair to cover two-thirds of his ears, was quite content with things the way they were. 'Don't know what you mean, my boy. You can't just absorb writers.'

'Of course you can, sir. Exactly like Rockefeller did with his oil companies. Simply buy 'em out, and if they won't sell, squeeze 'em out. It's easy!'

'Careful now, Knipe. Be careful.'

'I've got a list here, sir, of fifty of the most successful writers in the country, and what I intend to do is offer each one of them a lifetime contract with pay. All *they* have to do is undertake never to write another word; and, of course, to let us use their names on our own stuff. How about that.'

'They'll never agree.'

'You don't know writers, Mr Bohlen. You watch and see.'

'What about the creative urge, Knipe?'

'It's bunk! All they're really interested in is the money – just like everybody else.'

In the end, Mr Bohlen reluctantly agreed to give it a try,

and Knipe, with his list of writers in his pocket, went off in a large chauffeur-driven Cadillac to make his calls.

He journeyed first to the man at the top of the list, a very great and wonderful writer, and he had no trouble getting into the house. He told his story and produced a suitcase full of sample novels, and a contract for the man to sign which guaranteed him so much a year for life. The man listened politely, decided he was dealing with a lunatic, gave him a drink, then firmly showed him to the door.

The second writer on the list, when he saw Knipe was serious, actually attacked him with a large metal paperweight, and the inventor had to flee down the garden followed by such a torrent of abuse and obscenity as he had never heard before.

But it took more than this to discourage Adolph Knipe. He was disappointed but not dismayed, and off he went in his big car to seek his next client. This one was a female, famous and popular, whose fat romantic books sold by the million across the country. She received Knipe graciously, gave him tea and listened attentively to his story.

'It all sounds very fascinating,' she said. 'But of course I find it a little hard to believe.'

'Madam,' Knipe answered. 'Come with me and see it with your own eyes. My car awaits you.'

So off they went, and in due course, the astonished lady was ushered into the machine house where the wonder was kept. Eagerly, Knipe explained its workings, and after a while he even permitted her to sit in the driver's seat and practise with the buttons.

'All right,' he said suddenly, 'you want to do a book now?'

'Oh yes!' she cried. 'Please!'

She was very competent and seemed to know exactly what she wanted. She made her own pre-selections, then ran off a long, romantic, passion-filled novel. She read through the first chapter and became so enthusiastic that she signed up on the spot.

'That's one of them out of the way,' Knipe said to Mr Bohlen afterwards. 'A pretty big one too.'

'Nice work, my boy.'

'And you know *why* she signed?'

'Why?'

'It wasn't the money. She's got plenty of that.'

'Then why?'

Knipe grinned, lifting his lip and baring a long pale upper gum. 'Simply because she saw the machine-made stuff was better than her own.'

Thereafter, Knipe wisely decided to concentrate only upon mediocrity. Anything better than that – and there were so few it didn't matter much – was apparently not quite so easy to seduce.

In the end, after several months of work, he had persuaded something like seventy per cent of the writers on his list to sign the contract. He found that the older ones, those who were running out of ideas and had taken to drink, were the easiest to handle. The younger people were more troublesome. They were apt to become abusive, sometimes violent when he approached them; and more than once Knipe was slightly injured on his rounds.

But on the whole, it was a satisfactory beginning. This last year – the first full year of the machine's operation – it was estimated that at least one half of all the novels and stories published in the English language were produced by Adolph Knipe upon the Great Automatic Grammatizator.

Does this surprise you?

I doubt it.

And worse is yet to come. Today, as the secret spreads, many more are hurrying to tie up with Mr Knipe. And all the time the screw turns tighter for those who hesitate to sign their names.

This very moment, as I sit here listening to the howling of my nine starving children in the other room, I can feel my own hand creeping closer and closer to that golden contract that lies over on the other side of the desk.

Give us strength, oh Lord, to let our children starve.

Claud's Dog

First published in *Someone Like You* (1953)

The Ratcatcher

In the afternoon the ratcatcher came to the filling-station. He came sidling up the driveway with a stealthy, soft-treading gait, making no noise at all with his feet on the gravel. He had an army knapsack slung over one shoulder and he was wearing an old-fashioned black jacket with large pockets. His brown corduroy trousers were tied around the knees with pieces of white string.

'Yes?' Claud asked, knowing very well who he was.

'Rodent operative.' His small dark eyes moved swiftly over the premises.

'The ratcatcher?'

'That's me.'

The man was lean and brown with a sharp face and two long sulphur-coloured teeth that protruded from the upper jaw, overlapping the lower lip, pressing it inward. The ears were thin and pointed and set far back on the head, near the nape of the neck. The eyes were almost black, but when they looked at you there was a flash of yellow somewhere inside them.

'You've come very quick.'

'Special orders from the health officer.'

'And now you're going to catch all the rats?'

'Yep.'

The kind of dark furtive eyes he had were those of an animal that lives its life peering out cautiously and for ever from a hole in the ground.

'How are you going to catch 'em?'

'Ah-h-h,' the ratman said darkly. 'That's all accordin' to where they is.'

'Trap 'em, I suppose.'

'Trap 'em!' he cried, disgusted. 'You won't catch many rats that way! Rats isn't rabbits, you know.'

He held his face up high, sniffing the air with a nose that twitched perceptibly from side to side.

'No,' he said, scornfully. 'Trappin's no way to catch a rat. Rats is clever, let me tell you that. If you want to catch 'em, you got to know 'em. You got to know rats on this job.'

I could see Claud staring at him with a certain fascination.

'They're more clever'n dogs, rats is.'

'Get away.'

'You know what they do? They watch you! All the time you're goin' round preparin' to catch 'em, they're sittin' quietly in dark places, watchin' you.' The man crouched, stretching his stringy neck far forward.

'So what do you do?' Claud asked, fascinated.

'Ah! That's it, you see. That's where you got to know rats.'

'How d'you catch 'em?'

'There's ways,' the ratman said, leering. 'There's various ways.'

He paused, nodding his repulsive head sagely up and

down. 'It's all dependin',' he said, 'on where they is. This ain't a sewer job, is it?'

'No, it's not a sewer job.'

'Tricky things, sewer jobs. Yes,' he said, delicately sniffing the air to the left of him with his mobile nose-end, 'sewer jobs is very tricky things.'

'Not especially, I shouldn't think.'

'Oh-ho. You shouldn't, shouldn't you! Well, I'd like to see *you* do a sewer job! Just exactly how would *you* set about it, I'd like to know?'

'Nothing to it. I'd just poison 'em, that's all.'

'And where exactly would you put the poison, might I ask?'

'Down the sewer. Where the hell you think I put it!'

'There!' the ratman cried, triumphant. 'I knew it! Down the sewer! And you know what'd happen then? Get washed away, that's all. Sewer's like a river, y'know.'

'That's what *you* say,' Claud answered. 'That's only what *you* say.'

'It's facts.'

'All right, then, all right. So what would *you* do, Mr Know-all?'

'That's exactly where you got to know rats, on a sewer job.'

'Come on then, let's have it.'

'Now listen. I'll tell you.' The ratman advanced a step closer, his voice became secretive and confidential, the voice of a man divulging fabulous professional secrets. 'You works on the understandin' that a rat is a gnawin' animal, see. Rats *gnaws*. Anythin' you give 'em, don't matter what it is, anythin' new they never seen before, and what do they do? They *gnaws* it. So now! There you are! You get a sewer job on your hands. And what d'you do?'

His voice had the soft throaty sound of a croaking frog and he seemed to speak all his words with an immense wet-lipped relish, as though they tasted good on the tongue. The accent was similar to Claud's, the broad soft accent of the Buckinghamshire countryside, but his voice was more throaty, the words more fruity in his mouth.

'All you do is you go down the sewer and you take along some ordinary paper bags, just ordinary brown-paper bags, and these bags is filled with plaster of Paris powder. Nothin' else. Then you suspend the bags from the roof of the sewer so they hang down not quite touchin' the water. See? Not quite touchin', and just high enough so a rat can reach 'em.'

Claud was listening, rapt.

'There you are, y'see. Old rat comes swimmin' along the sewer and sees the bag. He stops. He takes a sniff at it and it don't smell so bad anyway. So what's he do then?'

'He *gnaws* it,' Claud cried, delighted.

'There! That's it! That's exactly it! He starts *gnawin'* away at the bag and the bag breaks and the old rat gets a mouthful of powder for his pains.'

'Well?'

'That does him.'

'What? Kills him?'

'Yep. Kills him stony!'

'Plaster of Paris ain't poisonous, you know.'

'Ah! There you are! That's exackly where you're wrong,

see. This powder swells. When you wet it, it swells. Gets into the rat's tubes and swells right up and kills him quicker'n anythin' in the world.'

'*No!*'

'That's where you got to know rats.'

The ratman's face glowed with a stealthy pride, and he rubbed his stringy fingers together, holding the hands up close to the face. Claud watched him, fascinated.

'Now – where's them rats?' The word 'rats' came out of his mouth soft and throaty, with a rich fruity relish as though he were gargling with melted butter. 'Let's take a look at them *rraats*.'

'Over there in the hayrick across the road.'

'Not in the house?' he asked, obviously disappointed.

'No. Only around the hayrick. Nowhere else.'

'I'll wager they're in the house too. Like as not gettin' in all your food in the night and spreadin' disease and sickness. You got any disease here?' he asked, looking first at me, then at Claud.

'Everyone fine here.'

'Quite sure?'

'Oh yes.'

'You never know, you see. You could be sickenin' for it weeks and weeks and not feel it. Then all of a sudden – bang! – and it's got you. That's why Dr Arbuthnot's so particular. That's why he sent me out so quick, see. To stop the spreadin' of disease.'

He had now taken upon himself the mantle of the health officer. A most important rat he was now, deeply disappointed that we were not suffering from bubonic plague.

'I feel fine,' Claud said, nervously.

The ratman searched his face again, but said nothing.

'And how are you goin' to catch 'em in the hayrick?'

The ratman grinned, a crafty toothy grin. He reached down into his knapsack and withdrew a large tin, which he held up level with his face. He peered around one side of it at Claud.

'Poison!' he whispered. But he pronounced it *pye-zn*, making it into a soft, dark, dangerous word. 'Deadly *pye-zn*, that's what this is!' He was weighing the tin up and down in his hands as he spoke. 'Enough here to kill a million men!'

'Terrifying,' Claud said.

'Exackly it! They'd put you inside for six months if they caught you with even a spoonful of this,' he said, wetting his lips with his tongue. He had a habit of craning his head forward on his neck as he spoke.

'Want to see?' he asked, taking a penny from his pocket, prising open the lid. 'There now! There it is!' He spoke fondly, almost lovingly, of the stuff, and he held it forward for Claud to look.

'Corn? Or barley, is it?'

'It's oats. Soaked in deadly *pye-zn*. You take just one of them grains in your mouth and you'd be a gonner in five minutes.'

'Honest?'

'Yep. Never out of me sight, this tin.'

He caressed it with his hands and gave it a little shake so that the oat grains rustled softly inside.

'But not today. Your rats don't get this today. They wouldn't have it anyway. That they wouldn't. There's where you got to know rats. Rats is suspicious. Terrible suspicious, rats is. So today they gets some nice clean tasty oats as'll do 'em no harm in the world. Fatten 'em, that's all it'll do. And tomorrow they gets the same again. And it'll taste so good there'll be all the rats in the districk comin' along after a couple of days.'

'Rather clever.'

'You got to be clever on this job. You got to be cleverer'n a rat and that's sayin' something.'

'You've almost got to be a rat yourself,' I said. It slipped out in error, before I had time to stop myself, and I couldn't really help it because I was looking at the man at the time. But the effect upon him was surprising.

'There!' he cried. 'Now you got it! Now you really said something! A good ratter's got to be more like a rat than anythin' else in the world! Cleverer even than a rat, and that's not an easy thing to be, let me tell you!'

'Quite sure it's not.'

'All right, then, let's go. I haven't got all day, you know. There's Lady Leonora Benson asking for me urgent up there at the manor.'

'She got rats, too?'

'Everybody's got rats,' the ratman said, and he ambled off down the driveway, across the road to the hayrick, and we watched him go. The way he walked was so like a rat it made you wonder – that slow, almost delicate ambling walk with a lot of give at the knees and no sound at all from the footsteps on the gravel. He hopped nimbly over the gate into the field, then walked quickly round the hay-rick, scattering handfuls of oats on to the ground.

The next day he returned and repeated the procedure.

The day after that he came again and this time he put down the poisoned oats. But he didn't scatter these; he placed them carefully in little piles at each corner of the rick.

'You got a dog?' he asked when he came back across the road on the third day after putting down the poison.

'Yes.'

'Now if you want to see your dog die an 'orrible twistin' death, all you got to do is let him in that gate some time.'

'We'll take care,' Claud told him. 'Don't you worry about that.'

The next day he returned once more, this time to collect the dead.

'You got an old sack?' he asked. 'Most likely we goin' to need a sack to put 'em in.'

He was puffed up and important now, the black eyes gleaming with pride. He was about to display the sensational results of his craft to the audience.

Claud fetched a sack and the three of us walked across the road, the ratman leading. Claud and I leaned over the gate, watching. The ratman prowled around the hayrick, bending over to inspect his little piles of poison.

'Somethin' wrong here,' he muttered. His voice was soft and angry.

He ambled over to another pile and got down on his knees to examine it closely.

'Somethin' bloody wrong here.'

'What's the matter?'

He didn't answer, but it was clear that the rats hadn't touched his bait.

'These are very clever rats here,' I said.

'Exactly what I told him, Gordon. These aren't just no ordinary kind of rats you're dealing with here.'

The ratman walked over to the gate. He was very annoyed and showed it on his face and around the nose and by the way the two yellow teeth were pressing down into the skin of his lower lip. 'Don't give me that crap,' he said, looking at me. 'There's nothin' wrong with these rats except somebody's feedin' 'em. They got somethin' juicy to eat somewhere and plenty of it. There's no rats in the world'll turn down oats unless their bellies is full to burstin'.'

'They're clever,' Claud said.

The man turned away, disgusted. He knelt down again and began to scoop up the poisoned oats with a small shovel, tipping them carefully back into the tin. When he had done, all three of us walked back across the road.

The ratman stood near the petrol-pumps, a rather sorry, humble ratman now, whose face was beginning to take on a brooding aspect. He had withdrawn into himself and was brooding in silence over his failure, the eyes veiled and wicked, the little tongue darting out to one side of the two yellow teeth, keeping the lips moist. It appeared to be essential that the lips should be kept moist. He looked up at me, a quick surreptitious glance, then over at Claud. His nose-end twitched, sniffing the air. He raised himself up and down a few times on his toes, swaying gently, and in a voice soft and secretive, he said: 'Want to see somethin'?' He was obviously trying to retrieve his reputation.

'What?'

'Want to see somethin' *amazin'*?' As he said this he put his right hand into the deep poacher's pocket of his jacket and brought out a large live rat clasped tight between his fingers.

'Good God!'

'Ah! That's it, y'see!' He was crouching slightly now and craning his neck forward and leering at us and holding this enormous brown rat in his hands, one finger and thumb making a tight circle around the creature's neck, clamping its head rigid so it couldn't turn and bite.

'D'you usually carry rats around in your pockets?'

'Always got a rat or two about me somewhere.'

With that he put his free hand into the other pocket and produced a small white ferret.

'Ferret,' he said, holding it up by the neck.

The ferret seemed to know him and stayed still in his grasp.

'There's nothin'll kill a rat quicker'n a ferret. And there's nothin' a rat's more frightened of either.'

He brought his hands close together in front of him so that the ferret's nose was within six inches of the rat's face. The pink beady eyes of the ferret stared at the rat. The rat struggled, trying to edge away from the killer.

'Now,' he said. 'Watch!'

His khaki shirt was open at the neck and he lifted the rat and slipped it down inside his shirt, next to his skin. As soon as his hand was free, he unbuttoned his jacket at the front so that the audience could see the bulge the body of the rat made under his shirt. His belt prevented it from going down lower than his waist.

Then he slipped the ferret in after the rat.

Immediately there was a great commotion inside the shirt. It appeared that the rat was running around the man's body, being chased by the ferret. Six or seven times they went around, the small bulge chasing the larger one, gaining on it slightly each circuit and drawing closer and closer until at last the two bulges seemed to come together and there was a scuffle and a series of shrill shrieks.

Throughout this performance the ratman had stood absolutely still with legs apart, arms hanging loosely, the dark eyes resting on Claud's face. Now he reached one hand down into his shirt and pulled out the ferret; with the other he took out the dead rat. There were traces of blood around the white muzzle of the ferret.

'Not sure I liked that very much.'

'You never seen anythin' like it before, I'll bet you that.'

'Can't really say I have.'

'Like as not you'll get yourself a nasty little nip in the guts one of these days,' Claud told him. But he was clearly impressed, and the ratman was becoming cocky again.

'Want to see somethin' far more *amazin'n* that?' he

asked. 'You want to see somethin' you'd never even *believe* unless you seen it with your own eyes?'

'Well?'

We were standing in the driveway out in front of the pumps and it was one of those pleasant warm November mornings. Two cars pulled in for petrol, one right after the other, and Claud went over and gave them what they wanted.

'You want to see?' the ratman asked.

I glanced at Claud, slightly apprehensive. 'Yes,' Claud said. 'Come on then, let's see.'

The ratman slipped the dead rat back into one pocket, the ferret into the other. Then he reached down into his knapsack and produced – if you please – a second live rat.

'Good Christ!' Claud said.

'Always got one or two rats about me somewhere,' the man announced calmly. 'You got to know rats on this job, and if you want to know 'em you got to have 'em round you. This is a sewer rat, this is. An old sewer rat, clever as buggery. See him watchin' me all the time, wonderin' what I'm goin' to do? See him?'

'Very unpleasant.'

'What are you going to do?' I asked. I had a feeling I was going to like this one even less than the last.

'Fetch me a piece of string.'

Claud fetched him a piece of string.

With his left hand, the man looped the string around one of the rat's hind legs. The rat struggled, trying to turn its head to see what was going on, but he held it tight around the neck with finger and thumb.

'Now!' he said, looking about him. 'You got a table inside?'

'We don't want the rat inside the house,' I said.

'Well – I need a table. Or somethin' flat like a table.'

'What about the bonnet of that car?' Claud said.

We walked over to the car and the man put the old sewer rat on the bonnet. He attached the string to the windshield wiper so that the rat was now tethered.

At first it crouched, unmoving and suspicious, a big-bodied grey rat with bright black eyes and a scaly tail that lay in a long curl upon the car's bonnet. It was looking away from the ratman, but watching him sideways to see what he was going to do. The man stepped back a few paces and immediately the rat relaxed. It sat up on its haunches and began to lick the grey fur on its chest. Then it scratched its muzzle with both front paws. It seemed quite unconcerned about the three men standing near by.

'Now – how about a little bet?' the ratman asked.

'We don't bet,' I said.

'Just for fun. It's more fun if you bet.'

'What d'you want to bet on?'

'I'll bet you I can kill that rat without usin' my hands. I'll put my hands in my pockets and not use 'em.'

'You'll kick it with your feet,' Claud said.

It was apparent that the ratman was out to earn some money. I looked at the rat that was going to be killed and began to feel slightly sick, not so much because it was going to be killed but because it was going to be killed in a special way, with a considerable degree of relish.

'No,' the ratman said. 'No feet.'

'Nor arms?' Claud asked.

'Nor arms. Nor legs, nor hands neither.'

'You'll sit on it.'

'No. No squashin'.'

'Let's see you do it.'

'You bet me first. Bet me a quid.'

'Don't be so bloody daft,' Claud said. 'Why should we give you a quid?'

'What'll you bet?'

'Nothin'.'

'All right. Then it's no go.'

He made as if to untie the string from the windshield wiper.

'I'll bet you a shilling,' Claud told him. The sick gastric sensation in my stomach was increasing, but there was an awful magnetism about this business and I found myself quite unable to walk away or even move.

'You too?'

'No,' I said.

'What's the matter with you?' the ratman asked.

'I just don't want to bet you, that's all.'

'So you want me to do this for a lousy shillin'?'

'I don't want you to do it.'

'Where's the money?' he said to Claud.

Claud put a shilling piece on the bonnet, near the radiator. The ratman produced two sixpences and laid them beside Claud's money. As he stretched out his hand to do this, the rat cringed, drawing its head back and flattening itself against the bonnet.

'Bet's on,' the ratman said.

Claud and I stepped back a few paces. The ratman stepped forward. He put his hands in his pockets and inclined his body from the waist so that his face was on a level with the rat, about three feet away.

His eyes caught the eyes of the rat and held them. The rat was crouching, very tense, sensing extreme danger, but not yet frightened. The way it crouched, it seemed to me it was preparing to spring forward at the man's face; but there must have been some power in the ratman's eyes that prevented it from doing this, and subdued it, and then gradually frightened it so that it began to back away, dragging its body backwards with slow crouching steps until the string tautened on its hind leg. It tried to struggle back farther against the string, jerking its leg to free it. The man leaned forward towards the rat, following it with his face, watching it all the time with his eyes, and suddenly the rat panicked and leaped sideways in the air. The string pulled it up with a jerk that must almost have dislocated its leg.

It crouched again, in the middle of the bonnet, as far away as the string would allow, and it was properly frightened now, whiskers quivering, the long grey body tense with fear.

At this point, the ratman again began to move his face closer. Very slowly he did it, so slowly there wasn't really any movement to be seen at all except that the face just happened to be a fraction closer each time you looked. He never took his eyes from the rat. The tension was considerable and I wanted suddenly to cry out and tell him to stop. I wanted him to stop because it was making me feel sick inside, but I couldn't bring myself to say the word. Something extremely unpleasant was about to happen – I was sure of that. Something sinister and cruel and ratlike, and perhaps it really would make me sick. But I had to see it now.

The ratman's face was about eighteen inches from the rat. Twelve inches. Then ten, or perhaps it was eight, and then there was not more than the length of a man's hand separating their faces. The rat was pressing its body flat against the car bonnet, tense and terrified. The ratman was also tense, but with a dangerous active tensity that was like a tight-wound spring. The shadow of a smile flickered around the skin of his mouth.

Then suddenly he struck.

He struck as a snake strikes, darting his head forward with one swift knifelike stroke that originated in the muscles of the lower body, and I had a momentary glimpse of his mouth opening very wide and two yellow teeth and the whole face contorted by the effort of mouth-opening.

More than that I did not care to see. I closed my eyes, and when I opened them again the rat was dead and the ratman was slipping the money into his pocket and spitting to clear his mouth.

'That's what they makes lickerish out of,' he said. 'Rat's blood is what the big factories and the chocolate-people use to make lickerish.'

Again the relish, the wet-lipped, lip-smacking relish as he spoke the words, the throaty richness of his voice and the thick syrupy way he pronounced the word 'lickerish'.

'No,' he said, 'there's nothin' wrong with a drop of rat's blood.'

'Don't talk so absolutely disgusting,' Claud told him.

'Ah! But that's it, you see. You eaten it many a time. Penny sticks and lickerish bootlaces is all made from rat's blood.'

'We don't want to hear about it, thank you.'

'Boiled up, it is, in great cauldrons, bubblin' and steamin' and men stirrin' it with long poles. That's one of the big secrets of the chocolate-makin' factories, and no one knows about it – no one except the ratters supplyin' the stuff.'

Suddenly he noticed that his audience was no longer with him, that our faces were hostile and sick-looking and crimson with anger and disgust. He stopped abruptly, and without another word he turned and sloped off down the driveway out on to the road, moving with the slow, that almost delicate ambling walk that was like a rat prowling, making no noise with his footsteps even on the gravel of the driveway.

Claud's Dog

First published in *Someone Like You* (1953)

Rummins

The sun was up over the hills now and the mist had cleared and it was wonderful to be striding along the road with the dog in the early morning, especially when it was autumn, with the leaves changing to gold and yellow and sometimes one of them breaking away and falling slowly, turning slowly over in the air, dropping noiselessly right in front of him on to the grass beside the road. There was a small wind up above, and he could hear the beeches rustling and murmuring like a crowd of people.

This was always the best time of the day for Claud Cubbage. He gazed approvingly at the rippling velvety hindquarters of the greyhound trotting in front of him.

'Jackie,' he called softly. 'Hey, Jackson. How you feeling, boy?'

The dog half turned at the sound of its name and gave a quick acknowledging wag of the tail.

There would never be another dog like this Jackie, he told himself. How beautiful the slim streamlining, the small pointed head, the yellow eyes, the black mobile nose. Beautiful the long neck, the way the deep brisket curved back and up out of sight into no stomach at all. See how he walked upon his toes, noiselessly, hardly touching the surface of the road at all.

'Jackson,' he said. 'Good old Jackson.'

In the distance, Claud could see Rummins' farmhouse, small, narrow and ancient, standing back behind the hedge on the right-hand side.

I'll turn round there, he decided. That'll be enough for today.

Rummins, carrying a pail of milk across the yard, saw him coming down the road. He set the pail down slowly and came forward to the gate, leaning both arms on the topmost bar, waiting.

'Morning, Mr Rummins,' Claud said. It was necessary to be polite to Rummins because of eggs.

Rummins nodded and leaned over the gate, looking critically at the dog.

'Looks well,' he said.

'He is well.'

'When's he running?'

'I don't know, Mr Rummins.'

'Come on. When's he running?'

'He's only ten months yet, Mr Rummins. He's not even schooled properly, honest.'

The small beady eyes of Rummins peered suspiciously over the top of the gate. 'I wouldn't mind betting a couple of quid you're having it off with him somewhere secret soon.'

Claud moved his feet uncomfortably on the black road surface. He disliked very much this man with the wide frog mouth, the broken teeth, the shifty eyes; and most of all he disliked having to be polite to him because of eggs.

'That hayrick of yours opposite,' he said, searching desperately for another subject. 'It's full of rats.'

'All hayricks got rats.'

'Not like this one. Matter of fact we've been having a touch of trouble with the authorities about that.'

Rummins glanced up sharply. He didn't like trouble with the authorities. Any man who sells eggs blackmarket and kills pigs without a permit is wise to avoid contact with that sort of people.

'What kind of trouble?'

'They sent the ratcatcher along.'

'You mean just for a few rats?'

'A few! Blimey, it's *swarming*!'

'Never.'

'Honest it is, Mr Rummins. There's hundreds of 'em.'

'Didn't the ratcatcher catch 'em?'

'No.'

'Why?'

'I reckon they're too artful.'

Rummins began thoughtfully to explore the inner rim of one nostril with the end of his thumb, holding the nose-flap between thumb and finger as he did so.

'I wouldn't give thank you for no ratcatchers,' he said. 'Ratcatchers is government men working for the soddin' government and I wouldn't give thank you for 'em.'

'Nor me, Mr Rummins. All ratcatchers is slimy cunning creatures.'

'Well,' Rummins said, sliding fingers under his cap to scratch the head, 'I was coming over soon anyway to fetch in that rick. Reckon I might just as well do it today as any other time. I don't want no government men nosing around my stuff, thank you very much.'

'Exactly, Mr Rummins.'

'We'll be over later – Bert and me.' With that he turned and ambled off across the yard.

Around three in the afternoon, Rummins and Bert were seen riding slowly up the road in a cart drawn by a ponderous and magnificent black carthorse. Opposite the filling-station the cart turned off into the field and stopped near the hayrick.

'This ought to be worth seeing,' I said. 'Get the gun.'

Claud fetched the rifle and slipped a cartridge into the breech.

I strolled across the road and leaned against the open gate. Rummins was on the top of the rick now and cutting away at the cord that bound the thatching. Bert remained in the cart, fingering the four-foot-long knife.

Bert had something wrong with one eye. It was pale grey all over, like a boiled fish-eye, and although it was motionless in its socket it appeared always to be looking at you and following you round, the way the eyes of the people in some of those portraits do, in the museums. Wherever you stood and wherever Bert was looking, there was this faulty eye fixing you sideways with a cold stare, boiled and misty pale with a little black dot in the centre, like a fish-eye on a plate.

In his build he was the opposite of his father, who was

short and squat like a frog. Bert was a tall, reedy, boneless boy, loose at the joints, even the head loose upon the shoulders, falling sideways as though perhaps it was too heavy for the neck.

'You only made this rick last June,' I said to him. 'Why take it away so soon?'

'Dad wants it.'

'Funny time to cut a new rick, November.'

'Dad wants it,' Bert repeated, and both his eyes, the sound one and the other, stared down at me with a look of absolute vacuity.

'Going to all that trouble stacking it and thatching it and then pulling it down five months later.'

'Dad wants it.' Bert's nose was running and he kept wiping it with the back of his hand and wiping the back of the hand on his trousers.

'Come on, Bert,' Rummins called, and the boy climbed up on to the rick and stood in the place where the thatch had been removed. He took the knife and began to cut down into the tight-packed hay with an easy-swinging, sawing movement, holding the handle with both hands and rocking his body like a man sawing wood with a big saw. I could hear the crisp cutting noise of the blade against the dry hay and the noise becoming softer as the knife sank deeper into the rick.

'Claud's going to take a pot at the rats as they come out.'

The man and the boy stopped abruptly and looked across the road at Claud, who was leaning against the red pump with rifle in hand.

'Tell him to put that bloody rifle away,' Rummins said.

'He's a good shot. He won't hit you.'

'No one's potting no rats alongside of me, don't matter how good they are.'

'You'll insult him.'

'Tell him to put it away,' Rummins said, slow and hostile. 'I don't mind dogs nor sticks but I'll be buggered if I'll have rifles.'

The two on the hayrick watched while Claud did as he was told, then they resumed their work in silence. Soon Bert came down into the cart, and reaching out with both hands he pulled a slice of solid hay away from the rick so that it dropped neatly into the cart beside him.

A rat, grey-black, with a long tail, came out of the base of the rick and ran into the hedge.

'A rat,' I said.

'Kill it,' Rummins said. 'Why don't you get a stick and kill it?'

The alarm had been given now and the rats were coming out quicker, one or two of them every minute, fat and long-bodied, crouching close to the ground as they ran through the grass into the hedge. Whenever the horse saw one of them it twitched its ears and followed it with uneasy rolling eyes.

Bert had climbed back on top of the rick and was cutting out another bale. Watching him, I saw him suddenly stop, hesitate for perhaps a second, then again begin to cut, but very cautiously this time, and now I could hear a different sound, a muffled rasping noise as the blade of the knife grated against something hard.

Bert pulled out the knife and examined the blade, testing it with his thumb. He put it back, letting it down gingerly into the cut, feeling gently downward until it came again upon the hard object; and once more, when he made another cautious little sawing movement, there came that grating sound.

Rummins turned his head and looked over his shoulder at the boy. He was in the act of lifting an armful of loosened thatch, bending forward with both hands grasping the straw, but he stopped dead in the middle of what he was doing and looked at Bert. Bert remained still, hands holding the handle of the knife, a look of bewilderment on his face. Behind, the sky was a pale clear blue and the two figures up there on the hayrick stood out sharp and black like an etching against the paleness.

Then Rummins' voice, louder than usual, edged with an unmistakable apprehension that the loudness did nothing to conceal: 'Some of them haymakers is too bloody careless what they put on a rick these days.'

He paused, and again the silence, the men motionless, and across the road Claud leaning motionless against the red pump. It was so quiet suddenly we could hear a woman's voice far down the valley on the next farm calling the men to food.

Then Rummins again, shouting where there was no need to shout: 'Go on, then! Go on an' cut through it, Bert! A little stick of wood won't hurt the soddin' knife!'

For some reason, as though perhaps scenting trouble, Claud came strolling across the road and joined me leaning on the gate. He didn't say anything, but both of us seemed to know that there was something disturbing about these two men, about the stillness that surrounded them and especially about Rummins himself. Rummins was frightened. Bert was frightened too. And now as I watched them, I became conscious of a small vague image moving just below the surface of my memory. I tried desperately to reach back and grasp it. Once I almost touched it, but it slipped away and when I went after it I found myself travelling back and back through many weeks, back into the yellow days of summer – the warm wind blowing down the valley from the south, the big beech trees heavy with their foliage, the fields turning to gold, the harvesting, the haymaking, the rick – the building of the rick.

Instantly I felt a fine electricity of fear running over the skin of my stomach.

Yes – the building of the rick. When was it we had built it? June? That was it, of course – a hot muggy day in June with the clouds low overhead and the air thick with the smell of thunder.

And Rummins had said, 'Let's for God's sake get it in quick before the rain comes.'

And Ole Jimmy had said, 'There ain't going to be no rain. And there ain't no hurry either. You know very well when thunder's in the south it don't cross over into the valley.'

Rummins, standing up in the cart handing out the pitchforks, had not answered him. He was in a furious brooding temper because of his anxiety about getting in the hay before it rained.

'There ain't gin' to be no rain before evening.' Ole Jimmy had repeated, looking at Rummins; and Rummins had stared back at him, the eyes glimmering with a slow anger.

All through the morning we had worked without a pause, loading the hay into the cart, trundling it across the field, pitching it out on to the slowly growing rick that stood over by the gate opposite the filling-station. We could hear the thunder in the south as it came towards us and moved away again. Then it seemed to return and remain stationary somewhere beyond the hills, rumbling intermittently. When we looked up we could see the clouds overhead moving and changing shape in the turbulence of the upper air, but on the ground it was hot and muggy and there was no breath of wind. We worked slowly, listlessly, in the heat, shirts wet with sweat, faces shining.

Claud and I had worked beside Rummins on the rick itself, helping to shape it, and I could remember how very hot it had been and the flies around my face and the sweat pouring out everywhere; and especially I could remember the grim scowling presence of Rummins beside me, working with a desperate urgency and watching the sky and shouting at the men to hurry.

At noon, in spite of Rummins, we had knocked off for lunch.

Claud and I had sat down under the hedge with Ole Jimmy and another man called Wilson who was a soldier home on leave, and it was too hot to do much talking. Wilson had some bread and cheese and a canteen of cold tea. Ole Jimmy had a satchel that was an old gas-mask container, and in this, closely packed, standing upright with their necks protruding, were six pint bottles of beer.

'Come on,' he said, offering a bottle to each of us.

'I'd like to buy one from you,' Claud said, knowing very well the old man had little money.

'Take it.'

'I must pay you.'

'Don't be so daft. Drink it.'

He was a very good old man, good and clean, with a clean pink face that he shaved each day. He had used to be a carpenter, but they retired him at the age of seventy and that was some years before. Then the Village Council, seeing him still active, had given him the job of looking after the newly built children's playground, of maintaining the swings and see-saws in good repair and also of acting as a kind of gentle watchdog, seeing that none of the kids hurt themselves or did anything foolish.

That was a fine job for an old man to have and everybody seemed pleased with the way things were going – until a certain Saturday night. That night Ole Jimmy had got drunk and gone reeling and singing down the middle of the High Street with such a howling noise that people got out of their beds to see what was going on below. The next morning they had sacked him, saying he was a waster and a drunkard not fit to associate with young children in the playground.

But then an astonishing thing happened. The first day that he stayed away – a Monday it was – not one single child came near the playground.

Nor the next day, nor the one after that.

All week the swings and the see-saws and the high slide with steps going up to it stood deserted. Not a child went near them. Instead they followed Ole Jimmy out into a field behind the rectory and played their games there with him watching; and the result of all this was that after a while the Council had had no alternative but to give the old man back his job.

He still had it now and he still got drunk and no one said anything about it any more. He left it only for a few days each year, at haymaking time. All his life Ole Jimmy had loved to go haymaking and he wasn't going to give it up yet.

'You want one?' he asked now, holding a bottle out to Wilson, the soldier.

'No thanks. I got tea.'

'They say tea's good on a hot day.'

'It is. Beer makes me sleepy.'

'If you like,' I said to Ole Jimmy, 'we could walk across to the filling-station and I'll do you a couple of nice sandwiches? Would you like that?'

'Beer's plenty. There's more food in one bottle of beer, me lad, than twenty sandwiches.'

He smiled at me, showing two rows of pale-pink, toothless gums, but it was a pleasant smile and there was nothing repulsive about the way the gums showed.

We sat for a while in silence. The soldier finished his bread and cheese and lay back on the ground, tilting his hat forward over his face. Ole Jimmy had drunk three bottles of beer, and now he offered the last to Claud and me.

'No thanks.'

'No thanks. One's plenty for me.'

The old man shrugged, unscrewed the stopper, tilted

his head back and drank, pouring the beer into his mouth with the lips held open so the liquid ran smoothly without gurgling down his throat. He wore a hat that was of no colour at all and of no shape, and it did not fall off when he tilted back his head.

'Ain't Rummins goin' to give that old horse a drink?' he asked, lowering the bottle, looking across the field at the great carthorse that stood steaming between the shafts of the cart.

'Not Rummins.'

'Horses is thirsty, just the same as us.' Ole Jimmy paused, still looking at the horse. 'You got a bucket of water in that place of yours there?'

'Of course.'

'No reason why we shouldn't give the old horse a drink then, is there?'

'That's a very good idea. We'll give him a drink.'

Claud and I both stood up and began walking towards the gate, and I remember turning and calling to the old man: 'You quite sure you wouldn't like me to bring you a nice sandwich? Won't take a second to make.'

He shook his head and waved the bottle at us and said something about taking himself a little nap. We went on through the gate over the road to the filling-station.

I suppose we stayed away for about an hour attending to customers and getting ourselves something to eat, and when at length we returned, Claud carrying the bucket of water, I noticed that the rick was at least six foot high.

'Some water for the old horse,' Claud said, looking hard

at Rummins, who was up in the cart pitching hay on to the rick.

The horse put its head in the bucket, sucking and blowing gratefully at the water.

'Where's Ole Jimmy?' I asked. We wanted the old man to see the water, because it had been his idea.

When I asked the question there was a moment, a brief moment, when Rummins hesitated, pitchfork in mid-air, looking around him.

'I brought him a sandwich,' I added.

'Bloody old fool drunk too much beer and gone off home to sleep,' Rummins said.

I strolled along the hedge back to the place where we had been sitting with Ole Jimmy. The five empty bottles were lying there in the grass. So was the satchel. I picked up the satchel and carried it back to Rummins.

'I don't think Ole Jimmy's gone home, Mr Rummins,' I said, holding up the satchel by the long shoulder-band. Rummins glanced at it but made no reply. He was in a frenzy of haste now because the thunder was closer, the clouds blacker, the heat more oppressive than ever.

Carrying the satchel, I started back to the filling-station, where I remained for the rest of the afternoon, serving customers. Towards evening, when the rain came, I glanced across the road and noticed that they had got the hay in and were laying a tarpaulin over the rick.

In a few days the thatcher arrived and took the tarpaulin off and made a roof of straw instead. He was a good thatcher and he made a fine roof with long straw, thick and well-packed. The slope was nicely angled, the edges cleanly clipped, and it was a pleasure to look at it from the road or from the door of the filling-station.

All this came flooding back to me now as clearly as if it were yesterday – the building of the rick on that hot thundery day in June, the yellow field, the sweet woody smell of the hay; and Wilson the soldier, with tennis shoes on his feet, Bert with the boiled eye, Ole Jimmy with the clean old face, the pink naked gums; and Rummins, the broad dwarf, standing up in the cart scowling at the sky because he was anxious about the rain.

At this very moment, there he was again, this Rummins, crouching on top of the rick with a sheaf of thatch in his arms, looking round at the son, the tall Bert, motionless also, both of them black like silhouettes against the sky, and once again I felt the fine electricity of fear as it came and went in little waves over the skin of my stomach.

'Go on and cut through it, Bert,' Rummins said, speaking loudly.

Bert put pressure on the big knife and there was a high grating noise as the edge of the blade sawed across something hard. It was clear from Bert's face that he did not like what he was doing.

It took several minutes before the knife was through – then again at last the softer sound of the blade slicing the tight-packed hay and Bert's face turned sideways to the father, grinning with relief, nodding inanely.

'Go on and cut it out,' Rummins said, and still he did not move.

Bert made a second vertical cut the same depth as the

first; then he got down and pulled the bale of hay so it came away cleanly from the rest of the rick like a chunk of cake, dropping into the cart at his feet.

Instantly the boy seemed to freeze, staring stupidly at the newly exposed face of the rick, unable to believe or perhaps refusing to believe what this thing was that he had cut in two.

Rummins, who knew very well what it was, had turned away and was climbing quickly down the other side of the rick. He moved so fast he was through the gate and half-way across the road before Bert started to scream.

Claud's Dog

First published in *Someone Like You* (1953)

Mr Hoddy

They got out of the car and went in the front door of Mr Hoddy's house.

'I've an idea Dad's going to question you rather sharp tonight,' Clarice whispered.

'About what, Clarice?'

'The usual stuff. Jobs and things like that. And whether you can support me in a fitting way.'

'Jackie's going to do that,' Claud said. 'When Jackie wins there won't be any need for any jobs . . .'

'Don't you ever mention Jackie to my dad, Claud Cubbage, or that'll be the end of it. If there's one thing in the world he can't abide it's greyhounds. Don't you ever forget that.'

'Oh Christ,' Claud said.

'Tell him something else – anything – anything to make him happy, see?' And with that she led Claud into the parlour.

Mr Hoddy was a widower, a man with a prim sour mouth and an expression of eternal disapproval all over his face. He had the small, close-together teeth of his daughter Clarice, the same suspicious, inward look about the eyes, but none of her freshness and vitality, none of her warmth. He was a small sour apple of a man, grey-skinned and shrivelled, with a dozen or so surviving strands of black hair pasted across the dome of his bald head. But a very superior man was Mr Hoddy, a grocer's assistant, one who wore a spotless white gown at his work, who handled large quantities of such precious commodities as butter and sugar, who was deferred to, even smiled at, by every housewife in the village.

Claud Cubbage was never quite at his ease in this house and that was precisely as Mr Hoddy intended it. They were sitting round the fire in the parlour with cups of tea in their hands, Mr Hoddy in the best chair to the right of the fireplace, Claud and Clarice on the sofa, decorously separated by a wide space. The younger daughter, Ada, was on a hard upright chair to the left, and they made a little circle round the fire, a stiff, tense little circle, primly tea-sipping.

'Yes, Mr Hoddy,' Claud was saying, 'you can be quite sure both Gordon and me's got quite a number of nice little ideas up our sleeves this very moment. It's only a question of taking our time and making sure which is going to be the most profitable.'

'What sort of ideas?' Mr Hoddy asked, fixing Claud with his small, disapproving eyes.

'Ah, there you are now. That's it, you see.' Claud shifted uncomfortably on the sofa. His blue lounge suit was tight around his chest, and it was especially tight between his legs, up in the crutch. The tightness in his crutch was actually painful to him and he wanted terribly to hitch it downward.

'This man you call Gordon, I thought he had a profitable

business out there as it is,' Mr Hoddy said. 'Why does he want to change?'

'Absolutely right, Mr Hoddy. It's a first-rate business. But it's a good thing to keep expanding, see. New ideas is what we're after. Something I can come in on as well and take a share of the profits.'

'Such as what?'

Mr Hoddy was eating a slice of currant cake, nibbling it round the edges, and his small mouth was like the mouth of a caterpillar biting a tiny curved slice out of the edge of a leaf.

'Such as what?' he asked again.

'There's long conferences, Mr Hoddy, takes place every day between Gordon and me about these different matters of business.'

'Such as what?' he repeated, relentless.

Clarice glanced sideways at Claud, encouraging. Claud turned his large slow eyes upon Mr Hoddy, and he was silent. He wished Mr Hoddy wouldn't push him around like this, always shooting questions at him and glaring at him and acting just exactly like he was the bloody adjutant or something.

'Such as what?' Mr Hoddy said, and this time Claud knew that he was not going to let go. Also, his instinct warned him that the old man was trying to create a crisis.

'Well now,' he said, breathing deep. 'I don't really want to go into details until we got it properly worked out. All we're doing so far is turning our ideas over in our minds, see.'

'All I'm asking,' Mr Hoddy said irritably, 'is what *sort* of business are you contemplating? I presume that it's respectable?'

'Now *please*, Mr Hoddy. You don't for one moment think we'd even so much as *consider* anything that wasn't absolutely and entirely respectable, do you?'

Mr Hoddy grunted, stirring his tea slowly, watching Claud. Clarice sat mute and fearful on the sofa, gazing into the fire.

'I've never been in favour of starting a business,' Mr Hoddy pronounced, defending his own failure in that line. 'A good respectable job is all a man should wish for. A respectable job in respectable surroundings. Too much hokey-pokey in business for my liking.'

'The thing is this,' Claud said, desperate now. 'All I want is to provide my wife with everything she can possibly desire. A house to live in and furniture and a flower garden and a washing-machine and all the best things in the world. That's what I want to do, and you can't do that on an ordinary wage, now can you? It's impossible to get enough money to do that unless you go into business, Mr Hoddy. You'll surely agree with me there?'

Mr Hoddy, who had worked for an ordinary wage all his life, didn't much like this point of view.

'And don't you think *I* provide everything my family wants, might I ask?'

'Oh yes, and more!' Claud cried fervently. 'But *you've* got a very superior job, Mr Hoddy, and that makes all the difference.'

'But what *sort* of business are you thinking of?' the man persisted.

Claud sipped his tea to give himself a little more time and he couldn't help wondering how the miserable old bastard's face would look if he simply up and told him the truth right there and then, if he'd said, What we've got, Mr Hoddy, if you really wants to know, is a couple of greyhounds and one's a perfect ringer for the other and we're going to bring off the biggest goddam gamble in the history of flapping, see. He'd like to watch the old bastard's face if he said that, he really would.

They were all waiting for him to proceed now, sitting there with cups of tea in their hands staring at him and waiting for him to say something good. 'Well,' he said, speaking very slowly because he was thinking deep. 'I've been pondering something a long time now, something as'll make more money even than Gordon's second-hand cars or anything else come to that, and practically no expense involved.' That's better, he told himself. Keep going along like that.

'And what might that be?'

'Something so queer, Mr Hoddy, there isn't one in a million would even believe it.'

'Well, what is it?' Mr Hoddy placed his cup carefully on the little table beside him and leaned forward to listen. And Claud, watching him, knew more than ever that this man and all those like him were his enemies. It was the Mr Hoddys were the trouble. They were all the same. He knew them all, with their clean ugly hands, their grey skin, their acrid mouths, their tendency to develop little round bulging bellies just below the waistcoat; and always the unctuous curl of the nose, the weak chin, the suspicious eyes that were dark and moved too quick. The Mr Hoddys. Oh Christ.

'Well, what is it?'

'It's an absolute gold-mine, Mr Hoddy, honestly it is.'

'I'll believe that when I hear it.'

'It's a thing so simple and amazing most people wouldn't even bother to do it.' He had it now – something he *had* actually been thinking seriously about for a long time, something he'd always wanted to do. He leaned across and put his teacup carefully on the table beside Mr Hoddy's, then, not knowing what to do with his hands, placed them on his knees, palms downward.

'Well, come on man, what is it?'

'It's maggots,' Claud answered softly.

Mr Hoddy jerked back as though someone had squirted water in his face. 'Maggots!' he said, aghast. '*Maggots?* What on earth do you mean, maggots?' Claud had forgotten that this word was almost unmentionable in any self-respecting grocer's shop. Ada began to giggle, but Clarice glanced at her so malignantly the giggle died on her mouth.

'That's where the money is, starting a maggot factory.'

'Are you trying to be funny?'

'Honestly, Mr Hoddy, it may sound a bit queer, and that's simply because you never heard it before, but it's a little gold-mine.'

'A *maggot factory*! Really now, Cubbage! Please be sensible.'

Clarice wished her father wouldn't call him Cubbage.

'You never heard speak of a maggot factory, Mr Hoddy?'

'I certainly have not!'

'There's maggot factories going now, real big companies with managers and directors and all, and you know what, Mr Hoddy? They're making millions!'

'Nonsense, man.'

'And you know why they're making millions?' Claud paused, but he did not notice now that his listener's face was slowly turning yellow. 'It's because of the enormous demand for maggots, Mr Hoddy.'

At that moment Mr Hoddy was listening also to other voices, the voices of his customers across the counter – Mrs Rabbits, for instance, as he sliced off her ration of butter, Mrs Rabbits with her brown moustache and always talking so loud and saying, Well, well, well; he could hear her now saying, Well, well, well Mr Hoddy, so your Clarice got married last week, did she? Very nice too, I must say, and what was it you said her husband does, Mr Hoddy?'

He owns a maggot factory, Mrs Rabbits.

No thank you, he told himself, watching Claud with his small, hostile eyes. No thank you very much indeed. I don't want that.

'I can't say,' he announced primly, 'that I myself have ever had occasion to purchase a maggot.'

'Now you come to mention it, Mr Hoddy, nor have I. Nor has many other people we know. But let me ask you something else. How many times you had occasion to purchase . . . a crown wheel and pinion, for instance?'

This was a shrewd question and Claud permitted himself a slow mawkish smile.

'What's that got to do with maggots?'

'Exactly this – that certain people buy certain things, see. You never bought a crown wheel and pinion in your life, but that don't say there isn't men getting rich this very moment making them – because there is. It's the same with maggots!'

'Would you mind telling me who these unpleasant people are who buy maggots?'

'Maggots are bought by fishermen, Mr Hoddy. Amateur fishermen. There's thousands and thousands of fishermen all over the country going out every week-end fishing the rivers and all of them wanting maggots. Willing to pay good money for them, too. You go along the river there anywhere you like above Marlow on a Sunday and you'll see them *lining* the banks. Sitting there one beside the other simply *lining* the banks on both sides.'

'Those men don't buy maggots. They go down the bottom of the garden and dig worms.'

'Now that's just where you're wrong, Mr Hoddy, if you'll allow me to say so. That's just where you're absolutely wrong. They want maggots, not worms.'

'In that case they get their own maggots.'

'They don't *want* to get their own maggots. Just imagine Mr Hoddy, it's Saturday afternoon and you're going out fishing and a nice clean tin of maggots arrives by post and all you've got to do is slip it in the fishing bag and away you go. You don't think fellers is going out digging for worms and hunting for maggots when they can have them delivered right to their very doorsteps like that just for a bob or two, do you?'

'And might I ask how you propose to run this maggot

factory of yours?' When he spoke the word 'maggot', it seemed as if he were spitting out a sour little pip from his mouth.

'Easiest thing in the world to run a maggot factory.' Claud was gaining confidence now and warming to his subject. 'All you need is a couple of old oil drums and a few lumps of rotten meat or a sheep's head, and you put them in the oil drums and that's all you do. The flies do the rest.'

Had he been watching Mr Hoddy's face he would probably have stopped there.

'Of course, it's not quite as easy as it sounds. What you've got to do next is feed up your maggots with special diet. Bran and milk. And then when they get big and fat you put them in pint tins and post them off to your customers. Five shillings a pint they fetch. *Five shillings a pint!*' he cried, slapping the knee. 'You just imagine that, Mr Hoddy! And they say one bluebottle'll lay twenty pints easy!'

He paused again, but merely to marshal his thoughts, for there was no stopping him now.

'And there's another thing, Mr Hoddy. A good maggot factory don't just breed ordinary maggots, you know. Every fisherman's got his own tastes. Maggots are commonest, but also there's lug worms. Some fishermen won't have nothing but lug worms. And of course there's coloured maggots. Ordinary maggots are white, but you get them all sorts of different colours by feeding them special foods, see. Red ones and green ones and black ones and you can even get blue ones if you know what to feed them. The most difficult thing of all in a maggot factory is a blue maggot, Mr Hoddy.'

Claud stopped to catch his breath. He was having a vision now – the same vision that accompanied all his dreams of wealth – of an immense factory building with tall chimneys and hundreds of happy workers streaming in through the wide wrought-iron gates and Claud himself sitting in his luxurious office directing operations with a calm and splendid assurance.

'There's people with brains studying these things this very minute,' he went on. 'So you got to jump in quick unless you want to get left out in the cold. That's the secret of big business, jumping in quick before all the others, Mr Hoddy.'

Clarice, Ada and the father sat absolutely still looking straight ahead. None of them moved or spoke. Only Claud rushed on.

'Just so long as you make sure your maggots is alive when you post 'em. They've got to be wiggling, see. Maggots is no good unless they're wiggling. And when we really get going, when we've built up a little capital, then we'll put up some glasshouses.'

Another pause, and Claud stroked his chin. 'Now I expect you're all wondering why a person should want glasshouses in a maggot factory. Well – I'll tell you. It's for the flies in the winter, see. Most important to take care of your flies in the winter.'

'I think that's enough, thank you, Cubbage,' Mr Hoddy said suddenly.

Claud looked up and for the first time he saw the expression on the man's face. It stopped him cold.

'I don't want to hear any more about it,' Mr Hoddy said.

'All I'm trying to do, Mr Hoddy,' Claud cried, 'is give your little girl everything she can possibly desire. That's all I'm thinking of night and day, Mr Hoddy.'

'Then all I hope is you'll be able to do it without the help of maggots.'

'Dad!' Clarice cried, alarmed. 'I simply won't have you talking to Claud like that.'

'I'll talk to him how I wish, thank you, Miss.'

'I think it's time I was getting along,' Claud said. 'Good night.'

Claud's Dog

First published in *Someone Like You* (1953)

Mr Feasey

We were both up early when the big day came.

I wandered into the kitchen for a shave, but Claud got dressed right away and went outside to arrange about the straw. The kitchen was a front room and through the window I could see the sun just coming up behind the line of trees on top of the ridge the other side of the valley.

Each time Claud came past the window with an armload of straw I noticed over the rim of the mirror the intent, breathless expression on his face, the great round bullet-head thrusting forward and the forehead wrinkled into deep corrugations right up to the hairline. I'd only seen this look on him once before and that was the evening he'd asked Clarice to marry him. Today he was so excited he even walked funny, treading softly as though the concrete around the filling-station were a shade too hot for the soles of his feet; and he kept packing more and more straw into the back of the van to make it comfortable for Jackie.

Then he came into the kitchen to get breakfast, and I watched him put the pot of soup on the stove and begin stirring it. He had a long metal spoon and he kept on stirring and stirring all the time it was coming to the boil, and about every half-minute he leaned forward and stuck his nose into that sickly-sweet steam of cooking horseflesh. Then he started putting extras into it – three peeled onions, a few young carrots, a cupful of stinging-nettle tops, a teaspoon of Valentine's Meat Juice, twelve drops of cod-liver oil – and everything he touched was handled very gently with the ends of his big fat fingers as though it might have been a little fragment of Venetian glass. He took some minced horsemeat from the icebox, measured one handful into Jackie's bowl, three into the other, and when the soup was ready he shared it out between the two, pouring it over the meat.

It was the same ceremony I'd seen performed each morning for the past five months, but never with such intense and breathless concentration as this. There was no talk, not even a glance my way, and when he turned and went out again to fetch the dogs, even the back of his neck and the shoulders seemed to be whispering. 'Oh Jesus, don't let anything go wrong, and especially don't let me *do* anything wrong today.'

I heard him talking softly to the dogs in the pen as he put the leashes on them, and when he brought them around into the kitchen, they came in prancing and pulling to get at the breakfast, treading up and down with their front feet and waving their enormous tails from side to side, like whips.

'All right,' Claud said, speaking at last. 'Which is it?'

Most mornings he'd offer to bet me a pack of cigarettes, but there were bigger things at stake today and I knew all he wanted for the moment was a little extra reassurance.

He watched me as I walked once around the two beautiful, identical, tall, velvety-black dogs, and he moved aside, holding the leashes at arm's length to give me a better view.

'Jackie!' I said, trying the old trick that never worked. 'Hey, Jackie!' Two identical heads with identical expressions flicked around to look at me, four bright, identical, deep-yellow eyes stared into mine. There'd been a time when I fancied the eyes of one were slightly darker yellow than those of the other. There'd also been a time when I thought I could recognize Jackie because of a deeper brisket and a shade more muscle on the hindquarters. But it wasn't so.

'Come on,' Claud said. He was hoping that today of all days I would make a bad guess.

'This one,' I said. 'This is Jackie.'

'Which?'

'This one on the left.'

'There!' he cried, his whole face suddenly beaming. 'You're wrong again!'

'I don't think I'm wrong.'

'You're about as wrong as you could possibly be. And now listen, Gordon, and I'll tell you something. All these last weeks, every morning while you've been trying to pick him out – you know what?'

'What?'

'I've been keeping count. And the result is you haven't been right even *one half* the time! You'd have done better tossing a coin!'

What he meant was that if I (who saw them every day and side by side) couldn't do it, why the hell should we be frightened of Mr Feasey? Claud knew Mr Feasey was famous for spotting ringers, but he knew also that it could be very difficult to tell the difference between two dogs when there wasn't any.

He put the bowls of food on the floor, giving Jackie the one with the least meat because he was running today. When he stood back to watch them eat, the shadow of deep concern was back again on his face and the large pale eyes were staring at Jackie with the same rapt and melting look of love that up till recently had been reserved only for Clarice.

'You see, Gordon,' he said. 'It's just what I've always told you. For the last hundred years there's been all manner of ringers, some good and some bad, but in the whole history of dog-racing there's never been a ringer like this.'

'I hope you're right,' I said, and my mind began travelling back to that freezing afternoon just before Christmas, four months ago, when Claud had asked to borrow the van and had driven away in the direction of Aylesbury without saying where he was going. I had assumed he was off to see Clarice, but late in the afternoon he had returned, bringing with him this dog he said he'd bought off a man for thirty-five shillings.

'Is he fast?' I had said. We were standing out by the pumps and Claud was holding the dog on a leash and looking at him, and a few snowflakes were falling and settling on the dog's back. The motor of the van was still running.

'Fast!' Claud had said. 'He's just about the slowest dog you ever saw in your whole life!'

'Then what you buy him for?'

'Well,' he had said, the big bovine face secret and cunning, 'it occurred to me that maybe he might possibly look a little bit like Jackie. What d'you think?'

'I suppose he does a bit, now you come to mention it.'

He had handed me the leash and I had taken the new dog inside to dry him off while Claud had gone round to the pen to fetch his beloved. And when he returned and we put the two of them together for the first time, I can remember him stepping back and saying, 'Oh Jesus!' and standing dead still in front of them like he was seeing a phantom. Then he became very quick and quiet. He got down on his knees and began comparing them carefully point by point, and it was almost like the room was getting warmer and warmer the way I could feel his excitement growing every second through this long silent examination in which even the toenails and the dewclaws, eighteen on each dog, were matched alongside one another for colour.

'Look,' he said at last, standing up. 'Walk them up and down the room a few times, will you?' And then he had stayed there for quite five or six minutes leaning against the stove with his eyes half closed and his head on one side, watching them and frowning and chewing his lips. After that, as though he didn't believe what he had seen the first time, he had gone down again on his knees to recheck everything once more; but suddenly, in the middle of it, he had jumped up and looked at me, his face fixed and tense, with a curious whiteness around the nostrils and the eyes. 'All right,' he had said, a little tremor in his voice. 'You know what? We're home. We're rich.'

And then the secret conferences between us in the kitchen, the detailed planning, the selection of the most suitable track, and finally every other Saturday, eight times in all, locking up my filling-station (losing a whole afternoon's custom) and driving the ringer all the way up to Oxford to a scruffy little track out in the fields near Headington where the big money was played but which was actually nothing except a line of old posts and cord to mark the course, an upturned bicycle for pulling the dummy hare, and at the far end, in the distance, six traps and the starter. We had driven this ringer up there eight times over a period of sixteen weeks and entered him with Mr Feasey and stood around on the edge of the crowd in freezing raining cold, waiting for his name to go up on the blackboard in chalk. The Black Panther we called him. And when his time came, Claud would always lead him down to the traps and I would stand at the finish to catch him and keep him clear of the fighters, the gipsy dogs that the gipsies so often slipped in specially to tear another one to pieces at the end of a race.

But you know, there was something rather sad about taking this dog all the way up there so many times and letting him run and watching him and hoping and praying that whatever happened he would always come last. Of course the praying wasn't necessary and we never really had a moment's worry because the old fellow simply couldn't gallop and that's all there was to it. He ran exactly like a crab. The only time he didn't come last was when a big fawn dog by the name of Amber Flash put his foot in a hole and broke a hock and finished on three legs. But even then ours only just beat him. So this way we got him right down to bottom grade with the scrubbers, and the last time we were there all the bookies were laying him twenty or thirty to one and calling his name and begging people to back him.

Now at last, on this sunny April day, it was Jackie's turn to go instead. Claud said we mustn't run the ringer any more or Mr Feasey might begin to get tired of him and throw him out altogether, he was so slow. Claud said this was the exact psychological time to have it off, and that Jackie would win it anything between thirty and fifty lengths.

He had raised Jackie from a pup and the dog was only fifteen months now, but he was a good fast runner. He'd never raced yet, but we knew he was fast from clocking him round the little private schooling track at Uxbridge where Claud had taken him every Sunday since he was seven months old – except once when he was having some inoculations, Claud said he probably wasn't fast enough to win top grade at Mr Feasey's, but where we'd got him now, in bottom grade with the scrubbers, he could fall over and get up again and still win it twenty – well, anyway, ten or fifteen lengths, Claud said.

So all I had to do this morning was go to the bank in the village and draw out fifty pounds for myself and fifty for Claud which I would lend him as an advance against wages, and then at twelve o'clock lock up the filling-station and hang the notice on one of the pumps saying GONE FOR THE DAY. Claud would shut the ringer in the pen at the back and put Jackie in the van and off we'd go. I won't say I was as excited as Claud, but there again, I didn't have all sorts of important things depending on it either, like buying a house and being able to get married. Nor was I almost *born* in a kennel with greyhounds like he was, walking about thinking of absolutely nothing else all day – except perhaps Clarice in the evenings. Personally, I had my own career as a filling-station owner to keep me busy, not to mention second-hand cars, but if Claud wanted to fool around with dogs that was all right with me, especially a thing like today – if it came off. As a matter of fact, I don't mind admitting that every time I thought about the money we were putting on and the money we might win, my stomach gave a little lurch.

The dogs had finished their breakfast now and Claud took them out for a short walk across the field opposite while I got dressed and fried the eggs. Afterwards, I went to the bank and drew out the money (all in ones), and the rest of the morning seemed to go very quickly serving customers.

At twelve sharp I locked up and hung the notice on the pump. Claud came around from the back leading Jackie and carrying a large suitcase made of reddish-brown cardboard.

'Suitcase?'

'For the money,' Claud answered. 'You said yourself no man can carry two thousand pounds in his pockets.'

It was a lovely yellow spring day with the buds bursting all along the hedges and the sun shining through the new pale-green leaves on the big beech tree across the road. Jackie looked wonderful, with two big hard muscles the size of melons bulging on his hindquarters, his coat glistening like black velvet. While Claud was putting the suitcase in the van, the dog did a little prancing jig on his toes to show how fit he was, then he looked up at me and grinned, just like he knew he was off to the races to win two thousand pounds and a heap of glory. This Jackie had the widest most human-smiling grin I ever saw. Not only did he lift his upper lip, but he actually stretched the corners of his mouth so you could see every tooth in his head except perhaps one or two of the molars right at the back; and every time I saw him do it I found myself waiting to hear him start laughing out loud as well.

We got in the van and off we went. I was doing the driving. Claud was beside me and Jackie was standing up on the straw in the rear looking over our shoulders through the windshield. Claud kept turning round and trying to make him lie down so he wouldn't get thrown whenever we went round the sharp corners, but the dog was too excited to do anything except grin back at him and wave his enormous tail.

'You got the money, Gordon?' Claud was chain-smoking cigarettes and quite unable to sit still.

'Yes.'

'Mine as well?'

'I got a hundred and five altogether. Five for the winder like you said, so he won't stop the hare and make it a no-race.'

'Good,' Claud said, rubbing his hands together hard as though he were freezing cold. 'Good, good, good.'

We drove through the little narrow High Street of Great Missenden and caught a glimpse of old Rummins going into the Nag's Head for his morning pint, then outside the village we turned left and climbed over the ridge of the

Chilterns towards Princes Risborough, and from there it would only be twenty-odd miles to Oxford.

And now a silence and a kind of tension began to come over us both. We sat very quiet, not speaking at all, each nursing his own fears and excitements, containing his anxiety. And Claud kept smoking his cigarettes and throwing them half finished out the window. Usually, on these trips, he talked his head off all the way there and back, all the things he'd done with dogs in his life, the jobs he'd pulled, the places he'd been, the money he'd won; and all the things other people had done with dogs, the thievery, the cruelty, the unbelievable trickery and cunning of owners at the flapping tracks. But today I don't think he was trusting himself to speak very much. At this point, for that matter, nor was I. I was sitting there watching the road and trying to keep my mind off the immediate future by thinking back on all that stuff Claud had told me about this curious greyhound-racing racket.

I swear there wasn't a man alive who knew more about it than Claud did, and ever since we'd got the ringer and decided to pull this job, he'd taken it upon himself to give me an education in the business. By now, in theory at any rate, I suppose I knew nearly as much as him.

It had started during the very first strategy conference we'd had in the kitchen. I can remember it was the day after the ringer arrived and we were sitting there watching for customers through the window, and Claud was explaining to me all about what we'd have to do, and I was trying to follow him as best I could until finally there came one question I had to ask.

'What I don't see,' I had said, 'is why you use the ringer

at all. Wouldn't it be safer if we use Jackie all the time and simply stop him the first half-dozen races so he comes last? Then when we're good and ready, we can let him go. Same result in the end, wouldn't it be, if we do it right? And no danger of being caught.'

Well, as I say, that did it. Claud looked up at me quickly and he said, 'Hey! None of that! I'd just like you to know "stopping's" something I never do. What's come over you, Gordon?' He seemed genuinely pained and shocked by what I had said.

'I don't see anything wrong with it.'

'Now, listen to me, Gordon. Stopping a good dog breaks his heart. A good dog knows he's fast, and seeing all the others out there in front and not being able to catch them – it breaks his heart, I tell you. And what's more, you wouldn't be making suggestions like that if you knew some of the tricks them fellers do to stop their dogs at the flapping tracks.'

'Such as what, for example?' I had asked.

'Such as anything in the world almost, so long as it makes the dog go slower. And it takes a lot of stopping, a good greyhound does. Full of guts and so mad keen you can't even let them watch a race they'll tear the leash right out of your hand raring to go. Many's the time I've seen one with a broken leg insisting on finishing the race.'

He had paused then, looking at me thoughtfully with those large pale eyes, serious as hell and obviously thinking deep. 'Maybe,' he had said, 'if we're going to do this job properly I'd better tell you a thing or two so's you'll know what we're up against.'

'Go ahead and tell me,' I had said. 'I'd like to know.'

For a moment he stared in silence out the window. 'The main thing you got to remember,' he had said darkly, 'is that all these fellers going to the flapping tracks with dogs – they're artful. They're more artful than you could possibly imagine.' Again he paused, marshalling his thoughts.

'Now take for example the different ways of stopping a dog. The first, the commonest, is strapping.'

'Strapping?'

'Yes. Strapping 'em up. That's commonest. Pulling the muzzle-strap tight around their necks so they can't hardly breathe, see. A clever man knows just which hole on the strap to use and just how many lengths it'll take off his dog in a race. Usually a couple of notches is good for five or six lengths. Do it up real tight and he'll come last. I've known plenty of dogs collapse and die from being strapped up tight on a hot day. Strangulated, absolutely strangulated, and a very nasty thing it was too. Then again, some of 'em just tie two of the toes together with black cotton. Dog never runs well like that. Unbalances him.'

'That doesn't sound too bad.'

'Then there's others that put a piece of fresh-chewed gum up under their tails, right up close where the tail joins the body. And there's nothing funny about that,' he had said, indignant. 'The tail of a running dog goes up and down ever so slightly and the gum on the tail keeps sticking to the hairs on the backside, just where it's tenderest. No dog likes that, you know. Then there's sleeping pills. That's used a lot nowadays. They do it by weight, exactly like a doctor, and they measure the powder according to whether they want to slow him up five or ten or fifteen lengths. Those are just a few of the ordinary ways,' he had said. 'Actually they're nothing. Absolutely nothing, compared with some of the other things that's done to hold a dog back in a race, especially by the gipsies. There's things the gipsies do that are almost too disgusting to mention, such as when they're just putting the dog in the trap, things you wouldn't hardly do to your worst enemies.'

And when he had told me about those – which were, indeed, terrible things because they had to do with physical injury, quickly, painfully inflicted – then he had gone on to tell me what they did when they wanted the dog to win.

'There's just as terrible things done to make 'em go fast as to make 'em go slow,' he had said softly, his face veiled and secret. 'And perhaps the commonest of all is wintergreen. Whenever you see a dog going around with no hair on his back or little bald patches all over him – that's wintergreen. Just before the race they rub it hard into the skin. Sometimes it's Sloan's Liniment, but mostly it's wintergreen. Stings terrible. Stings so bad that all the old dog wants to do is run, run, run as fast as he possibly can to get away from the pain.

'Then there's special drugs they give with the needle. Mind you, that's the modern method and most of the spivs at the track are too ignorant to use it. It's the fellers coming down from London in the big cars with stadium dogs they've borrowed for the day by bribing the trainer – they're the ones who use the needle.'

I could remember him sitting there at the kitchen table

with a cigarette dangling from his mouth and dropping his eyelids to keep out the smoke and looking at me through his wrinkled, nearly closed eyes, and saying, 'What you've got to remember, Gordon, is this. There's nothing they won't do to make a dog win if they want him to. On the other hand, no dog can run faster than he's built, no matter what they do to him. So if we can get Jackie down into bottom grade, then we're home. No dog in bottom grade can get near him, not even with wintergreen and needles. Not even with ginger.'

'Ginger?'

'Certainly. That's a common one, ginger is. What they do, they take a piece of raw ginger about the size of a walnut, and about five minutes before the off they slip it into the dog.'

'You mean in his mouth? He eats it?'

'No,' he had said. 'Not in his mouth.'

And so it had gone on. During each of the eight long trips we had subsequently made to the track with the ringer I had heard more and more about this charming sport – more, especially, about the methods of stopping them and making them go (even the names of the drugs and the quantities to use). I heard about 'The rat treatment' (for non-chasers, to make them chase the dummy hare), where a rat is placed in a can which is then tied around the dog's neck. There's a small hole in the lid of the can just large enough for the rat to poke its head out and nip the dog. But the dog can't get at the rat, and so naturally he goes half crazy running around and being bitten in the neck, and the more he shakes the can the more the rat bites him.

Finally, someone releases the rat, and the dog, who up to then was a nice docile tail-wagging animal who wouldn't hurt a mouse, pounces on it in a rage and tears it to pieces. Do this a few times, Claud had said – 'Mind you, I don't hold with it myself' – and the dog becomes a real killer who will chase anything, even the dummy hare.

We were over the Chilterns now and running down out of the beechwoods into the flat elm- and oak-tree country south of Oxford. Claud sat quietly beside me, nursing his nervousness and smoking cigarettes, and every two or three minutes he would turn round to see if Jackie was all right. The dog was at last lying down, and each time Claud turned round, he whispered something to him softly, and the dog acknowledged his words with a faint movement of the tail that made the straw rustle.

Soon we would be coming into Thame, the broad High Street where they penned the pigs and cows and sheep on market day, and where the fair came once a year with the swings and roundabouts and bumping cars and gipsy caravans right there in the street in the middle of the town. Claud was born in Thame, and we'd never driven through it yet without him mentioning the fact.

'Well,' he said as the first houses came into sight, 'here's Thame. I was born and bred in Thame, you know, Gordon.'

'You told me.'

'Lots of funny things we used to do around here when we was nippers,' he said, slightly nostalgic.

'I'm sure.'

He paused, and I think more to relieve the tension

building up inside him than anything else, he began talking about the years of his youth.

'There was a boy next door,' he said. 'Gilbert Gomm his name was. Little sharp ferrety face and one leg a bit shorter'n the other. Shocking things him and me used to do together. You know one thing we done, Gordon?'

'What?'

'We'd go into the kitchen Saturday nights when Mum and Dad were at the pub, and we'd disconnect the pipe from the gas-ring and bubble the gas into a milk bottle full of water. Then we'd sit down and drink it out of teacups.'

'Was that so good?'

'Good! It was absolutely disgusting! But we'd put lashings of sugar in and then it didn't taste so bad.'

'Why did you drink it?'

Claud turned and looked at me, incredulous. 'You mean you never drunk "Snakes Water"!'

'Can't say I have.'

'I thought everyone done that when they was kids! It intoxicates you, just like wine only worse, depending on how long you let the gas bubble through. We used to get reeling drunk together there in the kitchen Saturday nights and it was marvellous. Until one night Dad comes home early and catches us. I'll never forget that night as long as I live. There was me holding the milk bottle, and the gas bubbling through it lovely, and Gilbert kneeling on the floor ready to turn off the tap the moment I give the word, and in walks Dad.'

'What did he say?'

'Oh Christ, Gordon, that was terrible. He didn't say

one word, but he stands there by the door and he starts feeling for his belt, undoing the buckle very slow and pulling the belt slow out of his trousers, looking at me all the time. Great big feller he was, with great big hands like coal hammers and a black moustache and them little purple veins running all over his cheeks. Then he comes over quick and grabs me by the coat and lets me have it, hard as he can, using the end with the buckle on it and, honest to God, Gordon, I thought he was going to kill me. But in the end he stops and then he puts on the belt again, slow and careful, buckling it up and tucking in the flap and belching with the beer he'd drunk. And then he walks out again back to the pub, still without saying a word. Worst hiding I ever had in my life.'

'How old were you then?'

'Round about eight, I should think,' Claud said.

As we drew closer to Oxford, he became silent again. He kept twisting his neck to see if Jackie was all right, to touch him, to stroke his head, and once he turned around and knelt on the seat to gather more straw around the dog, murmuring something about a draught. We drove around the fringe of Oxford and into a network of narrow open country roads, and after a while we turned into a small bumpy lane and along this we began to overtake a thin stream of men and women all walking and cycling in the same direction. Some of the men were leading greyhounds. There was a large saloon car in front of us and through the rear window we could see a dog sitting on the back seat between two men.

'They come from all over,' Claud said darkly. 'That one

there's probably come up special from London. Probably slipped him out from one of the big stadium kennels just for the afternoon. That could be a Derby dog probably, for all we know.'

'Hope he's not running against Jackie.'

'Don't worry,' Claud said. 'All new dogs automatically go in top grade. That's one rule Mr Feasey's very particular about.'

There was an open gate leading into a field, and Mr Feasey's wife came forward to take our admission money before we drove in.

'He'd have her winding the bloody pedals too if she had the strength,' Claud said. 'Old Feasey don't employ more people than he has to.'

I drove across the field and parked at the end of a line of cars along the top hedge. We both got out and Claud went quickly round the back to fetch Jackie. I stood beside the car, waiting. It was a very large field with a steepish slope on it and we were at the top of the slope, looking down. In the distance I could see the six starting-traps and the wooden posts marking the track which ran along the bottom of the field and turned sharp at right angles and came on up the hill towards the crowd, to the finish. Thirty yards beyond the finishing line stood the upturned bicycle for driving the hare. Because it is portable, this is the standard machine for hare-driving used at all flapping tracks. It comprises a flimsy wooden platform about eight feet high, supported on four poles knocked into the ground. On top of the platform there is fixed, upside down with wheels in the air, an ordinary old bicycle. The rear wheel is to the front, facing down the track, and from it the tyre has been removed, leaving a concave metal rim. One end of the cord that pulls the hare is attached to this rim, and the winder (or hare-driver), by straddling the bicycle at the back and turning the pedals with his hands, revolves the wheel and winds in the cord around the rim. This pulls the dummy hare towards him at any speed he likes up to forty miles an hour. After each race someone takes the dummy hare (with cord attached) all the way down to the starting traps again, thus unwinding the cord on the wheel, ready for a fresh start. From his high platform, the winder can watch the race and regulate the speed of the hare to keep it just ahead of the leading dog. He can also stop the hare any time he wants and make it a 'no-race' (if the wrong dog looks like winning) by suddenly turning the pedals backwards and getting the cord tangled up in the hub of the wheel. The other way of doing it is to slow down the hare suddenly, for perhaps one second, and that makes the lead dog automatically check a little so that the others catch up with him. He is an important man, the winder.

I could see Mr Feasey's winder already standing atop his platform, a powerful-looking man in a blue sweater, leaning on the bicycle and looking down at the crowd through the smoke of his cigarette.

There is a curious law in England which permits race meetings of this kind to be held only seven times a year over one piece of ground. That is why all Mr Feasey's equipment was movable, and after the seventh meeting he would simply transfer to the next field. The law didn't bother him at all.

There was already a good crowd and the bookmakers

were erecting their stands in a line over to the right. Claud had Jackie out of the van now and was leading him over to a group of people clustered around a small stocky man dressed in riding-breeches – Mr Feasey himself. Each person in the group had a dog on a leash and Mr Feasey kept writing names in a notebook that he held folded in his left hand. I sauntered over to watch.

'Which you got there?' Mr Feasey said, pencil poised above the notebook.

'Midnight,' a man said who was holding a black dog.

Mr Feasey stepped back a pace and looked most carefully at the dog.

'Midnight. Right. I got him down.'

'Jane,' the next man said.

'Let me look. Jane . . . Jane . . . yes, all right.'

'Soldier.' This dog was led by a tall man with long teeth who wore a dark-blue, double-breasted lounge suit, shiny with wear, and when he said 'Soldier' he began slowly to scratch the seat of his trousers with the hand that wasn't holding the leash.

Mr Feasey bent down to examine the dog. The other man looked up at the sky.

'Take him away,' Mr Feasey said.

The man looked down quick and stopped scratching.

'Go on, take him away.'

'Listen, Mr Feasey,' the man said, lisping slightly through his long teeth. 'Now don't talk so bloody silly, *please*.'

'Go on and beat it, Larry, and stop wasting my time. You know as well as I do the Soldier's got two white toes on his off fore.'

'Now look, Mr Feasey,' the man said. 'You ain't even seen Soldier for six months at least.'

'Come on now, Larry, and beat it. I haven't got time arguing with you.' Mr Feasey didn't appear the least angry. 'Next,' he said.

I saw Claud step forward leading Jackie. The large bovine face was fixed and wooden, the eyes staring at something about a yard above Mr Feasey's head, and he was holding the leash so tight his knuckles were like a row of little white onions. I knew just how he was feeling. I felt the same way myself at that moment, and it was even worse when Mr Feasey suddenly started laughing.

'Hey!' he cried. 'Here's the Black Panther. Here's the champion.'

'That's right, Mr Feasey,' Claud said.

'Well, I'll tell you,' Mr Feasey said, still grinning. 'You can take him right back home where he come from. I don't want him.'

'But look here, Mr Feasey . . .'

'Six or eight times at least I've run him for you now and that's enough. Look – why don't you shoot him and have done with it?'

'Now, listen, Mr Feasey, *please*. Just once more and I'll never ask you again.'

'Not even once! I got more dogs than I can handle here today. There's no room for crabs like that.'

I thought Claud was going to cry.

'Now honest, Mr Feasey,' he said. 'I been up at six every morning this past two weeks giving him roadwork and massage and buying him beefsteaks, and believe me he's a different dog absolutely than what he was last time he run.'

The words 'different dog' caused Mr Feasey to jump like he'd been pricked with a hatpin. 'What's that!' he cried. 'Different dog!'

I'll say this for Claud, he kept his head. 'See here, Mr Feasey,' he said. 'I'll thank you not to go implying things to me. You know very well I didn't mean that.'

'All right, all right. But just the same, you can take him away. There's no sense running dogs as slow as him. Take him home now, will you please, and don't hold up the whole meeting.'

I was watching Claud. Claud was watching Mr Feasey. Mr Feasey was looking round for the next dog to enter up. Under his brown tweedy jacket he wore a yellow pullover, and this streak of yellow on his breast and his thin gaitered legs and the way he jerked his head from side to side made him seem like some sort of a little perky bird – a goldfinch, perhaps.

Claud took a step forward. His face was beginning to purple slightly with the outrage of it all and I could see his Adam's apple moving up and down as he swallowed.

'I'll tell you what I'll do, Mr Feasey. I'm so absolutely sure this dog's improved I'll bet you a quid he don't finish last. There you are.'

Mr Feasey turned slowly around and looked at Claud. 'You crackers?' he asked.

'I'll bet you a quid, there you are, just to prove what I'm saying.'

It was a dangerous move, certain to cause suspicion,

but Claud knew it was the only thing left to do. There was silence while Mr Feasey bent down and examined the dog. I could see the way his eyes were moving slowly over the animal's whole body, part by part. There was something to admire in the man's thoroughness, and in his memory; something to fear also in this self-confident little rogue who held in his head the shape and colour and markings of perhaps several hundred different but very similar dogs. He never needed more than one little clue – a small scar, a splay toe, a trifle in at the hocks, a less pronounced wheelback, a slightly darker brindle – Mr Feasey always remembered.

So I watched him now as he bent down over Jackie. His face was pink and fleshy, the mouth small and tight as though it couldn't stretch enough to make a smile, and the eyes were like two little cameras focused sharply on the dog.

'Well,' he said, straightening up. 'It's the same dog, anyway.'

'I should hope so too!' Claud cried. 'Just what sort of a fellow you think I am, Mr Feasey?'

'I think you're crackers, that's what I think. But it's a nice easy way to make a quid. I suppose you forgot how Amber Flash nearly beat him on three legs last meeting?'

'This one wasn't fit then,' Claud said. 'He hadn't had beefsteak and massage and roadwork like I've been giving him lately. But look, Mr Feasey, you're not to go sticking him in top grade just to win the bet. This is a bottom-grade dog, Mr Feasey. You know that.'

Mr Feasey laughed. The small button mouth opened

into a tiny circle and he laughed and looked at the crowd, who laughed with him. 'Listen,' he said, laying a hairy hand on Claud's shoulder. 'I know my dogs. I don't have to do any fiddling around to win *this* quid. He goes in bottom.'

'Right,' Claud said. 'That's a bet.' He walked away with Jackie and I joined him.

'Jesus, Gordon, that was a near one!'

'Shook me.'

'But we're in now,' Claud said. He had that breathless look on his face again and he was walking about quick and funny, like the ground was burning his feet.

People were still coming through the gate into the field and there were easily three hundred of them now. Not a very nice crowd. Sharp-nosed men and women with dirty faces and bad teeth and quick shifty eyes. The dregs of the big town. Oozing out like sewage from a cracked pipe and trickling along the road through the gate and making a smelly little pond of sewage at the top end of the field. They were all there, all the spivs, and the gipsies and the touts and the dregs and the sewage and the scraping and the scum from the cracked drainpipes of the big town. Some with dogs, some without. Dogs led about on pieces of string, miserable dogs with hanging heads, thin mangy dogs with sores on their quarters (from sleeping on board), sad old dogs with grey muzzles, doped dogs, dogs stuffed with porridge to stop them winning, dogs walking stiff-legged – one especially, a white one. 'Claud, why is that white one walking so stiff-legged?'

'Which one?'

'That one over there.'

'Ah. Yes, I see. Very probably because he's been hung.'

'Hung?'

'Yes, hung. Suspended in a harness for twenty-four hours with his legs dangling.'

'Good God, but why?'

'To make him run slow, of course. Some people don't hold with dope or stuffing or strapping up. So they hang 'em.'

'I see.'

'Either that,' Claud said, 'or they sandpaper them. Rub their pads with rough sandpaper and take the skin off so it hurts when they run.'

'Yes, I see.'

And then the fitter, brighter-looking dogs, the better-fed ones who get horsemeat every day, not pig-swill or rusk and cabbage water, their coats shinier, their tails moving, pulling at their leads, undoped, unstuffed, awaiting perhaps a more unpleasant fate, the muzzle-strap to be tightened an extra four notches. *But make sure he can breathe now, Jock. Don't choke him completely. Don't let's have him collapse in the middle of the race. Just so he wheezes a bit, see. Go on tightening it up an extra notch at a time until you can hear him wheezing. You'll see his mouth open and he'll start breathing heavy. Then it's just right, but not if his eyeballs is bulging. Watch out for that, will you? OK?*

OK.

'Let's get away from the crowd, Gordon. It don't do Jackie no good getting excited by all these other dogs.'

We walked up the slope to where the cars were parked,

then back and forth in front of the line of cars, keeping the dog on the move. Inside some of the cars I could see men sitting with their dogs, and the men scowled at us through the windows as we went by.

'Watch out now, Gordon. We don't want any trouble.'

'No, all right.'

These were the best dogs of all, the secret ones kept in the cars and taken out quick just to be entered up (under some invented name) and put back again quick and held there till the last minute, then straight down to the traps and back again into the cars after the race so no nosey bastard gets too close a look, The trainer at the big stadium said so. *All right, he said. You can have him, but for Christsake don't let anybody recognize him. There's thousands of people know this dog, so you've got to be careful, see. And it'll cost you fifty pound.*

Very fast dogs these, but it doesn't much matter how fast they are, they probably get the needle anyway, just to make sure. One and a half cc's of ether, subcutaneous, done in the car, injected very slow. That'll put ten lengths on any dog. Or sometimes it's caffeine in oil, or camphor. That makes them go too. The men in the big cars know all about that. And some of them know about whisky. But that's intravenous. Not so easy when it's intravenous. Might miss the vein. All you got to do is miss the vein and it don't work and where are you then? So it's ether, or it's caffeine, or it's camphor. *Don't give her too much of that stuff now, Jock. What does she weigh? Fifty-eight pounds. All right then, you know what the man told us. Wait a minute now. I got it written down on a piece of paper. Here it is. Point 1 of a cc per 10 pounds bodyweight equals 5 lengths over 300 yards. Wait a minute now while*

I work it out. Oh Christ, you better guess it. Just guess it, Jock. It'll be all right you'll find. Shouldn't be any trouble anyway because I picked the others in the race myself. Cost me a tenner to old Feasey. A bloody tenner I gave him, and Dear Mr Feasey, I says, that's for your birthday and because I love you.

Thank you ever so much, Mr Feasey says. Thank you, my good and trusted friend.

And for stopping them, for the men in the big cars, it's chlorbutol. That's a beauty, chlorbutol, because you can give it the night before, especially to someone else's dog. Or pethidine. Pethidine and hyoscine mixed, whatever that may be.

'Lot of fine old English sporting gentry here,' Claud said.

'Certainly are.'

'Watch your pockets, Gordon. You got that money hidden away?'

We walked around the back of the line of cars – between the cars and the hedge – and I saw Jackie stiffen and begin to pull forward on the leash, advancing with a stiff crouching tread. About thirty yards away there were two men. One was holding a large fawn greyhound, the dog stiff and tense like Jackie. The other was holding a sack in his hands.

'Watch,' Claud whispered, 'they're giving him a kill.'

Out of the sack on to the grass tumbled a small white rabbit, fluffy white, young, tame. It righted itself and sat still, crouching in the hunched-up way rabbits crouch, its nose close to the ground. A frightened rabbit. Out of the sack so suddenly on to the grass with such a bump. Into the bright light. The dog was going mad with excitement now, jumping up against the leash, pawing the ground, throwing himself forward, whining. The rabbit saw the dog. It drew in its head and stayed still, paralysed with fear. The man transferred his hold to the dog's collar, and the dog twisted and jumped and tried to get free. The other man pushed the rabbit with his foot but it was too terrified to move. He pushed it again, flicking it forward with his toe like a football, and the rabbit rolled over several times, righted itself and began to hop over the grass away from the dog. The other man released the dog, which pounced with one huge pounce upon the rabbit, and then came the squeals, not very loud but shrill and anguished and lasting rather a long time.

'There you are,' Claud said. 'That's a kill.'

'Not sure I liked it very much.'

'I told you before, Gordon. Most of 'em does it. Keens the dog up before a race.'

'I still don't like it.'

'Nor me. But they all do it. Even in the big stadiums the trainers do it. Proper barbary I call it.'

We strolled away and below us on the slope of the hill the crowd was thickening and the bookies' stands with the names written on them in red and gold and blue were all erected now in a long line back of the crowd, each bookie already stationed on an upturned box beside his stand, a pack of numbered cards in one hand, a piece of chalk in the other, his clerk behind him with book and pencil. Then we saw Mr Feasey walking over to a blackboard that was nailed to a post stuck in the ground.

'He's chalking up the first race,' Claud said. 'Come on, quick!'

We walked rapidly down the hill and joined the crowd. Mr Feasey was writing the runners on the blackboard, copying names from his soft-covered notebook, and a little hush of suspense fell upon the crowd as they watched.

1. Sally
2. Three Quid
3. Snailbox Lady
4. Black Panther
5. Whisky
6. Rockit

'He's in it!' Claud whispered. 'First race! Trap four! Now, listen, Gordon! Give me a fiver quick to show the winder.' Claud could hardly speak from excitement. That patch of whiteness had returned around his nose and eyes, and when I handed him a five-pound note, his whole arm was shaking as he took it. The man who was going to wind the bicycle pedals was still standing on top of the wooden platform in his blue jersey, smoking. Claud went over and stood below him, looking up.

'See this fiver,' he said, talking softly, holding it folded small in the palm of his hand.

The man glanced at it without moving his head.

'Just so long as you wind her true this race, see. No stopping and no slowing down and run her fast. Right?'

The man didn't move but there was a slight, almost imperceptible lifting of the eyebrows. Claud turned away.

'Now, look, Gordon. Get the money on gradual, all in little bits like I told you. Just keep going down the line putting on little bits so you don't kill the price, see. And I'll be walking Jackie down very slow, as slow as I dare, to give you plenty of time. Right?'

'Right.'

'And don't forget to be standing ready to catch him at the end of the race. Get him clear away from all them others when they start fighting for the hare. Grab a hold of him tight and don't let go till I come running up with the collar and lead. That Whisky's a gipsy dog and he'll tear the leg off anything as gets in his way.'

'Right,' I said. 'Here we go.'

I saw Claud lead Jackie over to the finishing post and collect a yellow jacket with '4' written on it large. Also a muzzle. The other five runners were there too, the owners fussing around them, putting on their numbered jackets, adjusting their muzzles. Mr Feasey was officiating, hopping about in his tight riding-breeches like an anxious perky bird, and once I saw him say something to Claud and laugh. Claud ignored him. Soon they would all start to lead the dogs down the track, the long walk down the hill and across to the far corner of the field to the starting-traps. It would take them ten minutes to walk it. I've got at least ten minutes, I told myself, and then I began to push my way through the crowd standing six or seven deep in front of the line of bookies.

'Even money Whisky! Even money Whisky! Five to two Sally! Even money Whisky! Four to one Snailbox! Come on now! Hurry up, hurry up! Which is it?'

On every board all down the line the Black Panther was chalked up at twenty-five to one. I edged forward to the nearest book.

'Three pounds Black Panther,' I said, holding out the money.

The man on the box had an inflamed magenta face and traces of some white substance around the corners of his mouth. He snatched the money and dropped it in his satchel. 'Seventy-five pounds to three Black Panther,' he said. 'Number forty-two.' He handed me a ticket and his clerk recorded the bet.

I stepped back and wrote rapidly on the back of the ticket '75 to 3', then slipped it into the inside pocket of my jacket with the money.

So long as I continued to spread the cash out thin like this, it ought to be all right. And anyway, on Claud's instructions, I'd made a point of betting a few pounds on the ringer every time he'd run so as not to arouse any suspicion when the real day arrived. Therefore, with some confidence, I went all the way down the line staking three pounds with each book. I didn't hurry, but I didn't waste any time either, and after each bet I wrote the amount on the back of the card before slipping it into my pocket. There were seventeen bookies. I had seventeen tickets and had laid out fifty-one pounds without disturbing the price one point. Forty-nine pounds left to get on. I glanced quickly down the hill. One owner and his dog had already reached the traps. The others were only twenty or thirty yards away. Except for Claud. Claud and Jackie were only halfway there. I could see Claud in his old khaki greatcoat sauntering slowly along with Jackie pulling ahead keenly on the leash, and once I saw him stop completely and bend down, pretending to pick something up. When he went on again he seemed to have developed a limp so as to go slower still. I hurried back to the other end of the line to start again.

'Three pounds Black Panther.'

The bookmaker, the one with the magenta face and the white substance around the mouth, glanced up sharply, remembering the last time, and in one swift almost graceful movement of the arm he licked his fingers and wiped the figure 25 neatly off the board. His wet fingers left a small dark patch opposite Black Panther's name.

'All right, you got one more seventy-five to three,' he said. 'But that's the lot.' Then he raised his voice and shouted, 'Fifteen to one Black Panther! Fifteens the Panther!'

All down the line the twenty-fives were wiped out and it was fifteen to one the Panther now. I took it quick, but by the time I was through the bookies had had enough and they weren't quoting him any more. They'd only taken six pounds each, but they stood to lose a hundred and fifty, and for them – small-time bookies at a little country flapping track – that was quite enough for one race, thank you very much. I felt pleased the way I'd managed it. Lots of tickets now. I took them out of my pockets and counted them and they were like a thin pack of cards in my hand. Thirty-three tickets in all. And what did we stand to win? Let me see . . . something over two thousand pounds. Claud had said he'd win it thirty lengths. Where was Claud now?

Far away down the hill I could see the khaki greatcoat

standing by the traps and the big black dog alongside. All the other dogs were already in and the owners were beginning to walk away. Claud was bending down now, coaxing Jackie into number four, and then he was closing the door and turning away and beginning to run up the hill towards the crowd, the greatcoat flapping around him. He kept looking back over his shoulder as he ran.

Beside the traps the starter stood, and his hand was up waving a handkerchief. At the other end of the track, beyond the winning-post, quite close to where I stood, the man in the blue jersey was straddling the upturned bicycle on top of the wooden platform and he saw the signal and waved back and began to turn the pedals with his hands. Then a tiny white dot in the distance – the artificial hare that was in reality a football with a piece of white rabbit-skin tacked on to it – began to move away from the traps, accelerating fast. The traps went up and the dogs flew out. They flew out in a single dark lump, all together, as though it were one wide dog instead of six, and almost at once I saw Jackie drawing away from the field. I knew it was Jackie because of the colour. There weren't any other black dogs in the race. It was Jackie, all right. Don't move, I told myself. Don't move a muscle or an eyelid or a toe or a fingertip. Stand quite still and don't move. Watch him going. Come on, Jackson, boy! No, don't shout. It's unlucky to shout. And don't move. Be all over in twenty seconds. Round the sharp bend now and coming up the hill and he must be fifteen or twenty lengths clear. Easy twenty lengths. Don't count the lengths, it's unlucky. And don't move. Don't move your head. Watch him out of your eye-corners. Watch that Jackson go! He's really laying down to it now up that hill. He's won it now! He can't lose it now . . .

When I got over to him he was fighting the rabbit-skin and trying to pick it up in his mouth, but his muzzle wouldn't allow it, and the other dogs were pounding up behind him and suddenly they were all on top of him grabbing for the rabbit and I got hold of him round the neck and dragged him clear like Claud had said and knelt down on the grass and held him tight with both arms round his body. The other catchers were having a time all trying to grab their own dogs.

Then Claud was beside me, blowing heavily, unable to speak from blowing and excitement, removing Jackie's muzzle, putting on the collar and lead, and Mr Feasey was there too standing with hands on hips, the button mouth pursed up tight like a mushroom, the two little cameras staring at Jackie all over again.

'So that's the game, is it?' he said.

Claud was bending over the dog and acting like he hadn't heard.

'I don't want you here no more after this, you understand that?'

Claud went on fiddling with Jackie's collar.

I heard someone behind us saying, 'That flat-faced bastard swung it properly on old Feasey this time.' Someone else laughed. Mr Feasey walked away, Claud straightened up and went over with Jackie to the hare-driver in the blue jersey who had dismounted from his platform.

'Cigarette,' Claud said, offering the pack.

The man took one, also the five-pound note that was folded up small in Claud's fingers.

'Thanks,' Claud said. 'Thanks very much.'

'Don't mention,' the man said.

Then Claud turned to me. 'You get it all on, Gordon?' He was jumping up and down and rubbing his hands and patting Jackie, and his lips trembled as he spoke.

'Yes. Half at twenty-fives, half at fifteens.'

'Oh Christ, Gordon, that's marvellous. Wait here till I get the suitcase.'

'You take Jackie,' I said, 'and go and sit in the car. I'll see you later.'

There was nobody around the bookies now. I was the only one with anything to collect, and I walked slowly with a sort of dancing stride and a wonderful bursting feeling in my chest, towards the first one in the line, the man with the magenta face and the white substance on his mouth. I stood in front of him and I took all the time I wanted going through my pack of tickets to find the two that were his. The name was Syd Pratchett. It was written up large across his board in gold letters on a scarlet field – 'SYD PRATCHETT. THE BEST ODDS IN THE MIDLANDS. PROMPT SETTLEMENT.'

I handed him the first ticket and said, 'Seventy-eight pounds to come.' It sounded so good I said it again, making a delicious little song of it. 'Seventy-eight pounds to come on this one.' I didn't mean to gloat over Mr Pratchett. As a matter of fact. I was beginning to like him quite a lot. I even felt sorry for him having to fork out so much money. I hoped his wife and kids wouldn't suffer.

'Number forty-two,' Mr Pratchett said, turning to his clerk who held the big book. 'Forty-two wants seventy-eight pounds.'

There was a pause while the clerk ran his finger down the column of recorded bets. He did this twice, then he looked up at the boss and began to shake his head.

'No,' he said. 'Don't pay. That ticket backed Snailbox Lady.'

Mr Pratchett, standing on his box, leaned over and peered down at the book. He seemed to be disturbed by what the clerk had said, and there was a look of genuine concern on the huge magenta face.

The clerk is a fool, I thought, and any moment now Mr Pratchett's going to tell him so.

But when Mr Pratchett turned back to me, the eyes had become narrow and hostile. 'Now, look, Charley,' he said softly. 'Don't let's have any of that. You know very well you bet Snailbox. What's the idea?'

'I bet Black Panther,' I said. 'Two separate bets of three pounds each at twenty-five to one. Here's the second ticket.'

This time he didn't even bother to check it with the book. 'You bet Snailbox, Charley,' he said. 'I remember you coming round.' With that, he turned away from me and started wiping the names of the last race runners off his board with a wet rag. Behind him, the clerk had closed the book and was lighting himself a cigarette. I stood watching them, and I could feel the sweat beginning to break through the skin all over my body.

'Let me see the book.'

Mr Pratchett blew his nose in the wet rag and dropped it to the ground. 'Look,' he said, 'why don't you go away and stop annoying me?'

The point was this: a bookmaker's ticket, unlike a totalizator ticket, never has anything written on it regarding the nature of your bet. This is normal practice, the same at every racetrack in the country, whether it's the Silver Ring at Newmarket, the Royal Enclosure at Ascot, or a tiny country flapping track near Oxford. All you receive is a card bearing the bookie's name and a serial number. The wager is (or should be) recorded by the bookie's clerk in his book alongside the number of the ticket, but apart from that there is no evidence at all of how you betted.

'Go on,' Mr Pratchett was saying. 'Hop it.'

I stepped back a pace and glanced down the long line of bookmakers. None of them was looking my way. Each was standing motionless on his little wooden box beside his wooden placard, staring straight ahead into the crowd. I went up to the next one and presented a ticket.

'I had three pounds on Black Panther at twenty-five to one,' I said firmly. 'Seventy-eight pounds to come.'

This man, who had a soft inflamed face, went through exactly the same routine as Mr Pratchett, questioning his clerk, peering at the book, and giving me the same answers.

'Whatever's the matter with you?' he said quietly, speaking to me as though I were eight years old. 'Trying such a silly thing as that.'

This time I stepped well back. 'You dirty thieving bastards!' I cried. 'The whole lot of you!'

Automatically, as though they were puppets, all the

heads down the line flicked round and looked at me. The expressions didn't alter. It was just the heads that moved, all seventeen of them, and seventeen pairs of cold glassy eyes looked down at me. There was not the faintest flicker of interest in any of them.

'Somebody spoke,' they seemed to be saying. 'We didn't hear it. It's a nice day today.'

The crowd, sensing excitement, was beginning to move in around me. I ran back to Mr Pratchett, right up close to him, and poked him in the stomach with my finger. 'You're a thief! A lousy little thief!' I shouted.

The extraordinary thing was, Mr Pratchett didn't seem to resent this at all.

'Well, I never,' he said. '*Look* who's talking.'

Then suddenly the big face broke into a wide, frog-like grin, and he looked over at the crowd and shouted, '*Look* who's talking!'

All at once everybody started to laugh. Down the line the bookies were coming to life and turning to each other and laughing and pointing at me and shouting, '*Look* who's talking! *Look* who's talking!' The crowd began to take up the cry as well, and I stood there on the grass alongside Mr Pratchett with his wad of tickets as thick as a pack of cards in my hand, listening to them and feeling slightly hysterical. Over the heads of the people I could see Mr Feasey beside his blackboard, already chalking up the runners for the next race; and then beyond him, far away up the top of the field, I caught sight of Claud standing by the van, waiting for me with the suitcase in his hand.

It was time to go home.

Roald Dahl

Roald Dahl was born in Llandaff, Wales, on 13 September 1916. His parents were Norwegian and he was the only son of a second marriage. His father, Harald, and elder sister Astri died when Roald was just three years old, leaving his mother, Sofie, to raise her four children and two stepchildren.

At the age of nine, Roald was sent away to boarding school, first in Weston-super-Mare and later in Derbyshire (not far from Cadbury's chocolate factory). He suffered acutely from homesickness and his unhappy schooling was to greatly influence his writing in later life. His childhood and schooldays became the subject of his autobiography *Boy*.

At eighteen, instead of going to university, he joined the Shell Petroleum Company and after two years training was sent to Dar es Salaam (in what is now Tanzania) to supply oil to customers. However, the outbreak of the Second World War saw him sign up as an aircraftman with the RAF in Nairobi: of the sixteen men who signed up, only Roald and two others were to survive the war.

He detailed his exploits in the war in a further volume of autobiography, *Going Solo*, which included crash-landing in no-man's-land and surviving a direct hit during the Battle of Athens. Invalided out of active service, he was transferred to Washington in 1942 as an air attaché, where an opportune meeting with C. S. Forester, the writer of the *Hornblower* series, set him on a new path.

Roald's first piece of published writing was used to help publicize the British war effort in America. Appearing anonymously in the *Saturday Evening Post* in 1942, 'Shot Down Over Libya' earned him $900. He published several more pieces for the paper, many of which were fictional tales, and these were eventually collected together and published as *Over to You*.

Later stories appeared in the *New Yorker*, *Harpers* and *Atlantic Monthly*. They were widely regarded and he won the prestigious Edgar Award from the Mystery Writers of America three times. In 1953 he married the Oscar-winning actor Patricia Neal and together they had five children.

It was not until the 1960s, after he had settled with his family in Great Missenden in Buckinghamshire, that Roald began seriously to write children's stories, publishing first *James and the Giant Peach* and, a few years later, *Charlie and the Chocolate Factory*. It was not long before his stories were a worldwide success.

After he and Patricia Neal divorced, Roald married Felicity Crosland in 1983. Working to the end on new books, he died aged seventy-four on 23 November 1990.

Now, over twenty years later, Roald Dahl's legacy as a storyteller and favourite of readers around the world remains unsurpassed.

Ah, Sweet Mystery of Life

'Something extremely unpleasant was about to happen – I was sure of that. Something sinister and cruel and ratlike . . . but I had to see it now.'

The sweet scents of rural life infuse this collection of Roald Dahl's country stories, but there is always something unexpected lurking in the undergrowth . . .

Whether it is taking a troublesome cow to be mated with a prime bull; dealing with a rat-infested hayrick; learning the ways and means of maggot farming; or describing the fine art of poaching pheasants using nothing but raisins and sleeping pills, Roald Dahl brings his stories of everyday country folk and their strange passions wonderfully to life. Lacing each tale with dollops of humour and adding a sprinkling of the sinister, Roald Dahl ensures that this collection is brimful of the sweet mysteries of life.

'All the stories sparkle with vibrant characters, humorous dialogue and sly rustic lore and cunning' Sunday Express

Going Solo

'It isn't often one gets the chance to save a person's life. It gave me a good feeling for the rest of the day.'

'They did not think for one moment that they would find anything but a burnt-out fuselage and a charred skeleton, and they were astounded when they came upon my still-breathing body lying in the sand nearby.'

In 1938 Roald Dahl was fresh out of school and bound for his first job in Africa, hoping to find adventure far from home. However, he got far more excitement than he bargained for when the outbreak of the Second World War led him to join the RAF. His account of his experiences in Africa, crashing a plane in the Western Desert, rescue and recovery from his horrific injuries in Alexandria, flying a Hurricane as Greece fell to the Germans, and many other daring deeds, recreates a world as bizarre and unnerving as any he wrote about in his fiction.

'His account of life as a fighter pilot in the Western Desert and in Greece has the thrilling intensity and the occasional grotesqueness of his fiction' Sunday Times

We believe in doing good things.

That's why ten percent of all Roald Dahl income* goes to our charity partners. We have supported causes including: specialist children's nurses, grants for families in need, and educational outreach programmes. Thank you for helping us to sustain this vital work.

Find out more at roalddahl.com

The Roald Dahl Charitable Trust is a registered charity (no. 1119330).
*All author payments and royalty income net of third party commissions.